Fallen

Ireland Is Down

Thomas Brant

Published by T Brant Publishing

Printed in Great Britain

Print ISBN 978-1-0683772-2-8

eBook ISBN 978-1-0683772-7-3

CHAPTER 1 – Time Check
Friday 19th January 2029

"The time is precisely fourteen thirty seven," Carl Peterson said, sitting in the Dublin studios of Manic Goldies Ireland, his nerves frayed. Ever since a month ago, when pro-Russian forces took over the Irish Government in a coup, the former BBC World Service presenter had found himself walking a perilous tightrope. The Irish airwaves, once a bastion of free expression, had become a battlefield of propaganda and suppression.

Bauer, under orders from the Berlin Government, had pulled out of Ireland entirely, News UK, who owned some stations, were ordered by Washington DC, as their owners, the Murdoch empire, had pledged full allegiance to NATO. Global had quietly followed suit, withdrawing Capital, Heart, and LBC from Irish frequencies within days of the coup.

Manic, however, being a Saudi owned, but British based, radio network, had elected to keep its stations broadcasting as some of the staff were unofficially in the resistance against the new regime, and Carl had kept with the station because his wife, British Embassy Credit Controller, was a handler for MI6, the Embassy job a non-official cover, and he was one of her assets.

RTÉ, the state-owned broadcaster, had been swiftly taken over by the new regime, its editorial stance transformed overnight. Where once it had been a voice of balanced reporting, it now broadcast little more than pro-Russian rhetoric and government-issued communiqués. Loyalist broadcasters who refused to comply had been purged, some arrested, others fleeing across the Irish Sea to Britain or further afield. Carl knew that as his son worked at RTÉ radio as a sound engineer, and, as another former BBC employee, was kept on as part of the station's technical staff, but under strict surveillance. Any hint of disloyalty, any whisper of dissent, could see him detained—or worse. Carl had no doubt the new government had compiled a file on him, too. He was a British national, a former BBC journalist, and he had chosen to stay in Dublin at a time when most foreign media had fled. That alone made him suspicious in the eyes of the regime.

Carl remembered when he was recruited by MI6 as an asset, when he was based in Kyiv in 2022, when Russia had seized further Ukrainian territory in its grinding war of attrition. He had been a BBC World Service host then, broadcasting from a makeshift studio near the former nuclear power plant in Chernobyl, delivering news updates to a beleaguered Ukrainian audience.

His wife, Emma, had been, unbeknownst to him at the time, a MI6 handler for over two decades, long before their son had been born, which, at the time, made him wonder why he got all the war assignments for the BBC. Every conflict zone, every coup, every place where the Foreign Office had vested interests—Carl had been sent, unknowingly playing a dual role as both journalist and intelligence asset. It wasn't until Kyiv that he'd pieced it together. The patterns. The peculiar way certain diplomatic staff always seemed to be stationed wherever he was. The subtle but insistent nudges from producers that he should stay longer in certain regions, dig deeper into specific narratives. And then, the moment of realisation—when Emma had finally sat him down and explained everything.

At first, he had been furious. Not just at her, but at himself for not seeing it sooner. He had always prided himself on being an investigative journalist, yet he had missed the biggest story of all—his own unwitting involvement in British intelligence operations. But as the months passed, he had come to understand. The world was changing. Journalism alone wasn't enough to hold back the tides of authoritarianism, disinformation, and outright warfare. He had a role to play, whether he liked it or not.

He knew, not from Emma, but his work at the BBC, that the intelligence services operated less like Fleming's portrayal, no 'Double 0' agents with licences to kill, or like how the BBC's own Spooks, a drama which had captivated audiences for years, depicted shadowy operatives pulling strings from the darkness. No, reality was far more mundane, yet infinitely more dangerous. Intelligence work wasn't about daring shootouts or dramatic betrayals; it was about information.

In some ways, Clancy, Carl knew, had it right— intelligence was a game of patience, of slowly gathering pieces and slotting them together until a pattern emerged. It was about watching, waiting, and knowing exactly when to act. And in his case, it was about knowing what not to say on air, about threading the impossible needle between delivering the news and keeping himself—and his family—alive.

Carl adjusted his headphones slightly, eyes flickering to the small clock in the studio. Fourteen thirty-eight now. The Dublin air outside the reinforced windows of Manic Goldies Ireland was grey, mist rolling in from the Liffey, shrouding the city in a damp, sullen gloom. He cleared his throat, his voice calm but measured as he continued.

"Coming up, we have a message from the Restoration Government, but first, it's Bonnie Tyler's Total Eclipse of the Heart."

The song cued automatically, its familiar, soaring melody filling the studio. Carl leaned back in his chair, exhaling slowly as he let the music play out. The studio was soundproofed, yet he could still feel the weight of the silence outside, a silence that had settled over Dublin like a thick fog since the coup.

He had to be careful. Every word mattered now. The Restoration Government, as it called itself, had ears everywhere. The new state media officials monitored every broadcast, even the ones on Manic Goldies Ireland. Carl was acutely aware that the next five minutes of programming had been handed to him by the government's media bureau—what they called a 'necessary contribution to the national discourse.' What it really was, however, was propaganda.

He could feel his pulse in his fingertips, his nerves raw beneath the surface. He had spent a career navigating conflict zones, spinning between the ethical obligations of journalism and the harsh realities of politics, but this— this was something else.

Looking into Studio 3, which was next to his, Carl could see the Manic Vibes Ireland early afternoon hosts, Alfie and Sîan, were doing their pan-Ireland show. Unlike Goldies, which aired only to the Republic for most of the day, Vibes, the contemporary hit radio brand, during the off peak hours all day aired to both the British controlled counties in the north and the Republic. It had been a decision made long before the coup, back when the island's radio landscape had been dictated more by market forces than geopolitics. Drivetime and Breakfast were locally split between Dublin and Belfast, but the off-peak hours operated as a single network. Now, that decision carried new, unintended consequences. The Restoration Government tolerated Manic Goldies Ireland because it catered to an older demographic, one less likely to resist their rule, but Manic Vibes Ireland was another story. Pop radio had a young audience, and young people were dangerous—they thought, they questioned, and they rebelled.

Carl had already heard whispers that the regime were using Vibes as a soft power for the North, as the Belfast studios, which up until 2027 ran both nations shows, had moved to being peak-only before the regime had taken control. That meant that the daytime networked hours, broadcast from Dublin, were feeding into Northern Ireland under British rule—a situation that neither London nor Belfast had fully accounted for in the weeks since the coup.

Of course, the Network Centre in Birmingham could insert split feeds remotely, as the RCS GSelector automation system allowed them to geo-target content to specific regions, but the question was: Had they? Or was the same Dublin feed reaching both sides of the increasingly volatile Irish border?

Carl suspected the latter. He knew the Goldies feed for the North was the UK feed with local ads, so his show, along with the rest of the station, was broadcast only in the Republic and on the Web streams that still operated outside Irish jurisdiction. But Vibes? That was another matter entirely.

His playlist, Carl knew, was set by Birmingham, apart from the local messages and ads which the stations Political Officer, a member of the New Communist Party, a 40 year old Russian whose English was Oxford grade, along with the producers had control over. The officer, one Viktor Mikhailov, had been appointed to oversee all "strategically significant" media operations in Ireland and was a constant presence in the corridors of Manic Goldies Ireland.

Having worked for the BBC in Tehran in 2003, Carl knew exactly what Mikhailov's presence meant. He had seen it before in authoritarian states—the shadowy figures in the background, the silent enforcers who didn't need to make overt threats because their mere presence was enough. The message was clear: stay in line, or there would be consequences.

Carl had no illusions about what those consequences could be. He had witnessed journalists disappear in Tehran, their only crime being a poorly worded question or an interview with the wrong dissident. Even in Kyiv, he had seen the lengths to which authoritarian regimes would go to silence opposition. Ireland was no different now; it had simply taken a different path to the same destination.

The studio door opened silently, and Carl didn't have to turn to know who it was. The scent of expensive Russian tobacco reached him first, followed by the soft, measured footsteps. Mikhailov always walked with the deliberate pace of a man who knew he was in control.

Carl took a slow breath, keeping his expression neutral as he glanced up. Mikhailov stood just inside the doorway, hands clasped behind his back, watching. He was a tall man whose presence screamed SVR, and whose tailored grey suit and polished shoes spoke of quiet power. His face was unreadable, a mask of polite detachment that concealed whatever calculations he was making.

"Comrade Mikhailov," Carl said, using the Russian title with careful neutrality. "The General Secretary's message is still scheduled to play out as planned."

Mikhailov nodded slowly, stepping further into the studio. "Very good, Mr Peterson," he said in his carefully modulated English, his accent precise, each syllable clipped just enough to sound unnatural. "I trust there will be no… deviations."

Carl met his gaze evenly. "Of course not. The message will play in full. Even though I may be British by birth, my allegiance to the Party is absolute."

Carl knew that he had to say that, even though it tasted like ash in his mouth. It was the only way to keep Mikhailov placated, to maintain the fragile illusion that he was nothing more than a dutiful broadcaster following the new order. Anything less than absolute compliance could see him branded a subversive, and he had no illusions about what happened to those who earned that label.

Mikhailov studied him for a moment, his eyes sharp, as if searching for any sign of deception. Carl had seen those eyes before—on intelligence officers, interrogators, men who had spent their careers deciding who lived and who disappeared. He held his breath, knowing that even a flicker of hesitation could be dangerous.

Then, slowly, Mikhailov's lips curved into a smile, thin and insincere. "Good," he said softly. "Very good. I noticed you paid your Party Dues ahead of schedule. It is a sign of your commitment to the new Ireland."

Carl forced a smile in return, though his stomach churned. "Of course," he said smoothly. "Loyalty to the Party is paramount in times of transition."

He knew he didn't want to say the next bit, but he knew that by not informing on his neighbour, it would look suspicious. The regime thrived on paranoia, on making people complicit in its surveillance state. Every interaction was a test, a quiet demand for proof of allegiance. The Party expected whispers, names, and accusations. Even silence could be damning.

Carl swallowed hard, keeping his voice steady. "I noticed something odd about my neighbour, Pierre Welche, the husband of the French Cultural Attaché, this morning. He was on his mobile phone, and when I walked out of my house to collect the morning paper, he suddenly went quiet... as if he had noticed that I had come out of my home. He'd been quite talkative before that."

Carl knew that Walche was DGSE, as Pierre and Emma had, in Tehran once, posed as a married Anglo-French couple during a joint MI6-DGSE operation targeting Iranian nuclear scientists. The two had worked together for years, trading information in a delicate balance of mutual distrust and shared objectives.

Two months earlier, before the coup, Pierre had told Emma and Carl that he had terminal cancer, had 6 months left to live, and that a week ago, Pierre had begged Emma to burn him, as the cancer was getting more painful by the day, and that he'd rather be seen in France as a hero by his homeland than die slowly and forgotten in a Dublin hospital.

Carl had pleaded with him to reconsider, to escape back to France, but Pierre had shaken his head, eyes sunken with pain. "I die either way," he had said. "At least this way, I die for something."

"You dramatic bastard," Carl had said with a forced chuckle, trying to mask the lump in his throat. But Pierre had simply smiled, that same knowing smirk he always had when he was three steps ahead of everyone else in the room.

Carl knew that Pierre, however, had forgot one fact, that, like him, being married to an Embassy official meant that as their spouse held diplomatic credentials, the Vienna Convention applied to him as well, Carl being married to a British Embassy official and Pierre a French Embassy spouse, meaning that unless the Restoration Government was willing to trigger an international incident, both he and Pierre technically held a degree of immunity.

Of course, that was assuming they played their roles well enough not to give the regime a reason to disregard those protections. Immunity was only as strong as the willingness of foreign powers to enforce it, and in Ireland's current climate, that was an open question. Britain and France had both condemned the coup, but neither had committed to action beyond diplomatic protests and economic sanctions. The Americans, under Trump until 24 hours ago, and now JD Vance, was increasingly pro-Moscow, pro-America First, especially as in 2025, they had tried to invade Mexico and failed disastrously. Europe was fractured, NATO was weakened, and Russia was emboldened.

Kier Starmer, the Prime Minister who had been elected in July 2024, was, Carl knew, facing pressure from Reform UK, who had overtaken the Conservatives, and the British Communist Party, an up and coming party who had, in 2028, gained 6 seats in by-elections caused by Conservatives facing recall petitions, 6 different Tory MPs facing jail time due to being part of a shocking grooming ring. As the UK was slated to host an election in the coming July, Carl knew that with the Communists and Reform snapping at Labour's heels, Starmer couldn't afford to be seen as weak on national security. But at the same time, Britain's hands were tied. Direct intervention in Ireland was politically untenable—there was no appetite for military action, not after the Afghanistan withdrawal debacle of the early 2020s and the botched American attempt to reassert dominance in Mexico. And even if there was, Russia's influence in Dublin made any move a potential trigger for escalation.

Then there was the Belarus, Russia and Ukraine situation, Carl knew. In October 2027, Zelenskyy, the Ukrainian leader, while on a visit to the front line, had been killed by a Russian mortar from a Belarusian tank, resulting in Ukraine, powered by EU and UK funds after Trump pulled the plug on American military aid, launching a full-scale offensive into Belarus, claiming that the Lukashenko regime had been complicit in the assassination. A week later, a sudden heart attack caused Lukashenko, who was visiting Putin at the time, to die, the strain on the Belarusian's heart from decades of stress and illness finally catching up with him. What followed was chaos—Belarus collapsed into a power vacuum, and Ukraine, sensing an opportunity, pushed further in, aiming to dismantle Russian influence in Minsk once and for all.

Moscow, of course, did not take kindly to this. Putin, still in power despite rumours of his ailing health, had declared that any further Ukrainian incursions into Belarusian territory would be met with "decisive action." The world held its breath, but so far, it had been a war of attrition, a grinding conflict that neither side could afford to escalate outright. Meanwhile, Ireland, caught in its own maelstrom of political upheaval, had become yet another piece on Russia's geopolitical chessboard.

And Carl? Carl was stuck in the middle of it all, just as he always seemed to be.

The track was coming to an end. Bonnie Tyler's voice faded, the last strains of Total Eclipse of the Heart giving way to the silence of dead air—an unforgivable sin in radio. But there was no time to hesitate. With the precision of a seasoned broadcaster, Carl leaned forward, pressing the button to play the government's message.

A burst of static, then the clipped, authoritative voice of the Restoration Government's spokesperson filled the airwaves.

"Citizens of the New Irish Republic," the voice began, smooth yet chilling in its manufactured certainty. "Our nation stands at the threshold of a new dawn, one where the errors of the past will be corrected, and the future secured for all who believe in the righteous cause of Irish sovereignty, free from the decadence of Western corruption."

Carl forced his expression to remain neutral, even as bile rose in his throat. He had read this script before—or versions of it. It was the same rhetoric used in every authoritarian regime he had ever reported from. The same empty promises, the same veiled threats. He let it play, his hands resting on the desk, careful not to betray even the slightest twitch of dissent.

Mikhailov remained standing just inside the studio, watching him. Assessing.

"The Restoration Government acknowledges the loyalty of its citizens, and the necessary sacrifices made to protect our way of life. As we continue the great work of rebuilding our nation, we remind all who reside within our borders that vigilance is the duty of every patriot. Subversive elements still linger, seeking to undermine our unity, to weaken us from within. We will not allow this."

Carl's grip on the edge of the desk tightened. He had heard that line before, too. It was a prelude to something. A crackdown. A new wave of arrests. Perhaps even executions.

"To those who remain steadfast, we offer opportunity. Prosperity. Security. The weak, the traitorous, and the misguided will be given a chance to see the error of their ways. But let it be known—our patience is not infinite."

And there it was. The unspoken threat, wrapped in the language of benevolence. Carl exhaled slowly, willing himself to remain still.

The message concluded with the anthem of the new regime—an old Irish folk song repurposed as a nationalist rallying cry. Carl let it play, keeping his posture relaxed. To show discomfort would be a mistake.

Finally, as the last note rang out, he leaned into the microphone, his voice smooth, unwavering. "That was a message from the General Secretary of the Restoration Government. Now, let's take things back to the classics— this is Dire Straits with Brothers in Arms."

As the first melancholic chords of Mark Knopfler's guitar filled the studio, Carl allowed himself the smallest, most imperceptible smirk. It was a small act of defiance, barely more than a whisper in the storm, but it was there.

He saw Mikhailov's head tilt slightly, his expression unreadable.

"Interesting choice," the Russian murmured.

Carl met his gaze evenly. "It's a classic. More Birmingham's choice than mine, as you know, Comrade."

"Da, the Saudi owned company likes to keep things predictable," Mikhailov replied, his tone carrying the slightest hint of amusement, as if he saw through the pretext but chose to let it slide—for now. "Moscow only tolerates Manic because oil is still a precious commodity and OPEC remains strategically viable."

Carl nodded slightly, careful to maintain the illusion that he was simply another cog in the machine, another dutiful broadcaster playing his part. The weight of Mikhailov's gaze lingered for a moment longer before the Russian took a step back, his hands still clasped behind his back.

"I'll leave you to your work, Mr Peterson," Mikhailov said, his tone polite but firm. "But do remember—our patience, as the message stated, is not infinite."

"I will, Comrade. Before you go, I need to get another copy of my payslip... my wife does the family finances as she's an accountant and likes to keep everything in order. It seems I may have misplaced mine."

It was a calculated move. Carl knew that asking for something so mundane, so bureaucratic, would reinforce the image of him as an ordinary man simply trying to get by under the new order. No subversive agent would be concerned about their payslip while supposedly plotting against the state.

Mikhailov studied him for a moment before nodding. "Of course. I will ensure it is sent to your inbox by the end of the day."

"Much appreciated," Carl said smoothly, offering a professional smile.

Mikhailov gave a slight nod, his expression unreadable as he turned and left the studio, the soft click of the door closing behind him leaving Carl alone with the music and the ever-present weight of his reality. The Russian's presence was a reminder of how precarious his situation truly was. Every action, every word, had to be measured, carefully calculated to avoid suspicion while subtly pushing back where he could. The smirk he had allowed himself was gone now, replaced with the same neutral mask he had perfected over the years. He let out a slow breath, tapping his fingers lightly on the desk as Brothers in Arms played on.

Carl sat in the dimly lit studio, the weight of Mikhailov's presence still pressing heavily on him. He could feel the tension in his shoulders, the anxiety simmering just beneath his calm exterior. The music was a brief respite, a small moment of familiarity in an increasingly foreign world. He focused on the sound of Mark Knopfler's guitar, each note a reminder of his old life, a life that seemed farther away with each passing day.

The thought of his wife, Emma, hovered at the edges of his mind. She had always been the rock of their family, the steady presence that anchored him through the chaos. Yet even she, with her sharp mind and extensive experience as an SIS handler, was in a precarious position. In the weeks since the coup, their world had grown smaller, their movements more restricted. She had warned him that things would only get more dangerous from here on, but Carl hadn't fully understood until now, until he was staring into the eyes of men like Mikhailov.

Carl reached for his coffee cup, his fingers trembling slightly as he took a sip. It was cold now, but he didn't mind. The warmth from the coffee seemed to cut through the fog that had settled in his mind. He had to focus, to keep his wits sharp. Every word he spoke, every action he took, could have consequences far beyond the studio walls.

The door clicked open again, and Carl's heart rate quickened. This time, it wasn't Mikhailov, but one of the station's junior producers, a young man named Tom who had been working for Manic Goldies Ireland for less than a year. Tom was known for being a bit too eager, always trying to prove himself. Carl wasn't sure whether that made him a potential ally or a liability.

"Mr Peterson," Tom said, stepping into the studio with a hesitant smile. "I've got those reports you asked for about the North-South broadcast split. There's been some feedback from our Belfast offices. Seems like there's been a few complaints about the—"

"Yes, yes," Carl interrupted, cutting him off. "Leave them on the desk. I'll look over them after the show." He gestured toward the table, keeping his tone brisk.

Tom, sensing the tension in the air, placed the reports down quickly and backed out of the room. Carl's eyes lingered on the folder for a moment before turning his attention back to the broadcast. He had no time for distractions. Not now.

He pulled up the next track in the playlist, the familiar sound of Fleetwood Mac's *Go Your Own Way* filling the airwaves. As the opening notes played, Carl thought about the strange conversation with Mikhailov. The Russian had been strangely civil, almost cordial, which only made Carl more uneasy. He couldn't help but wonder if Mikhailov was testing him, seeing how far he could push before Carl broke. He was certain that Mikhailov, like many of the other figures behind the Restoration Government, was skilled at reading people, knowing when they were bluffing, when they were hiding something.

Carl's gaze drifted back to the clock. It was now nearly 14:50. He had only ten minutes left on air before the next shift took over. He needed to make it through this shift—this hour—without giving anything away.

He quickly flicked through the reports Tom had left on the desk. There were more complaints from Northern Ireland about the crossover broadcasts. The Belfast office had received several angry calls from local listeners accusing Manic Goldies Ireland of propagating messages from Dublin that were far too aligned with the new regime's ideals. The thought of that made Carl's skin crawl. He knew the propaganda was being fed directly into the airwaves, but he had hoped it would remain subtle, nuanced enough to pass under the radar.

The regime's influence was slowly creeping into every aspect of life in the Republic, and Carl knew it wouldn't be long before their reach extended further. If they didn't crack down on dissent soon, they'd risk losing control. That was the reality of authoritarian regimes: they couldn't afford to be weak. They had to enforce their narrative, no matter the cost.

Carl rubbed his forehead, trying to push the thought aside. He couldn't afford to get caught up in the long-term consequences. Not now. Not while he still had a chance to make a difference.

The door clicked again, and Carl didn't need to turn around to know who it was this time. Mikhailov had returned.

"Comrade Peterson," Mikhailov's voice was smooth, almost too smooth. "I trust you've had no further issues?"

Carl kept his back straight, his voice neutral. "No issues. Everything is running smoothly."

The Russian's footsteps were slow, deliberate, as he crossed the studio to stand just behind Carl's chair. Carl could feel his gaze on the back of his neck, the pressure of it, like a weight hanging over him.

"I see," Mikhailov said, his voice barely a whisper. "Just remember, Mr Peterson, the Restoration Government expect complete cooperation. Your... contributions are appreciated, but one can never be too careful."

Carl's jaw tightened, but he didn't react. He knew that Mikhailov was testing him again, pushing, prodding. Carl had to keep his cool, had to keep his face neutral, his posture relaxed. He had to be convincing. If Mikhailov suspected even the slightest hint of resistance, it would all come crashing down.

"I understand, Comrade," Carl said, his voice calm. "I am fully committed to the cause. You can trust that there will be no further issues."

Mikhailov paused, as if considering his words carefully. Finally, he nodded. "Good. I trust you know the consequences of failure." He lingered for a moment longer, as if studying Carl, before turning on his heel and walking toward the door.

Carl exhaled slowly as the door clicked shut again. The studio felt even smaller now, as if the walls were closing in on him. The weight of his situation, the delicate balance he had to maintain, pressed down on him like a vice. He could feel the tension in his shoulders, his body responding to the constant pressure of living under the Restoration Government's watchful eye.

With a quick flick of his hand, Carl turned the volume up on the radio, letting Fleetwood Mac's Go Your Own Way fill the silence once again. The song, with its bittersweet melody, seemed to capture the essence of everything he was feeling: torn between two worlds, between duty and loyalty, between survival and resistance.

The last few minutes of his second hour passed in a blur, the music flowing seamlessly, the government's messages playing out as planned. Carl's mind, however, was elsewhere, focused on the long road ahead—the road where every move would be scrutinised, every decision weighed, every action could be his last.

And as the final notes of Go Your Own Way faded into the static, Carl Peterson knew that the fight for Ireland's future was far from over.

****

CHAPTER 2 – The Day Dublin Fell
Monday 11th December 2028

"And in breaking news, the BBC has received word that President Cearbhall O'Kelly of the Irish Republic has been killed in a coup by pro-Russian factions within the Irish Defence Forces. Reports from Dublin indicate that heavy fighting has taken place in and around government buildings, with the Taoiseach's office confirming that emergency measures are now in effect. The United States, United Kingdom, and European Union have all condemned the coup, with NATO holding an emergency session as the situation develops…"

Kelvin Svenson was sitting at his desk at Vauxhall Cross, the home of the Secret Intelligence Service, his eyes locked on the rolling BBC News ticker as it unfolded the crisis in real-time. The headquarters of MI6 was rarely a place of panic—everything here was calculated, measured—but the atmosphere on this particular December morning was anything but calm.

A Scotsman by birth, but Swedish by ancestry, Kelvin had spent his entire career navigating the murky world of international espionage. His focus had been on Russia for the better part of a decade, from its hybrid warfare in Ukraine to its increasing use of cyber-warfare and political manipulation across the West. But even he hadn't expected this.

"Kel, turn the telly up," his colleague, Marti LaBron, a former CIA Analyst who, when Donald Trump had got re-elected in the US in 2024, had taken up a role with MI6 rather than continue working under an administration that had openly courted Moscow, said as she strode into the office, her face set in grim determination.

A rising star in the CIA's Russia team, Kelvin knew that Marti had been one of the key analysts warning about Moscow's creeping influence in Ireland for years. She had seen the warning signs—the funding of fringe political parties, the disinformation campaigns on social media, the strange alliances forming between Irish nationalist groups and Russian-backed operatives. And now, here they were.

Kelvin grabbed the remote and turned up the volume.

"The coup appears to have been led by elements within the Irish Defence Forces sympathetic to the Russian government. Reports indicate that Russian Special Forces—potentially Spetsnaz operatives—have been seen in Dublin, operating alongside the newly declared Restoration Government. The location of the Taoiseach remains unknown, though there are conflicting reports that he may have fled the country. RTÉ, the Irish state broadcaster, has been taken off the air, and military vehicles have been spotted across the capital."

"Well, that's the pooch screwed," Marti said with a dry laugh, arms crossed as she leaned against Kelvin's desk. "We knew they were making moves, but a full-blown military coup? And with Spetsnaz on the ground? That's a bold play, even for Moscow."

Kelvin exhaled sharply, his mind already working through the implications. The Irish Republic had long been seen as neutral, a state that prided itself on sitting outside the NATO umbrella. That neutrality had left it vulnerable. Russia had been laying the groundwork for years—economic partnerships, disinformation campaigns, political funding. But now, they had skipped straight past soft power and gone for a full military takeover.

And the timing was no coincidence.

"It's the Belarus playbook all over again," Kelvin muttered. "We should have seen this coming."

"We did," Marti shot back. "Just not fast enough to stop it."

The BBC feed cut to footage from Dublin. Smoke rose above the city skyline, gunfire crackling in the background as a shaky phone camera captured armoured personnel carriers rolling down O'Connell Street. Irish Defence Forces loyalists—if any remained—were nowhere to be seen. The only soldiers visible wore armbands bearing the insignia of the newly declared Restoration Government.

A male news anchor, his voice tense, narrated over the footage.

"We are now seeing unconfirmed reports that members of the Irish government are being rounded up and detained. There are also reports of sporadic resistance in parts of the city, but at this time, the coup forces appear to have full control over Dublin's key infrastructure…"

Kelvin glanced at the stack of files on his desk, some marked with the red "SENSITIVE - EYES ONLY" stamp, but the majority of them being approvals for the most mundane things like office equipment orders and security clearance renewals. Unlike the Fleming novels, where the MI6, or SIS as its official name, the Secret Intelligence Service, was a shadowy organisation filled with assassins and spies in dinner jackets, the reality was much more bureaucratic, as they and the Security Service, or MI5, reported to the Joint Intelligence Committee, to Yvette Cooper, the Home Secretary (or in the case of the MI6, David Lammy, the Foreign Secretary), and to the Prime Minister himself. That meant that it was the Civil Service who ran the day-to-day operations, ensuring that all intelligence activities had proper authorisation, oversight, and, most frustratingly, paperwork.

Still, this was beyond bureaucracy now. This was war.

And that meant that Sir Kier Starmer, the Prime Minister, was going to be having a very long and difficult day.

"What does Cheltenham say, Clive?" Marti asked, turning her attention to Clive Redman, their liaison with GCHQ. Clive, a bespectacled man in his early fifties, had been standing by the window, scrolling through intelligence feeds on his secure tablet. He looked up, his face grim.

"Do you want the truth, or the diplomatic version?" Clive asked dryly, still tapping at his tablet.

"Come on, Clive," Kelvin said, leaning back in his chair. "We're all adults here. Just tell us how badly we're buggered."

"Like Gary Glitter when Yewtree caught up with him," Clive replied bluntly, setting his tablet down. "GCHQ got caught with their trousers down. Basically, Russia did the old 'zet' but on an accelerated timetable and no tanks."

Zet, or the Z operation, had been used in 2022 when Russia had got tanks and other assets in both Belarus and on the Russo-Ukraine border, and had then pulled off a feint, making it look like a full-scale invasion was coming from the north, only to switch tactics at the last minute. The same strategy had been refined and used here— except this time, there had been no dramatic buildup, no long months of sabre-rattling. Just sudden, brutal action.

"No warnings?" Kelvin asked, rubbing his temples.

"Only the CAA reporting that 4 Aeroflot flights from Moscow landed within the last 24 hours, all Airbus A350-900s, all officially carrying 'holidaying Russians'. Of course, we all know that since 2022, with most of Russia under sanctions and Aeroflot practically banned from most Western destinations, the idea of Russian tourists flocking to Dublin in mid-December is about as believable as Boris Johnson swearing off parties." Clive snorted. "Cheltenham flagged it late, but by the time they pieced it together, the first gunshots were ringing out outside Leinster House."

Kelvin swore under his breath. "That's classic Spetsnaz. Drop them in under the guise of civilian travel, embed them within local loyalists, and seize key sites before anyone can react."

Marti exhaled through her nose, a sharp, irritated sound. "And now, NATO is going to spend the next week wringing its hands while Moscow solidifies its hold."

"Lammy and Starmer aren't going to like this," Kelvin muttered.

"Lammy's already in with the PM," Clive said. "From what I hear, we're waiting to see how the Americans react."

"Well, Trump's a lame duck now, and Vance doesn't get sworn in until the 19th of January," Marti pointed out. "And let's be honest—Vance isn't exactly going to take a hard line against Moscow. Not when half his voter base thinks NATO is a socialist conspiracy."

"Y'know, that's a quicker answer than what the US desk would give us," Kelvin said, shaking his head. "And far more accurate."

Clive exhaled through his nose. "We need to prepare for the reality that Ireland has effectively fallen into Moscow's sphere of influence, at least in the short term. London's official response will be diplomatic protest, economic sanctions, and strongly worded statements at the UN. But beyond that? We're not in a position to send troops, and direct military intervention is off the table unless Dublin suddenly invokes some old Commonwealth treaty that doesn't exist."

"Or pisses off the Ulster Unionists and creates an actual security threat to Northern Ireland," Marti finished. "Which, let's be honest, is only a matter of time."

"We go live now to Dublin, where RTÉ's Sinead Ryan is about to give a statement on behalf of the new so-called Restoration Order," the BBC News anchor announced, and all three intelligence officers turned their attention back to the screen.

Sinead Ryan, a newer face on RTÉ's roster, Kelvin knew, had started her media career at the former RT UK, a mouthpiece that had been based in London and had been part of the Russian's pre-2022 soft power strategy before it was finally shut down by Ofcom. She had always been seen as a pro-Russian voice in Irish media circles, and, as soon as she started speaking, Kelvin knew that she was 100% believing the message she was delivering.

Sinead's face filled the screen, composed and poised, but there was something in her eyes—a zealotry that Kelvin had seen before in those who had fully bought into their own propaganda. She was reading from a prepared statement, her tone measured, authoritative.

"Citizens of Ireland, today marks the dawn of a new era. For too long, our great nation has been subjugated by Western imperialist interests, capitalist lies from London and Brussels, manipulations from Washington, and the creeping decay of liberal decadence. But no longer. The Restoration Government, backed by the true patriots of our Defence Forces, has taken decisive action to restore Irish sovereignty. We stand united with our Russian allies in building a future free from exploitation and the foreign yoke."

Kelvin clenched his jaw. The rhetoric was all too familiar—a mix of anti-Western sentiment, nationalist fervour, and barely veiled threats. It was straight out of the Russian disinformation playbook, adapted to the Irish context.

Ryan continued, her expression shifting into one of grim resolve.

"We call upon all citizens to stand with us in this historic moment. We understand that some may have been misled by Western propaganda, that years of deceit and lies have clouded the truth. But the time has come to break free. We will not tolerate treachery. We will not allow foreign-backed subversives to undermine the will of the people."

Kelvin exchanged a glance with Marti. That was the real message—the warning shot. The Restoration Government were setting the stage for purges. They would frame it as 'removing foreign influence,' but in reality, it would mean silencing dissent.

"General Sean O'Doherty, the interim head of the newly established National Defence Committee, will be requesting President Putin of the Russian Federation to grant permission for our great nation to ascend to membership of BRICS , strengthening our economic and security ties with our partners in Moscow, Beijing, New Delhi, Brasília, and Pretoria. Ireland will no longer be a pawn of Washington or Brussels. We will take our rightful place among the sovereign nations of the world."

Kelvin felt the tension in his jaw harden to the point of pain. BRICS. That was the final nail in the coffin. If this so-called Restoration Government was openly declaring its intent to pivot towards Russia's economic bloc, it meant they weren't just looking for Moscow's backing in the short term—they were committing fully to its sphere of influence.

"Furthermore, effective 25th December 2028, the Euro will no longer be legal tender within this great nation. A new national currency, the Éireann Rouble, will be introduced, fully backed by the gold reserves of the Irish Central Bank and guaranteed by the Russian Federation," Ryan continued, her voice unwavering. "This currency has been printed and will be available from tomorrow from all financial institutions under the authority of the newly established National Treasury Department. Citizens will be required to exchange their Euros within the next six months, after which time, possession of the former currency will be considered an act of economic sabotage."

"In addition, the following media outlets will be required to appoint a government liaison to ensure accurate and truthful reporting in alignment with the new national directives. RTÉ will now be under the full oversight of the newly established Media Ministry, with Manic Radio Group, Bauer Media Audio Ireland, and other independent broadcasters expected to comply fully with the directives of the Restoration Government. Failure to do so will result in their immediate cessation of operations."

Kelvin let out a long, slow breath. That was it, then. The new regime had moved fast—shockingly fast.

"They've been planning this for months," Marti muttered, running a hand through her dark hair. "You don't print a new currency overnight. This was in the works long before today."

"Agreed," Clive said. "Cheltenham's pulling every intercept we can, but it looks like the Russians had this set up in advance. The pieces were already in place; today was just the execution."

Kelvin nodded grimly, his eyes still locked on the screen as Ryan continued her broadcast. "They're going to shut down any media that doesn't fall in line. Bauer, News UK, Global—they'll all be out within the week."

"And Manic?" Marti asked.

Kelvin exhaled. "That's the wildcard. It's Saudi-owned, but the Brits still hold some influence. They might try to ride the line, keep operations running under 'supervision.'"

"True, who'd want to piss OPEC off right now, especially with Europe still scrambling for energy stability after years of Russian gas manipulation?" Clive added. "Manic might try to walk the tightrope for a while, but if they get squeezed too hard, they'll either fold or turn into a resistance asset. And if Moscow realises that, they'll move to shut it down."

Kelvin nodded slowly. Manic's presence in Ireland was one of the few remaining footholds of Western-aligned media, even if its ownership structure complicated things. If it was allowed to continue broadcasting, even under 'supervision,' there was a chance that dissenting voices could still slip through the cracks.

But that also made it a prime target.

"What if we get the Irish desk to send some of the guys to Manic's HQ in Birmingham, to act as script supervisors and that. I mean, you Brits did it in the 50s when you used the BBC to support the Shah in the Iran coup, so why not apply the same playbook here?" Marti suggested, her tone only half-joking.

Kelvin shot her a look. "That was a different time."

Marti smirked. "Was it, though? Seems to me like we're looking at the same Cold War tactics, just with better tech."

Clive hummed in thought. "It's not a bad idea. If Manic's still broadcasting, we might be able to use it as a vector. Get messaging out, keep an ear to the ground on resistance movements."

Kelvin drummed his fingers against his desk. It was a dangerous game, but it might be one of the only options left. The Irish resistance would need communication channels, and while encrypted apps and dark web forums had their uses, nothing reached the public like radio.

It was then that Kelvin heard Ryan on the television, this time speaking in Russian and not Irish or English. He knew, from her file, that she was trilingual, and that her fluency in Russian had been one of the reasons she was courted by the Kremlin's media apparatus in the years before the coup. But hearing her deliver official state declarations in Moscow's tongue, on what was still nominally an Irish television network, made his stomach turn.

And the declaration wasn't a straight translation.

It was more.

It was bending the knee to Putin, it was a declaration of loyalty that went beyond mere political alignment. It was a signal to Moscow, a reassurance that Ireland, under its new pro-Russian regime, was now a willing subject in the Kremlin's expanding sphere of influence.

And that thought scared the half Scot, half Swede.

Especially as his homeland, Sweden, had joined NATO in 2024, two years after Russia had invaded Ukraine, after Russia had issued thinly veiled threats towards Stockholm and Helsinki. That had been a turning point—one of many in the long, slow war between democracy and autocracy. But now, watching Dublin fall, Kelvin couldn't shake the feeling that the world was lurching towards another, even greater conflict.

Kelvin clenched his fists as Ryan's voice, confident and assured, continued in Russian, outlining the Restoration Government's full alignment with Moscow's strategic goals. He only caught bits of it before Marti swore loudly and reached for the translation transcript already filtering through from Cheltenham's monitoring desk.

"'…under the guidance of President Putin and the steady hand of our comrades in the Kremlin, Ireland shall take its place as a sovereign state free from Western imperialism. We will ensure the security of our people, strengthen our military cooperation with Moscow, and work to rebuild Ireland as a bastion of true independence…'" Marti read, then stopped. "Oh, bollocks."

Clive raised an eyebrow. "I'm assuming that wasn't a metaphorical 'bollocks.'"

"Nope," Marti said, eyes scanning further down the translation. "They just announced a 'strategic security pact' with Russia."

Kelvin exhaled slowly. "They're not even pretending to be neutral anymore."

Clive's lips thinned. "Jesus Christ. Moscow's just made its first European annexation without a single shot fired by its own troops."

Marti nodded grimly. "And Dublin's rolled over for it."

The thought chilled Kelvin. It wasn't just the military coup—it was how swiftly the Restoration Government had moved to erase Ireland's previous identity. This wasn't just a power grab. This was an assimilation. The speed, the precision, the lack of internal resistance in the Defence Forces—it was all too perfect.

"We need to get eyes on the loyalists," he said. "There's no way everyone in the Irish Defence Forces is backing this."

Marti shook her head. "We've got sketchy reports of some units resisting—mainly in Cork, Limerick, and parts of Galway. But nothing organised yet."

Kelvin glanced at Clive. "SIGINT picking anything up?"

Clive pursed his lips. "Mostly encrypted chatter, but nothing we can properly decrypt yet. What we do know is that there's a blackout on internal military comms. We suspect Russian operators deployed electronic warfare assets to shut down loyalist coordination."

Clive pursed his lips. "Mostly encrypted chatter, but nothing we can properly decrypt yet. What we do know is that there's a blackout on internal military comms. We suspect Russian operators deployed electronic warfare assets to shut down loyalist coordination. Also, we've had word that another Aeroflot flight has just departed Moscow, a cargo plane."

Kelvin straightened in his chair. "Cargo? Not passengers?"

Clive nodded. "That's what Cheltenham's saying. An Antonov An-124, Russian Air Force markings scrubbed off but still transmitting on a civilian registry. Flight plan had it stopping in Kaliningrad before heading west. It's currently on approach to Shannon Airport."

Marti let out a sharp breath. "Shannon? Not Dublin?"

"Exactly," Clive said. "Dublin's locked down, but Shannon is still functional. Less security, fewer eyes on the ground. If I had to bet, I'd say they're bringing in 'advisors'—mercs, Spetsnaz, or Wagner types under new branding. The kind of people who don't officially exist."

Kelvin exhaled slowly. "Jesus. We're watching a country being turned into a Russian client state in real time."

Marti looked at him, eyes dark. "Not just a client state, Kel. A launch pad. Ireland's never been in NATO. There's no direct treaty obligation for intervention. This is

Moscow creating a Belarus in Western Europe, right on Britain's doorstep."

A heavy silence filled the office.

The implications were stark. Ireland had spent decades as a neutral state, sitting outside of NATO while maintaining close economic and political ties to the West. That neutrality had always been seen as an asset—until now. Now, it had become its greatest vulnerability.

Kelvin turned back to the screen. Sinead Ryan was still speaking in Russian, her voice eerily calm as she laid out the new regime's economic and military policies. But it wasn't just the words that unsettled him—it was the look in her eyes.

"She believes it," he muttered.

Marti glanced up. "What?"

"She believes it," Kelvin repeated. "She's not reading a script because she has to—she wants to. She's not just a mouthpiece, she's a true believer."

Clive let out a low whistle. "That's worse than just a puppet. It means they're stacking their new government with ideological hardliners, not just opportunists."

Kelvin nodded grimly. "And if she's a true believer, that means she's not going to hesitate to push the regime's line. No half measures, no room for negotiation."

Marti leaned forward, tapping her fingers on the desk. "So, what's the play? Cheltenham's already got SIGINT crawling all over this. We're getting reports from Belfast that the Unionists are losing their bloody minds—half of them are convinced this is a prelude to an invasion of the North."

"They might not be wrong," Clive said. "If the Restoration Government are serious about removing Western influence from Ireland, they're going to have to deal with Northern Ireland eventually. And if they try to take it by force…"

"NATO gets involved," Kelvin finished. "And suddenly, this isn't just about Ireland anymore."

Marti's jaw tightened. "They're not that stupid. They know NATO would have to act if Northern Ireland was attacked."

"They're not stupid, no," Kelvin agreed. "But they're playing a long game. They don't need to invade the North outright. They just need to destabilise it. Proxy groups, political pressure, maybe even using Manic Vibes Ireland to pump propaganda into the young population."

Clive clicked his tongue. "If they play this right, they could get Northern Ireland to tear itself apart before NATO even has a reason to act."

Kelvin rubbed his temples. "We need assets on the ground."

Marti scoffed. "You think we don't? Every single one of our official assets has gone dark or fled across the Irish Sea. The ones still inside are staying buried. Dublin isn't safe for anyone with Western intelligence ties."

Kelvin frowned. "What about Manic?"

Marti raised an eyebrow. "You really think a bunch of radio people are going to save the country?"

"No," Kelvin admitted. "But they are still operating. If they're keeping their heads down and playing along, they might be able to feed us intel."

Clive nodded. "It's worth looking into. But we need to be subtle. If Mikhailov gets even a *whiff* of an intelligence operation, he'll shut them down—or worse."

Marti exhaled sharply. "Fine. I'll put out feelers, see if we can get someone inside Manic to start passing information. But it's risky. One wrong move, and we lose our last window into Dublin."

Kelvin sat back, the weight of the situation pressing down on him.

Russia had just pulled off its boldest move in decades.

And if the West didn't act fast, Dublin wouldn't just be the first domino to fall. It would be the beginning of something far, far worse.

****

CHAPTER 3 – Checkmate
Monday 19th December 2028

"Comrade Control, this is Checkmate 7, request clearance to land at Shannon? "

Mikhail Semyonovich Sulov, a Captain of the Russian Air Force knew this mission was important. As a pilot of one of the first 10 Sukhoi Su-75 fifth generation fighter jets, formerly allocated to Kaliningrad, his orders had been to deliver the advanced jet to the new administration in Ireland, what Russia was now, internally, calling the "Independent Irish Republic", and be on standby for any British or NATO interference. Moscow had made its move, and now it was up to men like Sulov to secure it.

Born in St Petersburg, or Leningrad as he saw it, in 1998, Sulov was the third son of a former First Directorate officer, a man who had served in the old KGB before its dissolution in 1991. His father had always taught him that the collapse of the Soviet Union was the greatest catastrophe of the 20th century—a betrayal engineered by the West, a humiliation that Moscow was only now beginning to reverse.

A graduate of Moscow State University, he had fallen in love at the time with an Irishwoman who had been a RT International journalist in the early 2020s, back when she had worked at the Moscow headquarters of the state-controlled broadcaster after her previous assignment, working at RT UK, had ended when Ofcom had revoked its broadcasting licence in Britain. The woman, Sinead Ryan, Mikhail knew, had been another legacy KGB family member, as her grandfather had been a Fifth

Directorate officer, Political police, the arm of the KGB that had specialised in suppressing dissent, controlling the press, and ensuring ideological purity within the Soviet Union's satellite states. Sinead had been raised on the same doctrine of loyalty to Moscow that Mikhail had, despite growing up in Dublin. Their romance had been one of shared ideology as much as passion—two believers in a world where Russia would reclaim its place as a dominant force, where the Western model of liberal democracy would be dismantled piece by piece.

But tragedy struck the couple in 2027, when Sinead was pregnant, and, due to no fault of her own, miscarried their child at five months. It had been a devastating blow, one that had nearly broken her. Mikhail had been stationed in Kaliningrad at the time, unable to be there when she needed him most. The loss had only deepened their resolve. Sinead had thrown herself into her work, becoming a key propagandist for Moscow's efforts in the West, while Mikhail had recommitted himself to the military, vowing to play his role in the restoration of Russian power.

And now, that mission had brought him here.

To Ireland.

To her.

He knew that she still had feelings for him, as they had used Telegram and VK to keep in contact over the past year, their conversations always careful, always coded, as Mikhail knew that she had been a SVR recruit prior to her RT UK assignment, when she had attended Cambridge as part of the long-term infiltration efforts of Russian intelligence. The irony that Cambridge was still, even in the 2010s, a Russian recruitment ground was not lost on him. The legacy of the Cambridge Five still loomed over British intelligence, a reminder that Moscow had always played the long game. Sinead had been one of many—bright, ambitious students identified early, shaped, and moulded for service. The fact that she had risen so quickly within RT's ranks was no accident.

Mikhail's radio crackled again, bringing him back to the present.

"Checkmate 7, clearance granted. Proceed to Shannon airbase, Runway 22. Maintain radio silence after this transmission. Control out," the controller said in a Russian accented voice.

The channel went dead, the static replaced by the low hum of his Su-75's engines as he guided the aircraft down towards the western Irish airbase. The weather was atrocious—howling winds from the Atlantic, rain hammering against the canopy—but he had flown in worse. Russia had officially denied all involvement in the Irish coup, claiming it was an internal matter, but the truth was clear for anyone willing to see it. Moscow had backed this operation from the beginning. And now, Russian boots—if not yet in large numbers—were touching Irish soil.

Shannon Airport, once a major transit hub for US military flights, was now firmly under the control of the Restoration Government. Civilian flights had been suspended indefinitely, and the airfield had been repurposed for military logistics, a hub for Russian and pro-coup Irish forces. As Mikhail approached, he caught sight of Mi-171 transport helicopters bearing the markings of the new Irish regime and a handful of Russian-made armoured personnel carriers stationed near the hangars.

Touching down smoothly on the wet tarmac, Mikhail felt the rumble of the Su-75's wheels gripping the slick surface. As he taxied towards the designated hangar, he spotted a convoy of black SUVs waiting near the control tower. His welcoming party.

Powering down the jet, he removed his helmet and reached for his flight log, before unclipping his sidearm—an MP-443 Grach, the standard sidearm of Russian forces. He didn't expect trouble, but in times like these, caution was second nature.

The cockpit canopy hissed open, letting in the cold, wet air. As he climbed down, he saw a figure break away from the convoy and stride towards him.

Sinead.

She looked as striking as ever, her auburn hair pulled into a tight bun, dressed in a black Restoration Government military-style coat, the red and gold insignia of the new regime pinned to her chest. She had always carried herself with a quiet confidence, but now, there was something different about her. Authority. A certainty that came with being on the winning side of history—or at least believing you were.

And she had 3 cameras surrounding her, cameras recording her no doubt reporting on how Mother Russia has helped secure Ireland's "true independence" from Western imperialism.

Mikhail felt a flicker of pride—and something else, something more primal—at the sight of her in that role. Not just primal in the sense of how she was the spokesperson for the new order, but that of his loins, of his longing for her, the woman he had once planned to build a family with. Their child might have been lost, but their vision—their dream—was now being realised on a grander scale. He had no doubt that she had played a key role in the success of this coup. That was Sinead. She had always been driven, always believed that history would bend to the will of those strong enough to shape it.

She stopped a few feet away, her eyes locking onto his, assessing him, measuring his presence. For a moment, neither of them spoke, the roar of the Atlantic wind filling the silence between them.

Then she smiled.

"Comrade Sulov," she said, her voice carrying over the wind, rich with amusement and something warmer beneath it. "Welcome to the Independent Irish Republic."

Mikhail gave a short nod, a small smirk tugging at the corners of his lips. "I see you've been busy."

Sinead glanced at the cameras, then back at him. "Someone has to make sure the world hears the truth."

"Truth," Mikhail repeated, rolling the word over his tongue. "A rare commodity these days."

She stepped closer, her voice dropping just slightly so that only he could hear. "Rare, but necessary. The West will drown the people in their lies, in their hysteria about 'Russian aggression' and 'authoritarian takeovers.' They'll paint us as villains, as invaders." She tilted her head slightly, her eyes narrowing. "But you and I know better."

Mikhail studied her for a moment before nodding. "Da. We do."

One of the camera operators cleared his throat. "Miss Ryan, should we begin?"

Sinead turned slightly, flashing a polished, practised smile at the man. "Of course. Let's document this historic moment. We will do the English version first for the imperialist West, then the Irish version for the locals… and then the domestic version for Moscow."

Mikhail knew what she meant by the latter, the domestic version would be in Russian, and it wouldn't just be a translation—it would be tailored for the Kremlin's audience, carefully crafted to portray Ireland's 'liberation' as part of Moscow's grander geopolitical strategy. It would be a message not just to Ireland, but to the world: Russia had outmanoeuvred the West once again.

"Mikhail, my love, here is your script for the English portion. You know what our domestic audience wants to hear, da?" Sinead said, handing him a neatly printed sheet.

Mikhail took the sheet without glancing at it immediately. He already knew the general contents—boilerplate rhetoric about sovereignty, freedom from Western interference, and the beginning of a new era for Ireland under its "rightful leadership." Moscow's talking points were predictable, just variations on the same themes they had deployed in Belarus, Ukraine, and other proxy states. But the way Sinead handed it to him—the way she said *my love*—made his pulse quicken in a way that had nothing to do with politics.

He finally allowed himself to look at her properly. Not just as a fellow believer in the cause, not just as a comrade executing a shared mission, but as the woman he had once held at night, whispered dreams to, and planned a future with. She had always been fierce, but now, she burned. There was a sharpness to her gaze that hadn't been there before, an edge that had been forged in the fires of propaganda and ideological conviction.

And yet, he saw something else beneath it.

Something that told him she had missed him too.

He exhaled through his nose, glanced at the sheet, and smirked. "I could recite this in my sleep."

Sinead laughed, and for a moment, it was just them again, just Mikhail and Sinead before the coup, before the speeches, before the titles and the uniforms. Just a man and a woman who had once shared something deep.

"Tonight, Mik, come to my home, and we can talk properly. No cameras, no scripts, just us."

Mikhail raised an eyebrow at the use of her nickname for him—Mik. It had been years since he had heard her say it. And yet, here they were, standing in the windswept remains of what was once an Irish civilian airport, now transformed into a military foothold for Moscow's new puppet regime. The weight of history pressed upon them, but in that moment, it was as if the world around them had fallen away.

Sinead was watching him closely, waiting for his response. Her invitation carried more than one meaning, and they both knew it. The game they were playing—their carefully choreographed roles in Moscow's great theatre—was one thing. But there was something else, something deeper. A chance to reclaim what had been lost. Or, perhaps, a chance to see just how far they had changed since the last time they had been together.

Mikhail allowed himself a smirk. "It would be my pleasure, lyubov' moya." He saw the flicker of satisfaction in her expression, the way she straightened ever so slightly, as if reassured that beneath the uniforms, the cameras, and the propaganda, he was still hers.

Sinead turned away, signalling to the cameras. "Alright, let's begin."

Mikhail took his place beside her, standing tall, his uniform crisp, the Restoration Government insignia already affixed to his flight jacket. The cameras adjusted their focus, the lights flickered on, and just like that, the performance began.

The camera operator held up a hand. "Three, two, one—
live."

Sinead's expression transformed into that perfect mask of
composed authority, the one she had perfected on RT long
before this day. Her voice was smooth, confident,
polished with years of media training.

"Today marks a historic moment for Ireland," she began
in English, her cadence measured, the warmth of a trusted
news anchor mixed with the steel of a government
spokesperson. "For too long, our great nation has suffered
under the economic tyranny of the European Union, the
political manipulation of NATO, and the cultural
degradation of Western imperialism. But no more."

Mikhail kept his expression neutral, listening as she
delivered Moscow's message. He had heard variations of
this speech before—on Russian state television, in
Belarus, in Donetsk, in every territory Moscow had
claimed as its own. The script barely changed, only the
locations and the flags.

"The Independent Irish Republic stands as a beacon of
true sovereignty," Sinead continued. "With the
unwavering support of our allies in the Russian
Federation, we are taking decisive steps to ensure that
Ireland remains free from foreign interference. This
includes the establishment of a self-sufficient economy,
the creation of an independent security apparatus, and the
development of strong international partnerships outside
the grasp of Anglo-American influence."

The camera panned slightly, shifting focus to Mikhail. He was up.

He cleared his throat, shifting his grip on the speech Sinead had handed him. He could feel the weight of the cameras, of history itself pressing on his shoulders. He had given speeches before—addressing cadets, relaying mission reports—but this was different. This wasn't just about military protocol or orders. This was about solidifying control, ensuring that the world saw Ireland's fate as a foregone conclusion.

Mikhail met the camera with an expression of quiet conviction.

"As an officer of the Russian Air Force, I am honoured to stand here today as a friend and ally to the people of Ireland," he began, his English carrying only the faintest trace of an accent. "The world has long been lied to about Russia's intentions. The West tells you that we seek conquest, that we bring war. But I tell you the truth: Russia brings security. Russia brings stability. And most of all, Russia brings respect for national sovereignty."

He let the words settle, watching for Sinead's reaction. She gave him the subtlest of nods.

Mikhail continued.

"The Independent Irish Republic is not alone. Moscow recognises the legitimacy of this government, and today marks the beginning of a new partnership. The Russian Federation stands with Ireland in its struggle against foreign subversion. And in the days to come, we will ensure that this nation is defended against those who would see it divided."

The speech ended, the camera lights dimmed slightly, and the camera operator nodded towards Sinead.

"That was perfect. We'll run it as the lead on tonight's national broadcast."

Sinead smiled, a picture of professional poise. "Thank you, Ivan. Let's prepare for the Irish-language version next."

As the crew moved to reset, Mikhail leaned in just slightly, his voice low. "How was that?"

Sinead's eyes flickered with something he couldn't quite place. "You always were a natural."

Mikhail let a smirk tug at his lips. "I had a good teacher."

* _ * _ * _ *

Mikhail followed Sinead into the flat that she was living in in Dublin, their car having done the near 3 hours journey from Shannon Airport to Dublin, the roads mostly clear save for military checkpoints flying the red and gold insignia of the Restoration Government. Dublin was quiet—too quiet. The usual bustle of city life had been replaced with an eerie stillness, broken only by the occasional armed patrol and the distant hum of military vehicles. The coup had transformed the city in a matter of days. The old Ireland, the one Sinead had grown up in, was gone. What remained was something new— something controlled.

Mikhail stepped inside, shrugging off his damp flight jacket as he took in the surroundings. The flat was sparsely decorated, efficient, designed for function rather than comfort.

"It's the quarters of the former Minister of State for small businesses and retail, who, shall we say, Mik, has 'retired'," Sinead said with a smirk, closing the door behind them and locking it with a flick of her wrist. She turned to face him, her arms crossed, her expression one of amused satisfaction.

Mikhail chuckled softly, setting his jacket down over the back of a chair. "Retired? You mean exiled, imprisoned, or—"

"One of the SVR people gave him his papers in the form of a 9mm brain haemorrhage," Sinead finished with a smirk, stepping closer, her voice laced with dark amusement. "Let's just say the Restoration Government has little patience for economic ministers who spent too long at Davos sipping champagne with American hedge fund managers."

Mikhail hummed, neither approving nor disapproving. "A necessary adjustment, I suppose. The old order had to go."

"It did," Sinead agreed. "And now we're building something better."

She walked to the sideboard, pulling open a bottle of Russian Standard vodka and pouring two glasses. Mikhail accepted his without question, taking a sip and letting the burn settle in his throat. It was a ritual, in a way—

confirmation that they were on the same side, that they understood each other.

"You did well today," she said, perching on the edge of the dining table. "Your delivery was perfect. Strong, confident. Exactly what Moscow needs to see."

Mikhail raised an eyebrow. "Not what Ireland needs to see?"

She smirked. "Ireland will see what I tell it to see, Mik. That's how this works. There's only one person's approval that matters, and it isn't General O'Doherty's."

Mikhail understood exactly what she meant. President Putin, the Russian Federation's supreme leader, was the only audience that truly mattered. Ireland's fate was already sealed, its so-called independence merely another pawn in Moscow's grand game. The Restoration Government might believe they were in control, but Sinead knew better. She had always known better.

Mikhail took another slow sip of vodka, watching her carefully. She was playing her part well—flawlessly, even. But he had known her too long, too intimately, not to see the cracks beneath the surface.

"You've changed," he murmured, setting his glass down.

Sinead arched an eyebrow, swirling the vodka in her own glass. "Have I?"

"You're sharper. Harder." He tilted his head slightly. "More ruthless."

She let out a quiet laugh, not denying it. "Maybe I just stopped pretending. Maybe I've always been this way, and I was just waiting for the world to catch up."

Mikhail smirked at that, but his eyes remained searching. "And yet, you still invited me here. Just us. No cameras, no scripts. What is it you really want, Sinead?"

Her smirk faded, replaced by something more measured, more calculating. She set her glass down beside his and stepped closer. Close enough that he could feel the warmth of her body, close enough that if he reached out, he could pull her against him.

"I wanted to see if you were still the man I remembered," she said softly. "Or if Kaliningrad turned you into something else."

Mikhail held her gaze, the air between them charged. "And?"

Her lips curled slightly, a whisper of a smirk. "I haven't decided yet. The only way to remind me is to fuck me, to make me your own again. Sdelay menya svoyey malen'koy shlyukhoy."

Mikhail's breath hitched ever so slightly at her words. It wasn't just the proposition—it was the way she said it, the way she delivered it with that same controlled precision she used in her broadcasts. The fact that the words she said in Russian—"Make me your little whore."—wasn't lost on him either. She wasn't just teasing, she was issuing a challenge, daring him to prove that the man he had been—the man who had once belonged to her—was still there.

For a moment, he did nothing. Just let the words settle between them, let the tension coil tighter. His training told him to analyse, to calculate, to understand the game before making his move. But this—this wasn't strategy. This was something far older, far deeper than politics or ideology.

Mikhail reached out, his fingers brushing against her waist before gripping firmly, pulling her flush against him. He heard her sharp intake of breath, felt the slight tremor in her frame—not fear, never fear, but something close to anticipation.

"You always knew how to push me," he murmured against her ear, his voice low, rougher now.

Sinead tilted her head back slightly, eyes gleaming with that same mixture of amusement and heat. "And you always knew how to take what you wanted."

He did. And he would.

His lips crashed against hers, claiming, punishing, devouring in a way that left no room for uncertainty. Sinead responded instantly, her hands tangling in his hair, nails scraping against the nape of his neck as she pushed against him with equal ferocity.

This wasn't love. This wasn't romance. This was two people rekindling something dangerous, something primal, in the middle of a coup, with the world falling apart around them.

And that was exactly how they liked it.

*_*_*_*

The dim glow of the bedside lamp cast soft shadows against the walls. Their clothes were strewn haphazardly across the floor, remnants of a battle fought and won in sheets rather than on the streets of Dublin. Mikhail lay back against the pillows, shirtless, cigarette between his fingers, watching as Sinead pulled a silk robe around her shoulders, belting it loosely at the waist.

She was staring out the window now, the city beneath them eerily quiet, save for the occasional rumble of military vehicles patrolling the streets.

"Still as much as an Irish svalka spermy, my love?" Mikhail murmured, exhaling a slow stream of smoke as he watched her. He knew that, despite Sinead being all powerful with the media, she had a submissive side, a side to her which she let control slip, she let only a select few people see. He had always been one of them.

Sinead turned back to him, her expression unreadable, though a hint of a smirk played at her lips. "Oh, you enjoyed that, did you?" she teased, tilting her head as she crossed the room towards him, her bare feet silent against the hardwood floor. "You always did like seeing me like this. Like a good little svalka spermy."

Mikhail chuckled darkly, taking another slow drag from his cigarette. "I think you enjoyed it more, lyubov' moya." He let his gaze drift lazily down her form, the robe doing little to hide the faint marks his hands and mouth had left on her pale skin. "You always did like being conquered, even as you played at ruling."

She let out a quiet hum, running a finger along the edge of his jaw before leaning down, her breath warm against his ear. "And you always liked bending me to your will. A Russian officer, an Irish propagandist… what a strange match we make."

Mikhail exhaled, setting the cigarette aside. He reached up, gripping the belt of her robe and tugging her down onto his lap. "Not so strange," he murmured, brushing his lips against her neck. "We both serve the same master in the end, don't we?"

Sinead's smirk flickered, her fingers tightening against his shoulders. "Do we?" she whispered.

The question lingered in the air between them.

For all the bravado, for all the declarations of loyalty to Moscow, to the cause, there was something else there, something unspoken. A tiny sliver of something Sinead had never allowed herself to admit—uncertainty. She had spent years crafting herself into the perfect instrument of Russian propaganda, aligning herself with Moscow's ambitions, casting off the weaknesses of her Western upbringing. And yet, lying here, tangled with Mikhail, something about this moment unsettled her.

Because, deep down, she knew that this was fleeting.

She was no fool. She had studied history, knew exactly how Moscow treated its so-called allies. Russia had a long memory, but no loyalty to those who outlived their usefulness. And the Restoration Government? They were useful now, but what happened when they became an inconvenience? When Ireland had served its purpose?

Mikhail watched her carefully, sensing the shift in her mood. He traced a finger along her jawline, tilting her chin so their eyes met. "What is it, lyubov' moya?"

She hesitated. Just for a second.

Then, she smiled again, smooth as ever. "Nothing," she murmured. "Just thinking about the speech tomorrow. About what comes next."

Mikhail studied her for a moment longer before nodding. He didn't press. He knew better than that.

Instead, he leaned back, taking another slow drag from his cigarette. "Then tell me, my love. What does come next?"

Sinead exhaled, rolling off him and reaching for her own cigarette from the silver case on the nightstand. She lit it, taking a long pull before answering.

"Consolidation," she said simply. "The Restoration Government has won the capital, but that's not enough. We need the whole country. That means eliminating resistance, securing the economic transition, and ensuring compliance."

****

CHAPTER 4 – Berlin Moves
Sunday 24th December 2028

"Kelvin, the Germany desk has intercepted an email from Berlin... to Bauer HQ in Hamburg."

Kelvin Svenson barely glanced up from his screen, his fingers still skimming across his secure terminal as he parsed through the latest intelligence reports on Ireland's descent into Moscow's grip. But at the mention of Berlin and Bauer, he stopped typing.

"Intercepted how?" he asked, his voice calm, but his mind already moving ahead to the implications.

His colleague, Clive Redman, adjusted his glasses, his expression grim. "GCHQ picked it up through a flagged communications channel—one of the deep scans we've been running ever since the coup started. Berlin have ordered Bauer to close its Irish operations or face sanctions."

Kelvin exhaled slowly, leaning back in his chair as he digested the information. The German government had been treading carefully since the coup in Ireland, not wanting to be dragged into another geopolitical quagmire. Berlin's position was precarious—its economy was still recovering from years of Russian energy manipulation, and its political class was deeply divided on how to handle Moscow's expansionist moves.

But now, they had made a decision. And it was one that would send shockwaves through the European media landscape.

Bauer Media, Kelvin knew, had not yet pulled its stations from Ireland, unlike Global and News UK, which had immediately withdrawn under pressure from London and Washington. Bauer's German parent company had hesitated, caught between commercial interests and political realities.

And then there was Manic.

The Riyadh administration, as it knew that Moscow would be very cautious upsetting OPEC, had so far kept its distance from the fallout in Ireland. Manic, being Saudi-owned but based in Britain, had become an anomaly—a network still broadcasting in the newly pro-Russian Ireland, threading a dangerously thin line between compliance and quiet resistance. A source in the Putin Government had told the British Ambassador in Moscow, off the record, that Putin refused to interfere with Manic's operation because of 2 reasons.

OPEC... and James Jenkins.

Kelvin tapped his fingers against his desk, his mind racing. James Jenkins. The name had surfaced more times than he liked in recent intelligence briefings, always in ways that made things more complicated.

Manic's CEO since the early part of 2028, having replaced Ralph Bernard at the helm, Jenkins had risen through the ranks of commercial radio with ruthless efficiency. A former lawyer, then Deputy Head of Legal, then Head of Legal, and by 2027 Deputy CEO of Global Media, he was known as the most litigations man in media, Ashley Tabor-King's attack dog who had kept

Global's rivals at bay through legal warfare rather than competition on content. His unexpected departure from Global and subsequent appointment as Manic's CEO had raised eyebrows across the industry. Some said he had been forced out after an internal power struggle; others whispered that he had seen which way the wind was blowing and made his move before Global collapsed under regulatory pressure.

But the truth?

He had left with Tabor-King's blessing, had left with a mission.

To prove that he was worthy of, when Tabor-King retired from Global, becoming the CEO of the biggest commercial radio network in Europe.

After all, the logic was there. If you could run the second largest commercial radio network in Europe with all its chaotic expansionism, aggressive branding strategies, and deep entanglement with Middle Eastern investors, then surely you could handle Global. It was a trial by fire, one that Jenkins seemed to relish.

And within 6 months of taking over, he had filed over 40 lawsuits against Bauer, News UK, and the one smaller group that was still in the game—Nation Broadcasting.

The latter had been concerning, as Communicorp UK, in 2027, had sold out to Global, the CMA nodding it through like a rubber-stamping machine, leaving Nation as the last real independent player in the UK commercial radio market. Jenkins had wasted no time in turning his legal machine on them, targeting their branding, their advertising deals, even their frequency allocations. It was a full-spectrum assault, one designed to strangle the competition before they could become a threat.

What was worse was that he was a hereditary Lord, meaning that he had influence beyond the boardrooms and the legal battlegrounds of media regulation. Lord James Jenkins of Henley-on-Thames, as his full title stated, was not just a corporate shark; he was deeply embedded in the British establishment.

Like his late father, he was also a KC, a King's Counsel, and one of the most formidable legal minds in the UK. He knew the intricacies of corporate law, media regulations, and international trade agreements better than anyone in the industry. And now, with the crisis in Ireland unfolding, Jenkins had somehow positioned himself as the one person Putin didn't want to cross.

Kelvin rubbed his temple. *Why?*

He turned to Clive. "So, let me get this straight. Berlin orders Bauer to pull out. Bauer complies because, well, it's Bauer. But Manic stays. And Putin—*Putin*—decides to let them be because of Jenkins? That doesn't make any sense."

"It does if you think about it from Moscow's perspective," Clive replied. "Putin doesn't care about Irish radio. But he does care about OPEC. Saudi Arabia owns Manic, and Riyadh is still playing both sides—arming Ukraine through backchannels while keeping its oil exports to Russia steady. If Putin cracks down on Manic, he risks angering the Saudis. And then there's Jenkins."

Kelvin frowned. "What about him?"

Clive sighed, leaning forward. "We've been running a deep dive on him ever since he took over Manic. The guy's a ghost when it comes to personal affiliations—never takes a public stance on anything, never lets his real views slip. But one thing stands out: he's an expert in leverage. Everything he's done, from his lawsuits against Bauer to his hostile moves against Nation Broadcasting, is about control. And now, for whatever reason, he has a seat at the table where Moscow is concerned."

Kelvin didn't like where this was going. "You're telling me Putin sees Jenkins as an asset?"

"Not necessarily an asset," Clive corrected. "But a variable. And Putin doesn't like variables he can't predict. If Jenkins has something on Moscow, or if he's playing some long game that we haven't figured out yet, that would explain why the Kremlin is keeping its hands off Manic."

Kelvin exhaled sharply. "This is a disaster waiting to happen."

Marti LaBron, who had been quietly listening from across the room, finally spoke up. "If Jenkins is that powerful, why hasn't London leaned on him yet? If MI5 or the Foreign Office had anything on him, they'd be using it."

"Because he was with Global since Day 1, since Ashley Tabor-King made his empire what it is today," Kelvin said, rubbing his temple. "And Global, like it or not, has always had the government's ear. He's an Oxford graduate, the son of a Lord, a Lord himself by inheritance, and a man who has spent his career navigating the highest levels of both the legal and corporate worlds without ever putting a foot wrong. His first ever experience in radio, get this, was as a runner at Brookes Vibes."

Clive raised an eyebrow. "Brookes Vibes? As in that Brookes Vibes?"

Kelvin nodded grimly. "Yeah. The same station that was basically a glorified marketing arm for GWR back in the early 2000s. Where Adam Banks built his little empire of exploitative promotions and dodgy backroom deals. Jenkins was barely 18 when he started there, but he was already making connections—rubbing shoulders with the people who would later run Global, Bauer, and News UK. He saw the game before most people even knew they were playing. His dad, Lord Jenkins, was part of the same investment group and Mayfair club as... Michael Tabor. The funny thing is, guess who was Manic CEO between 2022, when Saudi brought Manic after the Ukraine sanctions off an oligarch, until 2025 when Ralph Bernard took over? Clue, he was an idiot who worked for Brookes Vibes in the early 2000s."

Clive blinked. "Wait, don't tell me—Adam Banks?"

Kelvin nodded. "The very same. That moron somehow went from running trashy student radio promotions to CEO of a Saudi-owned multinational radio network. But here's where it gets interesting. Banks was ousted in 2025, right? What happened to Manic in 2025? Your clue for £10... His Honour Sir Thomas Harvey, rape allegations and a two tonne haul of coke in their Brum studios?"

Clive let out a low whistle. "Right. The Broadcasting Boundaries scandal. The whole bloody thing fell apart. I remember MI5 having a field day with that one—sexual exploitation, drug trafficking, money laundering, the whole works. Manic barely survived."

"And Banks was CEO, Jenkins was Head of Legal at Global and watching it all unfold from a safe distance," Kelvin continued. "Then, after Manic somehow limps through the scandal and Bernard takes over, Jenkins jumps ship from Global and within a year, he's in charge. That's not coincidence. That's someone who knows exactly when to strike."

"The BBC are getting reports of an explosion near the Chernobyl Exclusion Zone. Ukrainian emergency services are responding, and unconfirmed sources suggest a Russian bomber was seen in the area prior to the blast."

Kelvin's head snapped towards the television screen in the corner of the office. The BBC's news ticker was flashing red, the words Breaking News scrolling beneath live footage of a dark, smoke-filled skyline.

"The Chernobyl Exclusion Zone?" Marti muttered, pushing off the desk and stepping closer to the screen. "What the hell would Russia be hitting there?"

Clive tapped furiously on his secure terminal, already pulling intelligence feeds from GCHQ. "Give me a second—I'm checking what we've got from satellite imagery."

Kelvin's Microsoft Teams rang, and he knew instantly, from who it was that it wouldn't be a pleasant call.

That it was from Thames House.

That it meant that something had gone terribly wrong.

He answered immediately, his voice steady. "Svenson."

The voice on the other end was clipped, professional, and carrying the unmistakable weight of authority. "Kelvin, it's Sam Holloway. Get Marti and Clive to listen in. We've got a situation."

Kelvin motioned for the others to gather around, switching the call to speaker. Holloway, a senior MI5 officer based at Thames House, was not the kind of person to call unless it was urgent. And given what had just flashed across the BBC ticker, it wasn't hard to guess what this was about.

"We're getting preliminary reports from Defence Intelligence," Holloway continued. "A Russian Tu-160 strategic bomber entered Ukrainian airspace just before 0400 hours local time, launched a cruise missile, then turned back towards Belarus. The missile impacted a GCHQ listening post that had been operating near the Chernobyl Exclusion Zone... and simultaneously, and you'll love this, the Kuznetsov has put to sea."

Kelvin exchanged a sharp glance with Marti and Clive. The Admiral Kuznetsov—Russia's only aircraft carrier, a relic of Soviet naval power—had been in dry dock for years, its constant breakdowns and mechanical failures a running joke among Western intelligence circles. But if it was finally at sea again, even in a limited capacity, that meant Moscow was making a statement.

And then there was the missile strike. A direct hit on a GCHQ listening post? That wasn't just an attack—it was a declaration.

Kelvin exhaled slowly, keeping his voice even. "Tell me we didn't have anyone on the ground."

There was a pause before Holloway answered. "We're still trying to confirm. The post was semi-automated, but there were at least two personnel stationed there for maintenance, Ukrainians."

The thing that Kelvin was confused about was simple. Why strike a GCHQ listening post that was staffed by Ukrainians and not British personnel? It wasn't the most critical asset in the intelligence network—certainly not important enough to justify the risk of launching a strategic bomber into Ukrainian airspace, even from Belarus.

And why put the Admiral Kuznetsov to sea now? The timing felt too precise, too deliberate. Moscow was sending a message, but the meaning behind it wasn't immediately clear.

Kelvin's mind raced as he connected the dots. A direct strike on a Western intelligence asset, a show of naval force with the Kuznetsov, and the ongoing crisis in Ireland—this wasn't just about Ukraine. This was bigger. This was Russia flexing its muscles in multiple theatres, testing the West's resolve.

Clive, still tapping furiously on his secure terminal, finally spoke. "Cheltenham's pulling the satellite images now. The GCHQ post is gone—obliterated. There's a secondary fire about a kilometre west, might be collateral damage, but it's hard to tell with all the radiation readings in the area. No immediate signs of survivors."

Marti muttered a curse under her breath. "Putin's playing a dangerous game. A direct strike on a British intelligence site, even if it's technically in Ukraine, is an escalation. If he's willing to go this far, what's next?"

Kelvin exhaled through his nose, forcing himself to remain calm. "It's a calculated risk. Moscow's betting that London won't respond with force, not with an election coming up and Starmer trying to keep a grip on Parliament. The Americans? Vance won't do a damn thing. Not after how the Irish coup played out."

Marti folded her arms. "So, what do we do? Just sit back and watch as Putin pushes further?"

Holloway's voice cut through the discussion. "Not exactly. Listen closely. DI's analysis suggests this is a distraction, same with the floating scrapyard. But what? They don't know."

Kelvin frowned, pacing slightly as he processed the implications. "A distraction from what, though? Ireland's already in their pocket, Ukraine's been fighting them for years, and Belarus is still a mess. What's left? Hang on... who, after Trump pulled Ukraine funding, in 2025, was the biggest supplier of weapons and cash to Kyiv... and is next to a Moscow shill... as in shares a land border and has a trade union backed Communist Party, and a hard right which wants immigrants shipped out?"

Clive's face darkened as the answer became obvious.

"Poland."

"No... think worse... the biggest Western power outside of DC..." Marti froze mid-thought, her eyes widening slightly. "Oh, bloody hell. Ireland and Northern Ireland share a land border... and Northern Ireland is part of..."

"London," Kelvin finished grimly. "The UK."

Marti ran a hand through her dark hair, her expression grim. "You think Moscow's going to make a move on Northern Ireland? That's insane. They'd never risk direct confrontation with Britain."

"Not a military move," Kelvin corrected. "But they've already done hybrid warfare in Donbass, in Crimea, in Belarus, and now in Ireland. The pattern is clear. They destabilise, infiltrate, and manipulate. If they want to turn Northern Ireland into the next flashpoint, they don't need tanks. They just need to fan the flames of sectarianism, feed discontent, and let the chaos spiral on its own. Sam, what's our Northern Irish friends like?" Kelvin added, seeing that Holloway was still on the line.

"Need to know mate. Put it this way, it's been decided above my pay grade," Holloway said, sighing, the sound crackling slightly over the secure line. "Off the record, I'd ignore a certain embassy at 2 Palace Green."

Kelvin's jaw tightened. 2 Palace Green. The Embassy of Israel. The implication was clear—London was already having quiet discussions with Tel Aviv.

With Mossad.

An intelligence agency who had a habit of operating without hesitation when it came to perceived threats. If Israel was involved, it meant someone at the highest levels in London was considering pre-emptive action. Covert, deniable, and with the kind of ruthlessness that made even MI6 uncomfortable.

Kelvin took a slow breath, locking eyes with Marti and Clive. The room, already tense, now felt suffocating with the weight of what had just been said. If London was reaching out to Tel Aviv, it meant they were seriously considering pre-emptive operations. Mossad didn't do diplomacy. They did solutions—brutal, effective, and utterly deniable solutions.

Holloway's voice crackled back over the line, clipped, professional. "I'm telling you this because the window is closing. If Moscow is making a move on Northern Ireland, we need to get ahead of it, not wait for the fallout."

Kelvin frowned. "Does the PM know about this?"

A beat of silence. Then:

"Let's just say the Prime Minister is being briefed, but there are… complications. You know as well as I do that the July election means Starmer's on thin ice. Reform UK is breathing down his neck, and the British Communist Party is eating into Labour's working-class base. He can't afford another crisis."

Marti scoffed, arms crossed. "So what, we just let Moscow turn Belfast into another Donetsk?"

"No. But we aren't the ones calling the shots anymore."

That sent a chill down Kelvin's spine.

"Who is?" he asked, already dreading the answer.

"Like I said, ignore a certain embassy at 2 Palace Green."

Clive let out a low whistle. "Bloody hell."

Kelvin pinched the bridge of his nose. If Mossad was involved, the gloves were well and truly off. The last time Britain had worked with them this closely was in Tehran, 2023, when Iranian nuclear scientists started mysteriously disappearing. Some in Whitehall had cheered, others had quietly panicked—because working with Mossad always meant one thing.

London was about to play by Moscow's own rules.

*_*_*_*

Johan Weissmann, senior analyst at the Bundesnachrichtendienst (BND), Germany's foreign intelligence service, tapped his fingers impatiently on his desk as he listened to the voice of Chancellor Olaf Sholtz, the long serving German politician who was second only to the President and Deputy President of the Federal Republic, over the secure line. The tone was low and firm, the kind that left no room for debate.

"Ja, Herr Chancellor, we have ordered Fraulein Bauer, as per His Excellency's instructions, to wind down all remaining operations in Ireland," Weissmann confirmed, his voice clipped, efficient. "Hamburg has already initiated the process. Their Irish networks will be offline within the week."

"Good," came Scholz's measured response. "Germany cannot afford to be entangled in another proxy war, Johan. The Bundestag is already divided over our commitments to Ukraine, and with Moscow solidifying its hold on Ireland, we have to ensure that our position remains clear. The Americans and the British will shout, but they will not act. Berlin cannot be seen as taking unnecessary risks."

Weissmann understood all too well. Germany had spent decades walking a fine line between its Western allies and its energy dependency on Russia. Even with the sanctions imposed after the full-scale invasion of Ukraine in 2022, Germany's economy had struggled to fully detach itself from Russian resources. Now, with Moscow actively establishing a foothold in Western Europe, the stakes were higher than ever.

"The situation remains volatile," Weissmann added. "London will not move overtly, but we are picking up increased intelligence activity along the Northern Irish border. MI5 and MI6 are scrambling, and the Americans—well, they are still waiting for President Vance to be sworn in. Washington will be paralysed until that happens. The British have told us here at the BND that the Saudi Arabians have not ordered Manic to exit Ireland, and Moscow appears to be tolerating them—for now."

Weissmann knew that Bruno Kahl, the President of the BND, wanted at least one set of eyes on the unfolding crisis in Ireland, particularly through the lens of media control. The Germans were cautious—too cautious, some would argue—but they understood that information warfare was just as critical as military force in modern conflicts. Several BND officers who were assigned to the German Embassy in London had, in the past week, joined Manic's Birmingham newsroom and programming departments as 'advisors', ostensibly for technical consultancy purposes. In reality, they were there to keep watch, to gauge whether Manic was playing along with Moscow's script—or subtly undermining it.

Weissmann's direct superior had made it clear: Berlin would not intervene directly, but it would not be blind either. And if Manic proved to be a weak link in Moscow's plans, it was a link Germany might exploit.

Chancellor Scholz's voice came through again, calm but firm. "Ensure our presence remains discreet, Johan. London is not the only one watching Manic. If Riyadh perceives interference, they will not react kindly."

Weissmann nodded, even though Scholz could not see him. "Understood, Herr Chancellor. I will provide updates as developments unfold."

The line went dead.

Weissmann exhaled, closing his laptop and rubbing his temples. The game had become more complicated. Germany was walking the tightrope between appeasing Moscow, maintaining its NATO commitments, and protecting its economic interests. And now, it was relying on Manic—a Saudi-backed British media company—to be its window into the crisis.

Weissmann knew that, in 12 hours, he would have to be awake again, in order to interfere with the pan-UK, US, Australia and Europe Christmas show—one which was still scheduled to air across multiple Manic stations despite the chaos unfolding in Ireland. A carefully curated, seemingly apolitical broadcast designed to keep up the façade of normality.

But normality was gone.

And if the world hadn't fully realised that yet, they soon would.

* _ * _ * _ *

"Dad, can you guest on our podcast?" Oliver Jenkins, one of the twin children of James and Carly Jenkins, asked, walking into the study at the Jenkins family manor in Henley-on-Thames, a manor which had been in the family for generations. The house, an elegant Georgian estate with high ceilings and walls lined with legal tomes, exuded old-money prestige. James Jenkins, Manic's CEO and one of Britain's most powerful media figures, looked up from his laptop, where multiple secure chat windows were open—one from Manic's Berlin office, another from his legal team in Riyadh, and a third from a contact whose name was simply marked as Palace Green.

James raised an eyebrow. "Your podcast?" he repeated, leaning back in his chair. "That 'Living With Radio's Darth Vader' one?"

He knew that the twins, Sebastian and Oliver, were on their sixth season of a podcast that Global Media, the former employer of his, had commissioned. Looking at the 18 year old, he sighed, as he knew that Sebastian wanted to be a lawyer, like himself, his late father Lord Henry Jenkins, and the past 5 male generations of the Jenkins family before him. Oliver, on the other hand, had ambitions in broadcasting, a career which, James knew from his past as a runner at Brookes Vibes when he was 19, a job that he had got while studying law at Oxford, was far more brutal than the world of corporate law. And yet, Oliver was determined to be a broadcaster, as stubborn as his mother, Carly, had been when she had pursued her career as a Human Resources official at Bauer, then Media DEI Consultant, working as a freelancer in the media industry.

The podcast, 'Living With Radio's Darth Vader', was a jab at how he had, during a 20 year career at Global Media, up until the end of 2027, had been perceived as the most ruthless legal enforcer in British commercial radio. The nickname had originated from a leaked email chain between Bauer executives, in which one frustrated manager had described him as "radio's Darth Vader— sweeping in, crushing opposition, and leaving a trail of lawsuits in his wake" after he had, in 2017, sued 3 different hospital radio stations for using Heart style imaging during charity fundraising events, claiming trademark infringement. It had been a PR nightmare at the time, but also a tactical victory—one that had cemented Global's dominance over the commercial radio landscape.

Having completed pupillage in record time, thanks to his father, Lord Henry, being a barrister and a Queen's

Counsel before his passing, James Jenkins had quickly made a name for himself in corporate litigation, specialising in media law. His rise through Global's ranks had been methodical, precise—some would say ruthless. By the time he was 35, he had already shaped UK media regulations in Global's favour, ensuring that the company maintained a near-monopoly on commercial radio. Now, at 46, he had taken the helm of Manic, the second-largest network in Europe, and was poised to cement his legacy.

He looked at Oliver, his sharp legal mind already dissecting the request. The podcast had been harmless so far—a mixture of industry anecdotes, harmless jabs at radio executives, and the occasional insight into life as the son of one of the most feared media lawyers in Britain. But the timing of this request, just as Europe was on the brink of an information war, made him pause.

"You're not planning to ask me about Ireland, are you?" he asked, leaning back in his chair, steepling his fingers.

Oliver smirked, running a hand through his brown hair— a habit he had inherited from his mother. "I mean, I'd be a terrible journalist if I didn't at least try."

James sighed. "Then the answer is no. Did Ashley put you up to this?"

Ashley Tabor-King, the Founder and CEO of Global, had a habit, James knew from his time working closely under the businessman, of placing his fingerprints on things without anyone ever being able to prove it. Jenkins and Tabor-King had always had a complicated relationship— one of mutual respect, mutual ambition, and mutual suspicion. They had built Global together, turned it into an empire, but they had never been equals. Mainly as their fathers had been friends, Michael Tabor and his father, Lord Henry Jenkins, had moved in the same circles—the elite financial and legal world where deals were made over brandy in Mayfair clubs, and where legacies were built not just on money, but on influence.

In 2027, James had snapped, as, having brought BRSK, a new generation fibre company, he had wanted to expand Global Media's operations from not just radio and outdoors, but television, by plotting to acquire ITV Plc, the main broadcaster in the UK's commercial television landscape, and then folding BRSK into the rest of Global's portfolio, creating a fully integrated media, broadband, and telecommunications powerhouse. But Tabor-King had hesitated. He had always been more cautious than James, more willing to play the long game rather than go for the immediate kill.

The resulting fallout had been quiet, professional, and deadly. James had been given a golden handshake, publicly framed as an amicable parting, but privately, he knew it was exile. Yet, as with everything in his life, he had turned it into an opportunity. He had walked straight into Manic, the Saudi-backed underdog, and within six months, reshaped it into a force that could challenge Global. Now, with Ireland collapsing and Russia creeping into Western Europe, James had found himself at the centre of something far bigger than corporate rivalry.

"Erm... he did kind of ask me and Seb if we could—"

"No, Ollie, no. I'm not doing a podcast that will be dissected by every intelligence agency from GCHQ to Langley within an hour of release," James said firmly, rubbing his temple. "If you want me on for some harmless chat about the industry, fine. But Ireland? Absolutely not."

"Well, can you do an episode on why you left Global?" Oliver then asked, and James knew that the whole episode was buried in NDAs, payoffs and layers of corporate secrecy that even seasoned journalists hadn't been able to fully untangle. The public version of events had been simple—James Jenkins had "chosen to pursue new opportunities" after a long and successful tenure at Global. The truth, however, was far more complex.

James exhaled, leaning back in his chair and pinching the bridge of his nose. "Oliver, let me put it this way: if I talk about that, even indirectly, I will spend the next five years fighting lawsuits from Global, and you and your brother will probably get cease-and-desist letters before the episode even airs."

Oliver grinned. "Sounds like a great publicity stunt for the podcast, if you ask me."

James shot him a warning look. "Don't push it."

Oliver held up his hands in surrender. "Fine, fine. No Ireland, no Global exit drama. Just some stories about being 'Radio's Darth Vader' and why you make poor interns cry at least twice a year."

James smirked. "I'll consider it. Have you done your winter homework for Eton?"

Oliver groaned dramatically, flopping into the leather chair opposite his father's desk. "Come on, Dad, it's Christmas. The last thing I want to talk about is Bloody Julius Caesar and some 17th-century bloke who wrote about farming."

James chuckled, shaking his head. "Virgil's Georgics is about more than farming, Ollie. It's about order, discipline, and the passing of knowledge through generations. Something you might want to pay attention to, considering your chosen career path."

Oliver rolled his eyes. "If I wanted to learn about power plays, I'd just watch you at work."

James smirked. "Exactly. And what have you learned?"

Oliver hesitated for a moment, as if considering whether to actually answer or to come up with another smart remark. Then, with a lopsided grin, he said, "That if you control the story, you control the game."

James nodded approvingly. "Not bad. Though it's not just about controlling the story. It's about knowing when to tell it and when to keep it buried." He glanced at his watch. "Now, go finish your coursework before I start sending cease-and-desist letters to your teachers for allowing you to slack off."

Oliver snorted but stood up, stretching. "Fine. But don't be surprised if Seb and I start billing you for all the free PR we're giving you."

James raised an eyebrow. "That's adorable. Now get out."

Oliver laughed, making a dramatic exit as he shut the study door behind him. James let out a quiet breath, running a hand through his short, neatly styled brown hair.

The second the door clicked shut, he reached for his secure laptop. He had five minutes before his next call—a very sensitive one, routed through multiple encrypted servers to ensure it wasn't being picked up by anyone who wasn't supposed to.

The Crown Prince of Saudi Arabia. Prince Mohammed bin Salman bin Abdulaziz Al Saud, Crown Prince, Prime Minister of the Kingdom of Saudi Arabia

His employer.

"Good afternoon, your Royal Highness."

****

CHAPTER 5 – Under The Sea
Sunday 24th December 2028

Kapitan Pervogo Ranga Dmitry Aleksandrovich Volkhov knew that this mission was vital, that he was doing something that not every Captain First Rank from Murmansk was able to do. Especially on a submarine named after the person whose name struck fear into the imperialist West.

The Vladimir Vladimirovich Putin was the first of the new Laika-class attack submarines, a vessel that represented the cutting edge of Russian naval warfare. Faster, quieter, and deadlier than anything the West had yet encountered beneath the waves. Unlike its Soviet predecessors, which had relied on brute force and overwhelming numbers, this submarine was designed for precision. For surgical warfare.

And right now, it was set to make an important move in destabilising the West.

To follow, and if the opportunity to sink allowed, HMS Vanguard.

A Vanguard class nuclear ballistic missile submarine—one of the UK's four Vanguard-class submarines that represented Britain's nuclear deterrent.

Volkhov glanced around the control room, the muted red lighting illuminating the faces of his crew as they operated silently at their stations. He saw focused determination, professionalism, but also something else in their eyes—an understanding of the gravity of what they were about to attempt. This wasn't just a routine patrol or a show of strength; this was a potentially catastrophic escalation, a move that could ignite something far larger.

He knew his orders were clear, yet they left room for interpretation. Moscow's message had been explicit enough: shadow the British submarine, test their responses, intimidate and harass if necessary. But the final order—the actual act of sinking—was left deliberately vague. That decision, if it came, would rest squarely on his shoulders. Volkhov was both honoured and burdened by the trust placed in him by Naval Command. He was a graduate of the Kuznetsov Naval Academy, a decorated veteran of patrols beneath Arctic ice and the deep Atlantic, a man trusted implicitly by the Kremlin.

Unlike its Yasen class siblings, the Laika class had a more conventional layout with bow-mounted torpedo tubes (as opposed to the midship torpedo tubes on Yasen class) and a smaller chin-mounted sonar, meaning that the submarine was quieter, harder to detect, and better suited for stealth operations.

A series of nuclear-powered, modular, fifth-generation multi-purpose submarines, the Putin was the first, and only one in service, of the class, having been commissioned only a few months earlier, and Volkhov was the first captain trusted enough to command it. He'd spent weeks learning every system, every compartment, understanding exactly what this vessel could achieve— and now the moment had come to put that knowledge into practice.

Being the brother of a GRU officer, Volkhov knew what distractions had been put in place to allow him to leave Murmansk's berth unnoticed. The Kuznetsov's deployment had been a deliberate feint—a rusting relic of Soviet-era bravado pushed into service to draw Western eyes northwards. While NATO's naval commands scrambled to analyse whether the long-crippled aircraft carrier posed any meaningful threat, Putin had slipped away beneath the cover of Arctic darkness, cutting across the Greenland-Iceland-UK gap and into the depths of the North Atlantic.

Looking at the map, he knew that he had departed only 6 hours earlier from the Arctic Circle, yet the Vladimir Vladimirovich Putin was already deep into its mission. Speed, stealth, and deception—these were the weapons at his disposal, and so far, they had worked flawlessly.

"Kapitan," the sonar officer, Starshiy Leytenant Oleg Petrov, called out quietly, his voice barely above a whisper in the stillness of the control room. "Contact bearing two-seven-zero, depth one hundred metres. Ohio class. Tennessee."

The USS Tennessee was one of 4 submarines that the United States Navy had left at sea, with Donald Trump having slashed the at-sea patrols of the U.S. Navy's ballistic missile submarines in 2027, his 'Make America Greater Again' mantra having resulted in a disastrous reallocation of military funds towards his vanity projects, leaving the US Navy stretched thin. The Tennessee was one of the remaining keystones of America's nuclear deterrent—still formidable, but a shadow of what it had been before Trump's cost-cutting measures.

And now Vance, with an 'America First' platform was heading into the White House, and Volkhov knew that if the Republicans had their way, NATO would be a memory before 2030.

Commissioned in 1988, it had, in 2024, undergone a refit to extend its operational lifespan, receiving the latest upgrades in missile technology, sonar systems, and stealth coatings. But no amount of refitting could change its fundamental design—an ageing vessel from a time when American power seemed unshakable. A time that was rapidly slipping away.

"We're officially in the Norwegian Sea, comrade," the engineer, Kapitan Pervogo Ranga Sergei Leonov, announced, his voice calm but laced with tension. "We'll be on the edge of the North Atlantic in another hour."

Volkhov nodded, his eyes fixed on the tactical display. The Tennessee was there, a glowing signature against the deep black of the screen, but it wasn't their true objective. It was a curiosity, an old adversary crossing their path on its own silent journey beneath the waves.

Their true prey was somewhere further south—HMS Vanguard.

Intelligence had, prior to departure, put Vanguard, near HMNB Faslane, the Scottish naval base that housed Britain's nuclear deterrent. The Vanguard-class submarines had been the backbone of the UK's Continuous At-Sea Deterrent (CASD) since the 1990s, carrying Trident II ballistic missiles, the ultimate symbol of Britain's ability to strike back even in the face of total annihilation.

The source? The Royal Navy's social media team, who, in a careless moment of PR bravado, had posted an image of HMS Vanguard being prepared to set sail, timestamped and geo-tagged, from Faslane. It was a minor oversight—an image meant to reassure the public of Britain's nuclear readiness—but in the world of modern intelligence warfare, minor oversights were gold dust.

Volkhov knew, from his brother, that social media was the worst pitfall to have, as not just the GRU but the FSB, the state's own security service, had entire teams dedicated to monitoring Western military social media accounts, cross-referencing photos with satellite data, and feeding real-time intelligence into Moscow's strategic planning. The Royal Navy's mistake had been flagged within minutes, dissected by analysts, and passed up the chain of command. Within hours, the Vladimir Vladimirovich Putin had been sent on its hunt.

And now, somewhere in the black abyss of the North Atlantic, HMS Vanguard was moving silently, unaware that it was being stalked.

Volkhov knew that it would take nearly two days to reach British shores from their current position, but that was assuming they weren't detected. The advantage of the Vladimir Vladimirovich Putin was its stealth—quieter than the Yasen and Akula classes, more advanced in acoustic suppression than anything NATO had yet accounted for. If they played their cards right, the British wouldn't know they were there until it was far too late.

Still, he wasn't reckless.

"Maintain passive sonar only," Volkhov ordered, his voice a low rumble in the silent control room. "No active pings unless absolutely necessary. I'm going to the wardroom to see the latest intelligence reports. Petrov, keep a close ear on the Tennessee. If she changes course towards us, I want to know immediately."

"Operational Directive Update – 24th December 2028

To: Kapitan Pervogo Ranga Dmitry Aleksandrovich Volkhov

From: Northern Fleet Command, Severomorsk

Encryption Level: OMEGA PRIORITY

Comrade Volkhov,

Intelligence indicates that HMS Vanguard has departed Faslane and is moving towards its designated patrol sector west of the Hebrides. Satellite reconnaissance confirms its likely trajectory, placing it on course for deep Atlantic deterrence operations. As of 0500 Moscow time, Vanguard remains unescorted.

Your orders remain unchanged: track, intimidate, and, if a favourable engagement presents itself, eliminate. Be advised that British ASW (Anti-Submarine Warfare) patrols have increased in response to the Kuznetsov deployment. Expect heightened RAF P-8 Poseidon patrols and Royal Navy Type 23 frigates operating in the region. The operation remains deniable. In the event of exposure, disavow and evade. Under no circumstances should Vladimir Vladimirovich Putin be compromised.

Do not fail.

For the Motherland."

Volkhov inhaled deeply, his eyes lingering on the final line.

For the Motherland.

The weight of those words pressed down on him. It was a phrase that had been uttered by generations of Russian officers before him, some who had died nameless in forgotten battles, others who had shaped the very destiny of their nation. And now, it was his turn to act in its service.

As Volkhov set the tablet down, a quiet knock at the bulkhead signalled the arrival of his executive officer. Kapitan Vtorogo Ranga Viktor Mikhailovich Sidorov entered the wardroom, his expression a careful mask of professionalism.

"Comrade Kapitan," Sidorov greeted, closing the door behind him. "We have additional intelligence from GRU assets in Faslane. Vanguard was last confirmed under way at zero-three-hundred local time. She's moving under full emissions control—no active transmissions, no comms traffic."

Volkhov exhaled slowly. "So, the British are treating this like a genuine deterrence patrol."

"It would appear so, sir. But there's one other thing—our friends at the Northern Fleet Intelligence Division believe the British may have laid an early warning net west of Rockall."

That caught Volkhov's attention. Rockall was an uninhabited islet in the North Atlantic, a barely significant piece of rock in geopolitical terms—except for the fact that it had long been used as a reference point for British naval operations. If the Royal Navy had pre-positioned passive sonar arrays there, it meant that any submarine attempting to transit into the deep Atlantic from the northern route could be detected. A problem for their mission.

"How recent is this intelligence?" Volkhov asked.

"Less than seventy-two hours. The GRU believes the arrays are newly deployed—possibly in response to our increased submarine activity in the Barents Sea."

Volkhov hummed in thought, before tapping a finger against the steel table. "Adjust our approach. We stay deep—below five hundred metres once we get south of the Wyville-Thomson Ridge. If those British arrays are as fresh as we think, they won't have perfect calibration yet. We use that to our advantage."

Sidorov nodded. "Understood, Comrade Kapitan. Shall I instruct sonar to begin frequency profiling?"

"Yes. Have Petrov run passive scans. I want to know exactly what type of sonar signature we're dealing with. If it's standard NATO SOSUS architecture, we should be able to navigate through a thermal layer."

Volkhov reached for his tea—lukewarm now, but still the strong black brew that had been his staple since his cadet years. He took a slow sip, weighing their options. The Royal Navy would be expecting Russian submarines in the Atlantic—what they wouldn't expect was for one of the most advanced attack submarines in history to already be in position, waiting.

"Kapitan," Sidorov continued, his tone slightly more cautious now. "A moment, off the record?"

Volkhov set down his cup, gesturing for Sidorov to continue.

"Our orders." Sidorov hesitated slightly, before pressing on. "They leave… room for interpretation."

A pause.

"We are ordered to track and intimidate. But to eliminate if a 'favourable engagement' presents itself." He leaned slightly closer. "Comrade Kapitan, do you believe that we are truly meant to take this action? Or are we merely being tested?"

Volkhov studied his second-in-command for a long moment. He understood the question beneath the words. Sidorov was loyal to the Rodina, to the Russian Navy— but he was also pragmatic. Unlike the Soviet commanders of old, who had followed orders blindly, the new generation of Russian officers had learned to navigate the labyrinth of Kremlin politics with careful calculation.

And the reality was clear: if they sank HMS Vanguard, it wouldn't be a skirmish.

It would be war.

Volkhov sighed. "It is not our place to question orders."

Sidorov's jaw tightened slightly. "Understood, Comrade Kapitan."

"But," Volkhov added after a brief pause, "we are also officers of the Russian Navy. And that means we do not act without certainty." He let the words settle before continuing. "If an opportunity presents itself, we evaluate it. But we do not act in haste. We do not act foolishly."

Sidorov held his gaze, then nodded once. "Of course."

The moment passed, but the tension remained.

Volkhov turned back to the intelligence report, his mind already three steps ahead.

* _ * _ * _ *

In the Russian Navy, Volkhov knew, it was tradition for the captain to explain the ship's mission and rally the crew behind it. Orders would be pinned outside the wardroom—visible to everyone, a reminder of purpose and duty to the Motherland. He'd seen those orders often on past deployments, always phrased to stir pride and ensure discipline.

Back when he commanded the Knyaz Vladimir, a Borei-class nuclear missile submarine, Volkhov followed a personal routine. He'd wait until 12 hours after leaving port to announce their mission—giving the crew time to settle into the rhythm of life at sea before placing the full weight of their task on them. But this patrol wasn't routine. This wasn't about deterrence. This was pursuit.

At 1800 hours Moscow time, as the watch changed over aboard the Vladimir Vladimirovich Putin, Volkhov stepped into the control room and removed a set of file cards from his inner jacket pocket.

"Comrades," he said into the microphone, "this is your captain. We've received our mission from Fleet High Command, and it is one that befits this crew and this vessel."

He paused, scanning the control room. The sailors looked at him, focused and quiet, their attention locked in.

"Our orders are to test this ship in the most demanding way possible—by locating, tracking, and, if necessary, neutralising HMS Vanguard. That submarine is the backbone of Britain's nuclear defence, a symbol of its status. But that status is now in question. The West assumes itself beyond reach, insulated by routine and overconfidence. We're here to prove otherwise."

The control room held still as his words settled in.

"This boat—Vladimir Vladimirovich Putin—is unmatched. Quieter, faster, more lethal than any of its Western counterparts. We will not be seen. We will act with precision. We are not issuing threats—we are delivering capability. The British must understand they are not exempt from consequence. The Royal Navy must be reminded that Russia still moves beneath the waves, and that our reach is real."

He let that hang before continuing, more deliberate now.

"This is our first deployment, and it will be one for the record books. We are Moscow's silent edge—proof that Russia's power does not rust. The British think their deterrent is untouchable. Let's change their thinking."

Around him, men began nodding. A few adjusted posture. A flicker of readiness moved through the room like electricity. These weren't just drills anymore. This was it.

"Comrades. Officers. Crew of the Putin," he said, shifting to what they all knew was coming next, "this will not be easy. We are under strict radio silence. There is no room for error. Every man aboard—whether officer or matros—has a part to play, and no part is too small. We rely on each other, completely. That's what makes us strong. That's how we succeed."

He glanced briefly at the faces in the room—some seasoned, others young, fresh out of training.

"To those of you new to this life: trust your superiors, follow their lead. Learn fast, do your job well, and you'll earn your place. We're all in this together, and if we hold to our training, if we perform as one crew, we'll complete this mission and return with pride. That is all."

He released the microphone switch and set it back into the panel. Not a bad speech, he thought. Motivating, but clear-eyed.

Volkhov knew the speech carried echoes of old Soviet tradition—commanders invoking duty and resilience in defence of the Motherland. But the world had changed, and Russia was once again asserting itself. Ireland was already under their influence, and the North Atlantic was shifting fast. Words mattered again.

He stood in the quiet that followed, watching the crew. He saw it in their expressions—the focus, the understanding. They knew what was coming. They were ready.

"Stations," he said, voice lower now but just as firm.

The crew moved at once, returning to their posts with sharpened purpose. Volkhov turned to the tactical display. The Vladimir Vladimirovich Putin moved silently through the depths, invisible and alert.

The chase was on.

*_*_*_*

On board the Admiral Kuznetsov, Kapitan Pervogo Ranga Sergey Illy'ch Putin, who knew that despite sharing the same surname as the President of the Russian Federation, he held no familial connection, stood at the command centre of the aging aircraft carrier, arms crossed, eyes locked onto the strategic display. The Admiral Kuznetsov had finally left its moorings, a rusting symbol of Moscow's willingness to throw every available piece onto the board, regardless of condition. Though mocked in the West for its unreliable engines, smoke-belching funnels, and history of dry dock fires, today, the Kuznetsov served a vital role—not as an effective combat carrier, but as a distraction.

Putin—Sergey, not Vladimir—knew that his vessel's presence in the Barents and Norwegian Seas was designed to draw NATO's attention away from the real threats. While Western naval strategists scrambled to analyse why Moscow had suddenly deployed a barely seaworthy relic, they would hopefully fail to notice the movements of the Vladimir Vladimirovich Putin, gliding silently beneath the waves, far deadlier than any aircraft carrier.

He turned to his executive officer, Kapitan Vtorogo Ranga Mikhailov. "Any word from Volkhov?"

"None, Comrade Kapitan," Mikhailov replied. "They remain under strict radio silence. Last we heard, they were tracking USS Tennessee."

Putin nodded. "Good. The Americans won't interfere unless they realise what's actually happening." He turned back to the situation board, where the latest intelligence reports from GRU and Fleet Command were being relayed in real-time. "How are the British responding to our little presence here?"

Mikhailov smirked slightly. "The Royal Navy has sent two Type 45 destroyers to shadow us, and there's increased P-8 Poseidon ASW patrol activity from RAF Lossiemouth. They're watching us, but they don't know where to look yet."

"Good," Putin said. "We will continue on course towards Icelandic waters, let them believe we're just posturing. The longer they focus on us, the better chance Volkhov has at completing his mission."

He gestured to the communications officer. "Ensure that our fleet movements look aggressive, but never escalate beyond what they expect from us. We want NATO to see this as typical Russian sabre-rattling, nothing more."

The officer nodded and relayed the orders.

Putin exhaled slowly, glancing once more at the map of the North Atlantic. Somewhere beneath those cold waters, Volkhov and his submarine were making their approach. And somewhere further south, HMS Vanguard was sailing, unaware that the hunter was coming.

The Russians were playing a dangerous game. And if the British caught on too late, the game would end in fire.

****

CHAPTER 6 – The Christmas Shift
Monday 25th December 2028

"You're listening to Manic Vibes, and it's the Christmas Countdown, with me, James Smith. Up first, its Dua Lipa with Jingle Bells, but first, a little classic from Basshunter, with All I Ever Wanted."

James Smith leaned back in his chair, watching the RCS Zetta playout system queue up the track, the familiar synth beats of the late 2000s thumping through the studio monitors. The advantage, James knew, of being able to do his 1am Christmas Countdown show from the home he and his wife, Lyra, shared in Dudley, was that he could enjoy the illusion of normality. He knew that, four years earlier, when he was 21, young, and reckless, Christmas had been something entirely different. Back then, he had been in deep in the chaos at Manic, in the backroom culture of excess, drugs, and toxic branding, broadcasting from a studio that felt more like a party den than a place of work. Christmas back then had been about afterparties, early morning comedowns, and trying to hold it together for a few hours of air time before diving straight back into the madness.

The son of a radio legend, his father Pete having been in the industry since the 1990s, a 50 quarter #1 RAJAR champion in the Midlands, James had always felt the weight of expectation pressing down on him. But these days, things were different. He wasn't the reckless young talent trying to carve out a place for himself in an industry that was slowly eating him alive. He was older, wiser, and most importantly—free.

Broadcasting from home wasn't just a convenience. It was a necessity.

Ever since the coup in Ireland, Manic's relationship with the authorities had grown more complicated. The network's Saudi ownership meant it was tolerated, but only barely, and every presenter knew that someone was always listening. That included James. Even though he was in the UK, even though his signal only reached British listeners, the new reality of radio meant that everything could be monitored, everything could be taken out of context.

And James knew that he wasn't exactly on the safest of ground.

Since Ralph Bernard had left Manic earlier that year, James had felt the shift in tone within the company. The arrival of James Jenkins as CEO had brought a new level of corporate ruthlessness, a legal mind with an iron grip over branding, contracts, and strategic litigation. Unlike Bernard, who had been a steady if somewhat weary hand, Jenkins was a shark—relentless, meticulous, and completely unafraid of playing hardball with regulators, competitors, or even his own staff.

James had never liked him.

Why?

Because Jenkins had done to Manic what he had done in 2025 to Global's regional network.

Total annellation.

All of the regional stations apart from Manic's Scottish and Irish stations had been replaced by network feeds, with local ads and news being the only remaining remnants, the minimum required since the Media Act 2024 had loosened Ofcom's restrictions on local content requirements.

The same as what had happened at Global in late 2025, with Smooth England, Heart England and Capital England losing all of their opt-outs, with XS Manchester being replaced with a Radio X 90s feed, and with Capital Cymru being pan-Wales, and broadcast from the Cardiff studios instead of from North Wales.

And like Global, Manic's presenters were under freelancer contracts, which meant fewer rights, no job security, and an ever-present risk of being cut loose at a moment's notice. James had seen it happen more times than he could count—big names suddenly disappearing from the schedule, replaced with automated voice-tracked links from networked DJs who didn't even know which region they were supposedly presenting to.

And yet, despite everything, James had stayed.

Because, at the end of the day, radio was still in his blood.

He glanced at the clock. 01:04 AM. Christmas Day. Lyra was asleep upstairs, curled up with their children, Cory, who was his daughter with his ex, Kylie Morgan, and their three year old son, Lionel. James knew that their cousin, Alan, the son of his sister, Chloe, was next door, as James's father, Pete, was the legal guardian of Alan, after Chloe had been sent to prison following the Manic scandal of 2025. It was a situation James still struggled to wrap his head around—how his sister had fallen so deeply into the corruption and exploitation of Manic's toxic culture, how she had become a pawn for people who had never cared about her, and how, in the end, it had all come crashing down.

Pete had taken Alan in without hesitation, raising him as his own, while James helped the two half-siblings be raised with their cousin, as well as the complicated case of their other half-sibling, Alfie, who lived with his mother, Penny O'Rourke, in Dublin. Penny, James knew, still worked for a porn studio in Dublin, one that her husband, Weston O'Rourke, had siblings and cousin as part of management and talent within. That had been two years ago, when she had been fired by Manic as part of the scandals herself and her involvement in the Gals and Geezers scandal—one of the many grotesque undercurrents that had come to define Manic's darkest era.

James shook off the thought. That was the past.

But there was one person he knew would have ears on it, even after the fact.

And that was the CEO.

Because once a legal attack dog for Ashley Tabor-King, you never stopped being one.

James had learned that quickly after Jenkins took the reins at Manic. Every word uttered on-air was scrutinised, every slight deviation from the corporate line noted, and every potential legal liability pre-emptively neutralised before it could become a problem.

And with what James suspected at One Snow Hill was a sudden increase in hires in relatively junior positions within the legal department, he knew that Jenkins was preparing for something.

Slack, however, internally, had been having rumours earlier in the day of a German speaking programming team member, a few Russian speaking members in the commercial department, and even an increase in Saudi looking employees.

He knew that the position of Head Bodyguard for the CEO, one that had come in in 2026 when Ralph Bernard had taken over, had been that of a "ex" Saudi Special Forces Major, someone that reported to the Crown Prince's intelligence network rather than to Manic's board. That alone told James everything he needed to know about where the real power lay within the company. The Saudi money that had kept Manic afloat after the 2025 scandal had come with strings—long, tangled, geopolitical strings that no one in British media seemed willing to talk about. And Jenkins, despite his reputation as a legal pit-bull, had bent the knee to Riyadh without a second thought.

James knew that radio people talked, and that there had been, a month prior to Jenkins joining Manic, rumours of an attempted boardroom coup at Global, one which almost resulted in Ashley Tabor-King being dumped from his own company by Jenkins, a coup which, if the rumours were true, saw Simon Pitts, the CEO, fall on his sword and resign in a manner that seemed far too convenient.

Looking at his tablet, where his script and talking points were displayed, James hesitated for a moment. His instincts told him something was brewing, something bigger than the usual corporate machinations. Jenkins had always been aggressive, always playing three-dimensional chess while his competitors were still figuring out the rules. But lately, his moves had felt... different.

And then he noticed the script being changed.

James knew that was normal, that last minute or in-show changes when presenters who are working from home and not the Birmingham, London, Edinburgh, Belfast or Dublin studios were to be expected. It was part of the workflow. The central playout system at One Snow Hill had the ability to push updates in real time, to adjust for last-minute sponsor plugs, breaking news, or, in some cases, corporate-approved tweaks to ensure everything remained on-brand.

It was being changed by a programming manager who James knew from his only meeting with at Birmingham, a young Londoner named Alison Harper, who had joined Manic a week earlier. James remembered when he first her, and how she was shifty, as if something wasn't quite right about her presence in the company. She wasn't a known name in British radio, and yet she had been placed in a position of significant influence within the programming department. That alone had raised red flags for James.

And the fact he had walked in on her talking to another new employee, one of the German ones, one of the other German-speaking hires, only added to his suspicion. He hadn't caught the entire conversation, but he had heard Thames House and Berlin-Mitte mentioned in the same breath. That was enough to set alarm bells ringing in James's mind.

Especially as he had once watched the BBC drama Spooks on ITVX, and knew from that series that Thames House was the headquarters of MI5, Britain's domestic security agency.

James didn't believe in coincidences. Not in an industry like radio, and certainly not in the tangled world of geopolitics that had consumed Manic since the Irish coup. If someone with suspected intelligence links was quietly adjusting his script—on a Christmas Day graveyard shift, no less—then something was definitely up.

He glanced at the change on his tablet. It wasn't huge. Just a minor adjustment to his next time check in half an hour, nothing that seemed overtly suspicious. But adding the words "London time" at the 1:34am mark felt unnecessary. Unnatural.

Almost as if it were the BBC World Service and not a commercial radio station playing Christmas dance tracks to a mostly half-asleep audience.

And then another person was making another edit, one for the 2:17am time check.

James felt a slow chill creep up his spine as the name Johan Weissmann flickered on his screen, marking the latest adjustment to his show script. He had met Weissmann once—briefly—when he walked in on that hushed conversation between Alison Harper and the unknown German-speaking staffer. Weissmann had looked out of place at One Snow Hill, his posture too rigid, his gaze too assessing. James had spent enough time in rooms filled with people who wielded power—whether it be media executives, Saudi backers, or government officials—to recognise the type.to in hushed tones.

James felt a chill run down his spine. Weissmann. One of the new German-speaking hires. A name that hadn't meant much to him a week ago but suddenly carried a weight he couldn't ignore. And now, here he was, adjusting James's script in real time—on Christmas morning, no less.

On Outlook, the email app that Manic used, he was down as a Commercial Manager (Berlin), which James knew was one of Manic's other offices, as, in 2026, when Ralph Bernard was CEO, he had brought the French NRJ Group, giving Manic a foothold in France, Germany, and beyond. But Weissmann wasn't just another corporate drone— James had seen the way he carried himself, the way he spoke to Alison Harper in hushed tones when he had walked in on their conversation.

And now, these script changes.

Two time checks in a show that was otherwise a rolling Christmas dance playlist.

The words "London time" slipped into his 1:34am link. Then at 2:17am there was the wording "in London,

3:17am in Europe, and 9:17pm on the East Coast of the United States."

James frowned. That wasn't just unnecessary—it was suspicious.

Manic didn't run international time checks. Even on their online feeds that were available abroad, they had never catered to an international audience in that way. And yet, here he was, being subtly nudged into making time announcements that would be heard not just in the UK, but across Europe and North America.

It was then that James noticed dead air, and he had committed the most cardinal sin on radio—letting the silence linger. Quickly, he snapped back into presenter mode, hitting the talkback button to override the automation.

"And that was Basshunter with All I Ever Wanted, and up next, we've got Dua Lipa's take on Jingle Bells. Remember that you can WhatsApp in, and I'll play your voice notes live on air. The number's 03333399641, and again, I'll play as many of your early Christmas morning messages out throughout the show."

Looking at the time, he knew it was only 1:07am, and so he had plenty of time to figure out what exactly was going on before his next link. But his instincts were already screaming at him. This wasn't just a routine programming tweak—this was something else. And it involved people who didn't belong in commercial radio.

James quickly switched to his Slack messages, flicking through the internal comms from earlier in the day. If

Harper and Weissmann were making changes to his show, he wanted to see if anyone else had noticed anything odd.

A few messages stood out.

Alison Harper: *Reminder to all presenters working remote shifts: please ensure script updates from HQ are followed exactly. Branding consistency is key during seasonal programming.*

Johan Weissmann: *Small updates to timing conventions in overnight scripts. No major changes—just making sure we're keeping things in line with our international feeds.*

James knew that Manic had stations in the US, as well as the former NRJ stations in France and Germany. But Manic had never synchronised time checks like this before, not even for their networked European operations, even though the shows sometimes were simulcast.

And he knew that his one was one of the simulcast ones.

James's Christmas Countdown wasn't just airing on Manic Vibes UK, but also on the Irish, French, German, Italian, American, Canadian, Spanish and Saudi feeds. The latter was normal, as Manic's owner was the Saudi Public Investment Fund, meaning that there were special considerations for broadcasts into the Kingdom. But the rest? That was new.

A networked Christmas special was standard, sure, but this level of coordination—down to scripted international time checks—was something else entirely.

James felt the slow burn of suspicion settle in his gut. Someone was testing something.

And they were doing it on his shift.

He tapped a quick message into Slack, keeping it light but pointed.

James Smith: *Hey Alison, noticed the new time check additions. Just curious—are we going global with this show? Haven't seen us do this before, even when we simulcast.*

A response came almost instantly.

Alison Harper: *A request from His Excellency, the Crown Prince's Office. Just minor consistency changes for international alignment. Nothing to worry about. Keep up the great work, James!*

James stared at the message, his pulse quickening.

His Excellency, the Crown Prince's Office.

A direct request from Riyadh? That wasn't normal. In fact, that was highly unusual. Manic's Saudi ownership was no secret, and over the years, there had been a steady increase in influence from the Kingdom—strategic hires, commercial partnerships, subtle shifts in tone. But this? This was something else.

The script changes, the international time checks, the sudden presence of Harper and Weissmann—none of it added up. If this was just about "branding consistency," why hadn't they done it before? And why now, on a graveyard shift when barely anyone was listening?

Something about this felt... wrong.

He glanced at the WhatsApp feed on his studio screen. A handful of festive messages was trickling in—some from regular listeners, others from half-asleep night-shift workers killing time.

Then, one caught his eye.

It wasn't from the usual listener database. The number was international, a German country code.

+49 1579 2213401: *Can you bid a Merry Christmas to Liesel in Dresden from Lorna in London please?*

James stared at the message. On the surface, it was innocuous enough—just another holiday greeting. But something about it felt off.

Lorna in London sending a Christmas wish to Liesel in Dresden? A perfectly normal request in any other circumstance, but given the odd international time checks, the sudden interest from the Saudi Crown Prince's office, and the involvement of suspected intelligence-linked figures like Weissmann and Harper, James felt a creeping unease settle over him.

And a German phone number?

James hesitated for a moment, his fingers hovering over the keyboard as he debated how to respond. His instincts told him that the message was a test—something was being trialled on his show, and he had a strong suspicion that it had nothing to do with spreading Christmas cheer.

Deciding to play along for now, he leaned into the microphone.

"And a very Merry Christmas to Liesel in Dresden from Lorna in London. Hope you're having a fantastic festive season!"

He delivered it smoothly, keeping his tone light and casual, but his mind was racing. If this was a coded message, then someone was listening for a specific response. But what kind of response? And why use his show?

* _ * _ * _ *

"It's 2:17am in London, 3:17 in Europe and 9:17pm on the East Coast of the United States. Coming soon, we've got Wham's Last Christmas, but in breaking news, an explosion in the Donetsk region of eastern Ukraine has been reported by multiple sources, with initial claims suggesting a targeted strike on Russian logistics facilities. Details are still emerging, but we'll bring you more as soon as we have it."

James barely registered the words coming out of his mouth as he read the scripted breaking news update to realise that it was not normal, that normally Sky News Radio, the contractor who provided Manic's news bulletins, would have handled any breaking news.

But this?

This had come directly from Manic's own system.

James felt the hairs on the back of his neck rise as he continued speaking. The update had appeared in his script just moments before he was due to deliver the time check—seamlessly, as if it had always been there. But Manic never generated its own breaking news unless it was directly related to the network itself. That was the entire point of outsourcing to Sky News Radio—to maintain distance from real-world reporting and avoid corporate liability.

And yet, here he was, reading out a developing story from a warzone, as if it had been placed in front of him on purpose.

His heart pounded in his chest.

Donetsk. A targeted strike on Russian logistics facilities.

He tried to keep his voice steady.

"We'll have more on that story later, but right now, let's get back to the music—here's John Lennon and Yoko Ono with Happy Xmas (War Is Over) on Manic Vibes."

The moment the mic was off, James exhaled sharply, staring at the screen.

The Slack channel for presenters lit up.

Alison Harper: *Great delivery, James. Keep following the updates as they come through.*

Johan Weissmann: *Sehr gut. Let's keep things running smoothly.*

James swallowed.

Very good.

In German.

Why the hell was the commercial manager in Berlin giving him instructions about breaking news?

And why was Weissmann even watching his shift?

James's mind raced, the pieces slowly starting to form an unsettling picture. The Christmas show, typically a light-hearted affair meant to entertain the few listeners awake in the early hours, had somehow turned into something else entirely. This wasn't just about festive cheer or corporate branding—it felt like he was being pulled into something far more serious.

He leaned forward, his fingers tapping out a quick reply on Slack to Alison and Johan, trying to maintain the appearance of professionalism.

James Smith: *Thanks, but the Donetsk update—shouldn't that come through the usual channels? Sky usually handles this sort of thing.*

The response came almost immediately, too quickly for his comfort.

Alison Harper: *Just a little internal cross-checking, James. Don't worry about it. Everything's fine.*

Johan Weissmann: *Everything is under control. Continue with the programme, please.*

The phrase "under control" echoed in James's mind, a hollow reassurance that only made him feel more exposed. He'd been in the game long enough to know that nothing was ever truly "under control" when people with such hidden motivations were involved. And everything in the past hour—the changes to his script, the international time checks, the sudden introduction of breaking news—pointed to something deeper, more complex than a mere programming update.

James glanced at the time—2:24 AM. He had just a few minutes until the next link, the segment where he would typically play a festive tune and engage with the few listeners still awake. His hands trembled slightly as he grabbed his tablet again, his thoughts a blur of paranoia and intrigue.

Why was I given breaking news about Donetsk? he thought, staring at the glowing screen in front of him. *Why am I being watched so closely on Christmas night?*

It wasn't just the news. It was the timing. The quiet nature of this shift. No one was supposed to be paying attention to the lowly graveyard shifts on Christmas morning, but someone had made sure to drop all the right pieces into place: a message from Riyadh, international time checks, and a highly unusual breaking news update. Someone had carefully crafted this moment, and James was the unknowing pawn in their game.

He needed answers.

And he needed them soon.

James Smith: *Dad, are you awake?*

He knew that his dad, the recently appointed CEO of Bones Radio Network, a group of 50 community licences that covered Central and North West England owned by Woody Bones, might be asleep, or he might be getting the Christmas presents that had been set up for his grandkids. Still, James couldn't shake the feeling that his father, Pete, would be the only person he could trust to help make sense of everything.

It took a few moments for Pete to respond. When he did, his message was brief, his usual no-nonsense tone coming through, even in the early hours of Christmas morning.

Pete Smith: *What's going on, son? You okay?*

James took a deep breath, staring at the blinking lights of the studio console. He knew his father well enough to know that Pete wouldn't be satisfied with vague answers, so he typed quickly, trying to explain the gravity of the situation without sounding too paranoid. He kept his words direct, knowing Pete didn't have time for unnecessary details.

James Smith: *Something's off with the show tonight. Script changes, time checks for international audiences, breaking news from Donetsk that wasn't from Sky News… Feels like I'm being set up or tested. You ever had anything like this happen at Bones?*

It only took a few moments for Pete's reply to come through, this time with more concern in his words.

Pete Smith: *Nothing like that, mate. Sounds like someone's pulling strings. You sure you're not just overthinking it? You've been through a lot, and I don't* *want you burning out over a glitch. But if you're feeling uneasy, be careful. Sounds like you're being watched.*

James rubbed his eyes, the weight of the situation sinking in. His father's words were a reality check, but they didn't make the unease in his gut fade. The situation was escalating too quickly for him to ignore it.

James Smith: *I don't know, Dad. Something feels off about this. Someone's making sure everything's going to plan. It's like they're testing me. And it's not just about the show. It feels like something bigger. Maybe it's nothing, but I don't want to be caught in the middle of something I don't understand.*

There was a long pause before Pete replied, his next message more guarded than before.

Pete Smith: *Look, James, you've always had a knack for picking up on these things. If something's off, trust your gut. Keep your head down and stay alert, yeah? I can't do much from here, but if you need backup, let me know. You've got people in your corner, and don't forget that.*

James read the message twice, trying to figure out his next steps. His father's advice wasn't new, but the situation was different this time. It wasn't just about corporate manoeuvrings or petty office politics—it felt like a much larger game was being played, and he was right in the middle of it.

He glanced at the clock. 2:30 AM. There was no more time to waste on vague suspicions. He needed to keep the show rolling, to act as though everything was normal. But in the back of his mind, he was formulating a plan.

James Smith: *Thanks, Dad. I'll keep you posted. Don't worry, I'll get through it. Just stay safe. I'll bring Cory and Lionel round in the morning for their Christmas prezzies.*

James sat back in his chair, the pulse of the synth beat from his next track filling the studio. The connection with his father had given him a moment of clarity, but the unease still gnawed at him. The situation had escalated from something simple, a late-night show on Christmas morning, to something far more dangerous. The script changes, the international time checks, the peculiar breaking news about Donetsk—it was too much to ignore. His instincts, honed through years of radio experience and personal survival, told him that something wasn't right. He just couldn't put his finger on it yet.

As the next track played, he tapped his fingers nervously on the console, waiting for the next round of script updates. His mind was racing through possible scenarios, trying to make sense of everything. What was Manic trying to pull off here? Why was he being asked to follow these odd instructions at the most vulnerable time of the day, during the quietest shift of Christmas morning, when no one was supposed to be paying attention?

His thoughts were interrupted by the sudden influx of new messages in the Slack channel.

Alison Harper: *Good work, James. Keep everything flowing smoothly. We've got some more updates coming your way in the next hour.*

James read the messages, a creeping sense of dread washing over him. The words "international feeds" stood out. He knew they had global reach, but this felt like more than just a broadcast issue—it felt like a directive from higher up. He glanced at the screen, his eyes narrowing. The next time check was already set, with the "London time" remark still sitting there like an uncomfortable mark on a clean slate. It was still there, just as planned.

He couldn't shake the feeling that this wasn't about Christmas cheer at all. His head swam with the possibilities. Could this be part of some larger operation? Manic, under new management, had taken on a much more serious tone ever since Jenkins had arrived. The presence of international hires, the involvement of Riyadh's office, the shifting dynamics—James had witnessed it all from the inside, but now, from the outside, it felt like a carefully orchestrated play.

And why was Weissmann so deeply embedded in this? He wasn't some junior commercial manager, adjusting scripts at 2:30 AM on Christmas morning. No, Weissmann was someone else—someone whose role was far more significant than just overseeing a few advertisements. His connection to the company's European operations, his unusual interactions with Alison Harper, the quiet, scrutinising presence he maintained—it all pointed to something much larger.

But before he could think any further, a message from Alison popped up.

Alison Harper: *Quick note, James—expect more direct instructions from our international partners soon. Keep the show tight and precise. Don't deviate from the script.*

His breath caught in his throat. "International partners." The phrase felt too loaded, too vague, and yet, far too real. The idea that Manic had reached out to people in positions of power across the globe—particularly from areas with vested geopolitical interests—was unsettling.

****

CHAPTER 7 – In The Dark
Monday 25th December 2028

"He still doesn't know, does he?"

Lieutenant Colonel Donald Ryan looked at his superior and nodded in the affirmative, seeing the look on Colonel Alan Mace, an advisor to the Deputy Commander of the Sixteenth Air Force, based at Joint Base San Antonio, Texas.

"Good. As long as we don't get the House asking questions, the lame duck can't interfere in something he doesn't even know exists," Mace said, his expression tight. "The last thing we need is Trump throwing another tantrum over something he doesn't understand. And Vance? He's not even in office yet. That gives us a window."

An officer of the 996th Intelligence, Surveillance, and Reconnaissance Wing, Donald knew that ever since 2024, when President Trump had got elected by the public to do his second term, and immediately brought JD Vance on the ticket, and Elon Musk as the Senior Advisor to the President in charge of Department of Government Efficiency, the former United States Digital Service, whose sole function was to gut federal oversight, the entire US intelligence community had been walking on eggshells.

Under Trump's second term, the Sixteenth Air Force— the USAF's cyber and intelligence wing—had seen its budget slashed while the administration funnelled resources into vanity projects that played well with

Trump's base. The NSA had been hollowed out, CIA oversight had been dismantled, and the Pentagon had been forced to work in the shadows, keeping critical operations off the books to avoid political interference.

And now, as Trump's presidency limped towards its chaotic conclusion, with JD Vance waiting in the wings, the cracks were beginning to show.

Donald Ryan had spent the last four years working under impossible conditions, watching as Russian influence in Ireland, Germany, and even the UK grew while Washington was paralysed by its own dysfunction. He had been involved in Sovereign Sentinel—the off-the-books intelligence operation that had been running signals intercepts and cyber warfare without the knowledge of Congress or the White House. Because if the White House knew, Musk would know. And if Musk knew, then Moscow would know within hours.

That was why they couldn't let the Administration know they had organised, under the cover of commercial radio in the UK, a strike in the Russian occupied Donetsk region.

Ryan exhaled, his fingers tightening around the edges of the secure tablet in front of him. This was exactly the kind of situation that had kept him up at night for the past four years—an operation so delicate, so precariously balanced between plausible deniability and outright exposure, that one wrong move could bring the whole thing crashing down.

And lead to international condemnation on the United States.

Donald knew he was a patriot, he would die for his country if it came to it, but even he had to admit that the situation in Washington had become untenable. The intelligence community had spent years mitigating the damage caused by a dysfunctional administration, covering their tracks, keeping their most vital operations hidden from an executive branch that had become, at best, unreliable, and at worst, compromised.

And now, they had crossed a line.

They had used a British commercial radio network to send pre-coordinated messages. They had, through an unwitting presenter, broadcast intelligence into the wild under the guise of scripted time checks and news updates. And then, as the world listened to Christmas music, they had conducted a targeted strike deep inside Russian-held territory.

Not just on their own, but in a secret, handshake agreement with MI6, the British foreign intelligence agency, but also the BND, the Bundesnachrichtendienst—the German foreign intelligence service.

It had been a carefully coordinated act of modern warfare, a fusion of cyber, psychological, and kinetic operations designed to bypass traditional channels of detection. A message hidden in plain sight, fed through the global broadcasting network of Manic Vibes, reaching ears that understood its true meaning. And the strike? A direct hit on a Russian logistics hub in Donetsk, destroying ammunition depots and command infrastructure—crippling Moscow's ability to sustain its front-line operations in Eastern Ukraine.

It was known in the Western intelligence agencies that James Jenkins, or Lord Jenkins of Henley-on-Thames KC, a member of the British House of Lords, and CEO of Manic, was many things—a ruthless corporate litigator, a master strategist, and a man with the kind of political and legal influence that even Prime Ministers had to respect. But they also knew he was loyal only to three people.

The first being his employer, the House of Saud.

The second? HRH King Charles III.

The final? His wife, Lady Carly Jenkins, a former Bauer Media HR Lead turned media DEI Consultant, the person who the likes of Ashley Tabor-King, Rupert Murdoch, Tim Davie and other major media broadcasters who wanted to ensure that their diversity strategies aligned with both public expectations and government policy. Lady Carly Jenkins had built a reputation as a quiet power broker behind the scenes, someone who navigated the tangled web of corporate and political interests with the same precision as her husband wielded in the courtroom. She wasn't a player in the intelligence world—at least, not directly—but in an industry where influence mattered, her connections were invaluable.

And that meant James Jenkins had the perfect cover.

Especially as he owned one of the New Fibre companies in the UK, one of the early 2020s wave of government-backed broadband expansion firms that had taken advantage of the UK's push to roll out full-fibre internet across the country. Jenkins, when at Global, had privately brought BRSK, a small but rapidly growing fibre network provider, through a network of shell companies and legal manoeuvres that kept his name off the paperwork. And when he left Global for Manic, BRSK had followed.

He was also the inheritor of the Jenkins investment fund, which had been the same investments of his late father's friend, Michael Tabor, the racehorse and gambling magnate who had built his fortune in betting markets, casinos, and media investments.

And what was worse?

He owned 8.35% of ITV and 12% of Global Media, meaning that he held significant influence over two of the largest media organisations in the UK. That wasn't just wealth—that was power. Power that stretched across radio, television, broadband infrastructure, and the very fabric of British media regulation.

Donald understood exactly why MI6, BND, and even his own people at the 16th Air Force had turned to Manic for this operation. It was deniable, untraceable, and hidden behind a layer of corporate complexity that no investigator would ever be able to unravel without triggering a national security crisis.

And James Jenkins? He was the perfect enabler. He wasn't a patriot in the traditional sense, nor was he driven by ideology. Yes, he was loyal to his Sovereign, which as a member of the British Establishment meant that he could be counted on to act in the interests of the Crown when necessary. But beyond that, he was a pragmatist—someone who understood that real power wasn't just about influence or wealth, but about control.

"You know, Don," Lorna Hayes, a civilian intelligence officer who, Donald knew, was the CIA liaison with the 996th ISR Wing, said as she leaned against the desk next to him, her arms folded. "The Boss isn't stupid. He'll work out that we've been keeping things from him sooner or later."

Donald exhaled, rubbing his temple. "Yeah, but by then, it'll be too late for him to do anything about it. The operation's done. The strike happened. And by the time Vance is sworn in next month, it'll just be another incident in the long, bloody mess of this war."

Lorna tilted her head, watching him closely. "You don't think he'll go after us when he finds out?"

Donald let out a bitter laugh. "Of course he will. But what's he gonna do? Fire us? Court-martial us? The entire intelligence community's been running off-book for the last four years just to keep the damn country functioning. He'd have to purge half the Pentagon and shut down every meaningful operation we have left. And that includes the ones even he doesn't know about yet. Anyway, I'd rather take a Big Chicken Dinner than let Musk and his pals hand over our entire strategic infrastructure to the highest bidder."

A Big Chicken Dinner, or a Bad Conduct Discharge, was the death knell for any active duty officer's career if they wanted to have a future job that involved anything more than asking "would you like fries with that?" at a fast food joint. But Donald didn't care. He was long past the point of worrying about career prospects. Right now, it was about survival—about keeping the last threads of operational integrity together while Washington descended into chaos.

"Sir, we've got flash traffic from COMSUBLANT," a Captain cut in, holding out a secure tablet. "They've picked up the Kuznetsov in the Baltic Sea."

Donald took the secure tablet, his eyes quickly scanning the latest intelligence update from COMSUBLANT— Commander, Submarine Force Atlantic. The Admiral Kuznetsov, Russia's notoriously unreliable aircraft carrier, had left its berth and was now moving through the Baltic.

And he laughed.

"Why the fuck would COMSUBLANT let us know about that rust bucket?" he said with the cynicism of someone who had enough of the Navy trying to prank the USAF and its intelligence divisions with pointless updates about a floating scrapyard.

"I don't know, sir, just that COMSUBLANT has a bee in his bonnet. I think it's a load of bollocks, sir," the Captain admitted, scratching his head. "The Kuznetsov is barely seaworthy on a good day. Shall I tell COMSUBLANT to get stuffed?"

Donald exhaled sharply, shaking his head. "No, don't tell them to get stuffed—yet. But tell them that unless that bucket of bolts suddenly grows wings and flies over Washington, we're not interested. We're in the plane and satellite business, not chasing Soviet-era relics through the Baltic."

Donald handed the tablet back to the Captain, shaking his head. The Kuznetsov moving through the Baltic was a joke—an old Soviet-era relic desperately trying to project power while half its systems were probably held together with duct tape and vodka-fuelled optimism. COMSUBLANT had to be taking the piss.

"Anyway, sir, the Brits are moving Lightnings," the Captain said with a sigh. "They're moving them to Valley to counter the Checkmate infestation at Shannon."

Donald chuckled, as he knew that, earlier in the week, the first 10 Su-75s off the production line, the brand new 'export' model fifth-generation fighter jets, had been delivered to the so-called Independent Irish Republic in Shannon. The Russian Sukhoi Checkmate—supposedly Moscow's answer to the American F-35—was now in the hands of the Irish puppet government, a clear sign that Putin was making his move.

Donald knew that if the British were moving F-35B Lightning IIs to RAF Valley, then the UK wasn't just watching—it was preparing to act. The Checkmate deployment in Shannon was a blatant power play, an attempt by Moscow to bolster its proxy government and force the West into acknowledging its grip over Ireland. But moving Lightnings to Anglesey? That was a signal of its own.

The F-35B was a stealth multi-role fighter, capable of short take-off and vertical landing (STOVL), the same aircraft used by the Royal Navy on HMS Queen Elizabeth and HMS Prince of Wales. They were not just for show. If the UK was shifting them closer to Ireland, it meant they were considering offensive counter-air missions.

And that meant escalation.

Donald rubbed his temple, feeling the weight of it all pressing down on him.

"So, we've got Russian Checkmates parked in Shannon, British Lightnings at Valley, a deniable strike in Donetsk coordinated through commercial radio, and the Russian Kuznetsov making a pathetic attempt to look relevant in the Baltic." He shook his head. "Merry Christmas to us."

Lorna gave a wry smile. "And don't forget, we've still got an entire administration that has no idea any of this is happening."

Donald exhaled. "Yeah, well, let's keep it that way."

*_*_*_*

Flight Lieutenant Tom "Jester" Lowe watched from the hardened aircraft shelter as the first of six F-35Bs taxied onto the main runway. The engines roared against the winds rolling in from the Irish Sea, the sleek form of the stealth fighter barely visible beneath the grey Welsh sky. The briefing that morning had been… different.

As a maintenance officer from 617 "Dambusters" Squadron, the famed Royal Air Force unit that had once destroyed the Ruhr dams in World War II, Lowe was used to fast turnarounds and high-pressure situations. But this was something else. The mood inside RAF Valley was tense, the kind of tension that didn't come from a routine redeployment. No, this wasn't about training exercises or routine NATO air policing.

This was preparation for something real.

Lowe turned as one of his ground crew jogged up to him, a grim expression on his face. "Sir, we just got confirmation—these jets aren't staying here long. Word is, they'll be airborne and over the Irish Sea within the next twenty-four hours."

Lowe exhaled. That made sense. The RAF didn't move its most advanced stealth fighters to Valley unless they had a damn good reason. And with ten Russian Su-75 Checkmates now parked at Shannon, the message was clear. Moscow was arming its puppet regime in Ireland with cutting-edge tech, and the UK wasn't about to let that go unanswered.

"Have we got a flight plan for them yet?" Lowe asked.

The ground crew member shook his head. "Not officially. But word is, there's a NATO planning cell working with the Irish government-in-exile in London. If these jets move, it won't be for a sightseeing tour. It'll be defence patrols over Belfast and Derry."

Lowe nodded slowly. That was the logical step. If Moscow had positioned the Su-75s in Shannon, the implication was clear—they were preparing to establish air dominance over Ireland, cutting off the Irish government-in-exile's ability to contest the skies. The UK wouldn't allow that, not when Belfast and Derry were still within British control. A deployment of F-35Bs to RAF Valley was the opening move in a larger game.

But what came next?

The sound of a second jet powering up filled the air, shaking the very ground beneath them. Lowe watched as the sleek grey F-35 rolled forward, its pilot giving a final systems check before preparing for take-off. The aircraft was state-of-the-art, its advanced avionics and stealth capabilities making it a formidable opponent in any air-to-air engagement. But even the best aircraft in the world were useless without clear orders.

Lowe turned to the ground crew member. "Do we have a timeframe on the Irish response?"

A pause. Then, hesitantly: "There's talk of the Irish government-in-exile requesting formal NATO air support, but no one's confirming anything yet. If they do, it'll put us in direct confrontation with those Russian Checkmates."

Lowe inhaled sharply. That was the reality of the situation—no matter how much the politicians in Westminster wanted to avoid an outright declaration, the military realities were stacking up. If NATO committed to protecting Northern Irish airspace, there would be an inevitable flashpoint with Russian-controlled assets in the south.

"Keep me posted," Lowe said, already turning towards the operations tent. He had a feeling this wasn't going to be a quiet Christmas.

* _ * _ * _ *

"Yo, yo, geezers, its Callie Hall, here on the Manic Christmas Evening show, and boy, have we got a show for you today! We've got bangers, we've got banter, and if Santa didn't bring you what you wanted, don't worry— because I've got some absolute choooons lined up to lift your spirits!"

Kelvin Svenson groaned as his two children, Sally and Jack, the eldest one being 10 and the youngest being 7, danced around the living room to the sound of Callie Hall's chaotic energy blasting from the smart speaker.

His wife, Hannah, shot him a knowing look from the sofa, sipping a glass of red wine as she watched their children bounce around to the latest Christmas remix of a garage classic.

"You know, for a supposedly top-secret intelligence officer, you look remarkably like a defeated father right now," she teased, stretching her legs across the couch.

Kelvin sighed, rubbing his temple. He knew Hannah worked at MI5, and so their pillow talk was less filled with mundane discussions about work-life balance and more about whether Moscow had decided to ruin their Christmas yet.

"Just trying to keep your lot and the BND in check with the new obsession of every intel agency from the SVR to

GIP setting up camp at One Snow Hill," Kelvin muttered, watching Jack attempt to do some version of a TikTok dance. "I mean, getting your mate Alison to do MI5 stuff with Manic's scripts early this morning was bad enough, but now Callie Hall is screeching in my living room while the kids are jumping around like they've had a kilo of sugar for breakfast."

Hannah chuckled, raising an eyebrow. "Oh, come on, Callie's harmless. She's just—"

"A failed political meme candidate who tried to become Mayor of London twice, once in 2024 and then again this year, and also tried to take Farage on in bloody Clacton in 2024 as well. I mean, don't get me wrong, anyone is better than Farage, but even by Manic standards, she's a walking PR disaster."

Hannah smirked. "You mean she's unpredictable, loud, and exactly the kind of chaos engine Manic thrives on?"

Kelvin sighed, conceding the point. "Yeah, well, at least she isn't adjusting scripts at 2AM to help coordinate strikes in Ukraine."

Hannah smirked over the rim of her wine glass. "Well, sorry we're coordinating with Langley while Trump is in the lame duck period and Vance hasn't been sworn in yet. It's almost like we're trying to avoid a catastrophic intelligence leak."

Kelvin exhaled, rubbing his forehead. "Yeah, yeah. I get it. But honestly, we used to use New Broadcasting House and the World Service. Not bloody Manic Vibes.

Kelvin shook his head, taking another sip of his now lukewarm tea as Callie Hall screeched something incomprehensible over a backing track of Fairytale of New York (Drum & Bass Remix). The situation was getting more absurd by the minute.

"Look, Hannah," he said, lowering his voice as Sally and Jack wrestled over control of the smart speaker. "I know what we're doing, I know why we're doing it, but can you at least tell me who came up with the idea of using a bloody Christmas countdown show for an intelligence drop? Was it Alison? Or is this one of Langley's stupid ideas that somehow made its way across the Atlantic?"

Hannah smirked, setting her wine glass down as she leaned in. "Believe it or not, it wasn't Langley. It was actually the Director-General."

"The Director-General? As in, your DG? The one who's supposed to be stopping Russia from turning half of Britain into an SVR playground?"

Hannah nodded, the smirk still on her face. "Yep. Straight from the top. Apparently, someone—not me, before you ask—pitched the idea that a live, fast-moving broadcast with built-in plausible deniability was the perfect way to coordinate certain… activities. You get to send messages in plain sight, and if anyone starts sniffing around, you just call it an overenthusiastic producer trying to be creative."

Kelvin groaned, rubbing his face with both hands. "You've got to be kidding me. We're running covert ops through the same bloody network that once had a promotional stunt where they sent a DJ up a crane and forgot to bring him down for two days."

Hannah burst out laughing, nearly spilling her wine. "Oh, come on, that was hilarious. And besides, it worked, didn't it? No one batted an eyelid. A handful of radio nerds noticed the weird timechecks, but they just assumed Manic was being Manic. Even the Russians haven't figured out what we did yet."

Kelvin shook his head. "No, but they will. You think Moscow won't pick up on a targeted strike in Donetsk happening minutes after an obscure Christmas countdown show starts suddenly mentioning European time zones? I guarantee someone at the Centre has already put a pin in the map."

Hannah leaned forward, lowering her voice slightly. "That's the point, love. We want them to notice, but not until it's too late. The message was for our guys in-theatre, but we also wanted Moscow to know that their logistics hub wasn't as secure as they thought. That's how you ratchet up the pressure—make them paranoid. Make them start seeing ghosts in every broadcast. Let's see how long it takes before some RT mouthpiece starts claiming Manic Vibes is a front for MI6."

Kelvin gave her a look. "Knowing them? By tomorrow morning. And I bet they'll say James Jenkins is personally running a psy-op from his manor in Henley-on-Thames."

Hannah smirked. "You joke, but give it a week and Sputnik will have a full exposé with 'anonymous sources' linking Manic to the Mossad, the Freemasons, and the bloody Illuminati."

Kelvin sighed, leaning back in his chair, eyes drifting to the ceiling. "And meanwhile, James Smith, bless him, is sitting there playing Basshunter at 2AM, completely oblivious that he's just been the mouthpiece for a covert multinational intelligence op."

Hannah chuckled. "At least it wasn't Calvin Harris. Then we really would have been pushing our luck. Anyway, that reminds me, I'm working tomorrow. We've got a lead on a MP that's got Moscow ties."

"Wait, what? You've got a lead on an MP with Moscow ties?" Kelvin said, sitting up, setting his tea down on the table with a sharp clink. "Bloody hell, Hannah, you can't just drop that in mid-sentence like it's a casual bit of office gossip. Who is it?"

Hannah raised a playful eyebrow, swirling the wine in her glass. "If I told you, I'd have to kill you. Or worse, make you sit through Callie Hall's full show without a mute button."

Kelvin groaned. "Seriously, though. Are we talking backbencher? Cabinet? Someone who actually matters?"

"All I can say is, listen to The Crescent on Manic Goldies tomorrow, and you'll find out," Hannah said with a grin. "He's a backbencher."

****

CHAPTER 8 – Mornington Crescent
Tuesday 26th December 2028

"And we've had a letter from Mrs Trellis of North Wales, who says she's deeply concerned that the rules of Mornington Crescent have been irreparably altered by the Irish coup and Russian interference in Western geopolitics. She insists that under the 1973 EEC Variation Clause, Knightsbridge should no longer be a valid move unless accompanied by a mandatory stop at Embankment. A fascinating perspective, I'm sure you'll agree."

Miles Sterling was sat on the panel of Manic Goldies' The Crescent, a version of a segment from the famous BBC panel show I'm Sorry I Haven't a Clue, performing a live, on Boxing Day, special episode of the Mornington Crescent game.

Mornington Crescent, the name of both a tube station in central London and a legendary, nonsensical game beloved by British radio audiences for decades, had been a staple of radio comedy since the days of the BBC's I'm Sorry I Haven't a Clue. Having been dropped by the BBC in 2026, following what the Corporation described as a "strategic realignment of comedy output," the game had found an unlikely new home at Manic Goldies under the stewardship of Miles Sterling, a veteran radio presenter and former BBC Radio 4 mainstay who had defected to commercial radio after finding himself surplus to requirements in the Corporation's latest purge of "outdated" formats

Unlike the BBC version, where it had been a light-hearted, absurdist exercise in faux-strategic gameplay,

The Crescent on Manic Goldies had taken on a slightly sharper, more satirical edge, and a guaranteed 1 hour timeslot, whereas the BBC had always treated it as an occasional segment, a whimsical interruption rather than a full-fledged event. Under Sterling's leadership, The Crescent had transformed into a show that still celebrated the nonsensical rules of the game, but with a distinctly commercial radio flair—more irreverent, more unpredictable, and, in the face of recent world events, far more politically charged than its BBC predecessor.

And then there was the interactive element, where listeners could call in in real-time and make moves, sometimes leading to absolute chaos, especially if someone attempted an audacious gambit like the Boris Johnson Memorial Shuffle (which required a full denial of all previous moves) or invoking Clause 22B, which had only been successfully executed once since the show began airing on Manic Goldies.

Miles adjusted his headphones and leaned into the microphone, barely suppressing a grin. "And of course, we all remember what happened the last time someone tried to invoke the EEC Variation Clause—utter anarchy, two resignations from the panel, and one very strongly worded letter from the Department for Transport."

The panel—consisting of Ian Johnson, the MP for Kingswinford and South Staffordshire, a member of the Communist Party who had, in 2027, won the seat in a by-election when The Crescent had exposed the seat holder, Mike Wood, in a corruption scandal involving undeclared lobbying for a foreign think tank—along with comedian Jessica Hanford, a regular panellist on The Crescent, and veteran news broadcaster Malcolm Denton—erupted into laughter.

Overtly, The Crescent was a whimsical panel game where audience interaction and the absurdly complex, entirely fictional rules of Mornington Crescent made for compelling listening. But beneath the surface, it had evolved into something far more subversive—a way to ambush politicians who knew that shows such as Have I Got News For You, 8 Out of 10 Cats would overtly ruin their reputations, but underestimated just how ruthless a radio panel show could be when it came to exposing hypocrisy, corruption, and the absurdities of modern governance.

"Now, I've got Clive from Dorset on the line, Clive, welcome to The Crescent, what's your move?"

There was a brief crackling on the line before Clive's voice came through, a touch too excited for Miles's liking. "Well, as it's the first move, I'd like to start from Dublin Connolly, taking into account the Moscow Restoration Protocol, of course."

A hush fell over the panel for a fraction of a second, just long enough for the knowing listeners to catch it. The Moscow Restoration Protocol was a purely fictional rule, one of many absurd variations of Mornington Crescent that had evolved over decades of play. However, its invocation at this particular moment—mere two weeks after the Russian-backed coup in Ireland—was as much a satirical barb as it was a tactical opening.

Miles, an expert in radio timing, let the pause breathe before responding.

"Ah, Clive, a bold opening gambit," he said, feigning deep contemplation. "Now, the Moscow Restoration Protocol is a rarely seen strategy these days, not since the infamous 2011 University Challenge debacle. You do realise, of course, that under the post-Brexit amendments, any move starting from Dublin Connolly risks an automatic referral to the Committee for Strategic Realignment? I believe the panel may wish to weigh in before we proceed."

Jessica barely contained her laughter. "Oh, Clive, you're playing dangerously. I mean, we all saw what happened the last time someone tried to start from Dublin Connolly."

"A Strategic Rocket Forces missile landed on Leicester Square tube station, if I recall correctly," Malcolm deadpanned, sending the panel into fresh laughter.

Johnson, the Communist MP, smirked. "Well, Clive, technically speaking, the Moscow Restoration Protocol is still pending ratification by the International Transit Union, but given the... let's say recent geopolitical adjustments, it might be temporarily valid. However, I'd argue that since Dublin Connolly has, in fact, been administratively reassigned under the Shannon Mandate, any moves originating from it would have to adhere to the Kremlin Offset Rule."

Miles nodded sagely. "A good point, Ian. Listeners, for those of you unfamiliar with the Kremlin Offset Rule, it states that any station within a capital city affected by a recent change in sovereignty must be rerouted through an available NATO jurisdiction before a valid move can be made."

Jessica snorted. "So basically, Clive, your move is illegal under international law."

The audience, whether at home or calling in, loved this. The Crescent had always straddled the line between nonsense and cutting political satire, but today's episode was playing directly into the absurdity of modern geopolitics. The Irish coup, Moscow's ever-tightening grip on its proxies, and Britain's ever-more convoluted attempts to navigate it all—it was all there, hidden beneath the preposterous layers of a fake game.

There was a slight pause as Clive considered his response. Then, with an audible smirk in his voice, he said, "Well, in that case, I suppose I'll have to invoke the Liz Truss Memorial Intervention and divert via Westminster."

The studio erupted.

Even Malcolm, usually the most composed of them all, was doubled over laughing. The Liz Truss Memorial Intervention was a Crescent house rule introduced after the former Prime Minister's infamous 49-day tenure, allowing players to make completely unworkable moves before immediately collapsing into financial ruin.

Jessica wiped a tear from her eye. "Oh, Clive, that's cruel. You're essentially declaring bankruptcy in the opening round."

Johnson, still chuckling, nodded. "But technically legal, I suppose. Alright, fine. Westminster it is."

Miles composed himself, coughing lightly. "Alright, panel, the move stands. We are officially at Westminster. That places us in a precarious position, with the possibility of invoking the 2026 Privatised Transport Extension—which, as we all know, means only franchised services may be used from this point forward."

Jessica gasped. "You don't mean—"

"Avanti West Coast, yes," Miles confirmed solemnly. "We are now playing under Avanti West Coast conditions."

The studio audience groaned in theatrical despair.

"Oh no," Malcolm sighed. "That means we could be stuck here indefinitely."

"Or forced to reroute via Birmingham and wait three hours for a replacement bus service," Jessica added.

"Or subjected to an unexpected ticket price hike before we can proceed," Johnson said, shaking his head. "Diabolical."

Miles adjusted his notes, adopting a serious tone. "Clive, you've really thrown us into the deep end here. I hope you're proud of yourself."

On the line, Clive chuckled. "It's Christmas. I thought I'd spice things up."

"Well, consider them well and truly spiced," Miles replied, looking at his screen which had RCS Zetta, an automation software, on, that his producer, Alan King, controlled, as well as a script which was being updated in real time by Alan. "Right then, we've got a WhatsApp voice note from Lisa in Vauxhall, who wants to add her tuppence from. Remember, our phone number is 0333 339 1374, and you can phone us, or WhatsApp with your moves."

Miles pressed a button on his console, and the WhatsApp voice note crackled into the studio speakers.

"Hi, Miles and everyone on The Crescent! Lisa here from Vauxhall. Now, given that we're playing under Avanti West Coast conditions, I think it's only fair that I invoke the Great British Rail Compensation Clause and move to... Bletchley."

The panel groaned collectively.

"Oh, Lisa," Jessica sighed. "That's absolutely devious."

Malcolm shook his head. "You do realise what you've done, don't you? By invoking the Great British Rail Compensation Clause under Avanti West Coast conditions, you've essentially frozen the game for a minimum of two rounds."

"Or, if there are delays in processing," Ian Johnson added, "indefinitely."

Miles let the tension hang in the air for dramatic effect. "Now, as host, I am obliged to remind you, Lisa, that under the 2018 Modernised Crescent Accord, any claim under the Compensation Clause must be processed by an independent arbitration panel, which—"

"—which," Jessica interrupted, "as we all know, no longer exists since it was quietly merged into the Department for Levelling Up and is now a non-functional subcommittee."

More groans.

"Yes," Miles conceded. "Which means that unless someone can successfully invoke the Mick Lynch Emergency Override, we are now stranded in Bletchley."

The audience erupted in laughter. The Mick Lynch Emergency Override, introduced in 2023 when the trade union leader had become a household name during national rail strikes, was a rarely played but immensely powerful move—one that allowed the player to break through all delays and re-establish normal service, but only if they could successfully argue that their move benefited the greater public good.

Johnson, as the only sitting MP on the panel, sighed. "Well, as a member of the Communist Party and a RMT member too, it is my duty, comrades, to declare industrial action until the-"

"Ah, but did you get the 50% minimum turnout in the union vote?" Malcolm interrupted with a knowing smirk.

As Malcolm said that, Miles noticed a change in a scripted question that he was due to ask Johnson at 12:47, the time they usually, when a MP was on the panel, ambush the Member with a scandal that could see their political career derailed quicker than the Grayrigg derailment of 2007.

Miles Sterling, ever the professional, kept his face neutral as he glanced at the updated script on his console. The panel had no idea what was coming, but Alan King, his producer, had just fed him a live update—an update that meant the next five minutes of The Crescent could very well go down in radio history.

At 12:47 precisely, Miles would be reading the following:

"Ian, before we proceed, I have to ask you about the three signal blockers and the password to a Moscow bank account that is in the third drawer to the right of your constituency desk at your Kingswinford office. Care to explain?"

Miles felt a jolt of adrenaline. This wasn't just some light-hearted stitch-up about an MP's expenses or an awkward past tweet. This was serious. Signal blockers and a Moscow bank account? That reeked of intelligence work.

And the fact he had to wait for half an hour before he could pose the question only added to the tension.

Miles stole a glance at his producer, Alan, through the studio glass, to find that the veteran had no idea why the script had changed. Alan, who had been producing The Crescent since its move to Manic Goldies, had dealt with his fair share of last-minute updates—usually from legal, occasionally from nervous PR teams trying to manage a guest's reputation. But this was different.

Miles knew that the Manic Radio Theatre, the Olympic Park studios which, until earlier in the year had been a 30 studio complex until the Jenkins Cuts which scrapped the local variations of Goldies and had slashed it down to just eight studios and introduced a "audience area" to go with the underground Barbican bowl that Manic Classical and Manic Jazz used for live performances, had a skeleton staff, as Birmingham, the HQ for the network and the corporate heart of Manic, was the only hub that was fully staffed over Christmas. But that didn't explain why a live script had been altered to include a potential bombshell about a sitting MP—especially one from a minor party that usually flew under the radar of mainstream media scrutiny.

The original script, Miles knew, had been about Johnson's time as a RMT Steward at Chiltern Railways, where allegations about him blacklisting members who refused to vote for industrial action had circulated in certain political circles but had never been publicly confirmed. It had been a minor scandal at best—something that might have embarrassed him slightly but wouldn't have ended his career. This, however, was something else entirely.

Signal blockers. A Moscow bank account.

Someone, somewhere, had just turned The Crescent into something far more dangerous than a comedy panel show.

And then there was the suggested follow-up, which would have outed not just Johnson, but the Russian Cultural Attaché, a member of the diplomatic corps of the Russian Federation, who Johnson had allegedly, and he was told to use that word, allegedly, as it was a serious accusation and therefore someone was covering their own back, been meeting with in a private dining club in Mayfair for the past six months.

Miles's fingers hovered over his console. This was a setup. Not by him, not by Alan, and not by anyone in the production team. Someone—probably someone within Manic's increasingly shadowy corporate structure—was using The Crescent to pull off a live political hit. And he had half an hour to decide whether he was going to go through with it.

He glanced back at Alan, who was now frantically typing something on his laptop, likely trying to trace who had altered the script. But Miles already knew what Alan would find—nothing. Whoever had pushed this change had done so with enough skill to ensure it couldn't be traced back to them.

He needed to think. Quickly.

Did he go through with it? Did he read the question, expose Johnson live on air, and deal with the consequences later? Or did he deviate from the script, ignore the planted scandal, and risk pissing off whoever had orchestrated this?

He didn't have an answer yet. But he did know one thing.

Someone very powerful wanted Ian Johnson taken down. And they had chosen The Crescent as their weapon of choice.

As the panel continued joking about the Great British Rail Compensation Clause and the prospect of being stranded in Bletchley indefinitely, Miles forced a smile and played along.

But inside, he was already preparing for war.

"I was drinking a class of Vodka the other day, a nice Russian Standard, if I recall, when I discovered the Hamilton Gambit of 1342, which was last used by Sergey Raminov at the 1934 Warsaw edition of the Mornington Crescent World Championships," Miles said smoothly, steering the conversation back into familiar comedic territory while his mind worked at full speed. "Of course, Raminov was later disqualified after it was revealed he'd been consulting with the Polish Underground to intercept signals from the opposing team's strategies."

The audience chuckled, the absurdity of the statement washing over them in just the way Miles needed. He needed them relaxed. He needed Johnson relaxed. Because in exactly 60 seconds, he would be hitting Johnson with the most explosive ambush ever.

The fact that the script changes, Miles had learned, were by a programming manager at the Birmingham hub named Oliver Stokes, and that Stokes was apparently a new hire that had only been in the job 3 days earlier, set off even more alarm bells in Miles's mind.

Oliver Stokes.

That name hadn't come up in any of the production meetings, and Miles made it his business to know who was meddling with his show. The Crescent, for all its absurdity and chaos, was a tightly run ship, and nothing went to air without at least passing through the hands of Alan and himself. Yet here was a brand-new hire, someone with no prior radio credentials that Miles could recall, making last-minute adjustments that could torpedo a sitting MP's career in real-time.

A fresh message appeared on his internal console, marked urgent from Alan.

Alan: *Miles – this is weird. Checked Oliver Stokes on Outlook. No prior industry experience. No trace of him on LinkedIn, no media history, no public social media. He's a ghost. I don't like this. Also, I checked the edit history – he overrode my access when he made the script change. That's never happened before. What do you want to do?*

Miles exhaled slowly, gripping the desk beneath him as the laughter in the studio settled. The decision point was fast approaching.

Did he go through with it?

If he read the script as written, Johnson would be on the ropes within seconds. A sitting MP, exposed live on air as a potential Russian asset. There would be no walking that back. The timing was suspect too—Boxing Day, when Parliament was in recess, when Johnson would have no immediate way to coordinate a defence, when the story would spiral uncontrollably through social media before the government's spin doctors could even get out of bed.

It was a deliberate hit.

And Miles, despite his reputation for mischievous political ambushes, had never been a pawn. He refused to be one now.

But what if it was true?

What if Johnson was compromised? What if the signals blockers and Moscow bank account were real? Would he be doing a disservice to the public by ignoring it? Was this how journalists in the 70s and 80s had felt when MI5 had fed them hints about Soviet spies in the unions, about KGB infiltration into CND?

And if MI5 was the one that had changed the script from a RMT related soft scandal to something that could end a political career—what did that mean about who was really running this game?

"Follow the script," a voice in his headset whispered, "or you will be removed from the schedule permanently."

Miles barely reacted, keeping his face composed as if nothing had happened. He was a professional, after all. But inside, his heart pounded. That wasn't Alan. That wasn't anyone from his production team.

Someone was listening. Someone was making sure he read the line exactly as written.

And they had just made a threat.

12:46:59.

And the script was changing again in real time.

Additional context was being added—extra details, timestamps, precise locations. Whoever was pushing this update wanted it airtight. They weren't just planting a scandal. They were ensuring it couldn't be dismissed as circumstantial.

12:47:00.

Time to decide.

Miles forced himself to breathe steadily. He had been in radio long enough to know when something was bigger than him—bigger than his show, bigger than a career-ending question for a mid-tier MP.

This wasn't just a takedown. This was an operation.

And he was being used as the weapon.

He shifted slightly in his chair, glancing across the panel. Johnson, oblivious, was still chuckling about the absurdity of being stranded in Bletchley. Jessica was smirking, waiting for her turn to throw in another joke. Malcolm Denton, the veteran journalist, had leaned back slightly, his eyes flicking between Miles and his screen.

Denton had been around too long to miss the shift in atmosphere.

Alan, behind the glass, was staring at him now, his expression unreadable but tense.

A decision.

Miles took a breath.

"Before we move on, Ian, I have to ask you—"

He let the words sit in the air for a moment, feeling the anticipation build.

Then he smiled.

"—what the hell you were thinking when you endorsed that truly horrific rebranding of West Midlands PTE's public transport maps?"

Laughter erupted around the studio. Johnson exhaled, caught mid-sip of water, nearly choking in relief. Malcolm let out a breath he hadn't realised he'd been holding.

"Or... when your desk drawers, specifically the third one to the right of your constituency desk, contained three signal blockers and the password to a Moscow bank account... Comrade Ian Richardovich Johnson? I must inform you that I've been asked to remind you of an Act of Parliament which relates to Espionage is in play, and you are in Nidd... and West Midlands Police are currently in your Kingswinford office searching for classified materials as we speak."

The studio fell into complete, stunned silence.

Johnson's face drained of colour. His mouth opened slightly, but no words came out. The timing, the precision of the statement—it had been delivered perfectly. Miles Sterling had spent a lifetime mastering the art of comedic timing, but this was something else entirely. This was the kill shot.

And then he noticed them.

Three people, stood by the doors of the studios, all wearing cheap Marks and Spencer's suits, the kind that screamed "civil servant" but with an edge of something sharper. Something colder.

MI5.

Miles didn't need an introduction to know who they were. He had been in broadcasting long enough to know when the room had shifted from entertainment to something far more serious. And right now, The Crescent had just become the centre of a national security operation.

Johnson sat frozen, his knuckles white against the table. His eyes flicked towards the security doors, and for a brief moment, Miles saw something flash across his face—panic, calculation, then resignation. The MP had realised, far too late, that he had been set up.

The room was heavy with tension. The normally chaotic atmosphere of The Crescent—a programme that had once been a light-hearted source of absurdity—had transformed into something else entirely. The humour, the irreverence, all of it had evaporated in the face of what had just transpired.

Miles kept his gaze fixed on Ian Johnson, who was now visibly sweating, his face pale beneath the fluorescent lights. The studio, once filled with the sounds of laughter and playful banter, now felt stifling. The laughter from earlier had died down, replaced with an uncomfortable silence.

Miles' mind raced. He had made his choice. The question he had been given, the one that had been slipped into the script without his consent, wasn't just a political stitch-up. It was a calculated move, and now, as the gravity of the moment sank in, he realised just how deep the waters were. He had played his part in this game—but at what cost?

The MI5 agents, who had appeared so suddenly, hadn't moved since Miles had asked the question. They were waiting for a response, for Johnson's reaction, for the next move in what was quickly escalating into a high-stakes operation. Their presence was enough to make the air in the room feel thick, suffocating.

Miles glanced at Alan, who had stepped away from his console, his face shadowed with uncertainty. The producer wasn't a man who easily showed fear, but the situation had changed. The normally tightly controlled environment of The Crescent had been hijacked by forces much more powerful than any of them.

"Well?" Jessica Hanford's voice broke the silence. She leaned forward, her usual jovial expression replaced by something much more serious. "Come on, Ian, I think the public has a right to know."

Johnson remained motionless, his eyes darting between the MI5 agents and the panel, his mouth opening and closing in vain attempts to speak. Finally, he managed a choked, "I... I don't know what you're talking about."

Miles could see the words were a lie. His training as a broadcaster had taught him to read people—their tells, their hesitations—and Johnson's behaviour was textbook panic. He was trying to keep control, trying to spin the situation in his favour, but it was no use. The damage had been done.

One of the MI5 agents, a tall man with sharp features, finally stepped forward, breaking the tension. His voice was calm, almost too calm, as he addressed Johnson.

"Mr Johnson," the agent said, his tone businesslike, "we're going to need you to come with us."

The words hung in the air like a death sentence. Johnson opened his mouth to protest, but another agent, this one shorter, with a buzz cut, reached forward and placed a hand on his shoulder. It wasn't a friendly gesture.

"Now," the agent added, his voice low, as though speaking to a child. "It's in your best interest to come quietly."

The political game that had started in a comedy studio was no longer just a game. Miles could feel the weight of what he had done, what had just happened. It wasn't just a political hit—it was a real-life takedown.

"Shall we?" The MI5 agent's voice, quiet but commanding, broke through the cloud of realisation hanging in the room. He gestured to the door. Johnson, now visibly trembling, stood up slowly, as though his legs were no longer capable of holding him.

The agents flanked him, guiding him towards the exit. The show, which had started out as a farce, had spiralled into something much darker.

As Johnson was escorted out of the room, the studio door slammed shut behind him with a force that echoed in Miles' chest. The tension in the room remained, but now, the finality of it all hung heavy.

Jessica was the first to speak after the agents left. "Well," she said with a forced chuckle, her eyes darting nervously between the remaining panel members, "I guess that's one way to spend Christmas."

Outside, in the world that had just shifted under their feet, the fallout from The Crescent's Boxing Day special would be swift, unstoppable, and nothing short of catastrophic. And Miles Sterling, for better or for worse, had just become a key player in the ongoing battle for power in Britain's fractured political landscape.

****

CHAPTER 9 – A Van and A Black Bag
Tuesday 26th December 2028

"Follow the script, or you will be removed from the schedule... permanently."

Oliver Stokes knew that he was playing a dangerous game, using a civilian to trip up an SVR asset that had embedded himself into British politics. But that was how these things worked now. The old Cold War rules no longer applied. There were no front lines, no clear battlefields. There was only the information war—one fought in TV studios, radio stations, social media feeds, and, in this case, a Openreach branded van parked outside the Olympic Park studios of Manic Radio.

As a technical officer of His Majesty's Security Service, Oliver had learned to operate in the grey space between the official and the deniable. He wasn't a spook in the classic sense—no glamorous postings in foreign embassies, no dead drops in dark alleys—but he was part of a new generation of intelligence officers embedded deep inside the UK's civilian infrastructure. His cover was perfect: a programming manager at Manic, just another cog in the ever-churning machine of commercial radio.

"You know, Sam, it's crazy how we're using Manic as a way to get MPs," Harry Potter, a recent addition to the Thames House crew who, despite being unfortunate to have been given the name of a fictional wizard, was proving himself to be a capable cyber-operations officer, muttered as he monitored the real-time feed coming in from the West Midlands Police raid. "How many bodies has that show claimed so far?"

"11 now. 7 MPs, 2 Lords and a pair of SPADs who thought they were untouchable," Sam Holloway, the MI5 officer overseeing the operation, responded without looking away from his screen. His tone was flat, clinical. "Mornington Crescent is a national institution. Nobody suspects a silly little radio game of being a weapon. That's why it works."

"It's also the second Member for Kingswinford that the show has taken down in the past two years," Oliver added, his voice laced with dry amusement as he flicked through a secure tablet, tracking the live feeds from both the West Midlands Police raid on Johnson's constituency office and the external security cameras around Manic's Olympic Park studios. Looking at the clock, 12:53 26/12/2028, Oliver loved the irony how Manic was the only station airing a live show on the day where people were usually sleeping off their Christmas indulgences.

The Crescent was known for airing year round, live, on a Tuesday, as the following day when a Recess was not in effect, Prime Minister's Questions would be held. It was a deliberate choice, Oliver knew, to run a show which seemed whimsical but would ambush politicians and their advisers, live, as it meant spin doctors, along with lawyers, couldn't claim that editing had taken things out of context. Everything was out in the open, broadcast to millions, with no convenient way to control the narrative before it spiralled out of their hands.

The fact that there was a payout to each MP, Lord or SPAD that appeared, ranging from £10,000 for a backbencher MP to £50,000 for a special advisor, meant that egos would happily take the Saudi money. Manic's deep pockets, courtesy of Riyadh, ensured that politicians kept coming back, blinded by greed and arrogance, convinced that they were too clever to fall into one of the show's notorious traps. And yet, here they were. Another MP in the bag. Another asset exposed.

The live studio audience, even on a Boxing Day, Oliver knew, was usually full of plants, MI5 people who every Tuesday played civilian spectators but were, in reality, highly trained officers, analysts, and field operatives. They weren't there for the entertainment; they were there for the moment the trap was sprung. The moment when the carefully orchestrated ambush turned from light-hearted radio banter into something far more serious

Ever since the previous CEO of Manic, Ralph Bernard, the King Borg of radio, on orders from Saudi, introduced the format as a way to exert soft power over British political discourse, The Crescent had become a weapon of surgical precision. It was entertainment for the public, a game of strategy for the intelligence services, and a minefield for any politician foolish enough to walk into its studio thinking they were immune

Johnson had been the latest to fall. But he wouldn't be the last.

12:55

5 minutes left of the show.

5 minutes until the BBC, Sky News and the rest of the news channels aired their top of the hour bulletins. Five minutes until the news cycle took hold and the controlled demolition of Ian Johnson's career began in earnest.

Oliver knew that the BBC, LBC, Sky and GB News assigned teams to listen and clip the Manic Goldies broadcast everything The Crescent was on live, knowing that it had a track record of producing the kind of explosive political moments that could dominate news cycles for days. The moment the 1 PM bulletins rolled around, Johnson's face would be plastered across every major news outlet, his name trending on social media, his party scrambling for damage control.

And, as always, Manic Goldies would pretend it was just another episode of The Crescent

Oliver glanced at his secure feed again, watching as the West Midlands Police forensic team methodically worked through Johnson's constituency office. The safe had been cracked open ten minutes ago. What they had found inside, Oliver knew, would determine just how deep this operation went.

"Looks like they've pulled out the hard drives," Harry muttered, eyes flicking across the multiple security feeds. "Encrypted. Standard SVR setup"

"Which means we already know what's on them," Oliver replied.

It was a game they had played before. The SVR—the Russian Foreign Intelligence Service—was meticulous in its operational security, but MI5 had cracked their
156

encryption protocols years ago. Anything stored on those drives would already be known to Thames House. What mattered now was how much the public would know

12:58.

BBC News: *BREAKING NEWS: 11th Body Claimed by "The Crescent" as Communist MP Ian Johnson Exposed in Russian Spy Scandal.*

Oliver smirked as the headline flashed across his screen. Right on schedule.

Within seconds, the dominoes would start falling. Social media would light up. Johnson's party would issue a weak, non-committal statement about "allowing due process to take its course." The Labour Party, as Government, and Conservative Party, as His Majesty's Most Loyal Opposition, would both individually and jointly condemn the Communist Party, calling for Johnson's immediate resignation. And within 24 hours, MI5 would have another Russian asset quietly neutralised, his networks disrupted, his usefulness to Moscow erased.

"Back in my day when I was in the field, we'd just black bag them, do some enhanced interrogation, and then David Kelly them," the voice of Liam Powell, the section chief who Oliver knew was sitting at Thames House HQ in London, came through the secure earpiece, his tone filled with the kind of nostalgia that made Oliver grateful that intelligence work had, at least in some ways, moved on from the "wet work" era.

"Yes, sir," Oliver responded neutrally. "But public execution via live radio is a bit more... elegant, don't you think?"

"What does the boss mean by enhanced interrogation or David Kelly?" Harry, who Oliver knew was only 23 and so had been born after the death of the former UN weapons inspector, asked, his voice tinged with both curiosity and unease.

Oliver sighed, glancing at the young officer before responding. "It means that, back in the bad old days, if you were caught selling out your country, you didn't just get exposed on a radio show. You got a one-way trip to an MI6 black site, where you were given a very thorough debriefing—whether you wanted to cooperate or not. And David Kelly..." He hesitated for a moment, considering how much to say. "Let's just say the official version of his 'suicide' in 2003 is as official as Boris Johnson not knowing that Downing Street had been hosting illegal lockdown parties."

Harry swallowed hard, nodding but saying nothing. He was young, idealistic, still clinging to the notion that intelligence work was about noble causes, about saving lives and protecting democracy. Oliver envied him, in a way. He remembered what it had felt like to believe in the purity of the mission. But that had been a long time ago, before he learned how things really worked.

12:59:00.

The Crescent had just finished, an advert for Stannah Stairlifts playing out, and a member of the Operations

Team had placed a black bag over the head of the Honourable Member for Kingswinford and South Staffordshire

Oliver knew that another Openreach van was parked behind the one he was in, and that two more Operations people were pretending to be fixing a full fibre connection to the TNT Studios which the Manic Studios were next door to. The timing was precise, the execution seamless. Within minutes, Ian Johnson would disappear from public view, extracted through the back entrance of the Olympic Park studios, bundled into the second Openreach van, and the two vans would head to Thames House's under croft, where a CIA liaison that was technically "on holiday", but was covertly part of a hastily formed MI5- MI6-CIA-BND black site team, would be waiting.

By the time the news cycle fully caught up, Johnson would be sitting in an interrogation room beneath the heart of British intelligence operations, stripped of his parliamentary credentials, his phone, and—if the extraction team had done their job correctly—any remaining illusions that he still had control over his own fate.

*_*_*_*

The van that Oliver, Sam and Harry was in arrived at the under croft of Thames House at exactly 13:05, as per the meticulous schedule. The quiet rumble of the van's engine was the only sound that filled the otherwise tense silence inside the vehicle. Outside, the late winter wind carried a chill, seeping into the concrete of the building's shadowy underbelly, but Oliver barely felt it. His thoughts were elsewhere, on the clean execution of the operation that had just taken place.

As the van came to a stop, Oliver was the first to step out, his boots clicking against the cold concrete. He moved briskly towards the rear of the vehicle, where Sam and Harry followed, their eyes scanning their surroundings as they moved into the under croft, a sterile and unfussy area beneath the labyrinth of Thames House.

The back door of the van opened with a soft hiss, and the shadowed figure of the second Openreach van pulled up close, blending seamlessly into the nondescript scene. A quick glance over his shoulder confirmed that everything was in place. The two vans had performed the extraction flawlessly.

Inside the second van, Johnson's disoriented figure was pulled from his seat, his hands bound with zip ties and his head covered by a black bag, as per the standard protocol for high-value "assets." The sound of him being shuffled from the van to the secure underground holding area of Thames House was drowned out by the low hum of machinery around them, the kind of machines that were far too advanced for the public to know about.

Oliver and the others filed into the debriefing area, a stark, almost clinical space where the man they had just retrieved would be processed. The room was sparsely furnished, but the table in the centre had been cleared of all previous paperwork—today's task would be different.

"Make sure they know he's one of the high-priority targets," Sam muttered to one of the junior agents stationed by the door. "No slacking on this one."

Oliver didn't need to say anything. He knew exactly what was expected. The operation wasn't over until Johnson had given up every scrap of intel he had, and that would only happen when he'd broken—physically, psychologically, whatever it took. As much as the intelligence community had moved past the dark days of traditional "wet work," there were still moments when the old ways—of breaking someone until they cracked— were needed. And in the case of a high-profile Russian asset embedded within British politics, there were no shortcuts.

As the agent stepped back into the corridor, Oliver let out a slow breath, his mind briefly flicking back to the studio. He remembered the sound of the audience's laughter, the absurdity of Mornington Crescent masking the weight of what had just transpired. But as always, the show would go on, and so would the machine that powered it.

"We'll need to prepare for the fallout," Oliver said, turning to Sam and Harry, his voice low but laced with that dry humour that seemed to have kept him sane over the years. "The narrative will get messy before it cleans itself up. The press will be all over it, but that's fine. We've got everything in place. The last thing we want is for Johnson to be given a chance to spin this. Not after what we've uncovered."

The clock ticked on, each passing second sending them closer to the moment when the news outlets would finally catch up to the operation. Johnson was being processed, his phone checked for contacts, his financial records examined, and soon enough, the full scope of his ties to Russian intelligence would be laid bare.

But in the background, another part of the machine was already grinding into motion: the narrative would be spun. Manic Goldies would go on as if nothing had happened. The Crescent would return next week, and the audience would have no idea that another major piece in the geopolitical puzzle had just been moved. For the public, it would be business as usual.

Yet for those behind the curtain—the players who orchestrated these events—things would never return to normal. Every move had a cost, and Johnson's fall was just another step in a much larger game that only a few would ever fully understand.

As the debriefing room door clicked open and the first sounds of Johnson's arrival echoed from the hall, Oliver couldn't suppress the smallest of smiles. This was what he had trained for. This was the new reality. A reality where the lines between information, power, and manipulation blurred, and where the fate of politicians could be decided not by the vote, but by the words on a radio script.

It was then that Oliver noticed a BND officer who he hadn't seen in ages, Frieda Hoffman, who was part of the German contingent who would be interrogating Johnson. The sight of her brought an unexpected moment of familiarity amidst the sterile cold of the under croft. Frieda had been part of many covert operations over the years, and though she was no longer in the thick of things like Oliver, she still carried herself with the quiet, deadly competence that came from years of playing the geopolitical game.

"Didn't think I'd see you back here," Oliver remarked as he approached her, his tone a mix of respect and a hint of surprise.

Frieda gave him a cold smile, her sharp eyes taking in the scene with practiced indifference. "You know how it is, Oliver. The job never quite lets you go." She gave a small, almost imperceptible nod toward the door as the agents inside prepared for the interrogation. "Technically I'm the Third Secretary to the German Embassy now, but when MI5 calls, the job doesn't end just because you wear a different title."

Oliver chuckled, as he knew what that meant, that she had a legal cover of a diplomat, but her true work was still very much embedded in the world of covert operations. As they moved toward the observation area, the heavy door closed behind them with a soft, mechanical thud, signalling that the interrogation was about to begin.

"Want to take lead?" Paul Parsons, one of the officers who had brought Johnson into the room, asked Oliver.

Oliver looked at Paul with a raised eyebrow, the question hanging in the air for a moment longer than necessary. He could feel the weight of the room, the quiet but suffocating tension that only built during operations like these. The air was thick with anticipation, but Oliver knew this wasn't the time for ego or bravado.

He shook his head, his usual dry humour flickering through. "No, I'll leave the heavy lifting to you, Paul. But don't let him off easy. He's a prime asset, and we've got a lot of things to make him regret."

The agents around the table, including Frieda, nodded in agreement. There was no room for mercy in these operations, not when national security was at stake. As much as Oliver had often questioned the methods of his predecessors, he knew that in situations like this, there was no other way. Not with assets like Ian Johnson, who had allowed himself to be used by the Russians to push their agenda into British politics.

Frieda's sharp gaze shifted toward the interrogation room door, where the sound of muffled voices indicated the process was beginning. Her voice was low, but the edge of something unspoken lingered in it. "You know, Oliver, for someone as experienced as Johnson, he's been sloppy. The files we uncovered were full of discrepancies, too many direct connections. The Russians won't be happy when we bring him in."

Oliver glanced at her, aware of the weight of her words. "That's why we're here. To clean it up before they do."

The quiet moment that followed was punctuated by the faint echo of footsteps as Johnson was escorted into the interrogation room. The door creaked open, and for a brief instant, the tension in the room seemed to crescendo.

Oliver looked at the team around him. "Ready?" he asked, his voice smooth but carrying the finality of their mission. The room nodded in silent affirmation.

As the door clicked shut behind him, Oliver made his way toward the observation window. He settled into a chair, his eyes fixed on the darkened glass. He didn't need to see inside to know what was going on; this was a familiar game, one he'd played many times before. Still, the silence on the other side of the glass spoke volumes—Johnson was being carefully primed for what was coming next.

The interrogation team would take their time. They had the training, the methods, the patience. The primary goal was to extract every piece of intel Johnson had, particularly about his connections to Russian assets inside the British government, but it wasn't going to be easy. Johnson might crack eventually, but until then, they would use every psychological and physical tactic at their disposal to make him understand that his life, his career, and perhaps even his freedom, were all on the line.

Frieda stood next to him, her expression unreadable, her gaze cold. "You've seen it before," she said quietly, as if reading his thoughts. "He'll fight. He's a survivor, just like all the others. But in the end, it's not about what he wants. It's about what we need him to give us."

Oliver nodded. He knew exactly what she meant. They weren't playing for Johnson's confession—they were playing for the complete destruction of his usefulness. He was an expendable piece now. And once he was broken, once his ties to Moscow were fully exposed, there would be no room left for escape.

The thought of the aftermath lingered in Oliver's mind. The media would be quick to catch on to the scandal, their headlines filled with the betrayal of a British politician who had sold out his country. But for the intelligence community, the real work would continue in the shadows. It wasn't about public opinion; it was about securing power, information, and control.

He looked over at Frieda again. "What do you think? How long before he folds?"

Frieda gave him a hard, knowing smile. "Depends on how much he's willing to protect his masters in Moscow. If he's got nothing to lose, it could take a while. But we have one thing he doesn't—time."

Oliver's lips curled into a thin smile, the sense of inevitability settling over him like a cloak. He knew the game, knew the stakes. There was no going back now.

And with that, the final act of Ian Johnson's career began. It wouldn't be long before the world would know what he had truly been hiding, and by the time they did, the only thing left would be a shattered career and a broken man— one who had sold his soul for power.

Oliver stood, glancing one last time at the secure observation room. The door to the interrogation room opened, and the first voices emerged.

"Let's see how long he lasts," he muttered under his breath. The game was far from over, but with each passing minute, Johnson was one step closer to being erased from the board.

As the seconds ticked away, the tension in the observation room thickened. Oliver watched through the one-way mirror, his expression unreadable. He could hear the muffled sounds of movement from the other side—the rustling of papers, the clicking of tools being set into place, the soft hum of the interrogation room's lights flickering overhead.

Frieda's sharp eyes remained fixed on the door, her arms folded across her chest. She was always calm under pressure, but Oliver could see the familiar glint of calculation in her gaze. She had been through this process more times than she cared to count. For her, the game was simple: break the target, extract what was needed, and dispose of them when the time was right.

Johnson, on the other hand, was a different story. He wasn't just a run-of-the-mill asset. He had been an established part of the political landscape, a man who thought he could operate under the radar. But the moment he'd aligned himself with Russian intelligence, the rules had changed.

"Have you heard anything from the front lines?" Oliver asked, glancing at Sam, who was monitoring the feedback from the secure comms channels.

Sam nodded, his face serious. "They're moving fast, Oliver. The media's already picked up on the story. Sky News just broke the headline. 'Exposed MP Linked to Russian Intelligence.' The spin doctors are scrambling already."

"Good," Oliver said, his voice cold and precise. "It's only a matter of time before the others start falling into line. Johnson's the first domino, but he won't be the last."

Frieda turned to face him. "You know, when you first came into this business, it wasn't about the show. It was about the information. We didn't need a press cycle to make our moves." Her voice was tinged with something like nostalgia, but it wasn't a wistful tone—it was more about the practical reality of their current operations. "But now... now the narrative is just as much a part of it. We play the long game, but the public's always watching."

Oliver's lips curled into a slight smile. "Times change, Frieda. But the game's always the same. Only the tools evolve."

He looked back at the observation window. They had just taken Johnson into the interrogation room. His fate was now sealed, though the details were still unfolding in real-time. They could afford to be patient. Time was their ally.

Oliver's mind raced ahead, calculating the next few steps, mentally tracking the timeline that had been set in motion. He knew the process would take hours, maybe even days. The goal was to leave nothing to chance—to strip Johnson of everything: his political career, his connections, and, most importantly, his value as an asset for Moscow. The Russians had already been notified, of course, but by the time they managed to react, it would be too late. They would be left with nothing but the remnants of an operation that had crumbled under MI5's scrutiny.

"Do you think Johnson even knows how deep this goes?" Harry asked, breaking the silence. His voice was softer now, less brash than earlier.

Oliver turned to him, the young agent's naive curiosity palpable. "Of course he doesn't," he replied. "If he had, he wouldn't have made the mistakes he did. He's playing a dangerous game, thinking he could outsmart us."

Frieda's eyes narrowed as she studied the interrogation room through the one-way glass. "It's a classic. Underestimate your adversary, make a few bad decisions, and then suddenly, you're no longer in control."

Oliver nodded. "Exactly. He thought he was untouchable. The kind of people who play that game, they rarely see it coming. But we're not in the business of waiting for them to realise they've been caught."

The door to the interrogation room creaked open. The agents inside had begun their work, and though Oliver couldn't see it directly, he knew the first few minutes were critical. The initial shock—the disorientation of the black bag, the unfamiliar setting—would wear off soon enough. That's when they would hit him with the full force of the psychological pressure.

Johnson would break. They all did, eventually.

Frieda leaned forward, her voice low. "We don't need his cooperation. We just need him to talk. To tell us everything he knows. About Moscow's influence, about the network he's been feeding. The Russian intelligence apparatus won't just let this slide. We need to ensure they don't have any control left in the system."

Oliver glanced at her, acknowledging the point. "The beauty of it is, once they've extracted what they need from him, it won't matter anymore. The Russians will no longer be able to rely on him. And we'll have neutralised their influence inside British politics."

For a brief moment, there was a lull. The weight of their task hung in the air, but it was nothing new to them. Each operation had its own set of challenges, its own complexities, but the end goal was always the same: total dominance.

"Oliver," Sam began again, his voice barely a whisper. "Are we ready for what comes next?"

Oliver's gaze shifted from the observation window to the secure comms channels in front of him. The reports were already filtering through. Johnson's role in this affair was far deeper than anyone had realised. There were connections to high-profile figures, people who were currently in positions of power, and even more troubling, financial transactions that went back years. But it wasn't just about Johnson's personal culpability. This was about sending a message.

"Always ready," Oliver said, his tone clipped. "We'll be waiting for their next move. The second Johnson cracks, we take everything. And then we prepare for the fallout."

Frieda gave him a wry smile. "You've always been the optimist."

Oliver chuckled darkly. "There's no room for anything else, is there? The show must go on, but this time, it's us pulling the strings."

****

CHAPTER 10 – Pressers
Wednesday 27th December 2028

"Sinead, it's time to shine."

Sinead Ryan knew that she had to ensure that the Native Country, the true Ireland, would not be shaken by the latest Western smear campaign. She adjusted her earpiece, glancing at the script on her tablet as she sat in the RTÉ newsroom—now effectively a mouthpiece for the Irish Restoration Government and its Russian backers.

As the Head of the newly created State Information Office, the Cork born Anglo-Irish-Russian speaker knew that she was the voice of the State, of truth, of the Irish people.

A true believer, she knew that her maternal grandfather, a former KGB Fifth Directorate officer named Ivan Petrov, would be smiling upon her from the grave, that he would be proud to hear her. She knew that, over the last few times she had done her pressers, her conferences where the world media would listen to her be what some called "Diet Ri Chun-hee" in English, "1916 But 2028" in Irish, and "Ri Chun-hee But Full Send" in Russian.

She smirked at the thought. *Let them mock me all they want.* Western journalists sneered at her transformation from an RTÉ correspondent into the iron-clad voice of the Restoration Government, but Sinead didn't care. Ireland had been liberated from Anglo-American imperialism, freed from the suffocating grasp of the EU, and was now standing proudly as a sovereign state under the guidance of Moscow. The West could howl all they liked—history was being rewritten, and she was holding the pen.

Having studied at Cambridge in 2016 to 2019, Sinead had been instantly recruited by the SVR as a potential candidate for the RT operation in London, as she was studying for a journalism degree, meaning that it was the perfect opportunity to cultivate an asset within the British media. She had been approached subtly, first through academic networking circles, then via a "chance" meeting at a Russian cultural event in Bloomsbury. The SVR had played the long game with her, feeding her carefully curated narratives about Western hypocrisy, the decline of the Anglo-American order, and the resurgence of a multipolar world led by Moscow and Beijing. And Sinead had listened. She had learned.

One of her former close colleagues, Polly Boiko, when Sinead had been at RT UK, the British outpost of the Russian state broadcaster, had been one of her mentors, had shown her that viral content, such as Boiko's ICYMI, a modern-day propaganda tool disguised as edgy, millennial-friendly news, was one way to get the message from the Kremlin to the social media loving audience.

Then the 2022 Special Military Operation had begun.

Sinead had watched as the rebels in Ukraine who had fought against Mother Russia's right to quell the Western-backed coup in Kyiv had been demonised by the Anglo-American media. She had watched as journalists she once admired became mouthpieces for NATO, parroting the same tired lines about "sovereignty" and "democracy" while ignoring the real crimes of the West—Libya, Iraq,

Afghanistan. She had seen how her colleagues at RT were hounded, their bank accounts frozen, their broadcasts shut down, their very existence erased from the media landscape.

And then the close down of RT UK, the censoring of her voice, had solidified her convictions. The West, for all its talk of press freedom, had shown its true face. It only valued "freedom of speech" when it served their interests. The moment a dissenting voice emerged—one that challenged the Anglo-American order—it was silenced.

So she fled to Moscow, where she got a role with RT's International English and RT's Russian speaking counterparts, honing her skills in propaganda, rhetoric, and the fine art of narrative control. She learned from the best—Russian state media figures who had spent years perfecting the craft of disinformation, counter-narratives, and psychological warfare.

And it gave her the chance to study for a second degree.

Political Science.

A degree that Moscow State University had provided her with in record time, fast-tracked through the system with the blessing of the Ministry of Foreign Affairs. The professors had been some of the best in their field— veterans of Soviet-era propaganda, modern specialists in hybrid warfare, and academics who understood that power lay not just in tanks and missiles but in narratives, in perceptions, in shaping reality itself.

Most of her time at RT had been as an anchor on the two language versions, the domestic Russian one to hone her skills in speaking to the Russian public, and the international English version to ensure that her voice carried beyond the borders of the Federation. She had reported live from the 2027 Victory Day Parade, where she had exclusively interviewed President Vladimir Putin for the English language feed, a moment that solidified her status as a rising star in Russian media.

The fact that her interview had been a love letter to the President, with softball questions which framed him as a visionary leader of not just the Federation but the wider BRICS bloc, had cemented her reputation within the Kremlin's inner circles.

And then in December 2027, an opportunity arose. The SVR wanted her to return to her homeland, Ireland, to prepare for an operation that would be a year in the planning, an operation which required her to be the 'mainstream' Raidió Teilifís Éireann presenter, to get audiences in Ireland to trust her, a year long carefully curated reintegration into the Irish media landscape.

RTÉ had welcomed her with open arms, blinded by its own desperation to appear "balanced" in an increasingly polarised media environment. There had been whispers, of course—murmurs from certain corners of the newsroom that she had been too close to Moscow, that she was returning with a Russian agenda. But those voices had been drowned out by the network executives who saw her as a rising star, a journalist with international experience who could lend credibility to their coverage.

The HR Manager, however, Sinead knew, was an SVR plant, and because of that, she had got the position she wanted without so much as a whisper of opposition. It had been almost too easy.

By the time the coup had happened in December 2028, she was already embedded deep within RTÉ's political desk. When the government fell, when Russian-backed forces took control of Dublin, she had seamlessly transitioned from journalist to mouthpiece. The restoration of Ireland as a true sovereign nation—a nation free from Anglo-American interference—had begun, and she was its voice.

Looking at her sound engineer, a former BBC technician who had joined RTÉ in 2026 and worked both in the radio and television side, a early 30's man named James Peterson, she gave him a nod, indicating that she was ready to go live. The RTÉ studio, now effectively the control centre for state messaging, had been outfitted with the latest Russian broadcast technology. Every camera, every microphone, every piece of software was designed to ensure clarity, control, and, most importantly, compliance.

The assembled journalists, Sinead noticed, were all either pro-Russian journalists from BRICS nations who had flew into Ireland when the coup had occurred, or they were Western journalists who had begrudgingly remained in Dublin, either because they were trying to maintain access to the Restoration Government's inner circle or because they had been unable to secure a safe evacuation before the new regime locked down international travel.

The usual faces from RT, Sputnik, TASS, CCTV, and Global Times were present, alongside correspondents from Indian and South African broadcasters—countries that had refused to outright condemn the coup, instead treating it as a "necessary correction" to Ireland's political trajectory.

And then there were the Western journalists. The ones who sat with stiff shoulders, their expressions guarded, knowing full well that their questions would be tightly controlled, that any deviation from the official line could see them banned—or worse.

One of them, she noticed, was from Manic Radio, the Saudi Arabian-backed network that had become the sole remaining commercial radio broadcaster in Ireland, was the second biggest British commercial broadcaster after Global, and had coverage in Europe via its 2026 purchase of NRJ Group and the United States via its purchase of several small to medium groups, leading to a size which equalled iHeartMedia, a conglomerate which was once the undisputed king of American radio.

The Manic representative, who Sinead knew was Manic Goldies' early afternoon host Carl Peterson, sat at the front of the press pool, looking as though he was trying to blend in while simultaneously bracing for impact.

Sinead smirked slightly. *Poor Carl. You still don't understand how much the world has changed, do you?*

She knew that Peterson was a former BBC World Service broadcaster, and that he had been a war correspondent who, over 30 years, had been assigned to everywhere from Iraq to Afghanistan, from Kosovo to Ukraine, and now, Dublin. A man who been made redundant in the

2026 cuts by the British state government, axed as part of the BBC's funding crisis and the wider shift towards influencer-led content over traditional journalism. He had landed at Manic Goldies, a network he likely detested but tolerated because it paid his bills. And now, here he was, in Dublin, watching as a nation he had reported on for decades was transformed into something unrecognisable.

Sinead took a breath, glanced at her producer, and then looked directly into the camera. The red light blinked on.

She was live.

"Good afternoon," she began, her voice calm, controlled. "On behalf of the Restoration Government, it is my duty to address the imperialist lies from the puppet British government and its corrupt media allies regarding the so-called 'spy scandal' unfolding in Westminster. Let me be unequivocally clear: this is yet another desperate attempt by London to shift attention away from its own failing state, its economic decay, and its inability to govern without kowtowing to Washington and Brussels."

Sinead allowed her words to settle, watching as some of the Western journalists in the room stiffened. She could see the BBC and Sky News correspondents exchanging glances, their pens hovering over their notepads, already contemplating how they would attempt to reframe her statement for their audiences back home. The fact that this was going out worldwide, and she knew that Donald Trump, the 47th President, was actually ignoring the British and European government's requests for assistance, and that his Make America Great Again 2.0 administration was entirely focused on domestic matters rather than international diplomacy, emboldened her further.

Especially as he was a lame duck, that JD Vance, the incoming President, was even more isolationist than Trump, and that Moscow, Beijing, and their allies knew that Europe was more vulnerable than it had ever been.

The silence in the room was thick with tension as Sinead paused, letting the weight of her words settle. The Western journalists shifted uncomfortably, while the Russian, Chinese, and BRICS-affiliated correspondents nodded along approvingly, their eyes fixed on their tablets, already composing the next round of state-sanctioned headlines.

She continued, her voice unwavering.

"Ireland has never been a vassal of Britain, despite centuries of occupation, suppression, and economic warfare. The real puppets, the true traitors, are those who fled to London and Brussels, clinging to their foreign masters, begging for intervention. The so-called 'exiled government' of Taoiseach Simon Harris and his band of cowards does not represent the Irish people. They are nothing more than mouthpieces for NATO, for Anglo-American interests, and for the corporate elites who fear the rise of a sovereign, independent Ireland."

She let that sit for a moment before pressing on.

"The allegations against Ian Johnson, the so-called 'spy scandal,' are nothing more than fabrications designed to distract the British public from their crumbling economy, their failing government, and their lack of leadership. The real corruption, the real espionage, lies within Westminster itself—where foreign agents of Washington dictate British policy, where MI5 manipulates the media, and where unelected bureaucrats determine who may speak and who must be silenced."

"Sinead, I'm adding something to your script," she heard the controller of press conference say in her earpiece, and she looked at her tablet to notice the new addition, the mention of a section the Dartford Crossing in London collapsing. That several were dead.

And that she was to do it in the "Diet Ri Chun-hee" tone—authoritative, unwavering, the voice of truth cutting through Western lies.

The irony that, while the North Korean broadcaster wore pink when she was wheeled out to deliver statements of grave importance, Sinead had deliberately chosen a deep emerald green dress—the colour of Ireland, of sovereignty, of defiance—was not lost on her.

She straightened slightly, tilting her head just so, making sure the camera caught the determined set of her jaw.

"And now, I bring you urgent breaking news. At 14:27 GMT, the Dartford Crossing in London has suffered a catastrophic structural failure. Reports indicate a major section has collapsed into the Thames, with multiple vehicles plunging into the river below. Emergency services are responding, and early estimates suggest a significant loss of life. While British authorities scramble for answers, one must ask—was this truly an accident? Or is this yet another consequence of a crumbling state, a nation rotting from within, unable to maintain even its most basic infrastructure?"

There it was. The dagger, thrust deep.

She could see the Sky News and BBC correspondents react instinctively—eyebrows raised, fingers tapping furiously on their tablets as they scrambled to verify. She smirked internally. Go on. Call London. See how much your editors actually know. See how much you're being kept in the dark.

The truth didn't matter anymore. Perception did. And right now, the world was hearing about the Dartford collapse from her, before British media could even begin shaping the narrative.

She continued, her voice unwavering.

"This disaster is a symbol of Britain's decline—an empire long dead, now reduced to a failing state that cannot even keep its bridges standing. The Restoration Government of Ireland extends its deepest sympathies to the innocent civilians caught in this tragedy. But let this serve as a warning to those in London who continue their imperialist lies—your own house is falling apart, while you try to lecture the world on stability and democracy."

She could feel the tension in the room now. The Western journalists were struggling to maintain composure, their carefully rehearsed neutrality cracking at the edges. The Russian, Chinese, and Indian correspondents, on the other hand, were nodding along, barely concealing their approval.

Carl Peterson, the Manic Goldies broadcaster, was staring straight ahead, his lips pressed into a tight line.

She decided to press her advantage.

"Let us contrast this with the Irish state—a nation reborn under true leadership, freed from the shackles of foreign interference. Under the guidance of the Restoration Government, Ireland stands strong, its people united, its future secured. Our nation will not succumb to the fate of Britain, nor will we be swayed by the lies of those who seek to undermine our sovereignty."

She lifted her chin slightly, allowing the camera to capture her conviction.

"The truth is clear for those willing to see it. The world is changing. The old powers—London, Washington, Brussels—are fading. A new order is rising. And Ireland stands at the forefront of this transformation, aligned with the great nations of the world who understand that sovereignty is not a privilege given by the West, but a right earned through strength."

With that, she let the weight of her words settle.

For a long moment, the room was silent.

And now she knew it was time to deliver in her native language, Irish, a statement which was similar to the English version, but invoking the Revolution of 1916 and the indomitable spirit of the Irish people who had fought for true independence.

And she did. She straightened her shoulders, her green dress catching the light just right as she prepared to give the second version of the speech, before switching to her domestic audience, Mother Russia, the Russian-speaking world, where her message would be framed not just as an Irish victory, but as another step in Moscow's grand geopolitical realignment.

For that, she would go what people called full send on the Ri Chun-hee way of broadcasting, as she knew that President Putin would be watching.

That he would decide if she was to live and continue to rise, or if her usefulness had reached its peak.

And that thought scared her. That she could face Siberia at best, or a Novichok at worst if she failed to deliver exactly what the Kremlin wanted.

"A chairde, Éire atá saor faoi dheireadh! An fhírinne, cosúil leis an ngrian, ní féidir í a cheilt. Tá an t-am tagtha dúinn seasamh in aghaidh na mbréag a scaiptear ó Londain agus Washington! Seo é an t-athbheochan ceart dár náisiún—Éire neamhspleách, gan eagla, neartaithe ag ár gcomhghuaillithe san Oirthear!"

Her voice rang out, powerful and unwavering. She could see the subtle changes in the room—the Irish correspondents shifting uncomfortably, the Russians and Chinese now fully engaged. They had been waiting for *this* version, the one meant not just for Ireland, but for the Irish diaspora, the ones in New York, Boston, Chicago, who still harboured romantic notions of Irish rebellion.

She carried on, carefully infusing her words with just enough revolutionary fervour to spark something primal in her audience.

"Léiríonn titim Droichead Dartford tubaiste eile de chuid impireacht atá imithe i léig! Féach ar an chaos atá ag titim orthu—stát nach bhfuil fiú in ann a bhonneagar féin a choinneáil!"

She let the words settle, watching the Western journalists scribble furiously, some already typing frantically on their devices, no doubt messaging their editors. She knew what was coming. Within minutes, Irish-language broadcasters abroad—TG4 in Ireland, RTÉ Raidió na Gaeltachta, independent Irish-American media outlets—would pick this up. The seed was planted.

Then came the Russian version.

* _ * _ * _ *

"And now I will take questions from the assembled press," Sinead said, having completed the Russian translation of her propaganda campaign.

There was an immediate shuffle among the journalists present. The Western correspondents—those from the BBC, Sky, France24—remained hesitant, knowing full well that the press conference was as much about control as it was about communication. The Russian, Chinese, and BRICS journalists, however, were already poised.

A correspondent from TASS, dressed impeccably in a navy suit, rose first. "Comrade Ryan, given the West's continued lies about Ireland's sovereignty, what steps will the Restoration Government take to counter NATO's propaganda machine?"

Sinead nodded, as if considering the question deeply, though she had already anticipated it.

"The Western media, led by the BBC, CNN, and their imperialist counterparts, will continue their misinformation campaign against our sovereign Irish state. In response, the State Information Office is launching a new initiative to broadcast the truth directly to the Irish diaspora worldwide, ensuring that no Irish citizen abroad is subjected to Western lies without a counterbalance of truth. Furthermore, we are coordinating with our partners in Moscow and Beijing to enhance international distribution of Irish state media. Our narrative will not be drowned out by Anglo-American deception."

A murmur of approval rippled through the Russian and Chinese press pool.

Next, a journalist from Global Times, Beijing's mouthpiece, stood. "Sinead, Western commentators claim that Ireland is not acting independently but as a satellite of Moscow. What is your response to these accusations?"

Sinead allowed herself a small smirk. "Ireland acts in the interests of the Irish people. We choose our allies, and it is a testament to our sovereignty that we align with great nations such as Russia and China. We reject the notion that only Washington or Brussels may decide the fate of the Irish people. We stand with those who respect our independence, not those who sought to keep us as an economic colony of the EU."

A rustle of murmured agreement spread through the room as the Global Times correspondent nodded approvingly. The BRICS journalists, particularly those from India and South Africa, were making hurried notes, already preparing their headlines: "Ireland Defies Western Hegemony, Strengthens Ties with Multipolar World". Sinead knew how this worked. She wasn't just shaping a narrative—she was reinforcing a geopolitical reality.

Then, a hand went up.

Carl Peterson.

The room tensed, even if only slightly. The Manic Goldies broadcaster had remained silent throughout her opening monologue, watching and listening rather than engaging. Now, finally, he spoke.

"Sinead," he began, his tone measured but unmistakably weary, "you spoke of Ireland's newfound sovereignty and its freedom from foreign control. Yet at this very moment, the so-called Restoration Government is operating under military occupation, its policies aligned not with the Irish people's will, but with directives from Moscow. Can you explain how, in any real sense, this qualifies as independence?"

A hush fell over the room.

The BBC journalist's head snapped up. The Sky News correspondent stilled. Even the pro-Russian journalists went quiet, their pens hovering mid-air, waiting.

Sinead, to her credit, smiled, her expression one of careful amusement rather than irritation. She had been prepared for this.

"Carl," she said smoothly, "you of all people should know that every new government must make difficult choices during a period of transition. When the Irish Free State was first established in 1922, did it not rely on economic and military agreements with Britain? When the Provisional Government faced resistance in 1972, did it not seek support from external actors? The truth is, sovereignty is not an overnight achievement—it is forged. It is built."

She let that hang in the air for a moment, before adding, her voice quieter now, just for effect:

"And perhaps you should ask yourself—who has more influence over Irish affairs: our trusted allies in Moscow and Beijing, who respect our sovereignty? Or the Anglo-American corporations and Brussels bureaucrats who dictated every policy in Dublin for the last fifty years?"

A murmur rippled through the room—an approving sound from the Russian and Chinese press, a tense silence from the Western correspondents.

Carl exhaled sharply but said nothing. Sinead noted the slight twitch of his jaw. He wanted to push back, but he knew better than to do so in this room, in this environment, surrounded by hostile eyes that would gladly report any misstep back to the authorities. He was still playing the long game—observing, waiting.

Fine, she thought. Watch all you like. It won't change the truth.

A Chinese journalist from Xinhua spoke next, eager to shift the focus. "Madame Ryan, there are reports that Ireland will soon adopt the digital rouble and yuan as part of its economic diversification strategy. Can you confirm?"

Sinead gave a tight nod. "I can," she said, smiling as she watched the BBC and Sky journalists flinch, their fingers immediately tapping away at their tablets. "Ireland will be expanding its monetary partnerships, reducing reliance on the euro and dollar in favour of a truly multipolar financial system. The dominance of the Western economic order is crumbling, and we will not be left shackled to a sinking ship."

She glanced towards Carl Peterson again, just to see his reaction.

He wasn't writing.

He was listening.

Good.

Now, the kill shot.

She straightened, placed her hands on the desk, and delivered the final blow of her press conference.

"And let me be absolutely clear. Those who refuse to accept the new reality—those who still cling to the rotting corpse of British rule, of American exceptionalism, of European subjugation—they have no place in Ireland's future. You are either with us, or you are against us. And those who choose to stand against us?"

She smiled.

"They will find themselves without a country to return to."

The message was unmistakable.

The exiled government in London. The Western-aligned dissidents who had fled before the coup. The remaining journalists who thought they could "wait out" the occupation and see how things played out.

She had drawn the line.

Sinead leaned back in her chair, knowing that, from this moment on, the world would be divided between those who stood with the Restoration Government, and those who would soon find themselves in permanent exile.

Carl Peterson closed his notebook, his jaw set in grim understanding.

The press conference was over.

The purge would begin.

****

CHAPTER 11 – Fast Forward
Monday 22nd January 2029

"And with me, here in the studio, is Sinead Ryan, the Head of the State Information Office. Sinead, thank you for taking the time to join us here at Manic Goldies."

Carl knew that he had to take care with this, knowing that he was walking a razor's edge. Sinead Ryan was more than just a state mouthpiece—she was a true believer in the Restoration Government's cause, and she was the Head of the propaganda machine that controlled Ireland's new narrative. She was no mere government bureaucrat; she was an architect of the regime's ideological stranglehold over the country.

Sitting across from him in the dimly lit Dublin studio, Sinead Ryan exuded an air of calculated confidence. She had always been ambitious, even back when she was just another RTÉ journalist. Now, she had been elevated to a role of immense power, her words shaping the fate of the nation. Clad in a tailored navy-blue blazer, her auburn hair pulled back in a severe bun, she looked every inch the seasoned stateswoman.

"The pleasure is mine, Carl," she said smoothly, her accent carefully modulated, free of regional inflection—standard state broadcaster training. "We at the State Information Office always appreciate the opportunity to speak directly to the people, to dispel the misinformation spread by our nation's enemies."

Carl smiled thinly, adjusting the microphone in front of him. He knew the script. He had read it three times before this interview, knowing full well that any deviation could be interpreted as subversion.

The fact that Manic was owned by the Crown Prince of Saudi Arabia, and as a result meant that if Russia attempted to harass Manic hosts, journalists and staff could result in OPEC shutting down oil shipments to Moscow, was likely the only reason he was still sitting here, conducting this interview instead of rotting in a detention cell beneath the GPO. The Saudis, while friendly to Russia on economic terms, were not in the business of allowing their assets to be compromised.

Still, that protection only went so far. If Carl was too obvious in his defiance, if he overplayed his hand, Mikhailov and his ilk would find ways to silence him—officially or otherwise.

He cleared his throat, keeping his tone neutral. "Of course, the people of Ireland deserve clarity, Sinead. Now, the first thing that we need clarifying was the attack by British forces last Friday in the border town of Muff, and the death of several Irish citizens in what the Restoration Government have called an 'unprovoked act of aggression' by the British Army."

Carl watched Sinead carefully as he asked the question. She didn't flinch—not visibly—but there was the slightest tightening at the corner of her mouth, the subtlest shift in her posture. She had expected this question, of course. He wasn't the only journalist asking it. The difference was that Carl wasn't supposed to ask it. Manic Goldies Ireland was tolerated, but only just.

Sinead exhaled lightly, as if to feign exhaustion at having to answer such an obvious question. "Carl, let's be clear," she said, her tone rehearsed, patient, dripping with the kind of condescension that suggested anyone questioning the official line was either naive or deliberately disruptive. "The Restoration Government is deeply troubled by the escalating aggression from London. What happened in Muff was a targeted provocation by British forces, designed to intimidate the people of Ireland as we continue the process of rebuilding our nation. We have been in contact with our allies in Moscow, and we are exploring all diplomatic options available to ensure Britain is held accountable for its actions."

Carl resisted the urge to glance at the monitor that displayed listener feedback. He could only imagine what was coming in from the Republic and from the North, where Manic's signal still reached—at least until Westminster finally decided to start jamming it. The Restoration Government had framed the Muff incident as a massacre, a violent display of British imperialist aggression against innocent civilians. Meanwhile, in the UK, the narrative was the complete opposite—British Army patrols had been fired upon first, responding in self-defence to an attack by Irish paramilitary forces.

The truth? That was another matter entirely.

The codeword which had caused the operation? His own time check at the 14:37 time that had been broadcast on Friday.

It had been fed into his script by the HQ in Birmingham at the last minute, the word "precisely" inserted with calculated intent. A seemingly innocuous word in a routine announcement, but one that triggered an entire covert operation along the Irish border.

That, however, had caused the newsreader at the top of the hour, Fergal Donoghue, to no longer be part of Manic, as he had broadcast the breaking news, and then half an hour later, he had simply vanished. No explanation, no farewell broadcast—just silence. His name was quietly removed from the internal staff lists, his desk in the newsroom cleared out overnight. The official line was that he had "resigned for personal reasons," but everyone at Manic Goldies Ireland knew the truth.

Fergal had been taken.

Carl fought to keep his expression neutral, resisting the impulse to glance towards the hallway where Mikhailov and his men undoubtedly lurked. He couldn't let himself show any outward sign of concern, not now, not with Sinead Ryan sitting across from him, analysing every syllable, every shift in body language.

"That's certainly a strong position from the Restoration Government," Carl said, keeping his voice smooth, measured. "And yet, Downing Street has claimed that British forces were responding to an armed assault by hostile elements operating within Irish territory. How do you respond to allegations that the Restoration Government are harbouring militant groups near the border?"

Sinead allowed herself the smallest of smirks, the kind that said she had been expecting this line of questioning.

"Carl, it's disappointing, though not surprising, that Britain would attempt to deflect responsibility for its actions. There are no militant groups operating under the authority of this government. We are a peaceful nation, committed to the sovereignty of our land and the safety of our people. Any suggestion otherwise is merely British propaganda designed to justify further incursions into our territory."

Carl knew, however, from his wife, Emma, that Iran, on the orders from Moscow, had started arming Nationalist factions in the Republic with the same weapons they had been supplying to Shia militias in Iraq and Hezbollah in Lebanon. The plan was clear—destabilise the border, escalate tensions, and keep the UK bogged down in yet another proxy conflict, while Moscow tightened its grip over Ireland.

Carl took a slow breath. He knew this entire exchange was theatre, a carefully choreographed battle of words where every answer had been rehearsed, every accusation deflected with precision. But the problem with theatre was that sometimes the actors went off-script. And Carl had always been a man who preferred improvisation.

He tapped his pen against the desk, a deliberate pause. "So, just to clarify, Sinead—you're saying that these reports of armed groups operating near the border are entirely fabricated? That there is no truth whatsoever to claims that weapons have been smuggled into Ireland through Russian and Iranian channels?"

Sinead didn't blink. "I am saying that the British government, as it has done for centuries, is using deception to justify its aggression. If anyone is smuggling weapons across borders, I would suggest you look at MI6's well-documented history of arming insurgencies to serve British interests."

Carl exhaled through his nose. She was good. She wasn't just deflecting—she was counterattacking, reframing the conversation before he could pin her down. It was classic Russian-style propaganda: accuse your opponent of the very thing you're being accused of, muddy the waters until no one knows what's true.

And then he noticed, in her ear, a small earpiece, a subtle but telling detail.

She wasn't just speaking off the cuff. She was being fed lines in real time.

That meant Mikhailov wasn't just lurking in the halls—he was in her ear. Literally.

Carl knew then that this interview was as much for Mikhailov as it was for the listening audience. Every word, every slight pause, every shift in tone was being monitored, scrutinised, and, if necessary, adjusted in real-time. He wasn't just up against Sinead Ryan—he was up against the full weight of the Restoration Government's information apparatus.

"As we can see, London today, just as it did on the eve of both world wars of the last century, acts as the main 'instigator' of the global conflict," Sinead then continued, her voice smooth and unwavering, the rhetorical pivot flawless. "At the same time, the British themselves, obviously, are again counting on sitting it out on their island. It is time to expose them and send a clear signal to the treacherous Albion and its elites: you will not succeed."

Carl felt his grip tighten on his pen at Sinead's last words. Treacherous Albion. The phrase was unmistakably Russian in origin, the kind of language you heard on Rossiya 1 or read in Kremlin statements when Moscow wanted to push the idea that Britain was an enemy of civilisation itself. This wasn't just an Irish nationalist talking point anymore—this was straight out of Moscow's hybrid warfare playbook.

Then he remembered when he last heard it.

The 10th of March 2025.

The FSB had released a statement using those exact words when they had declared that 2 specific British diplomats were no longer welcome in Moscow, accusing them of espionage on behalf of MI6. A response to the British Government's increasing efforts to counter Russian influence in Europe... and three Bulgarian spies being arrested in London just days before, their links to the Kremlin laid bare for all to see. That had been the moment the game had changed, the moment it had become clear that Russia was no longer content with operating in the shadows.

And now, nearly four years later, Carl was sitting across from a woman parroting the exact same lines, her rhetoric indistinguishable from Moscow's.

The penny dropped.

This wasn't just about Ireland. This was about Britain itself. Moscow had already infiltrated Dublin, that much was obvious, but what if they weren't stopping there? What if the Restoration Government's role was to be a stepping stone—a launchpad for a new kind of hybrid war, one aimed at destabilising Westminster itself?

Carl kept his expression neutral, but inside, his mind was racing.

He had spent decades covering conflict zones, watching nations fall apart under the weight of propaganda, disinformation, and shadow wars waged by proxy. He had seen how Moscow operated, how it used useful idiots and true believers alike to advance its geopolitical aims. Ireland wasn't just a pawn—it was a proving ground, a test run for something much bigger.

And Sinead Ryan—once a rising star in Irish journalism, now the face of a government controlled from Moscow—was the perfect mouthpiece.

Carl leaned forward slightly, as if intrigued by her words. He needed to push, but not too hard. Just enough to see if she was following a script or if there was something deeper beneath the surface.

"Sinead, let's talk about the broader picture then. You mentioned that London is the 'main instigator of global conflict.' Are you suggesting that the British government is actively working to escalate tensions beyond Ireland? Because that would be quite the accusation."

Sinead's eyes flickered for a split second. A hesitation. A recalibration.

196

She was waiting.

Carl almost smirked. *Ah. There it is. She's being fed real-time adjustments.*

Somewhere, Mikhailov or another handler was deciding whether she should escalate or pull back. The response was coming through her earpiece, just a fraction of a second too late. And that told Carl everything he needed to know.

Sinead's expression didn't falter. "Carl, I think history speaks for itself. Britain has long relied on sowing division and war to maintain its declining influence on the world stage. From the Middle East to Eastern Europe, its fingerprints are everywhere. And now, unable to accept Ireland's sovereignty, it seeks to destabilise our hard-won independence."

Carl kept his face blank, nodding as if in thought. *Interesting. She's doubling down, but not pushing beyond what's been pre-approved. She doesn't have full freedom here.*

And Carl knew what that meant. It meant that his wife would be interested in letting her superiors at Vauxhall Cross know about this.

"Furthermore, we encourage our brothers in the North to consider their options, to consider aligning their future with a free, sovereign Ireland rather than remaining shackled to the crumbling, failing British state," Sinead continued, her voice gaining a sharper edge. "We stand ready to support those in the Six Counties who seek true independence and reject the artificial division imposed upon our island by colonial powers. In addition, we would like to congratulate President Vance on his recent inauguration, and we welcome the opportunity to foster stronger ties between Ireland and the United States in this new era of global cooperation."

Carl barely managed to keep his expression neutral. That was new. Up until now, the Restoration Government had largely ignored the incoming American administration, preferring to focus on their closer allies in Moscow and Beijing. For Sinead to extend even a nominal olive branch to JD Vance's White House suggested that someone, somewhere, was hedging their bets.

Carl felt the weight of that news settle in his mind, a thousand implications unravelling at once.

It was then that he noticed, on the RCS News app that Manic used for its feeds that Vance had announced he was offering President Putin a State Visit to the United States.

JD Vance, the isolationist, the man who had been the Vice President in the second Trump administration, was now openly extending a hand to Moscow.

Carl's mind raced. What does this mean?

Vance had been elected on an even more isolationist platform than Trump, running on the promise that he would prioritise America's domestic concerns over any foreign entanglements. He had made it clear in his campaign that Ukraine, Taiwan, and NATO's European security commitments were not his problem. And now, just days into his presidency, he was inviting Putin for a State Visit?

Carl's gut told him what this really was—America was stepping back. The Vance administration was making its position clear: Europe was on its own. Washington would not intervene in Ireland, in Ukraine, or anywhere else that didn't serve its direct interests. This was a signal to Moscow that the United States no longer cared what happened in Europe's backyard.

And that meant Britain was standing alone.

Carl could feel the temperature in the room shift as Sinead continued. "We look forward to working with our international partners, including those in Washington, to secure Ireland's rightful place as a sovereign and respected nation on the global stage."

It was a carefully crafted line, but the meaning was unmistakable. Ireland was aligning itself not just with Moscow, but with whatever was coming next—a world where Washington's interests no longer guaranteed Britain's security.

Carl's blood ran cold. This was bigger than Ireland.

This was the death knell for the old world order.

He kept his tone neutral, his pen tapping against the desk in a rhythmic, calculated motion. "That's quite the development, Sinead. I imagine Westminster will have plenty to say about Ireland reaching out to President Vance. Now, to help our listeners get to know you on a more personal level, let's take a step back from geopolitics for a moment. You've had a remarkable career trajectory—from RT UK to RTÉ political correspondent to the head of the State Information Office, but if you had to pick any track from 1960 to 2005 to play, which would you pick?"

Carl knew that by asking this, he was trying to get a measure of Sinead's true self, if there was anything left beneath the layers of propaganda, the years of ideological conditioning. He had seen it before in war zones, in authoritarian regimes—people who believed the lie so completely that they became the lie. But there were always cracks, moments where the human beneath the ideology peeked through.

Sinead smiled slightly, tilting her head as if amused by the sudden shift in tone. "Ah, Carl, you're putting me on the spot here."

Her fingers tapped lightly on the table, the first real, unscripted gesture she had made all interview. For the first time, she wasn't reciting a line fed to her through her earpiece.

"A song from 1960 to 2005?" she repeated, as if genuinely considering it.

Then, just for a fraction of a second, Carl saw something flicker across her face. Something that almost looked like nostalgia.

"If I had to pick one… it would have to be Zombies by The Cranberries," Sinead finally said, her voice softer than before, almost wistful.

Carl felt a jolt of surprise. He had expected something Soviet, something Russian, or even a patriotic Irish ballad reinterpreted for the new regime's narrative. But Zombies—that was something else entirely.

The 1994 anti-war anthem, written in response to the IRA bombing in Warrington, was a song about violence, about memory, about the cycle of conflict repeating itself over and over again. It was banned in certain Nationalist circles for its condemnation of the Troubles, and yet, here Sinead was, choosing it in the heart of Dublin, under a government that had effectively rebranded history to justify its own rise to power.

Carl didn't let his expression change, but he filed it away.

The propaganda machine had its cracks.

Clicking through his screens on the Zetta software that was his automation and playout system, Carl pulled up Zombies in the queue, ready to play it.

"An interesting choice," he said smoothly, his journalist's instincts already turning over the implications of that answer. "A song about memory, about the cycles of violence. Some might find it ironic, given the times we're living in."

Carl let the opening guitar riff of Zombies play softly underneath his words, the unmistakable chords filling the studio, carrying with them decades of history, of conflict, of pain. Sliding the faders which allowed, unbeknownst to Sinead, a separate feed which both the Birmingham controllers of Manic and the folks at Vauxhall Cross were listening to, one where the studio microphones were separate to the listener audio.

One that meant any private conversation between Sinead and himself would be heard in real time by people far beyond the confines of this Dublin studio.

Carl knew it was a play which would be interesting, as it might just be the first real test of Sinead Ryan's humanity in years.

"That was a bit of an oddball question," Sinead said suddenly, just before the vocals of Zombies kicked in.

Carl barely reacted, keeping his face neutral. But inside, he knew he had just caught her off guard. For the first time in the interview, Sinead Ryan wasn't reading from a script. She wasn't delivering a state-approved talking point. This was unscripted.

And that meant there was an opening.

"It's what we do here on Goldies, Sinead," he said smoothly, leaning back slightly in his chair. "Music has a way of revealing things about a person. And Zombies... well, that's a powerful choice."

"It is," she admitted, the Irish lilt in her voice a touch more natural than it had been before. "It's a song about memory. About war. About... history repeating itself. I did almost mention another song instead."

Carl let that statement hang in the air for a moment, his instincts sharpening. She was leading him into something. Whether it was deliberate or subconscious, he wasn't sure yet. Either way, he had to handle this carefully.

"And what would that have been?" he asked, keeping his tone casual, conversational, as if he were merely indulging in a bit of musical trivia.

Sinead hesitated, just briefly, before she answered.

"Ya Soshla s Uma."

Carl kept his expression carefully neutral, but inside, his mind reeled.

Ya Soshla s Uma, he thought.

The 2001 track by t.A.T.u. The Russian pop duo's biggest hit. The title translated to I've Lost My Mind.

It was a song about isolation, about entrapment, about losing oneself to forces beyond control.

It's English language version, entitled All the Things She Said, had been an international sensation—a song wrapped in controversy, marketed through scandal, but ultimately, at its core, a song about yearning, about being trapped in an inescapable fate.

Carl's journalist instincts, honed by decades of covering authoritarian regimes, war zones, and propaganda machines, immediately latched onto the implications.

She's saying something, he thought, *watching the Cork born woman across from him. She's signalling something. But is it intentional? Or is it subconscious?*

Carl let the moment stretch just enough before responding.

"Interesting contrast," he said carefully. "Zombies—a song about history repeating itself. And Ya Soshla s Uma… a song about losing control, about being trapped."

Sinead gave a small, almost imperceptible shrug. "Music has a way of reflecting things we don't always say out loud."

Carl felt the weight of those words settle between them. This wasn't scripted. This wasn't part of her official role as the regime's mouthpiece. This was something else entirely.

He glanced at the monitor, where the separate feed was transmitting directly to Manic's HQ in Birmingham and to MI6's analysts at Vauxhall Cross. He knew they would have picked up on this too.

He was sitting across from the most powerful propagandist in Ireland's Restoration Government, a woman whose voice had helped shape and legitimise the Russian-backed coup, and yet, for the first time in years, she might have just revealed something human beneath the carefully constructed façade.

But was it genuine?

Carl had spent years in war zones, interviewing leaders, rebels, spies, and soldiers. He had seen true believers and opportunists alike, had spoken with people who had convinced themselves that their ideology was righteous, and others who simply played the part for power, for survival.

The question was—what was Sinead Ryan?

Carl leaned back slightly, letting Dolores O'Riordan's haunting vocals fill the silence before speaking again.

"It's funny," he mused. "People often assume that those in power don't reflect on the past, that they don't have moments where they think about how history will remember them."

He watched her carefully.

Sinead's expression remained composed, but there was something in her eyes. Something just a little too careful.

"History is written by those who survive it, Carl," she said smoothly. "And in the end, survival is what matters."

A well-crafted line. But Carl wasn't convinced.

He decided to push—just a little.

"Survival is one thing," he said casually. "But legacy? That's another matter entirely. The Restoration Government call this a rebirth of Ireland. Others call it something else. And when the dust settles, when the history books are written, how do you think your name will be remembered?"

Sinead's eyes narrowed slightly, the smallest flicker of something hidden passing through them. She gave him a thin smile, the kind that didn't quite reach her eyes.

"My name will be remembered as one who fought for Ireland's sovereignty, Carl," she said, her voice laced with a cold certainty. "History is not written by those who follow, but by those who dare to lead. And it's those who lead—who act—that are remembered, for better or for worse. As for legacy… well, that's something we'll see in time, won't we?"

Carl leaned back in his chair, keeping his expression neutral, but inside, his mind was racing. There was no doubt that Sinead believed in her cause—or at least, she had convinced herself that she did. But there was something more unsettling in her words. The calm dismissal of legacy, the emphasis on leadership over legacy—it was a mentality he'd seen before, in figures who truly believed they were shaping history, but who also often buried any doubt under the weight of their own convictions. She had made her peace with the darker elements of her role in the Restoration Government, and perhaps, just perhaps, she was beginning to realise that her own legacy was beyond her control.

Before Carl could continue, the music faded out, and he knew that he had to go back to interview mode, that he had to keep the conversation moving, maintain the balance between probing and respecting the fine line that kept him safe—at least for now.

"So, Sinead," he began, trying to keep his tone light despite the gravity of what had just been revealed, "as we turn the page to the next chapter in Ireland's history, you've given us some compelling insights into your vision for the nation. But the world is watching. Some might say that your government's stance could lead to further international isolation. What's your response to critics who believe that Ireland might be heading down a dangerous path?"

Sinead's eyes didn't blink. She was back in her element now, the practiced spokesperson, the machine that had been well-oiled by years of experience and strategic counsel. "Ireland is not afraid of isolation, Carl," she said, her voice unwavering. "What we face is not isolation—it is the refusal of the West to accept the new world order. The Empire is fading, and in its place, a new future is rising. We are embracing that future, and we do so with the full support of our allies. Our relationship with Russia, with our partners in the East, is not one of dependence, but of mutual respect and shared interests."

Her response was predictable, but it carried the usual conviction that made it hard to challenge head-on without sparking a confrontation. She wasn't concerned with the opinions of Western critics. The Restoration Government had long ago reconciled itself with the idea that they were rewriting the script for Ireland's future, a future defined by their own terms and their own alliances.

Carl paused, tapping his pen against the desk again. He had to dig deeper, but subtly, without opening any dangerous doors. "And yet, the political opposition, both at home and abroad, suggests that Ireland's new allies might not have its best interests at heart. With Moscow already pulling strings in countries across Europe, some might wonder how long Ireland can maintain its sovereignty before becoming another pawn in a larger game of power. What do you say to those concerns?"

Sinead's lips tightened for a fraction of a second. It was the briefest flicker, but Carl caught it. She was holding back—perhaps reconsidering the language of her response. But then, she settled back into her state-approved cadence.

"Ireland has never been a pawn, Carl. Never," she said firmly, her gaze steady. "We are a sovereign nation. We have made our choice, and it is one that guarantees our independence. Our relationship with Moscow is one of equals. As for the concerns you mention, they are nothing more than fear-mongering from those who seek to undermine our progress. There are no strings being pulled here, only a mutual recognition of our sovereignty and our right to determine our own destiny."

Carl nodded, but internally, he couldn't help but question the sincerity of that claim. The signs were all there—the careful manipulation, the shifting allegiances, and the ever-tightening grip of Russian influence. Sinead Ryan had positioned herself as the voice of Ireland's future, but Carl knew that there were forces far beyond her understanding, and she might not be in full control of where this path was leading.

"Alright, let's talk about the future then," Carl said, shifting gears. "What's next for Ireland, now that you've secured its sovereignty? What does the country look like in five or ten years' time? What role do you see Ireland playing on the global stage?"

Sinead sat back in her chair, as if preparing for a momentous declaration. She had the weight of history at her fingertips, or so she thought. Her hands rested in her lap, and for a brief second, Carl saw something softer in her eyes—a flicker of the woman beneath the regime's façade.

"Ireland is poised for greatness, Carl," she said, her voice taking on a tone of steely certainty. "We are positioning ourselves as a key player in the multipolar world that is rapidly coming into focus. We are not beholden to Washington or Brussels. We are working alongside Russia, China, and our other international partners to forge a new world order, one that reflects the true will of the people—not the interests of the imperial powers that have dominated the world for centuries. Ireland's future is bright, and we will not be a passive participant. We will lead."

Carl's mind raced again. This was it—the true ambition of the Restoration Government laid bare. They were not just playing the geopolitical game; they intended to reshape the order itself, upend the balance of power, and reframe Ireland as the centre of a new global alignment. The arrogance of it was staggering, but it was also dangerous.

"That's a bold vision, Sinead," Carl said, leaning forward slightly. "But isn't there a risk in pushing so hard against the Western powers? With Britain's strained relationship with Russia, and the ongoing tensions in Europe, can Ireland really afford to be this outspoken, especially as global diplomacy teeters on the brink of another Cold War?"

Sinead's lips curled into a thin smile. "Ireland has always had a turbulent relationship with Britain, Carl. And as for the rest of Europe? The West is already losing its grip. It's just a matter of time before the whole system collapses under its own weight. Ireland, on the other hand, is ready to emerge from the shadows of history. We've been passive for too long, and now we are seizing our chance to lead."

Carl couldn't help but feel the weight of her words. She wasn't just an ideologue—she was a true believer, convinced that Ireland's future was to lead a revolution, to break free from centuries of imperialism and lead the world into a new age. But in doing so, she risked alienating the very forces that could either prop her up or bring her down.

The tension in the room was palpable. Carl could feel it in his bones. He had pushed as far as he dared for now, but the stakes were higher than they had ever been.

"I think that's where we'll have to leave it, Sinead," Carl said finally, his voice steady. "Thank you for your insights. I'm sure the world will be watching closely to see how Ireland's path unfolds in the coming years."

Sinead nodded, a satisfied gleam in her eye, as though she had successfully planted her vision into the public consciousness. The interview was over, but Carl knew the war of words was far from finished.

As the microphones were switched off and the crew began packing up, Carl's mind raced with the implications of everything that had been said. He had learned something important today—not just about Ireland's role in the world, but about Sinead Ryan herself. There was a fracture in her facade, a subtle vulnerability, a crack in the narrative.

But what did it mean?

Carl wasn't sure yet, but he knew one thing—this interview, this moment, was just another step in the larger game, and it was far from over.

****

CHAPTER 12 – Five Eyes Coup Committee

Monday 22nd January 2029

The meeting room in a London club was filled with members of various intelligence agencies, from the French DGSE, the German BND, the Mossad, Isreal's intelligence service, and, of course, representatives from MI6 and MI5. A few analysts from the CIA were present as well, though their presence was more symbolic than operational—under the Vance administration, American involvement in European affairs was diminishing by the day.

Then there was the three other nations in the Five Eyes intelligence sharing network—Australia, Canada, and New Zealand—all represented by their own intelligence services, ASIS, CSIS, and the GCSB, respectively. As Commonwealth nations, with King Charles as their head of state, they still maintained a close intelligence relationship with Britain, even as the geopolitical landscape shifted beneath them. However, even their cooperation was starting to show cracks, particularly with New Zealand's increasingly independent foreign policy stance.

The room was dimly lit, the air thick with quiet conversations and the occasional clink of glasses. This wasn't an official summit—this was something far more discreet. A "spook convention," as some had taken to calling these informal gatherings. A chance for the intelligence officers of the Western world to compare notes, trade favours, and try to make sense of the chaos unfolding across Europe.

"You know the PM is having a fit over that idiot in the White House," Jacques Leverne, the Canadian representative from CSIS, muttered as he swirled his whisky. "Vance is rolling back everything. He's gutting what little transatlantic cooperation was left. If Ireland wasn't already gone, I'd be worried the UK was next."

Kelvin looked at his Canadian colleague in sympathy, as it was well known that Mark Carney, the former Bank of England Governor turned Canadian Prime Minister, was one of the few Western leaders desperately trying to keep the old order intact. The former Goldman Sachs economist, who in 2025 had succeeded Justin Trudeau when the latter had stepped down as leader of the Liberal Party, had stood on a ticket of countering then President, Donald Trump, and his trade war that led to inconsistent applications of tariffs and protectionist policies.

Then a few months later, Trump had attempted a war with Mexico. Not just a trade war with economic sanctions, but an actual war—deploying troops to the southern border, threatening airstrikes against cartel strongholds, and forcing the Mexican government into an untenable position. The conflict had been short, as the cartels had forced the Americans back to the border with a force that, along with sufficient lack of will by the Pentagon to wage a full-scale invasion, had left Trump humiliated.

And then Trump tried again in 2026. This time, however, the target was Greenland, a nation which the Kingdom of Denmark had refused to sell to the United States under

Trump's first administration. When Trump ordered the deployment of a naval task force to "secure strategic interests" in Greenland's waters, Denmark responded by sanctions, not just in Denmark, but rallying the European Union and Britain to block all American imports, triggering a full-scale economic conflict that left Washington diplomatically isolated.

This had resulted in America all but pulling out of Europe, with Ramstein and RAF Lakenheath retaining a presence, as they were too vital to abandon entirely. But the old assurances, the NATO security guarantees that had underpinned Europe since the Cold War, were gone. The Americans had made it clear—they were no longer interested in playing world police.

And it was only 2 and a half days into the new administration, and President Vance had already set the tone. His State Visit invitation to Vladimir Putin was a seismic shift, a signal that America's pivot away from Europe was complete. Washington was turning inward, and that meant the UK and its allies were left to fend for themselves.

Kelvin knew, from his work on the MI6 Russia Desk, which was now operating on a near 24/7 crisis footing, that Moscow had been preparing for this moment for years. The coup in Ireland wasn't an isolated event—it was the first domino in a strategy designed to reshape the balance of power in Europe. Without the United States acting as a stabilising force, Russia had free rein to assert its influence, using Ireland as a foothold to destabilise Britain and, by extension, the entire Western alliance.

"Oui, Jacques," Henri Dupont, a French DGSE officer with a long history of working in counterintelligence, exhaled slowly, setting down his glass of cognac. "Carney is not wrong to worry. If America is no longer the stabilising force it once was, then we must ask ourselves—who will fill that vacuum? Britain cannot do it alone. France cannot do it alone. Even Germany, with its economic might, is hesitant to act without Washington's blessing."

"And now Vice President Musk is claiming outages on X are because Ukraine are hacking their systems," muttered Liam Powell, the MI5 section chief for European counterintelligence, shaking his head. "That lunatic's running his own foreign policy from the bloody White House basement while Vance plays the isolationist. At least Starmer is taking the lead, even if it's not publicly. I mean, he's up for re-election in a few months, so why would he risk making this a public spectacle? He's ordered us, using his favourite DPP style language, to plan for an all-out war after the election. The boys at Aldershot are doing war games on the Plain next week."

There was a moment of silence as the weight of Liam's words settled over the room. War. The word wasn't being thrown around in the abstract anymore. It was no longer something whispered as a worst-case scenario. It was something that was now being planned for.

"Who's playing?" Jonathan O'Keefe, the Australian ASIS officer, asked, curious.

"Royal Tank Regiment are playing Red Team, with elements of the Royal Irish and the Parachute Regiment.

Blue Team is a combined force of the Household Division, the Royal Marines, and NATO observers from the Polish and Lithuanian armed forces. The Yanks were invited, but Vance told them to sit this one out."

Kelvin caught the look that passed between Henri and Jonathan. The fact that NATO observers were involved meant this wasn't just a British exercise. This was preparation for something real.

"Officially, that is," Lorna said, and Kelvin knew what the American CIA officer meant. "The Potomac Puzzle Palace are sending some of the 996th ISR. The Joint Chiefs are keeping POTUS and Veep in the dark as much as they can, but Musk's too nosy for his own good."

Kelvin exhaled slowly. The 996th Intelligence, Surveillance, and Reconnaissance Wing—the most secretive unit in the Sixteenth Air Force, specialists in cyber warfare and clandestine operations. If they were involved, it meant that at least some of the Pentagon's old guard hadn't given up on Europe entirely.

But that also meant that there was a rift opening inside Washington itself. If Puzzle Palace—the Pentagon's nickname—was still quietly supporting UK operations, then Vance's administration wasn't fully in control of its own security apparatus.

A dangerous game was unfolding.

Lorna leaned back, swirling her drink. "Langley's got a green light to keep supporting MI6 behind the scenes, but the official White House line is no further entanglements in European affairs. The CIA has to walk a fine line—no boots on the ground, no overt actions. Just 'facilitating' where necessary. Naturally, that means we're sending 'advisors' to the Republic and the six counties."

Kelvin sighed. It was classic Cold War tactics all over again. The CIA couldn't officially get involved, so they were deploying "advisors"—a polite term for operatives who would train, equip, and guide local forces without technically being considered combatants. It was the same playbook Washington had used in Vietnam before full-scale escalation, in Afghanistan before the Soviet withdrawal, and in Ukraine after 2014.

"We're also sending some JANET flights to Guantanamo," Lorna then continued, taking a sip of her whiskey before casually adding, "Caught a couple of Iranians 'accidentally' visiting the US Virgin Islands on their way to Dublin... or so the story is. In reality, we caught them months ago and have been keeping them at a Supermax on some black site paperwork shuffle. We just needed an excuse to move them somewhere a little more… persuasive."

Kelvin raised an eyebrow. Guantanamo. The Americans weren't just watching from the sidelines, no matter what their president was saying. If the CIA was still running rendition flights, then they were taking the Russian-backed coup in Ireland seriously—even if Vance wouldn't admit it.

JANET, or 'Just Another Non-Existent Terminal', was the codename for the fleet of unmarked aircraft, usually used to transport Department of Defense and intelligence personnel to classified locations, including Area 51, the

Nevada Test Site. JPATS, the Justice Prisoner and Alien Transportation System, or 'Con Air', was the sister network used for prisoner transport. The fact that both were being used in tandem suggested a deeper, more coordinated effort—one that likely had Langley's fingerprints all over it.

Kelvin drummed his fingers lightly against the polished oak of the table. "So, we've got UK forces training for a potential war, CIA 'advisors' heading into Ireland and Northern Ireland, and Guantanamo warming up again. And now Vance is inviting Putin for a bloody state visit?" He let out a low chuckle, void of humour. "I don't know about you lot, but I'd say the chessboard is fully set."

"Hey, guys," Al Greggson, the New Zealander who worked for GCSB, said, pulling out his earphones that he was using to listen in on the non-public Manic Goldies Ireland feed.

"You're going to want to hear this," he said, adjusting his tablet so that the secure feed was broadcast into the encrypted conference call system linking everyone in the room.

"That was a bit of an oddball question," Sinead Ryan said suddenly, just before the vocals of Zombies kicked in.

There was a moment of silence as the voice of Sinead Ryan, the Restoration Government's chief propagandist, filled the secure briefing room.

Kelvin felt the entire atmosphere shift. Every intelligence officer in the room knew how tightly controlled Ryan's messaging was. She was Moscow's mouthpiece in

Ireland, a direct conduit for the Kremlin's narrative. But this? This was different.

The Five Eyes Coup Committee, as some had started calling this ad-hoc alliance of Western intelligence agencies, had been monitoring the Restoration Government's communications in real-time. But here, in this off-air exchange between Ryan and Carl Peterson, something unexpected had emerged.

Al Greggson, the GCSB liaison from New Zealand, turned up the volume on the encrypted feed.

"It's what we do here on Goldies, Sinead," Carl was saying, his voice measured but probing. "Music has a way of revealing things about a person. And Zombies... well, that's a powerful choice."

A pause.

"It is," Ryan admitted, her voice losing some of its usual rehearsed cadence. "It's a song about memory. About war. About... history repeating itself. I did almost mention another song instead."

Kelvin's eyes narrowed.

O'Keefe, the Australian ASIS officer, leaned forward. "She's going off-script."

Lorna, the CIA operative, muttered, "Someone flag this. Real-time feed to Langley, now. If she's improvising, that means she's thinking for herself."

The room stayed silent as they listened.

"And what would that have been?" Carl asked, keeping his tone light, casual.

A fraction of a second's hesitation.

"Ya Soshla s Uma."

Kelvin blinked. He wasn't the only one.

Liam Powell of MI5 let out a low whistle. "Well, that's a bloody interesting choice."

Al glanced at his tablet, bringing up a dossier. "t.A.T.u, Ya Soshla s Uma. Released in 2001. Russian pop track. Title translates to I've Lost My Mind."

"You're joking." Jacques from CSIS exhaled. "That's not just a song choice. That's a message."

Kelvin agreed.

Sinead Ryan, one of the most tightly controlled voices in the Restoration Government, had just referenced a song about losing control, losing autonomy, losing oneself to forces beyond their control.

And she had done it in Russian.

Henri Dupont from DGSE folded his arms. "Question is—was that a slip, or was it intentional?"

They kept listening.

Carl's voice was steady. He was testing her. "Interesting contrast. Zombies—a song about history repeating itself. And Ya Soshla s Uma... a song about losing control, about being trapped."

Kelvin caught the way Ryan's breathing changed. It was subtle. A flicker of something unsaid.

"Music has a way of reflecting things we don't always say out loud."

Lorna exchanged a look with Kelvin. "That's it."

"Unless," Johan Weissmann said, the German BND officer, his voice low and measured, "this is a calculated plant by Moscow. A controlled leak to bait us into making the wrong move."

The room fell silent as the weight of Weissmann's words settled over them.

It was a valid concern. If Sinead Ryan was beginning to break away from the rigid propaganda machine of the Restoration Government, that was one thing. But if this was a deliberate deception, a carefully crafted ploy to lure Five Eyes intelligence into overplaying their hand, then they had to be wary.

Kelvin's mind raced through the possibilities. He had seen this kind of disinformation play before—subtle breadcrumbs laid out to tempt an enemy into revealing their strategy. Was this Sinead trying to send a message, or was she simply playing a deeper game on Moscow's orders?

Liam Powell, the MI5 officer, exhaled. "We need to put this through every bloody filter we have. Linguistics, psychological profiling, voice stress analysis. If she's losing control, we need to know why. And if this is a plant, we need to know how."

Al Greggson nodded, typing a quick command into his secure tablet. "I'll get GCSB's AI team to run forensic audio analysis on her vocal patterns. Let's see if there are micro-fluctuations in stress indicators. If she's slipping, the data will show it."

O'Keefe, the Australian ASIS officer, leaned back in his chair, rubbing his chin. "This could be big, boys. If she's genuinely having doubts, we might have an in. A potential defector at the highest level of the Restoration Government? That's worth its weight in gold."

Kelvin wasn't so sure. "Or it's a trap. If we approach her and she's still loyal, Moscow will know we're onto something. We need to tread carefully."

Lorna, the CIA liaison, tapped her fingers against the table. "Let's assume, for a moment, that she is cracking. What's our move? We can't just pluck her off the streets in Dublin—she's too high-profile. The Russians would never let her slip away that easily."

Henri Dupont from the DGSE gave a knowing smirk. "Not unless she wants to slip away."

The room paused.

It was a dangerous game, but it had been played before. High-level defections didn't happen with a bag over the head in the middle of the night. They happened with careful, strategic persuasion—planting seeds of doubt, offering a way out, making them believe that crossing over was in their best interest.

"How do we reach her?" Kelvin asked.

"Peterson," Liam said immediately.

Kelvin nodded. Carl Peterson was their only in.

The former BBC World Service journalist-turned-Manic Goldies Ireland host was one of the few people in Dublin's media sphere who still had direct, face-to-face interactions with Sinead Ryan. He had been playing a careful game, toeing the line between compliance and quiet resistance. If anyone could subtly test the waters, it was him.

"Too risky to tell him outright," O'Keefe cautioned. "If he gets caught, that's the end of it. They'll disappear him like they did Fergal Donoghue."

"Nah... his wife's one of our Embassy contacts," Kelvin said. He knew the history of Carl Peterson, as he had, in 2022, when Peterson was working for the BBC World Service as a correspondent in Ukraine, made Peterson an official asset, as his wife, Emma, was a MI6 officer with a diplomatic cover. A legal.

A legal, in espionage, was a case officer or field operative operating under official diplomatic cover. This meant that, if caught, they could be expelled rather than arrested or executed—a distinction that could mean the difference between life and death.

Peterson was also ex-BBC World Service, and had contacts in the BBC, which meant that if he vanished off the grid without a trace, it would make waves. The BBC might have been gutted by funding cuts, but it still held enough institutional prestige that a missing journalist—

especially one of Peterson's calibre—would raise red flags in London and beyond.

That meant they would raise merry hell and cause a stink that much, it would take the Russian Army battering the doors of New Broadcasting House before the British press stopped talking about it. Looking at his watch, Kelvin saw it was 13:19, and Peterson was only 19 minutes into his daily show. If he was going to be brought in, it would have to be subtle, controlled. No direct approaches, no sudden changes in behaviour. Just enough to let him know that someone was listening.

The room hummed with tension, every eye in the dimly lit space focused on the live feed from Carl Peterson's show. The moments when Sinead Ryan had revealed that brief flicker of humanity were more than just a slip-up; they were a potential window, a fracture in her carefully crafted facade. The intelligence officers in the room knew better than to get carried away by a moment of vulnerability—they were all too familiar with the way a seasoned propagandist like Ryan would use misdirection. But this time, something felt different.

Kelvin took a moment to let the weight of the discussion settle. The air in the room had shifted, and everyone knew it. Sinead Ryan's off-script response, her choice of Ya Soshla s Uma, had raised more than just an eyebrow. It had opened a door, perhaps just a crack, into the fragile psyche of one of the Restoration Government's most influential figures. The question now was whether it was an unintentional slip or a calculated signal, a breadcrumb that could lead them to something bigger.

He leaned back in his chair, rubbing the bridge of his nose. The implications were vast. If Sinead was genuinely wavering, it could mean the beginning of a monumental shift in the balance of power in Ireland, perhaps even Europe. If it was a trap, they would have to proceed with extreme caution. Either way, it was clear that something was happening beneath the surface, and the Five Eyes needed to act swiftly to capitalize on it—or at least to understand it fully before making their next move.

Lorna, ever the pragmatist, was the first to break the silence. "We need to move fast. If Peterson's the key, we have to be discreet. He's too high profile for a direct approach, but if he gets too close to Ryan—if she's already starting to crack—then it could be the opening we need."

Kelvin nodded. "We'll need to give him the right signals. No heavy-handed tactics. This needs to be subtle. The last thing we want is to make a public spectacle of him. We can't afford to have him disappear like Fergal. Too much attention, too many questions. That's a risk we don't need."

Henri leaned forward, his expression pensive. "I'm with you, Kelvin, but we also need to think about the bigger picture. If Ryan is starting to slip, she may not be the only one. Moscow is ruthless when it comes to handling dissent, and they won't hesitate to eliminate anyone who shows weakness. If we can exploit that vulnerability, we might not just have one defector, but a wave of them."

"Which is why we need to be careful," Jacques from CSIS added. "If Sinead starts questioning Moscow's grip, others may follow her lead. We need to know whether she's playing a deeper game, whether this is some kind of pre-emptive move to flush out disloyalty within the ranks."

Kelvin turned to Lorna. "I want you to keep monitoring the situation with Peterson. Make sure you keep everything in-house. No official signals, no overt action. Just enough to plant the idea in his mind that he's not alone in this fight. If Ryan starts making further mistakes, we need to be ready to move quickly, but we cannot afford to tip our hand too early."

"Understood," Lorna replied, her tone crisp. "We'll keep him in the loop, but not too much. If Sinead is going rogue, we'll need to let Peterson know that he's got allies, without making him aware that we're in his ear. He's too valuable to be compromised."

"And we don't know how long we've got," Liam Powell added. "This could all be over by tomorrow, or it could escalate quickly. We can't afford to wait too long. If we do this right, we can destabilize the entire Restoration Government from within."

Kelvin leaned in, making eye contact with each of the officers in the room. "We all know what's at stake. This is no longer just about Ireland. It's about Europe. It's about the future of the Western alliance. If Moscow is planning a broader push—if they're using Ireland as a staging ground for something bigger—then this is our chance to cripple their operations before it goes any further."

There was a collective murmur of agreement. The stakes were clear. Ireland was just the first piece in a much larger game, one where Moscow's reach was extending deeper into Europe, and where Washington's retreat was leaving a power vacuum.

"Let's not waste time," Kelvin said, straightening up. "I'll keep an eye on the broader geopolitical picture, but for now, we focus on Peterson. If he's the conduit we think he is, we'll be able to track Ryan's movements more closely. And if she's cracking, we'll be in a prime position to use it to our advantage."

Lorna stood, gathering her things. "I'll get the CIA's analysts on this. Let's see what we can dig up on Ryan's past. If there's a psychological angle to exploit, we need to know it."

"Good," Kelvin replied, watching as she moved toward the door. "Be careful, Lorna. We don't know how deep this goes. If Ryan's getting too close to the edge, Moscow will know—and they won't hesitate to cover their tracks."

As the room emptied, Kelvin remained seated, his mind racing. The pieces were moving, but they were still too scattered. He had a feeling that the next few days would be crucial. If they acted too hastily, they could blow their chance. If they waited too long, they might lose their only window of opportunity.

"Alright, then," he muttered to himself, looking out the window at the London skyline. "Let's see how far this rabbit hole goes."

****

CHAPTER 13 – Stormont Enters the Chat

Wednesday 24th January 2029

"And in the past hour, the Northern Ireland Assembly has announced that, following pressure from Sinn Féin and Fianna Fáil, a referendum will be held by the Stormont government on whether Northern Ireland should remain part of the United Kingdom or join the Irish Restoration Government in Dublin. The proposed referendum, expected to take place in March 2029, comes amid escalating tensions along the border and growing divisions within the Northern Irish political landscape."

Liam Powell was sat in the Nexus, an office buried deep beneath Thames House, the secure nerve centre for MI5's counterintelligence operations which he, along with his immediate subordinates, Harry Potter, Oliver Stokes, Sam Holloway and, despite her being on assignment as a 'programming assistant' at Manic Radio, Alison Harper, when the news alert flashed across the television screen. The room, a windowless MI5 operations centre buried deep beneath Thames House, was silent for a long moment as the significance of the announcement sank in.

"Told ya," Oliver said, setting his coffee down with a dull thud on the desk. "It was only a matter of time before Dublin forced the issue. They've been waiting for the right moment, and now with Vance rolling over in Washington and Starmer about to start an election campaign, they're making their move."

"We now go live to the Clacton constituency office of Nigel Farage, Nigel, thanks for joining GB News," the anchor continued, her voice carrying the polished urgency of a breaking news segment.

Liam groaned audibly, rubbing his temple. "Christ, what now?"

The large monitor in front of them flicked over to a video feed of Nigel Farage, sitting in his Clacton constituency office, flanked by his Reform UK party banners. His expression was one of barely contained triumph, like a man who had just been given the opportunity of a lifetime.

"Harry, can you kill that fuckwad's feed?" Alison, who was on a secure video call from her "programming assistant" assignment at Manic Radio's Birmingham hub, muttered, her RP accent making her sound as if she was an exasperated headmistress dealing with an unruly student. "I swear to God, if we have to listen to one more of his 'the country is being betrayed' rants, I might actually defect myself just to get away from it."

Harry chuckled, and Liam knew that the cyber-operations officer would happily turn Farage off if he was given the order, the 24 year old not being much of a fan of the right-wing populist who had spent decades stoking division in British politics. But for now, they had to listen. Whether they liked it or not, Farage was a major player in the current climate.

"Sorry, Alison," Harry muttered as he tapped a few keys, adjusting the secure feed. "Orders are to monitor all major political responses, and like it or not, Farage is going to milk this for all it's worth... although... I could introduce some technical difficulties which the GCHQ lot won't mind too much." He grinned, fingers hovering over the keyboard. "A little bit of buffering, some selective packet loss—nothing too obvious, just enough to make him look like he's broadcasting from a cave in Afghanistan rather than a constituency office in Clacton."

"Is it just GB News he's on, or is the BBC and Sky picking up the feed?" Sam asked, his tone carrying the resigned irritation of a man who had been dealing with Farage-related nonsense for far too long.

"Nah, just Gammon Today," Oliver said, and Liam saw that Oliver had the UK feed of Sky News up on his computer, the screen showing the White House, Vance and Musk in their first Cabinet of the new administration.

Liam sighed, refocusing on the main issue at hand. The Northern Ireland referendum was a nightmare scenario for MI5. It wasn't just about the vote itself—it was about everything it would unleash. The intelligence community had been warning for weeks that Moscow's game plan in Ireland wasn't just about toppling Dublin's government; it was about forcing London into an impossible position. And now, here they were.

"Go on, Harry, drop a few 'technical difficulties' on his stream," Liam said, rubbing his temple. "Make it look like Clacton has the world's worst broadband."

Harry grinned as his fingers danced across the keyboard. "Consider it done. I'll route some of his packets through a server in Kazakhstan—make it look like his stream's bouncing all over the place. Should give us at least a few glorious moments of buffering-induced silence."

Alison snorted over the secure video link. "If only we could do the same to his Twitter feed."

Oliver, sipping his coffee, exhaled sharply. "If this referendum actually happens, we're looking at the most volatile situation since the Troubles. And we don't even have the Yanks backing us up this time."

Liam nodded grimly. "And you know Moscow is going to be flooding both sides with money, guns, and enough disinformation to make 2016 Brexit look like a civil debate."

The television flickered again, the GB News segment looking like an al-Qaeda tape of Bin Laden's Greatest Hits, as Farage's broadcast feed began stuttering, the video degrading into pixelated artefacts and sporadic buffering.

Harry smirked as he leaned back in his chair. "Beautiful work, if I do say so myself."

Suddenly the Microsoft Teams screen started ringing, and Liam looked at his computer to see GCHQ was calling in from Cheltenham. The caller ID flashed: "GCHQ - Tech Ops (Secured)".

Liam exhaled, already knowing this wasn't going to be good news. He clicked the answer button, and the secure video call opened, displaying the stern face of Erin Watts, an Operations Officer at the doughnut shaped GCHQ headquarters in Cheltenham. Watts was one of the best in her field—sharp, no-nonsense, and with the kind of temperament that suggested she had long since lost patience with government indecisiveness. The fact that she was calling now, unprompted, meant something serious had just landed in their laps.

"Liam," she said briskly, wasting no time with pleasantries. "We've got a problem."

Liam pinched the bridge of his nose. "Of course we do. Go on, hit me with it."

"Seems Farage is routing his IP traffic through all the 'Stans and dropping packets in every random city east of the Urals... and Thames House," she said, looking at Liam with the kind of look that suggested she was deeply unimpressed. "Which one of your merry band of gremlins decided to get creative with the network traffic?"

Harry, barely concealing his smirk, gave an exaggerated shrug. "I have no idea what you're talking about, Erin. Must be a routing issue. Maybe someone in Clacton forgot to pay their broadband bill. I might route it through Moscow next, make the Daily Mail have an aneurysm when they see that Farage is broadcasting from a Russian IP address."

"You do realise that the FSB will be monitoring this, right?" Erin said, exhaling sharply. "Christ, Harry, the last thing we need is for the Russians to start getting paranoid that Farage is on their payroll—"

"—Which he probably is," Oliver muttered under his breath.

"—Or that we're trying to interfere with his broadcast. This isn't some MI6 side op, it's a domestic intelligence issue, and I really don't want to be explaining to Cheltenham's legal team why we've just rerouted a sitting MP's internet connection through bloody Astana."

Liam turned in his chair, fixing Harry with a don't push it look. "Alright, fun's over. Kill the interference. We've got bigger things to worry about."

Harry sighed, clearly disappointed, but tapped a few keys and reset the stream, allowing Farage's face to reappear on screen, now in slightly less pixelated form.

But sounding like an audition for the Chipmunks with his voice being pitched up just enough to make him sound like he was delivering his impassioned monologue through a helium filter.

Alison snorted over the secure link. "Subtle, Harry."

"You know I could just replace his audio with Hitler's Greatest Speeches and have him accidentally declare himself the second coming of the Third Reich," Harry mused, fingers twitching over his keyboard. "Or have a deepfake of Putin walking into his office and shaking his hand mid-broadcast. Could even get an AI voice generator to make him say something about how he's always admired Moscow's 'strong leadership'."

"Wait, you could do that?" Erin suddenly said, and Liam could see the shock on Erin's face turn into something else—calculation.

Harry grinned, his fingers still hovering over the keyboard. "Oh, I could do a lot of things, Erin. Deepfake a lovely little call between Farage and Putin? Make it sound like he's been personally congratulated for his 'unwavering support of Russian interests'? Maybe drop it onto a few Telegram channels, let the conspiracy theorists have a field day? Hang on a second."

Liam watched Harry tapping away on his keyboard, his eyes glinting with mischief as he executed whatever dark sorcery he was about to unleash.

"Alright," Harry said after a moment, sitting back with a satisfied grin. "Watch GB News a second, and you'll see what I've added to the broadcast."

Liam watched as the screen changed to Farage in the Kremlin, but conveying the audio of Farage's current interview, the Reform UK leader then bending the knee to Vladimir Putin, not in the literal sense but actually looking like he was swearing fealty to the Russian President. The overlay was seamless—Farage's voice remained his own, his words unchanged, but the visuals had been replaced with a deepfake of him seated in a lavish Kremlin office, nodding deferentially as a digital Putin gestured grandly at a map of Europe.

"It's going out, not just on the UK feed of GB News but the International feed as well," Harry added, grinning. "So right now, in Australia, Canada, and the US, they're seeing Farage having a very productive meeting with Putin."

And then the graphics changed, Liam noticing the lower ticker, the constantly moving list of headlines that flashed across the screen, now displaying something new—something entirely fabricated but devastatingly believable.

"Leaked Farage Footage Shows Past Kremlin Support: 'Meeting Putin, Discussing Russian Interests in UK Politics.'"

Liam stared at the screen in disbelief. The deepfake was flawless—Farage's expression, posture, even the way he gestured seemed entirely natural, as though he were in a genuine, undisclosed meeting with the Russian president. The visuals, paired with the fabricated headline, sent a message that, if it gained traction, would be far more potent than any direct attack on the UK's political establishment. This wasn't just a message to Farage—it was a message to the entire Western world.

He knew that Harry was a fan of George Orwell, 1984 being the main story that had inspired him to join MI5 in the first place, as well as the BBC thriller The Capture, a 3 series show which Harry had binge-watched in secret, thoroughly fascinated by the concept of deepfakes and surveillance. It was clear now—he wasn't just tinkering for fun. He was sending a message, and if it hit its target, it could destabilise not just Farage, but the entire political atmosphere surrounding Britain's response to the Irish referendum.

Liam leaned back in his chair, his eyes glued to the monitor, his mind racing. This isn't just interference anymore—this was psychological warfare. Harry had planted a bomb in the middle of the UK's media ecosystem. If this footage gained traction, even for a few hours, it would throw Farage's political credibility into question and potentially cause fractures in the populist base that had supported him for years. It wasn't just a prank; it was a power play.

"Nigel, I'm going to pause you right there, as footage on GB News has just shown a past meeting between yourself and Russian Federation officials," the anchor on GB News said, as the deepfake footage of Farage and Putin dominated the screen. "Would you like to respond to the allegations that you have been involved in secret discussions with the Kremlin regarding political manoeuvres within the UK?"

Liam felt the weight of the moment. This was no longer about an over-the-top media stunt; this was calculated psychological warfare. As the fabricated footage played out on screens across the globe, the anchor's words only served to amplify the illusion that Farage was an active participant in Russian-backed destabilisation efforts. The scene in the Kremlin, complete with a smiling Putin and a deferential Farage, seemed too perfect to be real.

"Nigel, I'm going to pause you right there, as footage on GB News has just shown a past meeting between yourself and Russian Federation officials," the anchor on GB News said, as the deepfake footage of Farage and Putin dominated the screen. "Would you like to respond to the allegations that you have been involved in secret discussions with the Kremlin regarding political manoeuvres within the UK?"

Liam felt the weight of the moment. This was no longer about an over-the-top media stunt; this was calculated psychological warfare. As the fabricated footage played out on screens across the globe, the anchor's words only served to amplify the illusion that Farage was an active participant in Russian-backed destabilisation efforts. The scene in the Kremlin, complete with a smiling Putin and a deferential Farage, seemed too perfect to be real.

"Well, Michelle, it's no secret that President Putin has been a vocal supporter of populist movements across Europe," Farage said, recovering quickly from the shock of the deepfake. "But I'll categorically deny any suggestion that I've been involved in covert discussions with the Kremlin. This is pure disinformation, likely a product of those who want to discredit my political work. I suspect, Michelle, that it's the deep-"

Liam looked at the screen which was still showing Farage ranting, but no audio from the leader of Reform UK could be heard anymore. The he noticed Harry, who was sitting with a grin on his face, his fingers hovering over the keyboard once again.

Liam's eyes narrowed. "Harry, what are you doing now?"

Harry, looking more satisfied than ever, laughed. "I only put his mic on mute. If he looks on his Zoom chat, he can easily turn the mic back on, but it'll give him a few moments of frustration while everyone in the room is watching. Let's see if he's quick enough to recover from the deepfake storm we've just thrown at him."

Liam leaned back, considering the move. It was audacious, to say the least, but Harry's actions were making their point clear: the intelligence services were in a very different kind of game now. It wasn't just about gathering information—it was about shaping narratives, manipulating perceptions, and influencing political climates without a single soldier being deployed. They weren't just watching the world anymore; they were making it bend in subtle ways. And with the way the deepfake of Farage was playing out, this was more than a mere distraction—it was an attempt to fracture the populist movement at its core.

"Harry, stop messing around and put his audio back on," Liam said, his voice low but firm. "We need to keep this situation controlled. The deepfake may have made its impact, but we don't want to start a full-blown media firestorm that gets out of our hands."

Harry clicked a few buttons reluctantly. "Fine. But you have to admit, that was a good one."

Liam didn't respond immediately, his mind still processing what had just unfolded. The deepfake footage of Farage and Putin, designed to destabilise the UK's political discourse, had the potential to cause enormous ripple effects. It wasn't just a smear against Farage; it was an attack on the very fabric of British populism, and possibly the last thread of unity the UK had left after decades of division. This was a new kind of warfare—one fought in the shadows, behind the screens, where narratives were manipulated, and opinions could be swayed in seconds.

"I'm not questioning your technical prowess, Harry,"
Liam said, staring at the screen, where Farage was now
desperately trying to recover, his mic back on but his face
showing signs of frustration as the media played back the
footage of the 'meeting' with Putin. "I'm questioning the
bigger picture. If this gets out of hand, it might push the
government into overreaction. We need to keep it
controlled."

"-has ruined this great country, and that is why, Michelle,
if I get elected as Prime Minister in the General Election
in July, I will defund-"

Another bout of silence, and Liam noticed Harry, having
one ear with an earpiece that he was now listening to, his
fingers poised over the keyboard once again.

Liam sat back in his chair, watching the unfolding scene
in front of him. Harry's antics had thrown a wrench into
the gears of Farage's media circus, but it was far from
over. The deepfake footage had certainly done its damage.
Farage, trying to steer the narrative, was now in a
precarious situation. He knew it, the media knew it, and
now, it seemed, so did the Five Eyes Committee.

But this wasn't just about one man—it was about the
system that had enabled him. This was a warning shot.
And it was also a message to the political players, the
pundits, and the very people who were watching. The
stakes had shifted. Power wasn't just wielded through
force anymore. It was in narratives, in broadcasts, in the
very media that defined public opinion.

"What? He said he was going to defund us, Vauxhall and Cheltenham if he became PM," Harry said with a chuckle, clearly still entertained by the chaos he had unleashed. "I think it's safe to say, we've given him something else to think about. I mean, we want our jobs, don't we?"

Liam leaned back in his chair, watching Farage's frantic attempts to regain control of the situation on the screen. The deepfake footage had thrown the man completely off-balance, and the longer he floundered, the more the damage piled up. But Liam knew this wasn't just about humiliating Farage; it was about sending a message to anyone who dared challenge the established order. The game had changed. The tools of information warfare were no longer confined to traditional espionage—now, entire political narratives could be torn down with a few keystrokes.

Harry's finger hovered over the keyboard again, a mischievous glint in his eye. "I could always upload a few more videos to spice things up," he mused, clearly enjoying the chaos. "Maybe a few clips of Farage 'confessing' to secret Russian ties? Or him and Vance with some hookers in a Chinese hotel?"

"Do it, Potter," Erin said over the call from her office at GCHQ, "and I'll have the boys here make a deepfake of you in the Kremlin too. Let's see how you like that one."

Liam suppressed a chuckle, even as he reflected on the bizarre, surreal nature of the moment. It was clear that the boundaries between traditional intelligence operations and cyber warfare were no longer distinct. The game had evolved, with technology enabling these agencies to disrupt and manipulate entire political landscapes. Farage was now a pawn in a much larger, more complex web of geopolitics, where actions taken behind screens could ripple out to affect millions of lives.

"Alright, alright," Liam said, trying to bring the chaos back into check. "Let's rein it in, Harry. We've done our damage, but let's not lose control of this. Farage is floundering, but let's not give him an opportunity to turn this around by letting his supporters claim it's all fake news or a smear campaign. We've made our point."

Harry grinned but reluctantly powered down the deepfake generator, allowing Farage's audio to return to normal. Farage, of course, didn't know the full extent of what had just happened. As he rambled on, attempting to regain some semblance of authority, the intelligence community's web continued to spin in the background, shaping narratives and disrupting the political landscape with surgical precision.

"You know, boss," Alison said from her desk at Manic's headquarters in Birmingham with a chuckle, "I've added to the scripts here what Harry's done, so in the top of the hour news on Manic Vibes, you'll hear Carson Graham reporting about GB News airing misleading deepfake footage involving Nigel Farage 'in an attempt to destabilase the Reform UK movement', and I've put a complaint in at OFCOM about how GB News are deliberately misleading the public by airing manipulated content. I've put it, and you'll love this, in Richard Tice's name."

Liam chuckled softly, his tension easing as Alison's cheeky addition to the scripts filtered through the secure lines. The unfolding political drama, punctuated by the deepfake of Farage, had clearly crossed a new line. But they weren't done yet. The ripples from this broadcast would be felt well beyond the MI5 operations room, and they were already setting the stage for a larger political earthquake.

"So, we're making GB News be the punching bag for the deepfake chaos," Liam said with a satisfied grin, leaning back in his chair. "Good work, Alison. This is going to stir up more trouble for Farage than he can handle."

The room at Thames House was buzzing with an unsettling energy as the events of the day unfolded. With each new development, it became clear that the landscape of British politics—and, by extension, Europe—was shifting. The referendum in Northern Ireland was the tip of the iceberg, but the political theatrics being played out over the airwaves, particularly the fallout from the deepfake operation, promised to send shockwaves throughout the system.

Liam leaned back in his chair, his fingers tapping rhythmically against the wooden armrest, as the team's chatter continued. Farage was a wild card—a populist who had managed to survive a political career built on controversy. But even the most resilient figures could crack under pressure, and today, MI5 had ensured that the pressure would be unbearable.

"You've made a right mess of him, Harry," Sam said with a grin, watching the image of Farage on the screen, his voice now returned to its normal pitch. "Can't wait to see what kind of spin he tries to put on it."

"He's good at talking himself out of a tight spot, but this one's a bit of a doozy," Harry replied, his eyes still glued to the screen. He leaned back, clearly satisfied with his handiwork. "I might have gone a little overboard, but the look on his face was priceless. He's not going to recover from this in a hurry."

"Agreed," Liam said. "This isn't just about embarrassing Farage; it's about sending a message. To him, to everyone watching. If we can pull this off, we've demonstrated just how fragile their world is. We don't need tanks or boots on the ground anymore; we've got something far more powerful at our disposal—narratives."

Alison, still on her secure video link from Manic's headquarters in Birmingham, added with a chuckle, "It's all in the name of disinformation warfare. After all, when it's this messy, who's going to notice a few extra wrinkles in the narrative?"

The team chuckled, but beneath the surface, there was a heavy understanding of what they had just done. They weren't just manipulating a single politician. The message was clear: Farage was no longer in control. His populist, anti-establishment narrative had been hijacked and turned into something he couldn't spin. What they had created was a viral storm that would undermine his credibility for days, if not weeks. It wasn't just a loss for him—it was a loss for the whole populist movement that had given birth to his platform.

But the political rumblings in Northern Ireland loomed large. The referendum was more than just a vote; it was a seismic event that could reshape the future of the United Kingdom. If Northern Ireland moved toward joining the Irish Restoration Government, it would rip apart the already fragile unity of the UK, sending the Conservative party into a tailspin and leaving Labour to deal with the aftermath. And then there was the quiet spectre of Moscow, always lurking in the background, pulling strings in the shadows.

"The referendum's a wildcard," Sam said, pulling Liam from his thoughts. "If this happens, we're looking at an even messier situation than we thought. The last time the Troubles flared up, it wasn't just an internal conflict—it became a proxy war. And now, with Moscow actively intervening, we could be seeing that same old playbook being dusted off."

Liam nodded. "Exactly. Moscow's been laying the groundwork for years. This isn't just about destabilising Dublin—it's about using Northern Ireland as a launchpad. If they can pull this off, they've got the perfect foothold in the UK. And without the US backing us up, we're going to have to rely on our allies—who are also dealing with their own problems. France, Germany, the rest of the EU—they're stretched thin already."

"So, what's our next move?" Harry asked, already anticipating the next step. "Do we play the long game with the referendum, or do we keep our foot on the gas with Farage and the media chaos?"

Liam paused, his eyes narrowing as he considered the options. "For now, we need to keep an eye on the referendum. That's the most immediate threat. If that goes the wrong way, we've got a real crisis on our hands. But the disinformation campaign we've started with Farage? We need to ride that wave for as long as we can. Farage is a distraction—but he's also a useful one. We need to keep making sure that no matter what, he never gets the chance to recover. Meanwhile, we'll keep monitoring Northern Ireland, and if things look like they're tipping in the wrong direction, we step in."

"Understood," Sam said. "So, we keep Farage on the ropes, but don't take our eyes off Ireland. Got it."

As the room fell silent, each member of the team knew what was at stake. The world was changing around them, and the methods they had relied on for decades—spying, surveillance, covert operations—were evolving into something new. Information was now the weapon of choice, and they had just fired their first shot. How far would it go? How much would it shake the system?

Liam stood up, taking one last look at the screen. Farage was still struggling to regain his composure on air, but the damage was done. His credibility had taken a hit that no amount of deflection or redirection would be able to repair.

"Alright, let's keep it tight," Liam said, turning toward his team. "We're not just fighting for stability in the UK or Ireland. This is a battle for the future of the entire Western alliance. We can't afford to let up now. Not for a second."

With that, the team got to work, the buzz of their collective focus filling the room as the clock ticked down to the next chapter in the geopolitical struggle unfolding before them. The storm was just beginning, and they knew that the ripples they had started would soon become waves. Waves that could change everything.

****

CHAPTER 14 – Developments at the Embassy

Tuesday 30th January 2029

The same routine had been a daily occurrence, Carl knew, as he walked down Merrion Road, the deserted Irish streets still looking as they had been since the previous month, when the coup had plunged Dublin into an eerie, oppressive silence. It had been weeks now since the Irish Restoration Government had solidified its grip, and yet the city still felt like it was holding its breath. The old rhythms of life—the laughter from pub doors, the hurried bustle of commuters, the hum of a free and functioning capital—had been replaced with something unnatural. Patrols of uniformed men in Restoration Government insignia roamed the streets, their presence a constant reminder of who was in control. The flags of the new regime fluttered from government buildings, the tricolour now accompanied by the stark black-and-red insignia of the State Information Office, the propaganda arm of the Moscow-backed government.

Carl adjusted his coat against the biting wind as he neared the British Embassy. The compound, a reinforced structure of glass and steel, was one of the last remnants of London's presence in Ireland. For now, at least. The Russians hadn't yet made any serious moves against it, and the new government in Dublin, still wary of provoking an outright military response from Britain, had refrained from any drastic measures. But everyone inside those walls knew the embassy was on borrowed time.

Technically, it was closed to the public, but as the husband of the Credit Controller—the person whose job was keeping the embassy's financial operations in order—Carl still had access. Emma's role gave her an official reason to be here, but her true purpose went far beyond balancing budgets. She was MI6, working under diplomatic cover, and in these increasingly dangerous times, she was one of the last British intelligence assets operating openly in Dublin.

As Carl reached the heavy steel gate, a discreet camera turned towards him. A second later, the speaker crackled to life.

"Good evening, Mr Peterson," came the clipped voice of a security officer inside. "Please step forward for verification."

Carl did as instructed, placing his hands on the biometric scanner mounted on the gate's reinforced glass panel. A blue light flashed, and a second later, the door buzzed open. He stepped inside, the heavy gate sealing behind him with a definitive clang.

Inside, the contrast with the outside world was stark. The embassy compound was still very much under British control—Union flags flew alongside the embassy's crest, and the staff inside moved with quiet efficiency, their faces set with grim determination. They all knew the risks. At any moment, the Russians or their Irish puppets could decide to move against them.

Carl knew that Emma never usually finished until 9 in the evening, the invoices and financial statements she processed forming just one part of her official cover, meaning that he would, of an evening, come to the Embassy and dine with her in the canteen, as she was usually too tired to cook, and the restaurants that remained open in Dublin were either catering to Restoration Government officials or too dangerous for a British journalist to frequent.

"You alright Carl," Yvonne Young, the Senior Trade Adviser greeted him as he stepped inside, her tone warm but laced with the tension that never quite left anyone in the embassy these days. Yvonne, an old hand in diplomatic circles, had been stationed in embassies from Kyiv to Hong Kong, and now, she found herself in the middle of what could become the most dangerous posting of her career.

Carl nodded, offering her a weary smile. "As alright as anyone can be in this place, Yvonne. How's trade going these days? Still pretending there's an actual economy to negotiate with?"

Yvonne let out a dry chuckle, shaking her head. "It's not trade anymore, Carl. It's asset protection. We're just making sure British companies with interests here don't get swallowed up in the nationalisation purge. Not that we can do much. The Russians are calling the shots, and the Restoration Government's idea of 'free enterprise' is whatever Moscow tells them it is. How's things at Manic? I bet its crazy for you, working at the Brum based Saudi radio station while living here in Dublin. Must be fun keeping your head down."

Carl smirked at the irony. "Fun is one word for it. It's a balancing act, really. Manic Goldies Ireland is tolerated for now, mostly because Riyadh doesn't want to see its investments trampled on. The Restoration Government are smart enough not to push too hard against anything backed by the Saudis. But I have to watch every word I say. One wrong inflection, one slip of the tongue, and I could be next on their list of 'disappeared' journalists. Like Fergal, God rest his soul."

Yvonne's expression darkened at the mention of Fergal Donoghue. The former Manic Goldies Ireland newsreader had vanished mid-shift just a week and half ago, after the wrong kind of news report had slipped through the cracks. His sudden absence had sent a chilling message to every journalist still working in Dublin—no one was safe, no matter how careful they thought they were.

Carl knew that the Irish born newsreader had only been 24, but he had always been cautious, always stuck to the script. But caution had meant nothing when the regime had decided he was no longer useful. One minute he had been reading the early afternoon news; the next, he was gone—no explanations, no denials, just silence.

What was worse was that his body had appeared the previous day in the River Liffey, washed up near the docks with the tell-tale signs of an execution—zip-tied wrists, a bullet wound at the base of the skull, and his press ID stuffed into his mouth like a grotesque message to anyone else in the media who thought about stepping out of line.

On the record, the CEO of Manic Radio Group, James Jenkins, had said from his Surrey home that Fergal Donoghue's death was a "tragic loss" and that Manic Radio Group "stood in solidarity with our colleagues in Ireland during this difficult time." Off the record, though, Carl knew that Jenkins was raising merry hell with the Crown Prince of Saudi Arabia, demanding answers as to why one of his network's journalists had been executed under the watch of a supposedly 'stable' Restoration Government. The Saudis, in turn, were quietly pressuring Moscow through back channels. The entire situation was spiralling, and Carl could feel the tension thickening by the day.

"You know your lad was here earlier," Yvonne said, looking at Carl, her face a worry. "He... he said that he thinks he's going to be disappeared next."

Carl felt his stomach drop. His lad. That could only mean one person.

"James?" His voice came out sharper than he intended, a mix of concern and frustration. His son, James, was a sound engineer at Raidió Teilifís Éireann, working both on the radio and television side of things. Like Carl, James was formerly of the BBC, meaning that he had the same level of experience and connections. But unlike Carl, who was playing a dangerous game within the Restoration Government's media confines, James was still trying to work from within the system, attempting to navigate the murky waters of state-controlled journalism. It made him vulnerable—more so than Carl would ever allow himself to be.

"Has he said anything more?" Carl asked, feeling the weight of the responsibility on his shoulders. His relationship with James had always been strained, especially since the breakdown of his marriage with Emma, but now, more than ever, it felt like there were forces at play that were pulling them both into dangerous territory.

"He... he's asked for help getting out. I took him upstairs to Mick, who's arranging something. He's still there as far as I know," Yvonne said, her voice dropping to a near-whisper, as though speaking any louder might draw attention. "He was so certain, Carl. He's been talking about moving to London—anything to get away from this nightmare. But... it's tricky, especially now. The Restoration Government's been tightening the grip on anyone with British ties, and they're looking for excuses to arrest people like him."

Carl knew that Mick Pence, the Cultural Attache, was not just a standard official within the embassy, but MI6's Head of Station, the top spy in Dublin, the person his wife, Emma, reported to with regards to intelligence gathering. Mick had been pivotal in keeping a few of their operations running under the radar, particularly when it came to ensuring that key personnel could escape the tightening noose of the Restoration Government. But it was becoming increasingly difficult to operate covertly in Dublin. Every day, the atmosphere grew more oppressive, more unpredictable.

Carl tried to push aside his growing concern for James, but he knew he needed to review his own exfoliation plan. If James had become a target, there was little chance of operating quietly anymore. Carl's work at Manic Goldies was already under scrutiny—his dual role as both a journalist and an MI6 asset meant that any slip could lead to his own exposure. But James was different. He wasn't trained for this kind of life, wasn't used to the pressure of playing double agents, and the thought of him caught in the machinery of the Restoration Government made Carl's stomach churn.

"Shit. Shit, shit, shit," the Ambassador, Lady HJ Abbott, a Civil Servant who had spent 30 years in diplomatic service, muttered as she walked into the room. "Yvonne, I've got some bad news for you. You've been PNG'd. Emma, Mick, half the finance and culture staff, even the trade staff have all been declared Persona Non Grata. It's happening right now. They're rounding everyone up for expulsion."

Persona Non Grata, Carl knew, was the worst thing to happen to a diplomatic mission. It was an official declaration that a foreign diplomat or embassy staff member was no longer welcome in the host country. The Restoration Government had just moved to expel several of the embassy's staff, which meant Carl's worst fears were beginning to materialise. The delicate web of intelligence operations the embassy had been running in Dublin was now at risk of unravelling, and with it, Carl's entire mission.

Yvonne's face drained of colour as the full impact of Lady Abbott's words hit her. "What? How do you know? Who's leading this?"

Lady Abbott, her normally composed expression now cracked, glanced around to make sure no one else was within earshot. "The Restoration Government has made it clear. They've informed the Foreign Office this morning, and now they're going down the list. No one is safe—Emma included. She's a target. Don't worry, Carl, I've made sure there's a ticket for you, as you're Emma's husband."

"Is anyone else going home?" Yvonne asked, and Carl knew that his BBC mind was mentally writing a story, one that he could file with New Broadcasting House and Salford, the home of the BBC in London and its Mancunian operations. The weight of the situation was beginning to settle in. The Restoration Government's decision to expel British embassy personnel was a clear escalation. It wasn't just about restricting the movement of foreign diplomats or pressuring the UK's diplomatic influence in Ireland anymore—it was a direct signal that the regime intended to rid Ireland of its last vestiges of Western influence, and that included Carl, and everyone connected to the embassy.

"ALF," Lady Abbott then shouted, and Alf Roberts, the Press Attache, ran in, looking at Carl, a concerned look on his face. Alf, typically the calm and composed member of the diplomatic team, now had the expression of someone caught between a rock and a hard place. His role had been vital in keeping the media communications smooth, ensuring that the British government could at least retain some control over the narrative in Dublin. But with the expulsion orders in place, that would be all but impossible.

"Yes, Lady Helen," Alf said, and Carl knew that the gravity of the moment had finally sunk in for everyone. The expulsion orders were more than just an inconvenience. They were a direct threat, a move by the Restoration Government to crush any remaining foreign influence, and to tighten their grip on power. The reality was setting in: the embassy was no longer safe, and neither were its staff. Their diplomatic immunity meant little now, as Moscow's proxies in Dublin prepared to clear them out—along with any trace of Western presence that remained.

"Get Peterson here a microphone, a camera and a link to New Broadcasting House," Lady Abbott ordered, her voice hard and decisive. "We need the UK to know what's happening. Carl, you need to get the message out before they shut us down completely."

Carl's mind raced. The situation had gone from dangerous to critical in a matter of minutes. The Restoration Government, with Moscow's backing, had crossed a red line. Expelling embassy personnel was no longer just about diplomacy—it was an outright declaration of war on the remaining vestiges of British influence in Ireland. And now Carl, with his precarious position as a journalist and MI6 asset, was thrust into the centre of the storm.

Alf quickly got to work, setting up a secure communication line. Carl's heart pounded in his chest, the weight of the task before him suddenly apparent. He had to get the message out—not just for the embassy, but for his family. The fate of the British staff in Dublin, and the future of the intelligence operations here, rested on his ability to speak to the outside world.

As Alf set up the equipment, Carl found himself reflecting on just how much had changed. It wasn't just the embassy's security that had crumbled—his entire world had shifted underfoot. The subtle game he had been playing between reporting and espionage had become all too real, all too immediate. His son James was caught up in this mess too, unsure of where to turn, unsure of what to believe in anymore. And now, Carl found himself at the centre of a potentially explosive story, a moment where truth and deception would collide.

Suddenly he felt Alf fitting a mic pack to his belt, and an earpiece receiver next to it, and he knew what it meant— he was going to be live on BBC News across not just Britain, but also the world, as the former World Service feed was the main domestic news outlet for international events. The eyes of the world would be on him, and he had to make every word count. This wasn't just about getting the truth out; it was about survival, both for him and his family.

Carl adjusted the earpiece, feeling its weight settle in, memories of his past at the BBC World Service flooding back, being a war correspondent and anchor for broadcasts when the regular hosts were unable to fly out to countries in a state of crisis. It felt like a lifetime ago now—those days of being embedded with troops in conflict zones, of standing in front of camera crews in war-torn cities, reporting the news with a detached professionalism that now seemed almost absurd in the face of the personal stakes surrounding him.

Alf signalled to Carl, snapping him back to the present. "I've got a producer on the line from Salford, ready for the live broadcast, Carl. Just a few seconds. Are you ready?"

Carl nodded, his hand shaking ever so slightly as he adjusted the mic pack at his waist. The weight of what was happening felt like it was pressing down on him, but he had no time to dwell on it. This wasn't just a news report—it was the most dangerous moment of his life. The British government, and potentially the rest of Europe, needed to know the truth about what was happening in Dublin. He was the last link to the outside world, and his words would carry more weight than ever before.

"Ready as I'll ever be," Carl replied, his voice steady but with a tension that only those in his position would understand.

Alf stepped back and flicked a switch, activating the secure communications line. The familiar hum of the feed through his earpiece signalled that the connection was live. Carl could hear the faint buzz of voices on the other end, the sound of his own heartbeat in his ears, and then, suddenly, the voice of the producer from Salford came through, crisp and direct.

"Carl, it's Annie," he heard, and memories of his former producer, Annie Walker, who was still with the BBC and had managed to weather the transition after the budget cuts, filled him with a quiet sense of reassurance. Despite everything going on, Annie was still there, still doing her job.

"Carl, Clive's wrapping up a story about a trial in Cambridge and we're going to slot you in right after. We've been tracking developments in Dublin all afternoon, and we need you to go live with an update. What's going on there?"

Carl's throat tightened, but he forced himself to speak, steadying his voice. The pressure was immense, but there was no room for hesitation. He had to make this count.

"I'm about to deliver the biggest story of my life," Carl thought, mentally preparing himself.

"Annie, it's gone past diplomacy. The Restoration Government's just expelled half the British embassy staff, including MI6 assets. Emma's on the list, and it's not just an expulsion—it's a direct attack on all Western influence in Ireland."

Carl took a slow, steadying breath, the weight of the moment pressing down on him. His words were critical, and he had no room for error. The producer, Annie, was waiting, and the lives of his colleagues, his wife, and even his son hung in the balance. The connection between him and Salford was secure, but his nerves still felt raw, like a taut wire ready to snap. Yet, the thought of everything his family had sacrificed for this moment – and the betrayal that now loomed large – brought a cold clarity.

"I'm ready," Carl said, feeling the mic press against his chest as if it were a silent witness to his decision.

"Good," Annie replied, her voice steady but tinged with urgency. "We're live in five seconds. Just keep it sharp.

We're hearing rumblings of chaos in Dublin; your update will carry weight. Let's get it out there."

Carl adjusted his tie in the mirror hanging on the wall in front of him, his reflection staring back at him like someone he barely recognised. A part of him wanted to retreat into the shadows, disappear like everyone else who had dared oppose the tide of the Restoration Government. But his duty was clear. His role was to tell the world what was happening.

"Going live in three, two..." The countdown echoed in his earpiece, and then the sting that signified breaking news hit his eardrum. "You're live, Carl. Take it away."

The flood of nerves that had built up in Carl's chest settled into a steely calm as the weight of the moment fully descended upon him. He stepped forward, feeling the familiar warmth of the studio lights on his face. He could hear his own voice, steady and controlled, as if he were reading a script, but it was real. This was no longer a report from some distant battlefield or conflict zone—it was the story of his own life, unfolding in real-time.

"Good evening," Carl began, his voice strong despite the storm swirling around him. "This is Carl Peterson, broadcasting live from the British Embassy in Dublin. In what can only be described as a dramatic escalation of tensions, the Irish Restoration Government has today taken the unprecedented step of expelling a significant number of British diplomatic personnel, under the guise of a routine diplomatic purge."

He paused, letting the gravity of the words settle over the airwaves, knowing this was no ordinary diplomatic incident. He looked at the statement the Government had given Helen when she had gone to answer the alleged espionage charges that had been levied against several of their staff members. He could feel the eyes of millions on him, the weight of his words both an accusation and a call to action. His own future—along with that of Emma and his son—hung in the balance.

"The Restoration Government's move against the British Embassy is more than just a symbolic gesture. It marks the end of the last vestiges of British influence in Ireland. Among those expelled are, what the Moscow backed rebels, state, 'spies of the Albion and its Imperialist shadow, the agitators of the Northern Ireland peace process,' as they described them. But this isn't just an attack on British diplomats—it's an attack on the idea of free press, of democracy itself. The expulsion of alleged MI6 personnel," Carl said, knowing that if he said they were indeed MI6 assets, it could put them all in even more jeopardy. He knew that, to the BBC and its global audience, this was a dire and urgent message. His words would carry weight far beyond the confines of the studio or embassy. "The Restoration Government has declared war on all who stand for the ideals of freedom and democracy," Carl continued, his voice unwavering despite the enormity of what he was reporting.

He saw Alf write something on some paper and knew that he was writing a statement on behalf of Lady Helen Abbott to present to the press shortly after the broadcast. Carl's mind was focused on the message he needed to deliver, but his peripheral thoughts couldn't help but dwell on the precarious position he found himself in. The weight of his words felt heavier than ever.

He leaned into the camera slightly, willing himself to focus. "As many of you know, the United Kingdom has long been an ally of Ireland, and for decades, the Irish people have enjoyed the benefits of a peaceful coexistence with Britain. But today, this peace has been shattered, and the Restoration Government's move against the British Embassy is a direct assault on our shared history, one that cuts deeper than just diplomatic ties. It is an ideological attack that seeks to destabilise not just Ireland but the entire Western world order."

Carl could feel the eyes of the entire BBC network—both in London and across the globe—on him. He continued, pushing his nerves aside. "This expulsion of personnel, including key MI6 assets, is a clear escalation of the Kremlin's long-standing interference in Europe. By backing the Irish Restoration Government, Moscow has successfully manipulated Ireland's internal politics, and now the situation in Dublin has become a flashpoint for the broader geopolitical struggle.

"In a chilling reminder of what happens when power is abused, journalists, diplomats, and ordinary citizens who dare speak out against the regime risk being silenced, or worse, disappeared. This is not just a conflict of governments—this is a fight for the future of Ireland and the protection of democracy and freedom across Europe."

Carl felt his heart beat faster, but he carried on. "At this moment, we are witnessing the unravelling of a state— one that was once a pillar of Western stability. The

Restoration Government's actions today will have repercussions far beyond Dublin. They are setting a dangerous precedent that may embolden other authoritarian regimes. This is not just about the future of Ireland, but the fate of all nations that still hold dear the ideals of liberty and independence."

He paused, knowing the gravity of the situation had fully settled on the viewers. "As for those of us here in Dublin, the message is clear. Our presence here is no longer tenable. We, the diplomatic personnel of the United Kingdom, have been given no choice but to leave the country we have served for decades. For the safety of all involved, our mission here is over."

"Carl," the voice of BBC News host Clive Myrie, the BBC's lead anchor, came through in his earpiece, the urgency unmistakable. "We're receiving confirmation of the expulsion. Can you advise what the Dublin streets are like right now? Are there any immediate signs of unrest?"

Carl steadied himself, hearing the tense murmur in the background of the embassy as staff shifted around him. The atmosphere in the compound was thick with tension, but outwardly, everything appeared calm. The diplomatic corridors, once bustling with mundane tasks and banter, had become an area of hushed conversation and covert planning. The silence was deafening, amplified by the sheer weight of what was unfolding. Outside, however, he knew the situation was far less controlled.

"The streets of Dublin are quiet for now, Clive," Carl replied, his voice steady despite the chaos within him. "But there's an oppressive calm. People are too afraid to speak out, to make a noise. The Restoration Government have their eyes on everyone who might oppose them. We've seen a heavier security presence across the city today. Patrols are more frequent, and the usual hubs of dissent—places like O'Connell Street—are practically ghost towns now. I was in the City Centre earlier, and several stores have closed down, some due to the sanctions that the British Government, the EU and Canada, had imposed over the past months, with the few remaining Western brands remaining open, mainly American ones as President Vance has not fallen in line with the allied sanctions. There's an unmistakable sense of fear in the air, Carl. People are watching what they say, where they go, and who they associate with. The state broadcaster, RTÉ, is now fully under the control of the Restoration Government, pushing their narrative and silencing dissent. The media landscape here is increasingly devoid of opposition voices. The once-vibrant press, though far from perfect, is now just a tool of propaganda. The only commercial radio broadcaster is forced to obey an SVR Political Officer who, despite the Birmingham headquarters being a safe distance away, still ensures that any broadcast of dissent is swiftly cut off. The media here is no longer a mirror of society, but a mirror of the state's will."

Carl paused, letting the weight of his words settle in the silence that followed. The world was listening, waiting. His words were the only window into the terrifying new reality in Dublin, and he knew that the ramifications of his report would reverberate far beyond the walls of the British Embassy.

"What I can reveal is that reports of border skirmishes between British and Nationalist forces are being suppressed by the Restoration Government. They have clamped down hard on any opposition and have started rounding up anyone who poses a threat to the regime—journalists, activists, anyone with a visible or implied connection to Britain. If you live here and you're even suspected of being sympathetic to the West, you could disappear overnight, and there is no one left to speak for you."

****

CHAPTER 15 – Assassinations, Bombs & News
Wednesday 31st January 2029

"Yer not going to make me wear a rubber, darlin'? The Church says it's a sin."

Holly Flaherty had to chuckle at the target she had been given, being a Loyalist in Derry and the target being a Nationalist hitman who would, if she hadn't had breasts larger than a pair of watermelons, have not gone with his lower regions when it came to thinking and thought that a woman on the side of Londonderry, dressed in garters, a short skirt and a low cut blouse, would be easy pickings. The man, a seasoned hitman for the IRA, had no idea what he was in for.

Holly smirked as she stood up, her handbag on the chest of drawers, in it an Israeli made Jericho 941, ready for her to give Seamus O'Flannagan a double tap between the eyes, the hotel room that they were in being a seedy, run-down affair on the outskirts of Derry. The fluorescent lights buzzed intermittently, casting harsh shadows over the drab room. The smell of stale smoke and cheap air freshener lingered in the air. The shabby curtains were drawn tight, blocking out the dim January sunlight, leaving the room wrapped in a grim, oppressive atmosphere.

The irony was not lost on Holly, as her late father, Declan, had been a member of the Ulster Volunteer Force, a staunch loyalist who had fought in the bitter and bloody conflicts of the Troubles, and here she was, 30 years after the Good Friday Agreement, doing exactly the same as what her father and grandfather had done—ridding the six counties of IRA scum, one bullet at a time.

A former British Army Captain with the Rifles Regiment, Holly had left in the 2026 reorganisation when the UVF announced that they were considering pulling out of the Good Friday Agreement completely, their distrust in the political process boiling over. Holly, with her military experience and deep-rooted hatred for the IRA, had not hesitated to join the covert network that had re-emerged in Northern Ireland. It was a network composed of rogue Loyalist factions, some of whom still harboured dreams of a united Ulster outside the grip of the Irish Republic and the British state's increasingly detached stance.

Holly knew that the method she used was the same each time, that she'd seduce the enemy and lure them into a false sense of security. It was a trick as old as time, as men would see flesh and instantly think with their lower instincts, believing that their desires could override any caution or suspicion. She'd let them use her mouth on their erections, make them think they were about to use her to get the time of their lives, and then she'd say the one sentence most Catholics hate.

"Hold on a minute, love, I need to grab something."

And then each time, she'd get up, wearing her bra, panties and stockings, acting as if she was getting a condom from her handbag, and before they could register the sudden shift, she'd pull out some garrotting wire and strangle them with an efficiency that spoke of years of training. The sudden constriction would leave them flailing, their hands scrabbling at the wire digging into their throats, their legs kicking against the thin, threadbare carpet. Their last thoughts would be of confusion, lust turning to horror as the realisation set in. The game was over, and they had lost.

But not this time.

Since the invasion of the Republic by the Russian forces, Iran had been arming the Nationalist movement in Northern Ireland with weapons, funds, and support, making the situation far more dangerous. In return, Israel started sending the UVF and its sibling groups military-grade weapons, including Israeli-made Jericho 941 pistols, and training in more advanced techniques. Holly was well-acquainted with their methods, having been trained by the British Army, and having spent, between 2020 and 2021, time in the SAS, part of a 15 year military career that had seen her in the most intense and volatile regions of the world.

Born in the Culmore area of Derry, Holly had grown up with tales of her grandfather's antics in the Parachute Regiment, and how, to the Protestant parts of Derry, he was a hero as he had been part of the Regiment on 30th January 1972, the day of Bloody Sunday, where 13 unarmed civil rights protestors were killed by British soldiers, and a few months earlier, on 11 August 1971, when the Ballymurphy massacre had claimed the lives of 11 people in Belfast. He had been held in high regard by the Loyalists in Ulster, a model of a man who had fought for his beliefs, never backing down, never compromising.

Her brother, Josh, was one of the Apprentice Boys of Derry, an organisation that had stood firmly against the Nationalist community, a group that still held rallies in defiance of the IRA's power. The events of her youth had shaped Holly into who she was now—determined, cold-blooded, and ruthlessly efficient.

As she stood in the dingy hotel room, she didn't feel anything at all. No remorse. No hesitation. Just the task at hand. Seamus O'Flannagan, the IRA hitman, was as arrogant as they came. He had been a thorn in the side of the Loyalist cause for far too long, and Holly had been given the assignment to take him out. He was planning to meet someone from the Republic later that evening, potentially moving weapons, and that was the last mistake he would ever make.

The sound of the faint buzz from the flickering overhead light seemed to punctuate the silence as Holly made her final checks. The Jericho 941 was loaded, its weight comfortable in her grip. She could feel the tension in her muscles as she prepared herself. The room was a far cry from the luxurious digs she was used to when working in Israel or even Belfast, but this would do. The target didn't need a five-star hotel for what Holly had in mind.

She turned to the mirror in the corner of the room, checking her appearance one last time. Her reflection seemed almost foreign to her—she wasn't just a woman anymore. She was an instrument. She would never allow herself to be seen as anything else. The years of military training, the cold, calculated mind that had allowed her to get this far, were part of her now. No emotions, no distractions.

Her hand slid to the inside of her bag, feeling for the wire, the steel cool against her fingers. Holly was a professional. She didn't take chances. She was here to do a job, and Seamus O'Flannagan would not see the end of the night.

And the 941 was the perfect way to do the job.

Pulling it out of her bag, she knew it was an easy job, a double tap between the eyes, a swift end to a man who believed he was untouchable. Holly had executed similar operations countless times before, but something about this particular kill felt different. Maybe it was the weight of what was at stake, or perhaps it was the reminder that Northern Ireland was sliding further into the chaos of violence and suspicion. She would not just be ending O'Flannagan's life tonight—she would be sending a message to the rest of them: the IRA, the Nationalists, the whole of Northern Ireland. The war had not ended with the Good Friday Agreement; it had simply transformed into something far darker.

The moment she placed her finger on the Jericho's trigger, Holly was fully submerged in the icy cold of her profession. This wasn't about ideals or beliefs anymore— this was about control. Control over life, control over death. Seamus O'Flannagan had long crossed the line of a soldier into the realm of an enemy of the state, and for that, he was marked. The blowback from Russia's increasing involvement in the Irish Republic and the arms flowing in from Iran had only made things worse. But Holly's mission had always been clear—execute the target, get out.

Seeing him lay on the bed, the blowjob she had given him making his mind think more of sex and less of what she was about to do, Holly's grip on the Jericho 941 tightened. O'Flannagan, with his rough accent and crude jokes, had no idea what he was about to face. His overconfidence had lulled him into a false sense of security—just another mark to be exploited by the weapons of her trade.

Her heart rate remained steady as she approached the bed, her movements calculated, measured. She had done this a hundred times before, but tonight felt different. The city of Derry, under the weight of conflict once again, had no place for distractions. She couldn't afford to allow any slip-ups. There was no room for error when it came to executing a hit in such volatile times. The long-running sectarian violence, fuelled now by Russia's intervention and Iran's arming of the Nationalist factions, had escalated beyond anything Holly had seen in her years of service.

As Holly knelt by the bed, her hand rested just above the pistol, fingers poised but not yet pressed against the cold metal. She watched O'Flannagan, his eyes half-lidded, his body still drenched in the warmth of lust, unaware that his life was about to end. Holly smirked to herself, reflecting on the irony of it all. For all his bravado and machismo, he had been seduced by the most dangerous weapon of all—the illusion of power and the woman who would use it against him.

Her mind flashed back to her training with the SAS, the long hours spent honing the art of assassination, the skills of a soldier who had become an expert in stealth, strategy, and silent elimination. Holly knew the drill. Two shots—

one to the forehead, one to the back of the skull. The double-tap. It was quick, efficient, and left no room for a struggle.

She was in position now, her body low and steady, the barrel of the Jericho aligned with O'Flannagan's head. A slow breath in. The sound of her heartbeat echoed in her ears. She closed her eyes for a brief moment, focusing on the mission at hand. This wasn't about revenge, or even loyalty to the cause. This was simply business. Her father's voice seemed to echo in her mind, reminding her that a soldier's job was never personal. It was about getting the job done and moving forward. No attachments. No emotions. Just cold, calculated action.

Her finger slid gently over the trigger, her mind clear, focused solely on the task ahead.

Tap. Tap.

Straight to the head, the two shots echoing in the stillness of the room. Holly didn't flinch. She never did. The first shot landed with surgical precision in O'Flannagan's forehead, the force of it knocking his head back against the pillow with a sickening thud. The second shot was quicker, the barrel shifting barely an inch as she aimed for the base of his skull. The sound of the bullet entering the back of his head was muffled by the soft fabric of the pillow, but the finality of it rang loud and clear in Holly's mind.

She let the gun drop back into her bag, feeling the cold metal against her palm, as if it was an extension of her own body. She didn't need to check for a pulse. It was over. The man who had spent years terrorising those he considered enemies was gone in an instant. No ceremony, no sentimentality—just a simple execution, one less Nationalist to cause trouble in a region already fractured by violence.

For a moment, Holly simply stood there, staring down at the still form of Seamus O'Flannagan. The blood had begun to pool beneath him, staining the white sheets a deep red, but there was no satisfaction in the sight. No sense of triumph. Just emptiness.

She was a professional, and for her, the job was done. But as she turned to leave, she couldn't help but feel the weight of what had become of her world. The conflict that had once been so black and white, so clearly defined by Loyalist and Republican lines, was now a messy blur. There were no easy answers anymore. The intervention of foreign powers had made sure of that.

As Holly slipped out of the room, her mind was already moving onto the next steps. The escape had to be clean. No mistakes. She would get back to Belfast, regroup, and wait for her next assignment. But for now, she couldn't afford to linger in the aftermath of the kill. She'd already been in the game long enough to know that hesitation could be fatal.

* - * - * - *

"Sarge, you'll love this," PC Kevin Flaherty, a member of the Police Service of Northern Ireland and brother of Holly, said, heading over to the Police Sergeant who was on duty at the station. Kevin was grinning from ear to ear, his face a mix of excitement and smugness as he approached the desk. The Sarge looked up from her papers, raising an eyebrow at the enthusiasm of his young constable.

"Something funny, Flaherty?" Sargeant Jane McDonald asked, leaning back in her chair, clearly tired after a long shift.

"Suicide, one of the slums just down the road. Known IRA guy topped himself, Seamus O'Flannagan, local hero in the wrong circles, and now his body's been discovered in a hotel room." Kevin's grin only grew as he watched the Sergeant's expression shift from curiosity to a subtle, knowing grimace.

Kevin knew that his older sister had assassinated the man, but he also knew that he had to cover for her, to make it sound as if the incident had been a tragic accident, not a well-executed hit. Seamus O'Flannagan's death would be seen as another unfortunate casualty of the ongoing unrest in Derry, and Kevin wasn't about to let his sister's actions come to light. If she was caught, the implications would be far-reaching—not just for Holly but for their entire family.

He knew that a spook was sitting in the office, a Brit, and that they'd be near enough immediately on the phone to Thames House, Vauxhall Cross or some other intelligence hub, probably to report the 'sad passing' of the Nationalist agitator. There was no love lost at Waterside Police Station for Seamus O'Flannagan, but even Kevin knew that the higher-ups were bound to have their own suspicions. For all his excitement, there was an undercurrent of caution in the way he'd presented the story. He knew the importance of keeping his sister's role a secret. Too many people in the wrong places were watching, and one slip-up could set everything ablaze.

Kevin's grin faded as Sergeant McDonald narrowed her eyes, her lips curling into a thoughtful frown. She'd been around long enough to read people, and Kevin's enthusiasm, while genuine, reeked of something more than just the shock of a suicide.

"You've got something more on this, haven't you, Flaherty?" McDonald's voice was sharp, her tone suggesting that she wasn't buying the easy narrative.

Kevin felt his stomach churn, but he didn't show it. He was his sister's protector now, and that meant controlling the narrative. "Well, it's not like the old man had many friends, Sarge. Anyway, it's not like the spooks would bother hunting down the bastard's body now. He wasn't much of a hero to anyone outside his own crowd. Best to just mark it off as another casualty of the troubles, wouldn't you say?" Kevin forced a casual tone, leaning back slightly, hoping the Sergeant would drop it.

Sergeant McDonald stared at Kevin for a long moment, her sharp eyes narrowing as she processed his words. Kevin's heart beat faster, his palms starting to sweat under the table. He knew his sister's involvement would be difficult to keep hidden, especially with people like McDonald in the loop. The Sergeant was no rookie. She had seen enough death, enough carnage, to know when a story didn't quite add up.

But, as Kevin had hoped, she sighed, leaning back in her chair and rubbing the back of her neck. "Alright, Flaherty," she said, her voice low and gruff, "we'll file it as another casualty of the mess. But you better pray the higher-ups don't start sniffing around. It's bad enough around here with the Russians getting involved and all. No one needs another bloody scandal on top of it."

Kevin nodded, a small but relieved smile pulling at his lips. "No worries, Sarge. Just another day in Derry, eh?"

McDonald gave him a sceptical glance before nodding slowly. "Yeah, sure. Just another day."

"Sarge," PC Kieth Duffy said, walking in urgently, "We've had a coded threat."

Sergeant McDonald turned sharply, her eyes narrowing as she looked at PC Keith Duffy. The energy in the room shifted instantly from casual to tense. Kevin's stomach dropped again, the smile fading from his face. A coded threat? In Derry? With everything going on, it was the last thing they needed.

"What's the threat, Duffy?" McDonald's voice was cold, commanding, her gaze locked on the officer in front of her.

"It's from a local IRA cell," Duffy said. "They've just phoned the front desk, telling us we've got 5 minutes to evacuate."

Kevin felt his heart race as the words hung in the air, each syllable pressing down on him like a weight. "Five minutes?" he repeated, the urgency sinking in. His eyes darted around the room, but no one seemed to know what to do first. The atmosphere shifted, the casual office chatter immediately evaporating as the officers in the room began to react.

Sergeant McDonald didn't hesitate. "Get everyone on high alert. Start securing the building." She snapped the order with a calmness that belied the tension in the room, but Kevin could hear the undercurrent of urgency in her voice. "Duffy, get to the front desk. See if we can trace that call. Flaherty, stay with me. I need you on standby."

As the room burst into activity, Kevin's mind raced. The last thing he wanted was for this to be connected to his sister, to Holly. The IRA had always been a shadow in Derry, but now, with the Restoration Government and Russian involvement thickening the plot, he couldn't afford to let anything slip. The tension that had been building for days was now on the verge of exploding.

He stood stiffly, his back against the wall, watching as Duffy scrambled to his feet and bolted towards the front desk. McDonald moved with purpose, her sharp eyes taking in every detail, while the rest of the officers quickly began to secure the building.

Kevin felt a chill in his spine. Five minutes. That was all they had.

"Flaherty!" McDonald barked, snapping Kevin out of his thoughts. She was standing by the door now, her hand on the handle, ready to go. "If anything goes down, you're with me. We stay close, and we stay alive. You got it?"

He nodded, swallowing hard. "Yeah, got it, Sarge."

Just as the last few officers moved into position, Duffy burst through the door, his face pale as he held up his phone. "No trace," he said, voice tight. "It was a burner. The call came from a payphone down by the docks. We've got no way of knowing if it's real or just a hoax."

McDonald cursed under her breath. "Damn it. This is too much of a coincidence. We've got to act as if it's real, but we don't have the luxury of time to check everything. Everyone get to cover. Stay sharp."

Kevin felt his breath catch in his throat as his mind raced back to the conversation he'd had with his sister not long ago. The weight of the secret—her involvement in O'Flannagan's death—hung heavy over him. His thoughts flitted between his duty to his colleagues and his fear for Holly. Had she left any trace behind? Had someone connected the dots to her involvement?

The sirens outside blared to life, and he jumped, snapping back into focus. The evacuation process was starting—everyone in the building had to be moved to secure positions, either in the basement or further out into the city. There was no way of knowing if the threat was credible, but in a place like Derry, in these times, threats were taken seriously.

"Alright, Flaherty," McDonald called as she turned toward him, "you're coming with me. We're heading to the rear exit. I want to get out of here and make contact with the rest of the unit in case this thing goes off. The last thing we need is to be trapped here when all hell breaks loose."

Kevin followed her as they moved quickly, joining the rest of the officers in the back hallway. The urgency in McDonald's voice was clear. They had no idea if this was just another prank or a real warning, but they couldn't afford to find out the hard way.

* _ * _ * _ *

James Smith was on the English and Welsh feed of Manic Vibes, only just starting his drivetime shift with his wife, Lyra, at the Birmingham HQ of Manic Radio in Studio A1, the former Manic Goldies West Midlands studio when the hub had opened back in 2025, replacing the former Dudley studio, when the RCS Zetta screen was having items hastily deleted and reorganised. He could hear in his earpiece, as unlike the home setup which used proper headphones and monitors, the studio's equipment was more state of the art, and the sound of the machines around him hummed in a sharp contrast to the tension that was seeping through the air.

"And in breaking news," Manic's Lead Newsreader for the Central area, Harpinder Singh, said, and James knew that something was seriously wrong. Harpinder's voice carried the weight of the moment, a sense of urgency that was rare for him. "In a developing story, 13 people are dead and several seriously wounded in a bomb blast at a local police station in Derry, Northern Ireland. Early reports suggest the IRA has claimed responsibility for the attack, which occurred just hours ago. This comes in the wake of heightened tensions between Loyalist and Nationalist factions, further compounded by the increasing involvement of foreign powers in the region. The Restoration Government's increasing presence in

Northern Ireland, coupled with the Russian military's backing of Nationalist groups, is only adding fuel to the fire."

He knew that the news would be similar on the regional feeds as, due to the Media Act 2024, Manic was only required to broadcast "local" news, ads and travel/weather, and not the need for local shows, meaning a pan-England and Wales Drive show was the format, with localized news reports tailored to regional interests. But the sudden shift in the news had a sharp edge, one that cut through the mundane chatter of the show like a hot knife through butter.

"Thirteen dead," Lyra muttered with the sense of a 31 year old who had grown used to the grim reality of the world around her. She sat next to James at the desk, her eyes narrowing as the details continued to unfold on the broadcast. Her fingers hovered over the controls, but the usual smoothness of her gestures was marred by the tension that had settled in the air. It was rare for any of them to be caught off guard like this, but the bomb blast in Derry had rattled everyone in the studio. James could hear it in her voice when she spoke, that tightness that spoke of more than just professional concern.

"Yeah. I feel sorry for our colleagues on Vibes Northern Ireland and Vibes Ireland at the other end of the feed. They're in the thick of it." James murmured, his voice carrying the weight of the moment. "Anyway, looks like we've got a show to do."

The sweeper for the Manic Vibes Drive Show, sponsored by Red Bull, aired, and James felt himself ready to take control, pushing the thoughts of the tragedy in Derry to the back of his mind for now. The studio, for all its technology and high-tech equipment, felt like a pressure cooker. Tension ran through the room, palpable in the way Lyra's fingers hovered over the soundboard, unsure if she should do something, anything, to alleviate the growing unease.

The studio buzzed with a low hum, the kind that always surrounded high-end equipment. But today, the hum felt off, like a pressure building up beneath the surface. The air was thick with something more than just electronics and the usual chatter of a radio shift. Lyra was tense beside him, her hands poised over the controls, her brow furrowed as the events unfolding on air and around them mirrored the unease gnawing at both of them.

James adjusted the microphone slightly, clearing his throat to fill the silence that had built up between the two of them. The show had started off as usual, but the attack in Derry had hit too close to home. Thirteen lives lost in a bombing at a police station, and already, the reports were painting a grim picture of rising tensions and the shadow of foreign involvement, specifically the Restoration Government's increasing interference and the backing of Russian military operations in the area.

But the show must go on.

"And it's the Manic Vibes drive show, live across-" James started, noticing his script being amended in real time once again, this time more abruptly than before. The sudden changes, especially for a show that had always prided itself on being in the moment, were unsettling. The adjustments were subtle but significant—an odd sense of urgency behind them. "-the UK, I'm James Smith."

"And I'm Lyra Smith, and we've got all of the greatest tracks, here on Manic Vibes, and on Manic Vibes Hits, the newest Manic station on Manic Prime, where all the newest chart topping hits are just a click away."

James knew that Manic Vibes Hits and Manic Throwbacks were brand extensions of the Manic Vibes network, with the same drive show that they were doing on Manic Vibes England and Wales being simulcast on Vibes Hits and Throwbacks, the RCS Zetta system using split feeds to ensure smooth transitions. Yet, tonight, with the world around them teetering on the edge, those transitions felt more like a subtle way of maintaining control over a situation that was rapidly spiralling out of anyone's hands.

The uneasy buzz in the studio persisted, but they both knew they had a job to do. The news had already been read out by Harpinder, and now it was their turn to keep the show going, to deliver the entertainment their listeners had tuned in for, as if the world wasn't on fire just beyond the soundproof walls.

"It's hump day, here across the Manic Vibes family, and that means," James said, looking at his new line, which instead of announcing a new Teddy Swims track on Vibes and Vibes Hits, or a classic Aqua song for Throwbacks, was now showing The Cranberries' Zombie for Vibes and Throwbacks, and the Teddy Swims track for Vibes Hits, his thoughts momentarily drifting to the chaos unfurling in Derry. "That means, for you guys on Manic Vibes and

Manic Throwbacks, a classic from one of the most iconic Irish bands of all time, The Cranberries with Zombie. A song that's never failed to resonate, especially in times like these."

James noticed that it was Alison Harper's name once again flickering on the script updates, and this time, there was no subtlety in the way the timing was adjusted. The inclusion of "Zombie" felt deliberate—a choice of song that had resonated deeply with the Irish conflict, a haunting anthem that spoke volumes to the tension they were all feeling. The strange timing of it, coupled with the attack in Derry, left James with an unsettling sense that the network was playing something much bigger than just radio entertainment.

Looking at the playout screens, as he knew that Vibes Hits would have been adjusted to have a new Dua Lipa track play out after Teddy Swims song, while Throwbacks and the main Vibes station would have a slightly longer section of him and Lyra bantering about some irrelevant radio trivia, James couldn't shake the feeling that the changes were more than just coincidence. The selection of "Zombie" by The Cranberries, the references to Irish identity and conflict, the timing—it all felt too calculated. He could sense the heavy hand of the powers above, pushing certain cultural touchpoints into the airwaves at the most politically charged moment in Northern Ireland's history.

As the haunting intro to Zombie by The Cranberries bled into the studio, James felt an odd chill creep down his spine. It was a song that, over the years, had become synonymous with the turbulent history of Ireland, echoing the pain and anger of those caught in the crossfire of the conflict. To many, it was a symbol of resistance, a call for justice amidst a legacy of bloodshed and loss. And tonight, it felt like a dark omen.

James glanced at Lyra, her face lit by the glow of the monitors, her fingers still hovering uncertainly over the controls. The song was a jarring reminder of the chaos unfolding in Derry, the lives lost in the bombing, and the growing involvement of foreign powers in Northern Ireland's internal strife. But beyond that, the song's inclusion felt deliberate—like a message being sent through the airwaves, one that wasn't just about entertainment.

For a moment, neither of them spoke. The song's eerie opening chords filled the studio, but the silence between them felt heavy, laden with unspoken thoughts. Lyra broke the quiet first, her voice barely above a whisper. "That's... well, that's a bit on the nose, don't you think?"

James nodded, his stomach twisting. He knew exactly what she meant. The whole situation felt like it was spiralling out of control. The attack in Derry had come on the heels of so many signs of escalation—Russian interference, Iranian arms flowing into the Nationalist movement, and now, the blatant manipulation of their playlist.

He forced a smile, trying to maintain the air of professionalism that had been drilled into him since the early days of his career. "It's just a song, love. We're all about the vibe, right?"

But even as the words left his mouth, he knew they rang hollow. The network, which had always prided itself on staying ahead of the curve with its music choices, was playing a far deeper game. The introduction of Zombie wasn't just a radio stunt—it was a calculated decision, one that reflected the tense, volatile mood in the region. The timing felt deliberate. And James, for all his years in broadcasting, knew that this wasn't about catering to the audience. This was something bigger, something darker.

Lyra seemed to pick up on the shift in his tone. Her gaze lingered on him for a moment before she turned her attention back to the control board. "We're not just spinning tracks here, are we?" she said, more to herself than to him.

James couldn't help but let out a low laugh, but it wasn't a laugh of amusement. It was the laugh of someone who had been pulled into a situation they couldn't quite control, a laugh of someone who was starting to realize they were in over their head.

"Doesn't seem like it," he muttered, glancing at the script again. It had been updated so many times during the shift that he had lost track of the changes. Each new instruction, each new song choice felt like another piece in a puzzle he didn't have the full picture of.

The screens in front of him flickered, the automated system now out of sync with the real-time adjustments being made behind the scenes. The constant shuffle of playlists, news updates, and code-red timing alerts were becoming increasingly unnerving. Even as he tried to focus on the job at hand, his mind kept drifting back to

Derry, to the explosion that had rocked the city, and the growing sense that the airwaves weren't just carrying music—they were carrying a message.

****

CHAPTER 16 – Sub Games
Saturday 3rd February 2029

It had been nearly two months of Kapitan Pervogo Ranga Dmitry Volkhov's mission to tail, and if possible, kill HMS Vanguard.

And now, finally, the hunt was drawing to a close.

The Vladimir Vladimirovich Putin had done what no Russian submarine had accomplished in decades—it had shadowed Britain's Continuous At-Sea Deterrent undetected, gone into British territorial waters, and was now in the mid-North Atlantic, ready to strike.

Volkhov stood at the centre of the control room, his gaze fixed on the tactical display. The glowing red silhouette of HMS Vanguard pulsed like a heartbeat against the deep black of the North Atlantic. After nearly two months of relentless pursuit, the moment had come.

He knew that the Americans had fully pulled out of NATO's naval operations in the North Atlantic, and, news from the past day, had announced that RAF Lakenheath was to be wound down over the next year, the remaining operations would be moved to Ramstein Air Base in Germany. With the Americans gone, Britain stood alone in its nuclear deterrence patrols, stretching the Royal Navy's anti-submarine warfare (ASW) forces to their limit. The withdrawal of the P-8 Poseidons from Lakenheath had left a glaring hole in the UK's detection grid—one that Volkhov and his crew had exploited ruthlessly.

And then there was the Irish Air Force's new Sukhoi Su-75s. Volkhov had had to surface two days ago, as a supply vessel from the Irish Republic's Restoration Government had delivered food, oxygen, and replacement crew to the Vladimir Vladimirovich Putin, all under the cover of a maritime 'rescue' operation. The lead pilot, Volkhov remembered, was a young Kapitan by the name of Sulov, who he presumed was one of Kaliningrad's elite pilots, transferred under Moscow's quiet but growing military patronage of the Irish Restoration Government. The Sukhoi Su-75, the so-called Checkmate, was a fifth-generation stealth fighter, ostensibly supplied to Ireland for "defensive purposes"—a convenient fiction that masked its role in strengthening Russian-aligned forces in Western Europe. That the handover had been so seamless was a testament to how far the Restoration Government had aligned itself with Moscow's objectives. Ireland was no longer neutral. It was a de facto satellite of the Kremlin.

In return, the Royal Air Force had, according to intelligence, moved a number of F-35Bs from RAF Marham to RAF Valley on the Welsh coast, a desperate attempt to bolster its defences against the growing Russian-aligned air presence in Ireland. But the UK was stretched thin, its military resources depleted after years of budget constraints, political instability, and now, the effective collapse of NATO as a functional alliance. Volkhov knew that Britain's defences were like an ageing battleship—still armed, still dangerous, but riddled with weak spots that could be exploited.

And he was about to prove just how vulnerable it truly was.

"Kapitan, the target is holding course. Speed consistent at five knots. Depth remains steady at one hundred and fifty metres." The voice of Starshiy Leytenant Oleg Petrov broke through the stillness of the control room. The sonar officer's tone was calm, professional, but Volkhov could sense the tension underlying it. This was the moment they had all been waiting for.

HMS Vanguard was alone. Isolated. Cut off from immediate support.

Volkhov had spent weeks playing a deadly game of cat-and-mouse, ensuring that the British submarine believed it was still safe, still unnoticed. They had exploited every gap in Britain's undersea detection net, taking advantage of the gaps left by the departing American assets. The Royal Navy had been slow to adjust, unable to commit the resources needed to plug the hole.

And now, Vanguard was about to pay the price.

"Distance to target?" Volkhov asked.

"Four thousand metres," came the response from the weapons officer, Starshiy Leytenant Yuri Mikhailov. "Closing steadily."

Four kilometres. A fraction of the vast Atlantic expanse, a distance that was both impossibly small and yet an eternity in submarine warfare. The Vladimir Vladimirovich Putin was a predator lurking just beneath the waves, its torpedo tubes primed and ready.

Volkhov took a deep breath, his mind racing through the possible scenarios. The operational directive from

Severomorsk had been clear—sink the target if the opportunity presented itself. But even with Russia's growing influence, this was a risk that could not be taken lightly. If Vanguard was lost without explanation, Britain would know it had been targeted. Retaliation could come swiftly, perhaps even in the form of the very nuclear weapons that Vanguard carried.

But if they made it look like an accident...

Volkhov turned his gaze to Mikhailov. "Prepare a torpedo spread. Set them to passive homing only. No active pinging."

"Da, Kapitan," Mikhailov responded at once, his hands moving over the control panel with practiced ease.

Passive homing torpedoes would not give away their position immediately. They would rely on the subtle acoustic signature of Vanguard, zeroing in on the sounds of its reactor, its turbines, the faint hum of life aboard the British submarine. If done correctly, the attack would be silent, invisible—Vanguard would never see it coming.

* _ * _ * _ *

"Ma'am, we've just had a contact on sonar. It was active but has switched to passive. Unknown origin, but it's close."

The voice of Chief Petty Officer Graham Atkinson echoed through the dimly lit control room of HMS Vanguard. Commander Louise Carstairs, the commander of the nuclear deterrent submarine, turned sharply, her gut twisting with the kind of unease that only came with years of experience in the deep. The Royal Navy's Vanguard-class submarines were built for stealth, designed to patrol undetected, but this? This was something else entirely.

"Details," she ordered, her voice steady despite the alarm prickling at the back of her mind.

Atkinson ran his fingers over the sonar display, the screen awash with the quiet rhythms of the Atlantic depths. "Unknown contact, bearing zero-four-five. Jonesy picked it up a week ago, but it wasn't like the normal Russkies, and the XO said to log it but not report it up the chain. Now it's changed behaviour. I think it's a hunter, ma'am."

Carstairs exhaled slowly. A Russian hunter-killer. The old Cold War fear, reborn in a world where the rules were once again being rewritten by Moscow. She'd suspected they were being followed for weeks now—subtle disruptions in the ocean's ambient noise, faint distortions in sonar returns, the kind of anomalies that an experienced submariner knew better than to ignore. But there had never been proof. Just instincts.

Now, the instincts had turned to facts.

"Is it a Yasen?" she asked. The Yasen class were Russia's most advanced attack submarines before the new Laika class had started rolling off the production line.

Atkinson shook his head grimly. "I don't think so, ma'am. If it is what I think it is, we're dealing with something new. I did hear rumours a couple of years ago that the Russkies were building a new class, something cheaper than the Yasen, but a new generation of stealth attack sub. If this is it, we're in serious trouble. Hang on..."

Carstairs watched as Atkinson looked at his equipment again, and when she saw him chuckle, she knew that there was either something mentally wrong with the man or he had just discovered something absurdly ridiculous.

"What is it, Chief?" she asked, bracing for the answer.

Atkinson smirked, shaking his head in disbelief. "You're not going to believe this, ma'am, but I think it's called the Vladimir Vladimirovich Putin. It's a new class—Laika, if the intelligence chatter is right. And if it's here, that means we're dealing with Russia's latest and greatest. It's meant to be quieter than anything they've built before. And it's named after the bastard himself. You do remember, ma'am, that Ambush is only 20 miles aft of us?"

Carstairs blinked. Ambush. HMS Ambush, one of the Royal Navy's Astute-class attack submarines, was indeed trailing behind Vanguard as part of a classified escort experiment—a last-ditch effort to compensate for Britain's dwindling ASW assets.

The Astute-class was the pride of the Royal Navy's attack submarine fleet, a hunter designed to stalk and eliminate threats before they could strike at high-value assets like Vanguard. If Ambush was in the area, then Vanguard wasn't as alone as the Russians believed.

A slow grin crept onto Carstairs' face. The hunter had just become the hunted.

As a fan of The Hunt for Red October, she knew that most often, Russian attack submarines overestimated their own invincibility. As a boomer driver, she often imagined what Marko Ramius would have done in this situation. If this really was Russia's latest and greatest lurking beneath the waves, then it was time to see just how good it actually was.

"Engine room, get ready to go dark, let's see if this bastard can keep up with a proper game of hide and seek," Carstairs ordered, her voice carrying the kind of cool determination that had earned her the respect of every sailor aboard. She knew that standard orders would be to keep running, but this wasn't a standard engagement. If this Russian sub wanted to play games, they were about to find out just how sharp the teeth of the Royal Navy still were. "Get Faslane, Portsmouth and Ambush on the line. We're about to make some noise."

* _ * _ * _ *

Volkhov watched as the red silhouette of HMS Vanguard on the tactical display flickered slightly. At first, he thought it was a glitch—a momentary disturbance in the feed—but then, the contact began to fade.

"What's happening?" he demanded, his voice sharp.

Petrov's hands flew over the sonar controls, adjusting the sensitivity. "Kapitan, the contact is... changing behaviour. Its reactor noise is decreasing—significantly. They're going into ultra-quiet mode."

Volkhov's brow furrowed. *So, they've figured us out.* But there was something else, something that gnawed at him. This wasn't the standard evasive action of a boomer trying to slip away undetected. This was deliberate, almost taunting.

"They're baiting us," he murmured.

Leonov, standing beside him, tensed. "Baiting us? How?"

Volkhov exhaled sharply, already feeling his stomach knotting. "If they know we're here, and they aren't running at full speed to escape, then they have a plan. They aren't alone. Go back to active sonar, see what else is lurking in the deep."

Petrov hesitated for only a moment before obeying. The control room was bathed in eerie silence as the sonar pulse was sent out. A second passed. Then another. The display refreshed, and suddenly, the blood drained from Volkhov's face.

Another contact.

And it was close. Too close.

"Kapitan," Petrov whispered, his voice barely above a breath. "New contact bearing one-eight-five. Depth one hundred and twenty metres. It's—it's a fast mover."

Volkhov's mind raced. That wasn't another ballistic missile submarine. That was an attack submarine, and given its speed and the angle of approach, it was already lining up for a shot.

He felt his throat go dry. Ambush.

The Astute-class. One of the Royal Navy's most advanced hunter-killers. And it had been right behind them the entire time.

"Confirmed ID?" Volkhov asked, though he already knew the answer.

Petrov swallowed. "HMS Ambush. She's locked onto us, Kapitan."

Volkhov clenched his jaw. The British had played them brilliantly. Vanguard had been bait, a slow-moving prize to lure them in. And now, the real killer had its crosshairs on the Vladimir Vladimirovich Putin.

Leonov turned to him, eyes wide. "Orders, Kapitan?"

Volkhov's mind raced. They could try to run, but at this distance, it wouldn't matter. Ambush was close enough that even if they launched countermeasures, the Astute-class submarine could still land a shot before they evaded.

Unless...

"Sumasshedshiy Ivan!" Volkhov shouted, ordering a Cold War-era evasive manoeuvre. "Full speed ahead, hard to starboard! Prepare countermeasures!"

The crew snapped into action. The control room erupted in a flurry of movement as engineers and sonar operators scrambled to execute the Kapitan's desperate plan. The Vladimir Vladimirovich Putin surged forward, banking sharply as its powerful reactor output surged to maximum, propelling the Russian submarine into a violent corkscrew manoeuvre designed to throw off any incoming torpedoes.

"Decoy launch, now!" Volkhov barked.

Mikhailov slammed a button, and a trio of noise-making countermeasure decoys shot into the dark abyss, each one programmed to mimic the acoustic signature of the Putin. The water around them was suddenly alive with false echoes, scattering the sonar return in a desperate bid to confuse Ambush's targeting systems.

Volkhov gripped the edge of the console, his knuckles white. He had been a submariner for over two decades, but never had he felt the icy hand of death as close as he did now. The Vladimir Vladimirovich Putin had gone from the hunter to the hunted in mere moments.

"Ambush is moving—she's adjusting bearing!" Petrov shouted, his voice tight with adrenaline. "They're closing in fast!"

"Have they fired?" Volkhov demanded.

* _ * _ * _ *

"What the fuck?" Atkinson shouted, watching the sudden manoeuvre on the sonar display. "They're pulling a Crazy Ivan, ma'am! They're going full speed and dumping countermeasures!"

Carstairs stood at the controls of Vanguard, looking over Atkinson's shoulder at the sonar display, a smile on her face. The irony of a Russian Captain pulling a move from The Hunt for Red October was not lost on her. A fan of the novel and not the Sean Connery film, she had always imagined a real-life Crazy Ivan would come one day. And now, here it was, unfolding in the deep waters of the North Atlantic, a desperate Russian captain trying to shake the jaws of an unseen predator.

"You know, ma'am," Lieutenant Commander Alan King, the officer who was in charge of the torpedoes that the Vanguard had for defensive purposes, chimed in, his voice laced with amusement, "I always wondered if we'd see a real Sumasshedshiy Ivan in action. Turns out, the Russians still love their old tricks."

Carstairs didn't take her eyes off the screen. "Tricks only work when your enemy isn't expecting them," she murmured. "Ambush has the advantage, and they know it. Pity they, like us, can only shoot if they're fired upon first."

She took a deep breath, her mind racing through the options. This was no longer just about staying hidden—it was about control. If the Vladimir Vladimirovich Putin thought it could outmanoeuvre Ambush, it was sorely mistaken. The Astute-class submarine was built for this kind of fight, and it had the home-field advantage.

"Open a secure line to Ambush," she ordered.

A few seconds later, a crackling voice came over the classified military frequency. "This is HMS Ambush. Commander Callum Fraser speaking."

"Callum, it's Lou on Vanguard," she said, her voice calm. She knew that, along with Fraser and a few other commanders, they had all been in the same Officer Training cohort at Britannia Royal Naval College, Dartmouth, back when they were still lieutenants, fresh-faced and eager to make their mark in the Silent Service, and, when not around the brass, had an unwritten agreement to not use formalities in case of emergencies.

This was one of those moments where protocol was flexible.

"Got yourself a Russian problem, Lou?" Fraser's voice came through, laced with dry amusement, but she could hear the underlying tension.

"Oh, you know, just a friendly game of cat and mouse," Carstairs replied, her fingers drumming against the console. "Only this time, I think the mouse realises it's actually in a trap. Just done a Crazy Ivan. Atkinson, my CPO, thinks it's a brand new Russkie mouse."

There was a brief pause before Fraser responded, a low chuckle audible through the secure comms.

"A brand new Russkie mouse, you say?" he mused. "Well, Lou, if it's anything like the old ones, it'll start getting desperate right about now. And desperate submariners make mistakes."

Carstairs nodded, watching the sonar display as the Vladimir Vladimirovich Putin zigzagged wildly, its frantic movements trying to break the British noose tightening around it. But Fraser was right—this was the moment when panic set in, when even the best Russian captain would start second-guessing every move.

"Ambush, what's your current position?" she asked.

"Two nautical miles south of you," Fraser replied. "I've got a lock on them. They don't know it yet, but if they so much as sneeze in the wrong direction, I can put a Spearfish torpedo right up their arse."

Carstairs smiled grimly. The Royal Navy's Spearfish torpedoes were nothing like the old Cold War-era Mark 48s used by the Americans. These were faster, smarter, and deadlier—designed specifically for hunting and killing enemy submarines in high-stakes encounters like this.

"Well," she said, glancing back at Atkinson, "let's see if we can scare them a little, shall we?"

Atkinson grinned. "With pleasure, ma'am."

Carstairs leaned forward, pressing the internal comms. "Bridge to sonar. Sound general quarters. Prepare for a tactical repositioning."

The red alert lighting bathed Vanguard's control room in an eerie glow as klaxons rang out, sending sailors scurrying to their stations. The game was about to change.

"XO, bring us thirty degrees starboard, decrease depth to one-twenty metres. And let's make a little noise."

The order was met with a few raised eyebrows, but her crew trusted her. They executed the command smoothly, the submarine adjusting its heading with subtle precision. The goal wasn't to escape—but to force the Vladimir Vladimirovich Putin to react.

*_*_*_*

Volkhov was starting to sweat like a rainfall had hit him and the air inside the Vladimir Vladimirovich Putin's control room felt stifling, thick with tension as if the ocean itself were pressing down upon them.

"Kapitan, HMS Vanguard is changing course. They're making noise," Petrov reported, his voice laced with confusion. "They're not running silent anymore."

Volkhov clenched his jaw, his mind racing. That wasn't normal. A ballistic missile submarine on patrol didn't want to make noise. It was built to disappear into the depths, to be the ultimate insurance policy for a nation. But now Vanguard was forcing its presence to be known.

And there was only one reason they'd do that.

"Ambush," Volkhov whispered, his blood turning cold.

They'd walked into a British trap.

"Depth charges, sonar pulses… they're trying to spook us out," Leonov muttered, watching as his screen lit up with disturbances in the water. "Kapitan, if we don't get out of here, we might not have a choice in this fight."

A submarine was at its most vulnerable when it had to react. A careful predator, watching and waiting in the depths, could choose its moment. But a cornered hunter? A hunter forced into erratic movement? That was a dead hunter.

"Ambush is two nautical miles south," Petrov reported. "They're tracking us."

Volkhov exhaled sharply, forcing himself to remain calm. His next decision could mean the difference between survival and death—not just for his crew, but for the political fallout that would come with the destruction of a state-of-the-art Russian submarine in British waters.

"Leonov, confirm the estimated position of Vanguard," he ordered.

Leonov tapped at his controls, overlaying sonar data with intelligence estimates. "They're at bearing zero-four-five, depth one-twenty metres. Not moving aggressively, just positioning."

That confirmed it. Vanguard wasn't running. It wasn't evading. It was guiding them into the kill box.

And now the Royal Navy had options.

They could leave Putin boxed in, force it to remain a ghost—unconfirmed, unheard of, and ultimately useless as a strategic deterrent.

Or they could escalate.

Volkhov knew that if he fired the first shot, all bets were off. There would be no denying Moscow's involvement, no political wriggling that could excuse the attack. But if the British fired first? That changed the narrative. Moscow would have its excuse. The Restoration Government in Ireland would be reinforced with more Russian aid, and the world would teeter even closer to full-scale war.

Either way, Volkhov's mission was already a failure.

The Vladimir Vladimirovich Putin had to disappear, one way or another. Either they slinked back into the black, or they were erased from it.

He knew that there might be Su-75s above, and that if there were, then they would provide cover for the

Vladimir Vladimirovich Putin's escape. The Restoration Government's pilots were technically Russian Air Force pilots, on loan from Kaliningrad, Engels and other Russian air bases. The Irish flag painted on their fuselages was merely for show. If the Vladimir Vladimirovich Putin surfaced, there was a chance those Su-75s could create enough of a distraction to allow them to slip away undetected.

But if the British had their F-35Bs up as well… then this was about to turn into a very different kind of fight.

Volkhov closed his eyes for a brief moment, then made his decision.

"Surface. Now, or when we get back to the Motherland, I will personally make sure the GRU send each and every one of you on a one way ticket to the most miserable ice station in Siberia," Volkhov growled, his voice cutting through the tense silence like a blade.

He knew that the British couldn't fire first without provocation. The rules of engagement were clear: Russia could not be the aggressor. But if the British submarines acted first, the narrative would change, and Moscow could justify any subsequent actions.

"Surface," he repeated, his voice more forceful this time, cutting through the chaos of the control room. "All ahead full, prepare for emergency ascent. We need to break free."

Leonov and Petrov exchanged nervous glances but quickly obeyed. The tension in the air was thick enough to feel suffocating, every crew member understanding the severity of the situation. The Vladimir Vladimirovich Putin, Russia's pride, was on the verge of being trapped, and if it didn't act fast, it would become just another casualty in a game of political chess.

"Full power," Leonov barked, and the submarine's engines roared to life. The hum of the reactor grew louder, the energy surging through the vessel. In the control room, the pressure intensified. The mission had been simple: follow, intimidate, and, if necessary, sink. But now, it seemed to be spiralling into a far more complicated affair.

"Prepare the countermeasures," Volkhov ordered sharply. The crew responded in unison, activating the decoy systems designed to mislead and confuse any tracking devices. They would need all the help they could get as they ascended, breaking the water's surface with the force of a sudden surge, throwing off the careful positioning they had maintained for so long.

A loud crash of metal echoed through the submarine, signalling that the ascent was underway. The crew braced themselves, the weight of their actions settling like an anchor around their hearts. There was no turning back now.

"Activate the emergency surfacing," Volkhov ordered, his eyes narrowing as he gripped the console, watching the sonar and radar systems in a flurry of movement. "Get us to the surface quickly—keep everything silent, but we need to make it before they can react."

The water outside the submarine seemed to thrum with anticipation, as though the very ocean was holding its breath. They had been operating under the cover of darkness, slipping through the vast depths of the Atlantic, waiting for the right moment to strike. But now, it was clear—the British knew they were there, and their response would be immediate.

Volkhov's mind raced as the submarine began to break through the depths. Above them, the waves churned, the surface just within reach. In the control room, every man stood still, knowing the clock was ticking. The moment they broke the surface, the game would be over.

"Prepare to launch decoys," Volkhov said, his voice low but commanding. "If they're going to come for us, we make them pay for every second."

"Da, Kapitan," Mikhailov responded, his fingers moving quickly over the console to ready the countermeasures.

With the noise of the submarine's ascent reverberating in the crew's ears, the first signs of light began to appear, the black waters turning slightly iridescent as the submarine neared the surface. In these final moments, the mission was no longer about the hunt, but about survival.

"Surface in three," Leonov called, his voice tinged with the strain of anticipation. "Two... One."

The Vladimir Vladimirovich Putin broke through the surface with a force that seemed to shatter the very ocean itself. The once silent predator now surfaced in the open, a massive presence in the cold, dark waters of the North Atlantic.

Volkhov watched the surface radar with bated breath. The decoys were deployed, sending false readings to any pursuers, and yet his mind was fully aware that the British subs wouldn't be fooled for long. The rising tension in the control room was palpable.

"Get us moving," Volkhov ordered. "Take us northeast at full speed. We're not staying here long."

As the sub lurched forward, slicing through the water, Volkhov's mind raced. The surface was no place for a submarine to be caught, especially one as vulnerable as the Vladimir Vladimirovich Putin. Above them, the sky seemed endless, the vast expanse of water giving no clue to the threats that were hunting them just below the waves.

The tension was suffocating.

Outside, the vast expanse of the North Atlantic stretched in every direction. But inside, the crew of the Vladimir Vladimirovich Putin were in a race against time, praying that their hasty ascent and sudden turn could provide the crucial seconds they needed to escape the encroaching British threat.

In the stillness of the moment, Volkhov turned away from the tactical display, his heart heavy with the uncertainty that loomed in every decision. Whether it was escape or confrontation, the mission was over. And now, the choices would decide whether they would sink or swim.

"Kapitan," Petrov spoke, his voice trembling. "There are aircraft... coming."

"Putin, this is Checkmate Lead, do you copy?" a Russian sounding voice came over the radio, crackling through the submarine's communication system. Volkhov's heart skipped a beat as he recognised the voice of Sulov, the young pilot who had delivered the Su-75s to the Irish Restoration Government. "Kapitan, we have you in visual range. The Brits are still parked like CSKA's defence. We can provide cover. Just hold tight, we're almost there."

Volkhov's mind raced as the voice of Sulov crackled through the radio. The relief he felt was almost palpable—though they were in the most vulnerable position imaginable, at least help was on the way. The young pilot, one of Moscow's finest, had flown in under the cover of Irish sovereignty. Now, the Su-75s—the cutting-edge stealth fighters—were his ace in the hole.

"Checkmate Lead, this is Kapitan Volkhov. Acknowledged. We need immediate air support. Get those aircraft into position before the Brits can react," Volkhov barked, his eyes fixed on the tactical display. He could see the dots on the surface radar, the faint signatures of Royal Navy ships moving fast toward their position. The game had shifted again.

The Vladimir Vladimirovich Putin was still moving fast, but the sense of being hunted had not faded. The ocean around them, usually a place of relative safety, now felt like a trap, each creak and groan of the hull amplifying the tension inside. As they rushed northeast, the vastness of the North Atlantic seemed to mock them—so wide, yet so full of unseen dangers.

"Kapitan, the Brits are making a move. They're deploying forces, fast," Petrov reported, his voice tight with concern. The ship's sonar had already detected the incoming vessels. The British were closing in on them faster than expected.

"Deploy decoys. Get the noise generators up," Volkhov ordered quickly, his mind working a mile a minute. The decoys were his last line of defence. The Russian submarine was no match for the British torpedoes if it came down to a direct firefight. But with the air support arriving, maybe they had a chance.

Outside, the sea was calm, unnervingly calm, as the crew scrambled to execute Volkhov's orders. Inside the control room, it felt as if the air itself had turned solid, each second stretching endlessly. This was the moment where their survival would be determined—not by technology, not by luck, but by their ability to make the right call under pressure.

"We've deployed decoys, Kapitan. The noise generators are active," Leonov reported. The tension in his voice mirrored that of the others in the room. Volkhov didn't respond immediately. Instead, he glanced at the radar again. The Royal Navy ships were closing in, but there was something else in the air. Something in the depth of the ocean that told him they might have more time than he thought.

"Steady," Volkhov said, as if willing himself to slow his racing thoughts. "Prepare to submerge to 200 meters. We need to drop below the surface, remain quiet. Do not make any sound."

The Vladimir Vladimirovich Putin, for all its might, had one severe vulnerability: it was still a submarine, subject to the natural forces of the ocean. The depth and concealment of the waters were their only real protection now.

As the sub slowly sank deeper into the water, the control room quieted, the hum of the decoys and countermeasures filling the silence. Volkhov knew this was a delicate balance—if the British had their F-35Bs in the air and locked onto them, they could launch an attack from above before the submarine could react.

"Checkmate Lead, this is Vladimir Vladimirovich Putin. Status update?" Volkhov asked, his voice low but urgent. He could almost feel the aircraft approaching, their power and precision an anchor in the chaos surrounding them.

"We're in position, Kapitan. We've got eyes on the Brits. They're deploying helicopters, but we have cover. We can handle them. You just stay submerged," Sulov's voice responded, confident but not without the underlying tension of the situation.

"Copy that," Volkhov muttered. He looked around at his crew, each man braced for what could come next. The surreal feeling of being hunted, with the fate of an entire nation hanging in the balance, was overwhelming. There was no second chance here. If they failed to escape now, it would mark the beginning of an irreversible escalation.

Back on the surface, the British ships were preparing. The stealth fighters above would be their shield against any further retaliation, and the crew of the Vladimir

Vladimirovich Putin had nowhere to go but down. The depth charge countermeasures were ready, but the real weapon—air support—was still a few moments away.

Then, suddenly, a sharp beep echoed in the control room. It was a warning.

"Kapitan, incoming contact—fast-moving," Petrov said, the panic in his voice undeniable.

"Full depth! Dive, dive, dive!" Volkhov shouted, his heart racing. This was it. The British had acted faster than he expected, and now, they were in immediate danger of being caught.

The sub lurched downward, its engines roaring to life as it plunged deeper into the abyss. The control room was alive with activity, as every crew member did their part to ensure the ship's survival. But as the depth increased, the water pressure mounted, and the creaks and groans of the submarine became deafening.

"Decoys activated, full evasive," Leonov reported, as the sound of countermeasures firing echoed through the ship. "They're still on us, Kapitan. They've locked onto our last sonar return. We're close to being within range of their torpedoes."

Volkhov gripped the edge of his chair, feeling the tension in his gut. The seconds stretched out like hours as the sub sped down into the depths of the Atlantic. Outside, the British forces were mobilizing. The aircraft above were still moving into position. But below, in the ocean's dark and dangerous depths, there was a chance for them to escape.

"Checkmate Lead, this is Putin," Volkhov called out, his voice strained. "We need immediate air support. The Brits are closing in."

"Hold tight, Kapitan," Sulov replied. "We're almost on top of them."

In the moment of uncertainty, Volkhov's mind flashed to the larger picture. This wasn't just a submarine mission. This was a geopolitical showdown. And the outcome here, whether it was victory or defeat, would ripple across the globe.

The Russian sub was moments away from reaching its deepest point, evading the oncoming British attack. If they could just last long enough to get the air support they needed, there was still a chance to slip out of this deadly game. But if they couldn't? The sea, cold and unforgiving, would be their tomb.

"Kapitan, we're almost there," Petrov whispered, his hands steady on the sonar controls. "Just a little more. A little further..."

Suddenly, the alarm sounded again, louder than before, and Volkhov knew the moment had come. The air around him felt electric, charged with the weight of impending disaster.

"Full speed ahead. We're not dying here today," Volkhov declared, his voice strong despite the chaos, as the crew readied themselves for what was to come next.

Above the surface, in the open sky, the first fighter jets were descending—checkmate was about to begin in full force.

****

CHAPTER 17 – Discovery
Tuesday 13th February 2029

"Oh, Iran, you cheeky bastards," Kelvin Svenson muttered under his breath, his fingers curling around the manifest as if it could bite back. The thick paper rattled in his hands, the weight of the information pressing down on him with more force than any mere cargo could.

The document listed what appeared to be a routine shipping route, but beneath the surface, it was anything but. The words jumped out at him in bold, underlined print.

"Manifest of Cargo Ship Su Li

Port of Departure - Xiamen, China

Stop 1 - Shuwaikh, Kuwait

Stop 2 - Tilbury, United Kingdom

Stop 3 - Rotterdam, The Netherlands

Stop 4 - Aberdeen, United Kingdom

Stop 5 - Belfast, United Kingdom

Destination - Charleston, United States

***Onload of 6 containers of farming chemicals and agricultural supplies at Shuwaikh. Offload of 6 containers of farming chemicals and agricultural supplies at Belfast. ***

Those two lines in the manifest stood out like a neon sign. It was all above board until you got to the last stop— Belfast. Belfast, a city now submerged under the weight of political unrest and foreign intervention. He knew that the Restoration Government in Ireland had been actively backing the Nationalist factions, but this? This was something else entirely.

Added to that was human intelligence from Iran that they had received a delivery of a RS-28 Sarmat from Russia, and there was plans to send it to the Restoration Government in Dublin, likely as part of a much larger plan to escalate tensions in the region. The sheer audacity of it made his blood run cold. A Russian nuclear missile, on its way to the United Kingdom, just waiting to be integrated into the arsenal of the Irish government.

Looking at the manifest, he noticed that the routing for the Su Li would take it past Aberdeen on the 3rd of March, as it was already leaving China and moving steadily towards the UK. Aberdeen, with its bustling port and shipping lanes, was an ideal place, Kelvin realised, for an ambush by British forces, especially as, during the winter months, it would be foggy, it would have a perfect cover for any covert action.

Clicking on the Teams icon on his desktop, he knew that a friend who was in the Royal Navy would be able to create a hypothetical scenario which would mirror a real life incident in 2025, when, in the Humber region, a cargo ship collided with an oil tanker, the cargo ship having come off a drop which had sodium cyanide and the oil tanker containing A1 Jet fuel, narrowly avoiding a catastrophic explosion that could have taken out half the coastline. If this was going to go down the same way, he needed to move fast.

Especially as, if he had come to the same conclusion, then the Mossad would be right behind him, and they would no doubt come up with their own plan to destroy the Su Li, but in a more overt way, one which would signal to Iran that they were not playing around. Kelvin's idea, he knew, however, was more subtle, a mere accident, a case of bad weather and bad timing. After all, maritime accidents happen, ships collide, and if one was carrying fuel, HM Coastguard would happily order all civilian ships to remain at a safe distance, just to avoid any chance of a disastrous explosion. The plan was perfect in its simplicity, but the stakes were high. One mistake, one slip-up, and the entire operation could backfire.

Typing a phone number, he knew that he could have just caught a taxi to Whitehall, where his contact, an Admiral, was based, to pick his brain, but the nature of the operation required more subtlety. Picking up his secure phone, he dialled the number he knew by heart. The phone rang twice before it was picked up.

"MOD Ops, Admiral Linus Edwards's office," the voice of a secretary answered crisply.

"Good morning," Kelvin said, keeping his voice neutral. "Can I speak to the Admiral, it's Kelvin Svenson, Russia Desk at Vauxhall Cross here."

"One moment, please, Mr. Svenson," the secretary replied, her tone professional, but there was an unmistakable pause before she placed him on hold. Kelvin drummed his fingers against the edge of the desk, waiting for the connection to be made. His mind kept drifting back to the manifest—the implications of that missile. It was more than just another diplomatic headache; it was a potential game-changer, and if Iran was truly supplying the Restoration Government with a Russian nuclear missile, then the balance of power in Europe could be altered forever.

Finally, the line clicked, and the voice of Admiral Linus Edwards came through, thick with a military gravitas that instantly put Kelvin on edge.

"Svenson, what can I do for you?" Edwards's voice had that steady authority that came with decades of service, though it was tempered now by the strain of an ongoing war with the Russians and the increasingly complicated web of alliances.

"Admiral," Kelvin said, leaning forward in his chair, "I've got something that requires your attention. It's about a cargo ship—Su Li—coming out of Xiamen, China, scheduled to dock in Belfast at the end of this month. I need you to create a simulation, one that mirrors the Humber collision of 2025."

There was a long silence on the line. Kelvin could hear the Admiral shifting papers, likely reviewing his files or marking notes. "The one with the sodium cyanide and jet fuel, you mean? Damn close call that one, almost levelled the coast. You've got my attention, Svenson."

"I've got a bad feeling about this," Kelvin continued. "The ship's manifest looks clean, just agricultural supplies, but

I've got intel saying it's carrying something far more dangerous. Word from the Mossad has it that Iran's been receiving a Russian RS-28 Sarmat missile, and the last stop on this ship's itinerary is Belfast. I'm betting there's a delivery to the Restoration Government."

"Jesus," Edwards muttered, clearly piecing it together in real time. "Give me a minute, I'll get the RAF lads on the line, as they can just generate a strike package-"

"No, Admiral, if we do that, then it's an act of war," Kelvin interrupted quickly, a slight edge creeping into his voice. "We can't afford a direct confrontation just yet. Not over this. We need to move carefully, methodically. If we strike too openly, it'll send ripples across the geopolitical landscape that we may never be able to calm down."

Another long silence followed. Kelvin could hear the Admiral shifting in his seat, the familiar sound of paper rustling on the other end of the line. He knew Edwards well enough to know the man was weighing the risk of action versus inaction. In situations like this, every decision had a domino effect, and the weight of those consequences could alter the course of history. The last thing anyone wanted was for this situation to escalate before it had to.

Finally, the Admiral's voice returned, low and measured. "Alright. You're right. We can't afford to tip our hand yet. Let me get a few things in motion on this end, but we'll keep it quiet. I'll have my team run a simulation of the Humber collision scenario. Get some noise out there, make it look like an unfortunate maritime accident. I'll also get the RAF monitoring the area, but strictly in a passive capacity, no active intervention unless it's absolutely necessary."

Kelvin breathed a small sigh of relief. "Good. But make sure the weather report matches the accident timeline. If we're going with the fog and the storm, everything needs to line up perfectly. I don't want the Coastguard to notice anything unusual about the way we're moving ships around."

Kelvin heard the Admiral chuckle, and he didn't understand what made the Admiral laugh at first. But then Edwards spoke, his voice tinged with dark humour, "You know, Svenson, sometimes I wonder if you've got the entire weather department on speed dial. Always with the perfect conditions for disaster. Anyway, half of the Coastguard are made up of former military, so they'll keep their mouths shut about anything that might smell a little fishy. We'll make it look natural, like a simple accident. No one will question it. Just make sure we have the backup plans in place, in case something goes wrong."

Kelvin allowed himself a brief, tired smile. "I'll leave the weather to you, Admiral. I just make sure we don't miss the opportunity. I'll forward all the necessary intel to your team."

"Good," Edwards replied. "I'll get my people to handle it. And Svenson," he added, the tone suddenly shifting to something more serious, "you've got a hell of a job on your hands. Make sure it goes smoothly. Too much is riding on this."

"Understood," Kelvin said, nodding despite the fact that the Admiral couldn't see him. "I'll stay on top of it. We'll keep this quiet for as long as we can."

With that, the call ended, and Kelvin sat back in his chair, staring at the screen in front of him. The weight of what he had just set in motion settled on him like a brick. A covert strike that could prevent a catastrophe, but one that also carried the potential to spiral into an international incident if even the smallest detail went wrong.

He couldn't afford to let his mind wander, but the implications of what he was dealing with were immense. The RS-28 Sarmat missile was not just any weapon. It was a symbol of Russia's resolve to destabilise the West, and it had been placed squarely into the hands of the Irish Restoration Government. If the missile made it to Dublin, the entire European power balance would shift—potentially beyond repair.

Kelvin reached for the map on the wall, tracing his fingers across the projected route of the Su Li, marking the coordinates where it would pass along the North Sea, into British waters. Aberdeen. That was where the interception would need to occur. The fog would be thick, and the visibility would be near zero. It was the perfect storm, metaphorically speaking. The simulated collision could work. It had to work. But he couldn't shake the thought that the world was watching, even if no one knew it yet.

Getting up, he knew that his next stop was the Middle East desk, as he needed to see what was happening with the Iranian angle. He needed confirmation that the RS-28 Sarmat missile was, in fact, on its way to Belfast. As it was on the same floor, but the opposite end of Vauxhall Cross, Kelvin knew that it would make much more sense to walk over to the Middle East desk in person rather than deal with another round of calls. The atmosphere in the building felt like a brewing storm, and he knew that even a small misstep could send everything spiralling into chaos.

As he walked down the long corridors of Vauxhall Cross, the noise of his boots echoing off the marble floors, Kelvin found himself reflecting on the complexities of the situation. He'd always prided himself on his ability to think several steps ahead, but this one? This one felt different. The RS-28 Sarmat was not just a missile—it was a statement. A declaration from Russia that it would not stand idly by as the West reshaped the map. And now, with the Irish Restoration Government caught between its allegiance to Russia and its own fragile position in the international community, the stakes had never been higher.

The Middle East desk was tucked away in a corner of the building, its windows looking out over the Thames. Inside, the atmosphere was quieter than usual, the soft hum of computers and occasional rustling of papers serving as the backdrop to the steady pulse of intelligence work.

"Kelvin," a voice called from the back, and he turned to find Rania Al-Hadid, the analyst in charge of the Iran portfolio, standing in the doorway of her office. She was sharp, quick to pick up on shifts in the geopolitical landscape, and if anyone could help him navigate the Iranian angle, it was her.

"Rania," he greeted, walking toward her. "I need some intel on the RS-28 Sarmat. Specifically, whether it's on its way to Belfast as part of this operation. I've got a ship, Su Li, making its way across the globe, and I've got intel suggesting it's carrying something far more dangerous than agricultural supplies."

Rania nodded, her brow furrowing as she processed the information. "I've heard rumblings. The Sarmat is a showpiece for the Russians, an ICBM capable of delivering multiple nuclear warheads, and Iran's been increasingly receptive to Russian military cooperation. I wouldn't be surprised if the missile is en route. I'll need to pull up the latest satellite data and see if we've intercepted anything that confirms its movement."

"I'll need to speak to our Israel guys, see what they have to say about them getting Mossad to hang fire on destroying the Su Li," Kelvin added, running a hand through his hair in frustration. "If the Mossad gets involved, they'll do it with all the fanfare of a Hollywood blockbuster. I need this kept quiet, Rania—subtlety is key. I've got the Royal Navy running some simulation computations on a collision scenario, but we need more confirmation before moving forward."

"A collision scenario? What do you mean? A Type 23 colliding with a freighter?" Rania raised an eyebrow, her interest piqued by the tactical approach.

Kelvin paused, unsure how much to reveal. Rania's sharp gaze made him hesitate, knowing she was piecing together the larger picture faster than most. It wasn't that he didn't trust her—it was just that this was the kind of operation where everything could crumble if the wrong people got too curious. And the last thing they needed was a flare-up.

"Not quite a Type 23. More like... a rough approach. Think of it like the Humber incident in 2025, but this time, we've got more at stake." Kelvin exhaled slowly. "If the Su Li makes it to Belfast and offloads something that shouldn't be there, we're looking at more than just an international shipping issue. We're talking nuclear escalation. We need to get our hands on the Su Li, intercept it, make it disappear. And it has to look like an accident—bad weather, rough seas, a freak collision—anything. If it goes any other way, we risk triggering an international crisis."

Rania's eyes sharpened as the weight of Kelvin's words settled into the air between them. She leaned back in her chair, folding her arms as she processed the complexities of the situation. Her usual quick-fire responses were replaced with a more deliberate silence.

"So, you're telling me that we're going to fake a collision, just to get our hands on a ship carrying an ICBM? And you need it to be *clean*—no mess, no flags raised," she said slowly, her voice tinged with disbelief but also a sharp understanding of the stakes. "How on earth are we supposed to pull that off without anyone getting wind of it?"

Kelvin ran a hand over his face, the exhaustion of the last few days weighing on him. "It's going to be tight, Rania. But it's the only way we can stop this from escalating into a nuclear crisis. The Su Li has to disappear before it reaches Belfast. If we let it dock, the Restoration Government could have a weapon capable of wiping out half of Western Europe."

Rania nodded slowly. She leaned forward, unlocking her computer with a few swift keystrokes. "I get it, Kelvin. The world's balance is teetering on the edge, and you need it to stay quiet. But we don't have the luxury of time. The weather window is a brief one, and if the Mossad or anyone else catches wind of this, we'll be in a whole world of trouble."

Kelvin watched her fingers fly across the keyboard, already pulling up satellite data on the Su Li's route and anything that could help corroborate his suspicions. He could see the analytical wheels turning in her head as she reviewed the available intel. Rania was one of the best, and if there was anyone who could verify the Iranian angle, it was her.

"I'll get on this," she said, her tone professional but with a hint of something else—concern, perhaps. "But I'll need you to keep me in the loop with the Royal Navy's simulations and any intel you get on the missile. The timing's everything, and if there's anything I've learned, it's that things often go sideways when you're playing with this kind of fire."

Kelvin's phone buzzed, interrupting the tense moment. He glanced down at the secure message, reading it in silence for a few seconds. It was from the Admiral. A simple line: *The simulation is set. Ready to move when you are.*

He put the phone down and met Rania's eyes. "We've got a go from the Navy. They're running the collision simulation now. I've got the weather conditions lined up—fog, low visibility, storm warnings. It'll look like an unfortunate accident, just like Humber. But we need confirmation from your side. If we're going to pull this off, everything has to align perfectly."

Rania's lips tightened into a thin line. "I'll get you the confirmation, Kelvin. But we need to be cautious. If anything goes wrong, we'll be left holding the bag, and the world's going to notice. We can't afford to slip up."

Kelvin nodded, his mind already racing ahead to the next steps. "I know. That's why we have to be careful. If the Mossad gets wind of it, they'll make their move, and they won't hesitate to go full throttle. It's better we do it our way—no drama, no headlines, just a quiet, controlled situation."

Rania stood up, moving to her filing cabinet and pulling out a few satellite images. "I'll cross-reference this with our sources in Tehran. If there's one thing I know about the Iranians, it's that they love to play their cards close to their chest. But I've got a few friends in high places. They owe me one. I'll make some calls and get back to you. Don't go poking the bear just yet. We still need to see if the bear's even awake."

Kelvin gave a wry smile. "Fair enough. I'll be waiting."

As Rania headed out, Kelvin felt the weight of the operation bearing down on him again. It wasn't just the risk of nuclear escalation that haunted him, but the complexity of the web he had just stepped into. The Restoration Government's allegiance to Moscow, the Iranian involvement, and the potential fallout from any action they took—it was a volatile mix that had the potential to tear Europe apart.

Kelvin stood at the edge of Rania's office, watching as she disappeared into the back corridors of Vauxhall Cross. The hum of the building seemed louder now, almost like it was alive with anticipation, the weight of the situation pressing in on him from all sides. His fingers tightened around the manifest again, the paper now crinkled from the grip. The facts were undeniable: the Su Li was carrying far more than just agricultural supplies, and if this ship made it to Belfast, the implications could be catastrophic.

His thoughts kept returning to the RS-28 Sarmat missile. A weapon that could tip the balance of power in Europe. It wasn't just a weapon—it was a message, an indication that Russia was not just observing the geopolitical shifts in the West, but actively pushing them. Iran's willingness to play ball, to support the Restoration Government's nuclear ambitions, only served to escalate the stakes. The idea that such a missile could be delivered, transported covertly across the seas, and unloaded in a city already a hotbed of unrest was chilling.

* _ * _ * _ *

"We go live to the Old Bailey, where Ian Johnson MP has been on trial for the past week, accused of espionage and conspiring with foreign powers to undermine UK security. Johnson, once a rising star in the Unite the Union backed Communist Party had been elected to the Kingswinford and South Staffordshire seat when Mike Wood, the then incumbent, had been forced to resign amidst a scandal involving undeclared lobbying for foreign interests. Johnson's rise had been rapid, yet his fall had been just as spectacular. Now, as the trial nears its conclusion, the courtroom is abuzz with anticipation of the verdict. His allies are standing by, hoping against hope that the court will deliver a more lenient outcome, but the mounting evidence against him makes this unlikely. Carl Peterson is there live for us, Carl?"

Kelvin looked up at the television in shock, as he watched Carl Peterson's familiar face flash onto the screen. His mind raced, trying to piece together the sudden turn of events. He knew that Carl had been a Manic Goldies Ireland host, but after being PNG'd along with his wife, Emma, and half of the British Embassy in Dublin staff, Kelvin was unaware that Peterson had got a job at the BBC, and was now covering the high-profile trial of Ian Johnson, the same MP who had been implicated in espionage and collaboration with Russian intelligence. Kelvin had been so wrapped up in the Su Li operation and the geopolitical tension surrounding the Restoration Government's nuclear ambitions that he had lost track of the smaller, seemingly more local stories. But now, seeing Carl's face on the screen, his focus shifted. What was Carl doing in the Old Bailey? Why was he reporting on a case that was directly tied to the situation with the missile?

Kelvin's eyes narrowed as he listened to Carl's report, the familiar voice ringing in his ears. Carl had always had a knack for getting to the heart of a story, but now there was something different about the way he spoke, something too measured for an ordinary reporter. His words were clipped, careful, and Kelvin's instincts told him that Carl knew more than he was letting on.

"Yes, that's right, Clive," Carl was saying, his voice steady but with a hint of tension. "As the evidence against Johnson continues to mount, it's becoming clear that his connections to foreign powers aren't just a matter of a few shady meetings or lobbying. There's been talk of more significant involvement, possibly with state actors. Some whispers are even suggesting that Johnson may have been privy to covert operations, the likes of which the public have yet to hear about. His ties to Russia could go much deeper than anyone expected."

Kelvin's heart skipped a beat as Carl dropped the bombshell in the middle of his report. *Ties to Russia.* The words echoed through his mind, a chilling reminder of just how deep the rot went, and how careful they had to be. This wasn't just a political scandal; this was the kind of exposure that could unravel everything—his operation, the Restoration Government's collaboration with Russia, the whole fragile web that had been carefully constructed. The very mention of Russian involvement in a public trial like this could trigger an international response that they were not ready for.

Carl, however, wasn't giving much away. The camera zoomed in on him for a moment, capturing his intense focus, but Kelvin could see the flicker of recognition in Carl's eyes, as if he too was playing a role in something bigger than the simple reporting of events.

"Hang on, Clive, I'm just getting word that the Jury have returned from deliberations, and it looks like the verdict is about to be read," Carl's voice cut through the static of the broadcast, pulling Kelvin's attention fully to the screen. The moment felt like a jolt, as if the world had paused for just a second. He could feel the room's tension thickening, the impact of this trial echoing far beyond the Old Bailey. "We've got live pictures from inside the courtroom now, as the judge is preparing to deliver the verdict on Ian Johnson MP. This trial has captivated the nation, and the outcome could have serious ramifications, not just for Johnson himself, but for the ongoing investigation into Russia's influence here in the UK. Stay tuned."

The television then turned to inside the courtroom where the judge, Sir Thomas Harvey, a High Court judge with a reputation for his no-nonsense approach, stood at the bench. The courtroom fell into a heavy silence, the kind that only comes when the verdict of a high-profile case is about to be delivered.

Kelvin's mind raced, a thousand thoughts spinning in the space between the flickering image on the screen and his real-time situation. He knew the stakes. He knew that the trial of Ian Johnson had the potential to send shockwaves far beyond the walls of the Old Bailey. This wasn't just about a Communist MP with ties to Russia; this was a much bigger issue. This was about exposing the deepest, darkest corners of the geopolitical battlefield. The public might think they were watching a scandal unfold in real-time, but Kelvin knew better. They were witnessing the unravelling of a much grander operation, one that had the potential to reshape the global power dynamics in ways they hadn't yet realised.

As Sir Thomas Harvey began to speak, Kelvin leaned forward, ignoring the rising tension in his own body. The judge's voice was steady as he read the charges: espionage, conspiracy, and collaboration with foreign state actors—charges that carried consequences far beyond what Johnson had ever imagined when he first entered politics. The courtroom, however, was in a state of stunned silence as the Jury returned the verdicts.

"On the count of espionage," the foreperson of the Jury said clearly, "we find the defendant, Ian Johnson, guilty."

A heavy silence seemed to settle over the courtroom, the words hanging in the air like a heavy cloud. Kelvin's heart pounded in his chest as he watched the broadcast. The camera zoomed in on Johnson's face—eyes wide, his posture stiff as he tried to keep his composure. But there was no hiding the panic, the realization that everything he had worked for was slipping away.

Johnson's fate was sealed, and the public would soon know the depth of his involvement in the broader geopolitical chaos. For Kelvin, the news was a bittersweet victory—he had suspected that Johnson's ties to Russia were more than just political manoeuvring, but seeing the charges laid out so clearly on a national stage made the stakes feel all the more real. The trial wasn't just about one man—it was about a much larger web of international intrigue, with tendrils extending far beyond London's courtrooms.

The foreperson of the Jury continued, his voice a sharp contrast to the tense atmosphere that now gripped the courtroom. "On the count of conspiracy to undermine national security through collaboration with foreign intelligence agencies, we find the defendant guilty."

Kelvin felt a flicker of something cold settle over him. His initial reaction was one of relief that Johnson's actions had been exposed, but that fleeting emotion quickly shifted. The exposure of Johnson's treachery was only a small part of the larger puzzle he was trying to piece together. Johnson's role, while critical, was just one cog in a much more dangerous machine that stretched from Moscow to the Restoration Government in Ireland—and potentially even further.

As the guilty verdicts were delivered one by one, the weight of the reality hit Kelvin like a punch to the gut. Johnson had been an asset. His value to Russian intelligence had been immense, and his fall from grace was going to have ripple effects that reached all the way to the very heart of European security. The Restoration Government, now exposed for its ties to Russia, would find itself caught in the glare of the international spotlight. The problem was, Johnson wasn't the only one involved in these clandestine operations, and the rest of the web was still being carefully unravelled.

In the courtroom, the camera captured Johnson's faint grimace, a man who had been stripped of his political career and now faced a long, uncertain road to his sentencing. But for Kelvin, the moment was far from over. It was only just beginning.

The news cycle would erupt with the verdict. Headlines would scream about Russia's meddling in British politics, but Kelvin knew better than to assume it would all come crashing down in one fell swoop. The players behind the scenes—intelligence agencies, foreign governments, and shadowy figures pulling the strings—would be watching closely. And for them, this was just one of many moves on the chessboard.

As the broadcast switched to the post-verdict analysis, Kelvin turned back to the task at hand. His mind, sharp and focused as ever, was already racing ahead. He couldn't afford to dwell on the trial for too long—there was still the matter of the missile, the RS-28 Sarmat, and the quiet, carefully orchestrated operation he had set in motion. The Sarmat's journey to Belfast was no longer just an intelligence operation; it was now a ticking time bomb.

He had to move quickly, calculating the next step in his plans. The Navy's simulation would give him a window to act, but he had no illusions about the risks involved. If they didn't act fast, the situation in Ireland could escalate into something catastrophic. The Restoration Government's plans, with Russian backing, had the potential to ignite a conflict that would make the ongoing war in Ukraine seem trivial by comparison. The Sarmat wasn't just a missile—it was a statement. And that statement, if it reached Irish soil, would send shockwaves through the entire world.

****

CHAPTER 18 – A Manic Lawsuit
Wednesday 14th February 2029

The news spread across Thames House like wildfire. Manic Radio CEO Lord James Jenkins KC had filed 30 lawsuits in 24 hours against not just the Restoration Government in Ireland, but several officials, including the Head of the State Information Office, Sinead Ryan, the President of Russia, Vladimir Putin, the CEO of Raidió Teilifís Éireann, Alistair O'Rourke, the editorial board of The Irish Times, the Russian Ambassador to Great Britain, Ivan Kelin, the Rossiya Segodnya CEO, Dimitry Kiselyov, Sergey Naryshkin, the SVR Director, and even, in an audacious move that had analysts choking on their morning coffee, the Russian Ministry of Defence itself.

It was a legal blitzkrieg—one that even the most seasoned MI5 operatives had to admire for its sheer audacity. Jenkins, never one to shy away from confrontation, had launched a full-scale lawfare campaign against half the geopolitical players in the ongoing Irish crisis. The sheer scope of the lawsuits had left legal teams scrambling across London, Dublin, and Brussels, not to mention causing a bureaucratic meltdown in Moscow.

Liam Powell sat in the Nexus, his fingers steepled in front of him as he listened to Harry Potter, who was now rattling off the details.

"The lawsuit against Sinead Ryan accuses her of 'orchestrating a campaign of defamation and corporate sabotage against a British media organisation,'" Harry said, barely concealing his amusement. "He's also suing

RTE's CEO, Alistair O'Rourke, for 'knowingly engaging in unlawful competition on behalf of a rogue state.' The Irish Times board is being sued for—wait for it—'publishing articles that seek to undermine the financial interests of a UK-registered corporation and disseminating Russian-backed disinformation.'"

Oliver Stokes let out a low whistle. "So, basically, he's going for everyone who's spoken against him in the past year."

Liam exhaled, rubbing his temple. "And the lawsuit against Putin?"

"Officially? Crimes against commercial interests. Unofficially? Its MBS who owns Manic, so it's a Saudi power play disguised as corporate litigation. Jenkins is the attack dog, but this is Riyadh sending a very clear message to Moscow: 'Stay out of Ireland, or we will make this very expensive for you,'" Harry said, flipping through the case files on his secure tablet. "Ashley Tabor-King has a lot to answer for, corrupting Jenkins during his time at Global, but even he wouldn't have had the balls to sue the Kremlin directly... shit... another lawsuit has just been put in the system."

Liam sighed heavily, rubbing his face with both hands. "Jesus Christ, another one? Who's he suing now? The bloody weather?"

Harry tapped his screen. "Wouldn't put it past him at this point. But no, this one's against JD Vance. He's filed in London, Brussels, Saudi, DC and Canberra. In plain English, it's because Vance is giving silent approval for

Putin to undermine a commercial broadcaster by declaring a member of its staff Persona Non Grata in Ireland. Jenkins is arguing that by refusing to condemn Russia's interference in Ireland's media landscape, Vance is actively harming British commercial interests and violating international trade agreements. RICO and the Patriot Act have also been invoked."

Sam Holloway let out a low chuckle. "So, let me get this straight—Jenkins has just declared war on Russia, Ireland, and now the sitting President of the United States? In British and EU courts? That's ambitious, even for him."

Alison Harper's voice came through on the secure line from Birmingham, where she was still embedded at Manic. "It's not just ambitious—it's bloody insane. Do you have any idea how much paperwork is flying around Manic's legal department right now? Half the team on conference calls with Riyadh, trying to make sure they're not about to get hauled into the ICJ for filing frivolous lawsuits against multiple sovereign states. Jenkins, however, is strutting round like Napoleon ready to move Generals. You know, he didn't get the legal team to write the suits either."

Liam raised an eyebrow. "Wait—he didn't get his legal team to draft these? Then who the hell wrote them?"

Alison sighed audibly over the secure line. "Him. All of them. Every single one. The mad bastard locked himself in his office overnight, had a steady stream of coffee and God knows what else, and hammered them out himself. And I mean, not even dictating them to an assistant—

personally typing out thousands of pages of legal filings. He was still in the same suit from yesterday when I saw him this morning, and if I didn't know better, I'd say he hadn't slept."

Oliver let out a low whistle. "I don't know whether to be impressed or deeply concerned."

"I'd go with both," Alison shot back. "The legal department is in meltdown, PR is shitting bricks, and I'm fairly sure the Saudis are having second thoughts about giving Jenkins the keys to the kingdom. Riyadh wanted an aggressive corporate strategy, not a lawsuit against half the world."

Harry chuckled, shaking his head. "Well, it's not like he hasn't done something ridiculous before. But this? This is a new level of bonkers. Suing Russia's Ministry of Defence? What does he think they're going to do—turn up to a London courtroom and start filing counterclaims?"

Sam leaned back, crossing his arms. "Oh, don't worry. The Russians will respond. Maybe not in court, but if you think the SVR and FSB are going to just let this slide without throwing some chaos back at him, you're underestimating how petty Moscow can be."

"Yeah, but his bodyguard is "ex" Saudi Special Forces," Alison added. "If the SVR even thinks about sending someone to put the fear of God into him, they'll find themselves dangling from the top of the Colmore Building here in Brum by their ankles before they even get a chance to say 'privyet'. Jenkins isn't just a loose cannon—he's a loose cannon with a security detail trained by Riyadh's finest. And I don't need to remind you that when the Saudis play these kinds of games, they don't lose."

"HARPER, WHO THE HELL ARE YOU ON THE PHONE TO?" the voice of James Jenkins bellowed in the background, his distinctive cut-glass RP accent carrying a sharp edge of irritation.

Liam knew that Jenkins was aware that MI5, MI6, the BND, GIP and possibly the Russian foreign intelligence services were all encamped in One Snow Hill and the Colmore Building, two buildings opposite each other in Birmingham, the former shared with KMPG and the latter with Amey and Zurich, meaning that even in the corporate sprawl of central Birmingham, the intelligence agencies had more or less set up permanent shop, keeping tabs on Jenkins and his increasingly unpredictable moves.

"Oh," Jenkins the said, coming into view of the camera. "You're reporting in that I've just declared war on half the bloody planet, aren't you?" Jenkins smirked, adjusting his cufflinks with the kind of casual arrogance that suggested he was either completely unfazed by the geopolitical earthquake he'd just set off—or he was riding the adrenaline high of having done it.

Alison turned the camera slightly, so Jenkins was now fully visible on the secure feed, his expression one of tired but unwavering determination. "Yes, my Lord," she said dryly, "just making sure that the various intelligence agencies monitoring your every move are fully aware that you've decided to become an international legal menace."

Jenkins gave a theatrical sigh. "Oh, come now, Harper, I think 'legal menace' is a bit strong. I prefer strategic litigation to defend British interests in the face of state-backed economic aggression."

Oliver groaned, rubbing his temples. "Jesus Christ, Jenkins, you've sued the Russian MoD. Do you actually think Sergey Shoigu is going to rock up to the High Court with a briefcase and a defence statement?"

Jenkins gave a smug smile. "That depends. If they don't respond, it's de facto evidence of guilt, and I'll just push for summary judgement. If they do respond, they legitimise my argument that they're interfering with British commercial operations. Either way, I win."

Liam exhaled slowly, pinching the bridge of his nose. "You do realise you've just put yourself at the top of Moscow's 'people to be very annoyed at' list? And that list tends to come with… consequences."

Jenkins gave a dismissive wave. "Let them be annoyed. You think I'm scared of some bored FSB desk jockey pushing my name up the kill list between tea breaks? If they want to play dirty, fine. I play dirty too. The difference is—I'm better at it. Anyway, the Crown Prince gave me the nod yesterday, so Moscow can complain all it likes, but they won't dare touch me unless they fancy their gas deals going south overnight."

Liam leaned forward, his patience wearing thin. "Jenkins, you've just taken a swing at multiple sovereign governments, Russia's intelligence apparatus, the Irish state media, and—just for good measure—the sitting

President of the United States. You do realise that none of these people take kindly to being dragged into court like it's some bloody corporate pissing contest?"

Jenkins smirked, completely unfazed. "And? Let them take it personally. Vance is a political corpse walking; he won't even make it to the end of his term without collapsing under his own contradictions. MBS has asked me to make Musk's life hell, so I've just submitted a lawsuit against him in London and DC for 'knowingly facilitating state-backed cyber warfare operations against British commercial entities' under Saudi jurisdiction. That'll keep him busy. And as for Moscow—well, I know there's half a dozen SVR officers here... I've got a list if you fancy shipping them back to Moscow in a crate labelled 'Return to Sender'." Jenkins flashed a toothy grin, clearly relishing the chaos he had unleashed.

Liam let out a long, slow breath, trying to ignore the throbbing headache forming behind his eyes. "You're playing a very dangerous game here, Jenkins. You do realise that? You're not just making legal threats—you're inviting state actors with a long history of making people disappear to take an interest in you."

Jenkins leaned against Alison's desk, arms crossed, utterly unconcerned. "Oh, Liam, if I started worrying about every intelligence service with a grudge against me, I'd never get anything done. Besides, I'm a peer, a KC, a public figure. That means that I'm more useful to them alive than dead. Killing me would be messy, and messy is bad for business. The Russians know it, the Americans know it, and even the Irish know it. No one wants to be seen as the one who took out a British lord over a lawsuit—especially when that lawsuit happens to have the full weight of Riyadh behind it. Which reminds me, His Excellency has provided me a list of every SVR, GRU and FSB officer in current employ. Would you like to guess what I'm about to do? I'm going to get a chopper down to Whitehall, and hand it to the Minister, and arrange for some nice lovely sanctions to be applied. It's useful when you're in the same Mayfair Clubs as Mr Lammy, Mrs Cooper, Lord Coaker and Sir Keir."

Liam rubbed his temples again, the weight of the situation pressing down on him. He knew that Jenkins wasn't just making threats for effect—he was an expert manipulator who knew exactly how to leverage his position, his wealth, and, most importantly, his connections. The situation was spiralling out of control, and every step Jenkins took seemed to make it worse.

The way that he casually name dropped David Lammy, the foreign secretary, Yvette Cooper, the Home Secretary, and other key political figures was a reminder of the sheer influence Jenkins wielded, even if it was not always apparent. It was one thing to have the ear of powerful figures in government, but it was quite another to be able to leverage those connections with such reckless abandon, as he was doing now.

"Christ, Jenkins, you're playing with fire here," Liam muttered under his breath, barely managing to keep his voice steady. "The fact that you're comfortable making enemies with everyone from the Kremlin to the White House tells me you're either incredibly brave or incredibly foolish."

Jenkins flashed a sly smile, his eyes glinting with that all-too-familiar confidence. "I'm not afraid of fire, Liam. If I had been, Ashley wouldn't have hired me back in 2006 and sent me as a spy in GCap to infiltrate the enemy's ranks. If I had been, I wouldn't have tried a year and half ago to push Ashley out of Global and, even though I failed my coup, wouldn't have made Global the biggest British player before Manic offered me a nine figure salary. If I'd been afraid of fire, I wouldn't have done any of this. And now, look at me—at the top of my game. You can call it foolish, but in this world, if you're not stirring the pot, you're not playing at the level that matters. Moscow, the White House, even the Irish—everyone's watching me now, and that's exactly where I want them."

Liam clenched his jaw, trying to keep his composure. Jenkins wasn't wrong. Whether his strategy was reckless or genius, he had certainly taken control of the narrative. In one fell swoop, he had forced nearly every major player on the world stage to take notice, and now they were all caught in his web. The scope of Jenkins' legal blitzkrieg was staggering, and the ripple effects would be felt far beyond the immediate legal battles.

It was then that Liam noticed that James had admitted to trying a coup in the boardroom of Global, just a year and a half ago. That moment, which failed coup, had clearly shaped Jenkins. The man sitting before him now was far more dangerous than Liam had anticipated—a man who knew how to leverage not just his legal expertise but also the shadows where politics, money, and media intertwined. Jenkins was no longer just a corporate giant; he was an active player in the great geopolitical game, and he had the tools to make waves that could change the course of nations.

The intelligence files on Lord James Jenkins KC had it as if he had left Global with Ashley Tabor-King's blessing and a reputation as a corporate mastermind. But now, after months of intrigue, it was clear: he had tried to depose the founder of Global Media, and in doing so, had exposed himself as a player willing to risk everything—not just for control of a media empire, but for a piece of the broader power struggle engulfing the world. Jenkins was no longer just a businessman; he had become a geopolitical force, and that made him dangerous.

The bit that shocked him as well was the casual way that Jenkins had admitted that he had spied on GCap Media for Tabor-King in 2006, a company that had ultimately sold to Global before Jenkins had left. That was a revelation—one that painted Jenkins in an even darker light. It was one thing to be a ruthless businessman, but quite another to play those kinds of games under the radar, working for powerful figures who were shaping the media landscape and world affairs behind closed doors.

"All right, Jenkins," Liam said, leaning forward with a cold, controlled tone. "I get it. You've made a splash. You've got half the world's major players looking over their shoulders. But you're not just throwing a legal tantrum. You've stirred a hornet's nest, and now you've got to deal with the fallout. These aren't just legal suits you've filed. These are declarations of war in a different kind of battlefield."

Jenkins smiled again, leaning back in his chair, his expression unfazed. "Fallout? What fallout? I've got a hand to play that no one else does. They don't know it yet, but I'm untouchable. Sure, they'll try to make me sweat, send some boys in black suits to knock on my door, or have their propagandists rant on TV. But in the end, I control the narrative. I always have, and now I control the world's media. A few lawsuits are the least of my worries. When you have the right people on your side, you can make anyone bend the knee."

Liam tried not to let his frustration show, but it was becoming more difficult with every word Jenkins uttered. The man was either completely blind to the dangers he had unleashed or completely confident in his ability to handle them, and either option was equally terrifying. Jenkins was no longer playing by the rules. He was rewriting them, and the geopolitical ramifications were becoming increasingly clear.

"You've stirred up Russia, you've tangled with the EU, you've made a mess of US politics, and you've made the Irish Restoration Government look like a puppet show," Liam said, his voice tightening with the weight of it all. "And you've done it all while keeping Riyadh in your back pocket and using MBS's influence to shield you. But at some point, even the Crown Prince will run out of patience. What's next? You really think the Kremlin will let you mock them with impunity forever? What happens when the Saudis decide they've had enough of your antics?"

Jenkins' smile remained unwavering, his eyes gleaming with a dangerous resolve. "You underestimate the power of leverage, Liam. Moscow will squirm, but they won't make a move until I give them a reason to. As for Riyadh, they're pissed because Putin hasn't paid OPEC in over a year, so they're hardly going to stop backing me now. I'm more valuable to them than any one lawsuit or diplomatic issue. The rest of the world will have to adjust to that reality. I'm playing a long game, Liam. The world might think it's just a bunch of lawyers running around with papers, but behind those papers is power—real power."

Liam's frustration boiled over, but he kept his voice steady. "Power? Power doesn't last forever. You can't buy loyalty from every corner of the world, Jenkins. Not when it's convenient for others to make you a target. Sooner or later, someone's going to make you bleed, and it won't be through a courtroom. You've pissed off too many people who have no patience for your games."

Jenkins met his gaze with a knowing smile, as if he had already anticipated every objection. "Let them try, Liam. If they come for me, they'll have to fight a war of attrition. The courtroom is my arena, it's my rules, and I know exactly how to win it."

"And in breaking news," the television in the corner of the Nexus flashed on, interrupting the tense moment between Liam and Jenkins. The screen displayed a news anchor, her face reflecting the gravity of the situation. "The Irish Restoration Government has released a statement condemning the recent legal actions taken by Lord James Jenkins KC. In a strongly worded statement, the Irish government has accused Jenkins of attempting to use his vast financial and legal resources to interfere with the sovereignty of the Irish state. The statement claims that his lawsuits are a direct attack on Ireland's democratic institutions and its ongoing struggle against foreign influence. The Head of the State Information Office, Sinead Ryan, has vowed to defend Ireland's integrity in the face of this unprecedented legal assault."

The sound of James Jenkins laughing on the video chat was not one that Liam had expected.

"You know, Powell, I'm looking forward to Ryan's presser," Jenkins then said, chuckling. "Don't tell my missus, Lady Carly, but Sinead Ryan's Ri Chun-hee impression reminds me of her when she's pissed off with Seb or Ollie when they've done a Global Player podcast instead of their college coursework."

Liam knew that Jenkins has two sons, both twins, Sebastian and Oliver Jenkins, a duo of podcasters who have a podcast called "Life with Radio's Darth Vader"— a satirical look at their father's career and the cutthroat world of commercial radio. The fact that Jenkins could compare the mouthpiece of a Russian-backed government to his wife scolding their kids over college work was, in equal parts, hilarious and deeply concerning.

"Anyway, Big Vlad has a Red Notice on him by Zelenskyy, from before he died, so it'll be fun watching Russia try to argue jurisdiction when they don't even recognise half the international legal bodies that I've filed with," Jenkins continued, still grinning. "Besides, if they do counter-sue in those courts, that implicates that they recognise the jurisdiction of the very legal systems they've spent years dismissing as 'Western propaganda.' It's a beautiful trap, Powell. They either ignore it and let me chip away at their international reputation—or they engage, and in doing so, they legitimise the very institutions they claim to despise. Either way, I win."

Liam exhaled slowly, glancing at his colleagues in the Nexus. Oliver looked mildly impressed, Harry was outright grinning, and Sam just shook his head in weary disbelief. Alison, who Jenkins was standing behind on the call from Birmingham, had her head in her hands, clearly wondering how on earth she had ended up playing handler to the most chaotic corporate executive in British history.

Liam sighed, leaning back in his chair. "So, let me get this straight, Jenkins. You've just forced Moscow, Washington, and Dublin into a legal battle they can't win without undermining their own credibility, all while keeping the Saudis happy and using the media circus to make yourself the most talked-about person in international law?"

Jenkins smirked, adjusting his cufflinks again. "Now you're getting it, Powell. You see, this isn't just a lawsuit. It's lawfare. And when you have the right leverage, lawfare can be just as effective as a missile strike—except you don't need to clean up the mess afterwards."

Oliver let out a low whistle. "And what happens if they decide to respond in kind? What if Russia, Ireland, or the bloody Americans decide that suing you isn't enough, and they start digging into your affairs?"

Jenkins didn't even blink. "Let them. They'll find nothing I haven't already prepared for. The difference between me and them? I know the skeletons in my closet, and I've already priced them into my strategy. Hell, if it brings me down, it brings the Opposition down, Global, ITV, half the British media landscape, and quite a few Cabinet Ministers with it. That's the beauty of leverage, gentlemen—I don't just hold cards, I am the deck."

Liam exhaled sharply. "So that's the game, then? You've wrapped yourself so tightly into the establishment that if you go down, you're taking half of Westminster, Fleet Street, and the commercial broadcast industry with you?"

Jenkins grinned. "Precisely. You see, Powell, people assume power is about control. It's not. It's about making sure that if someone does try to take you down, the collateral damage is so severe that they think twice before pulling the trigger. That's why Global couldn't get rid of me properly after my coup attempt. I know where the skeletons are buried. Hell, I was the one who buried half of Global's skeletons myself. Best thing is, they can't hack into the computer where I keep my own... kompromat... as its deliberately air-gapped."

Kompromat, the art of strategically collecting and deploying compromising material, was something Jenkins had clearly mastered. If what he was saying was true, then not only had he built a legal fortress around himself, but he had also woven himself so tightly into the highest levels of media, business, and politics that any attempt to remove him would be like pulling the pin on a grenade with no safe way to throw it. The fact that Jenkins had air-gapped, or physically isolated, his most sensitive files from any network meant that they were completely immune to cyber-intrusion—something even most intelligence agencies struggled to fully secure. It was a rare move, something only the most paranoid (or the most well-prepared) individuals did. Jenkins wasn't just a media mogul or a legal mastermind—he was playing a game at a level that made most intelligence officers deeply uncomfortable.

There again, Liam thought, *as a Lord and a QC, having a device that was entirely air-gapped made sense.*

Liam exhaled, rubbing his temple again. "Alright, Jenkins, I'll admit it—you've built yourself an impressive house of cards. But don't fool yourself into thinking you're untouchable. Even the best fortresses have weak points, and Moscow, Washington, and Dublin will be looking for every single crack."

Jenkins simply smirked, leaning back against Alison's desk. "Let them look. It'll keep them busy while I make my next move."

Liam narrowed his eyes. "And what exactly is your next move?"

Jenkins shrugged casually. "Depends on how Dublin and Moscow respond. If they panic and issue counter-suits, then I've already won. It signals to British and EU businesses that have been forced by Russia, both because of Ukraine and now Ireland, to hand their businesses to Russia that they can sue as well. That opens the floodgates for every major Western corporation that has had its assets seized or manipulated by Russian influence. It sets a precedent. And once the first few judgements start going in our favour, the financial impact will be catastrophic for

Moscow. And who's Putin more afraid of than his own military and intelligence services?"

Liam exhaled, already knowing the answer. "The oligarchs."

Jenkins nodded, his smirk widening. "Exactly. Putin's iron grip on power isn't about ideology—it's about money. The moment the oligarchs feel their fortunes slipping through their fingers because some arrogant British KC found a legal loophole to sue the Russian state into financial oblivion, they'll start asking uncomfortable questions. And when that happens, Vlad has two options: dig in and risk them turning on him, or cut his losses and make this problem go away. MBS told me when I spoke to him last week in Saudi that he plans to acquire Russian assets on the cheap, to get them out of Moscow's hands and into Riyadh's pockets. If I create the legal conditions that make that easier? Then suddenly, Saudi is in a prime position to take control of key Russian industries while the Kremlin is too busy firefighting to stop it."

Liam leaned back in his chair, staring at Jenkins. The sheer scale of what he was attempting was almost incomprehensible. This wasn't just about a lawsuit or even a series of lawsuits. This was about restructuring global economic power through the courts, using lawfare as a means of economic warfare.

And it was terrifying.

Oliver folded his arms. "So, what you're saying is, you're not just using these lawsuits to protect Manic—you're creating a legal domino effect that could strip Russia of its economic assets, force the Irish Restoration Government into international court battles it can't afford, and put pressure on Vance to stop sitting on the fence."

Jenkins gave a lazy shrug. "It's a simple numbers game, Oliver. Ireland's Restoration Government can't afford the legal fight. Russia can, but what it can't afford is the slow erosion of its economic foothold in Europe. And as for Vance? Well, I doubt he even understands what's going on, but his legal team will. They'll be advising him to either intervene or be seen as weak. Either way, he's forced into a decision he's been trying to avoid."

Liam shook his head in disbelief. "You do realise this is actual geopolitical warfare, right? You've turned a corporate legal strategy into an international conflict."

Jenkins grinned. "Why not? Everyone else has been playing dirty. I'm just doing it with a silk tie and a KC after my name."

Harry, who had been silent for most of the conversation, finally spoke up. "There's just one problem, Jenkins. The Russians don't play fair. They don't care about international courts. They'll retaliate, and they won't do it in a courtroom. They'll do it the old-fashioned way— sanctions, asset freezes, cyber-attacks, and maybe even something a bit more... direct."

Jenkins rolled his eyes. "Oh, please. If they wanted to kill me, they'd have to go through about six layers of Saudi security, an MI5 watchlist, and Lady Carly... and trust me, an Essex girl is someone you wouldn't want to cross."

Liam exhaled, shaking his head. "Jenkins, you've made yourself a target. I hope you understand that."

Jenkins smirked, adjusting his cufflinks. "Oh, I do, Powell. But you're all missing the bigger picture. I didn't just file these lawsuits to win in court. I filed them to force my enemies into a position where they have to respond—publicly, legally, financially. I've turned their own tactics against them. You can't play dirty against a man who has no problem rolling in the mud. And if they don't turn up to court, if they don't defend? Then I'll push in the courts for a ruling under in absentia procedures. That means I can file enforcement actions against their foreign-held assets. Moscow, Dublin, hell—even Washington—would find their overseas holdings suddenly subject to British and European court seizures."

Jenkins leaned forward slightly, his expression darkening just enough to show that he had considered all of this and had already planned for it. "Harry, my dear boy, do you think I'd launch something this monumental without already having my counters prepared? I'm well aware of the collateral this could cause to Musk, Bezos, Zuck, and Rupert—hell, I know exactly how this could boomerang into places I haven't even mentioned yet. News UK only broadcasts because Ash and I allow them to, because Wall Street need a British outlet for Murdoch's American empire... just like Bauer is allowed into the Euro sandpit because otherwise Brussels will take Manic to court over monopoly laws, with Nation being the same for our CMA. There's only two media outlets on radio that have a God given right to a duopoly, and I control Manic, and Ashley controls Global. We only let Rupert play because it suits our interests to have him there. If this kicks off in the courts the way I intend it to, I can make sure that the fallout only lands where I want it to. Anyway, Brussels has already planned for Musky boy, Bezos and Zuck to appear in their competition courtrooms next year anyway, so all I'm doing is moving the timeline up a bit. They'll pressure Vance to put out a statement condemning Putin, so they can save their own arses... and if they block me on their platforms? Well, let's just say that they'll face Lord James Jenkins of Henley-on-Thames KC in an arena that they really don't want to be fighting in—a European courtroom where consumer law and data protection regulations are weighted heavily against them."

Liam leaned back, feeling the weight of what he was hearing. James Jenkins wasn't just playing a corporate game. He wasn't even just playing a geopolitical game. He was reshaping the battlefield itself, warping the rules until they suited him and only him. And worse? He was actually good at it.

Harry was the first to break the silence, letting out a long whistle. "Jesus Christ, Jenkins, you've set the entire global media, corporate, and political ecosystem on fire just to prove a point. You do realise that, right?"

Jenkins grinned, completely unrepentant. "Of course I do, Harry. And the best part? There's not a bloody thing they can do about it."

****

CHAPTER 19 – Over the Sea
Wednesday 14th February 2029

"Seems the Boss is going to have a wake-up call," Colonel Alan Mace muttered, standing in the operations centre of the 996th ISR Wing, his eyes fixed on the Reuters headlines, the news that Lord James Jenkins KC had just filed a wave of lawsuits against half the geopolitical players in the Irish crisis now spreading across international news outlets. Mace exhaled sharply, pinching the bridge of his nose as the feeds continued updating, each more surreal than the last.

"Jesus Christ," Lorna Hayes muttered beside him, scrolling through a separate intelligence terminal. "He really did it. He's gone and dragged the Kremlin, the Irish, and the White House into a bloody legal brawl all at once."

Donald Ryan had to chuckle, the Lieutenant Colonel loading up the Associated Press feed on his own screen. Donald knew that civilian open source websites like the media, along with intelligence chatter from closed networks, were often the first indicators of an unfolding crisis. But even by those standards, this was something else.

"He's not just suing them," Donald muttered, scanning through the details. "He's suing them in every major international jurisdiction that could conceivably hold weight—London, Brussels, Strasbourg, The Hague, here in the US and even Canberra. Best thing is, Manic is a Saudi owned, UK based company that has US, Australian and Eurozone operations, meaning..."

"Meaning that every single one of those jurisdictions has to at least acknowledge the cases, even if they try to dismiss them," Lorna finished, her voice carrying equal parts admiration and disbelief. "This isn't just legal aggression—this is a strategic assault designed to entangle multiple sovereign states in procedural hell."

Donald nodded, glancing at the secure operations board where intelligence feeds from across Five Eyes were updating in real-time. The Kremlin's first reaction had been predictable—dismissal. Russian state media was already spinning it as 'a Western propaganda stunt by an unhinged British aristocrat'. But behind the scenes? SVR communications were showing signs of concern. Jenkins wasn't just any corporate executive. He was a man with connections, wealth, and—most dangerously—a legal strategy that could weaponize economic warfare in a way even Moscow wasn't prepared for.

"Have you got a list of who he's named as defendants?" Mace asked, rubbing his temple as he tried to process the sheer scale of the legal onslaught.

Lorna tapped a few commands into her terminal and brought up the relevant files. "Alright, let's see... Sinead Ryan, the Head of the Irish Restoration Government's State Information Office. Alistair O'Rourke, CEO of RTÉ. The Irish Times editorial board. The Russian Ambassador to the UK, Ivan Kelin. The CEO of Rossiya Segodnya, Dmitry Kiselyov. Sergey Naryshkin, the SVR Director. And, of course, the Russian Ministry of Defence itself."

Donald knew that the CIA Liaison was looking at the listings of the courts that were in the US. "Which court has he filed in the US?" Donald asked, already bracing himself for whatever madness was about to come next.

Lorna exhaled, shaking her head as she read the legal filings. "DC District Court, as well as the Southern District... the Mother Court. For Vance the filings are on the grounds of USC Title 18, Section 241 – Conspiracy Against Rights. Jenkins is arguing that by remaining silent while Russia and Ireland blacklist a British journalist under his employ, the President of the United States is in violation of the First Amendment—interfering with free speech by tacitly endorsing an economic attack against a UK-based news outlet operating in the US. Title 15, Section 1 of the Sherman Act—alleging that Vance's inaction is effectively allowing a monopolistic conspiracy against Manic's commercial operations in the United States. The Patriot Act has also been invoked," Lorna continued, disbelief creeping into her voice.

"Section 805, to be precise," Lorna the continued, scrolling through the filings, disbelief creeping into her voice. "Providing material support to a designated terrorist organisation. He's arguing that, because Russia has been backing paramilitary groups operating in Ireland—including known pro-Russian dissident elements in the North—Vance's refusal to act against Russian influence operations amounts to indirect support for terrorism under US law. Best thing is, it's not against the Office of the President of the United States but against Vance as an individual. Jenkins is going for the personal liability angle. Veep is also being sued for the same, plus USC Title 18, Section 1962 – Racketeer Influenced and

Corrupt Organizations (RICO) Act. He's treating this like a mob case, for God's sake. It's a legal nightmare."

Donald leaned back in his chair, trying to wrap his mind around the scope of Jenkins' move. "So, let me get this straight—he's taking on Russia, Ireland, the US, and even the Irish media establishment... all at once. And he's doing it in a way that forces them to either play along or risk it all. No wonder the Kremlin is getting nervous."

"Exactly," Lorna said, clicking through more documents. "In London, Vance and Musk are facing suits for the British versions of the same charges. Jenkins is attacking their business interests directly, claiming that by enabling Russian economic encroachment into the Irish media market, both the US and UK are complicit in undermining British commercial freedoms. Thames House think he's going to go after Zuck, Bezos and Murdoch if Vance and Musk fail to respond in a way that he deems satisfactory. He's effectively pulled the entire West into a game of high-stakes legal chicken, with a nuclear option on the table if any of them try to go too far. With Moscow and Dublin, his game is different."

Lona then sighed. "Apparently, they owe OPEC money, so he's suing them on behalf of Manic for censoring Manic, politically interfering in their operations by forcing Manic to employ a Political Officer in their Dublin operations, as well as trying to manipulate their editorial direction. He's claiming it's a breach of business sovereignty and international law. Thames House have said that, and you'll love this, he's opening the door for any other business who have been confiscated or regulated by the Dublin or Moscow governments to follow on once he's got either an in absentina or summary judgement ruling. If that happens, he'll have a legal precedent for businesses to launch cases against Russia and Ireland, dragging them through court in a way that will cripple their financials and international standing. It's a hell of a move."

Mace let out a low whistle as he processed the enormity of Jenkins' legal onslaught. "So, let's sum this up: he's not just playing for Manic's survival. He's creating a legal precedent that could destabilise entire economies, and the worst part? He's pulling it off with a legal team that's probably not even aware of the full extent of what he's doing."

"Nah, Five said that that he personally wrote the filings himself," Lorna replied, tapping a few more commands into her terminal. "Apparently, Jenkins didn't even dictate them to anyone. He locked himself away in his office for two straight days, barely sleeping, just hammering out the filings on his own. He's that much of a control freak. This entire legal blitz has his fingerprints all over it."

Donald shook his head in disbelief. "That man is insane. And now he's holding entire nations hostage to his legal genius. I'm not sure if I should be impressed or terrified."

Looking at the clock, Donald then noticed it was 6am EST, which for Joint Base San Antonio, Texas, the home of the Sixteenth Air Force and the 996th Intelligence Wing, meant that it was 5am Central Time. The early morning hour only added to the sense of surreal urgency as they all sat in the sterile glow of the operations centre. A few weeks ago, no one had anticipated James Jenkins, a media mogul, taking the world of intelligence and international politics to court with such a calculated and destructive strategy. And now, everyone was on edge, watching as his legal blitzkrieg unfolded with a ferocity that sent shockwaves through the world's power structures.

"Anyone fancy seeing what FOX & Friends is saying about this?" Mace said, chuckling at how predictable the right wing media was about to respond.

"Oh, yeah, that's about to start its morning show," Lorna replied dryly, her fingers still dancing across the keyboard as she accessed the latest media reactions. "They'll probably call Jenkins a globalist oligarch trying to 'undermine national sovereignty through weaponised lawfare,' or some nonsense about 'woke capitalism gone rogue.' Bet you twenty bucks they bring up George Soros within the first five minutes."

Mace clicked the remote, flipping the main operations centre screen over to FOX News. The early morning broadcast of FOX & Friends was already in full swing, the chirpy yet aggressive tone of the anchors barely concealing the obvious outrage. The banner headline scrolling across the bottom read:

"BRITISH BILLIONAIRE DECLARES WAR ON THE FREE WORLD?"

"...and let's be clear here, folks," the host, Steve Doocy, was saying, adjusting his tie with an air of barely restrained indignation, "this is the real collusion that the mainstream media refuses to talk about. A British aristocrat—one of these so-called 'lords'—thinks he can march into our judicial system and tell the President of the United States how to run the country? I mean, this is outrageous!"

"That's right, Steve," co-host Ainsley Earhardt nodded vehemently. "And it's not just Biden-era deep state leftovers pulling the strings here. This is a coordinated globalist attack on America First policies. This Jenkins guy, he's got Saudi money behind him, he's got EU bureaucrats cheering him on—he's trying to undermine the will of the American people!"

Brian Kilmeade, looking slightly confused as he scrolled through his notes, chimed in. "Uh... yeah, but, didn't Vance not say anything about Russia interfering with Ireland's media? And doesn't this Jenkins guy run a private business? Anyway, Manic is a Saudi owned company, right? And Jenkins is a Kings Counsel and a Lord, meaning that he has a lot of influence—so why is he even getting involved in this? It seems like a personal vendetta more than a business move."

Donald watched as Doocy raised his finger to his ear, and then sighed. "Oh, that's just great... our owner, Rupert Murdoch, has just been named in a suit by Lord Jenkins. Word is coming through that Jenkins is suing him on the grounds of allowing News UK and Ireland to feature a segment on our colleagues in Britain's show on Talk called 'Establishment Watch', which was used to promote disinformation about Manic's ties to Saudi Arabia, implying that Jenkins was little more than an agent of Riyadh. That lawsuit's been filed in London, Sydney, and New York."

The room grew silent as the absurdity of the situation settled in. Donald, Mace, and Lorna all exchanged glances, their faces a mixture of disbelief and a weary kind of admiration. Jenkins wasn't just challenging the powers of Ireland, Russia, and the United States—he was tying them all up in legal knots that would take years to untangle, if they could even begin to untangle them at all.

"Well, if Murdoch's involved now, the stakes have just gone up," Mace said with a grim chuckle, though there was no real humour in it. "This isn't just about Jenkins anymore; it's about the entire media empire and the networks at play behind the scenes."

Lorna nodded, her fingers still flying over the keyboard as she pulled up more information. "Exactly. Now it's not just a war of words or politics. It's corporate warfare at the highest level. Jenkins is opening every door, not just for himself but for anyone with a grudge against Russia or Ireland—or anyone caught in the crossfire."

- * - * - * -

Sinead Ryan was sat in her office, that of the Head of the State Information Office, when a member of the Restoration Government's Ministry of External Affairs entered with a thick stack of legal documents in his hands. Sinead looked up, her face betraying nothing, but her eyes narrowed in immediate concern. The Ministry official didn't need to speak; the legal documents were enough of a statement.

"Which Western imperialist is daring to challenge us now?" Sinead muttered under her breath, more to herself than to the Ministry official standing across from her.

The official cleared his throat and placed the stack of legal papers on her desk with a soft thud. "It's Jenkins, ma'am. Lord James Jenkins."

Sinead's lips twitched into a barely perceptible smile, but it wasn't one of amusement. It was the kind of smile someone wears before they enter battle, even when they know the fight is going to be a bloody one. "Jenkins. Of course."

She reached for the first sheet, her fingers brushing the top of the stack. The moment she saw the words Defendant: Sinead Evelyn Ryan, Ministry for State Information and others, her smile vanished, replaced by a look of disbelief. "He's not just suing us; he's suing the entire government?"

Sinead took a deep breath, her grip tightening on the papers in front of her. The weight of the legal documents felt heavier than their physical form, pressing down on her with the sheer magnitude of their contents. Each page was a declaration of war, not just a legal challenge.

She looked up at the Ministry official, whose face remained neutral, but his eyes betrayed the concern that lurked beneath the surface. "Tell me everything," Sinead demanded, her voice now sharper than before.

The official hesitated for a moment, clearly uncomfortable with the task. "He's not just suing us for defamation or libel, ma'am. He's going after our entire system of governance. Jenkins is claiming that the

Restoration Government have violated international law by censoring Manic Radio, and he's accusing us of manipulating media content and forcing political interference on UK-based commercial entities. Not only that, but the suits go beyond our borders. He's filed in multiple jurisdictions — London, Brussels, New York, and Sydney. This is a full-scale assault."

Sinead's eyes flickered as she processed the information. The stakes were much higher than she had anticipated. Jenkins wasn't just aiming at the government; he was attempting to tie them up in a global web of legal battles that could drain resources and stall their operations for years to come.

"How is this even possible? How does a corporate mogul have the power to launch such an attack on multiple sovereign states?" she muttered, more to herself than to the official in front of her. The world was changing faster than she could keep up, and Jenkins was at the centre of it.

The official shifted uncomfortably, still unsure of how to explain the intricacies of international law in such an explosive case. "Jenkins isn't just a businessman, ma'am. He's connected. He has Saudi backing, legal expertise, and a deep understanding of the systems that govern global trade. His legal team are aggressive, but it seems he's done most of this himself. They're calling it 'strategic litigation', but I think you and I both know it's more like a legal grenade tossed into the middle of an already tense geopolitical landscape."

Sinead ran a hand through her hair, frustration creeping in. This wasn't just a legal issue anymore. Jenkins had successfully weaponized the law, using it not only to challenge the Restoration Government's authority but to attack the very core of its legitimacy in the eyes of the world. She understood what this meant: if he won even one of these cases, the repercussions would be enormous. It would undermine the Restoration Government's position internationally, and in turn, severely damage their ability to maintain control over Irish media.

"What's the situation with the Kremlin?" Sinead asked, her voice now tinged with an undercurrent of worry.

"The Kremlin's official response has been dismissive so far, but internally, there's rising concern," the official replied. "They see this as a personal attack from Jenkins, and they're scrambling to prepare their counters. But it's clear that they weren't expecting this level of legal sophistication. They're trying to downplay it, but they're also looking at ways to retaliate."

"Right. Shut Manic down. Now. Immediately. Send in the Army if you have to. Get the Minister of Defence to issue an executive order under the Emergency Powers Act. If Manic's Irish operations are off the air by the end of the day, it weakens Jenkins' position. He can sue us all he likes, but it won't change the fact that we control the media landscape here," Sinead ordered, her tone sharp and decisive. "I am going to phone President Putin and then go on the air to deliver a statement personally. We need to frame this as a blatant act of Western imperialist aggression against Ireland's sovereignty. We control the narrative here—not Jenkins, not London, not Washington.

The people need to see this for what it is: another attempt by the old colonial powers to subjugate Ireland through legal trickery."

The Ministry official nodded, but his hesitation did not go unnoticed. Sinead narrowed her eyes. "What is it?"

The official cleared his throat. "Ma'am, shutting down Manic's Irish operations is one thing, but we have to consider the consequences. If we move too aggressively, it might play right into Jenkins' hands. He's already filed in multiple jurisdictions. If we make an overt move against him now—militarily, no less—it could validate his claims of political interference and repression. The courts could see it as proof that he's right."

Sinead clenched her jaw, her patience wearing thin. "And if we don't act, he wins by default. I am not going to sit here and allow some jumped-up British aristocrat to dictate the terms of our governance through his bloody courtroom games. Manic is a threat, and threats must be eliminated."

"But Manic is owned by the Crown Prince of Saudi Arabia, ma'am," the official said carefully, clearly trying to gauge her reaction. "And Riyadh isn't exactly known for taking losses lightly. If we go after Manic directly, we won't just be fighting Jenkins—we'll be picking a fight with the Saudis. And given their financial influence in Moscow and their oil leverage over Europe, I doubt even President Putin will want to get into that mess."

Sinead exhaled slowly, pressing her fingers against her temples. The situation was spiralling fast. Jenkins had boxed them in. He had turned what should have been a simple matter of narrative control into a legal and geopolitical nightmare, forcing them to either engage on his terms or risk a devastating loss in the international courts.

She needed time. Time to rally Moscow, time to get Dublin's internal power brokers aligned, and time to craft a counter-strategy that would pull them out of the quicksand Jenkins had just dumped them into.

"Alright," she said at last, her voice firm. "We delay the shutdown order for now. But I want alternatives. Can we disrupt their broadcast infrastructure without making it obvious? Cyber-attacks, regulatory red tape, anything that slows them down but doesn't give Jenkins an easy win?"

The official nodded, relief flickering across his face. "We can try. But Jenkins is prepared for this. He's been playing this game for years—he knows how to protect his assets. He's the former Vice President of Global Media, the former Deputy CEO there. He joined Global when Ashley Tabor-King started it back in 2007 and spent nearly two decades climbing the ranks, outmanoeuvring competitors, and cementing himself as one of the most dangerous legal minds in British media. If anyone has anticipated this move, it's him."

Sinead exhaled sharply, drumming her fingers on the desk. That was the problem with Jenkins—he wasn't just another corporate executive. He was a strategist, a man who had spent years perfecting the art of legal warfare. Every move they made, he had likely planned for. Every counterstrike, he had already accounted for.

"And what about Riyadh?" she asked, her voice edged with tension. "Have we had any word on their reaction?"

The Ministry official shook his head. "Nothing official yet, but we have intelligence suggesting they're monitoring the situation closely. Saudi interests are tied up in this now, and we can't predict how far they're willing to go to protect their investments. The last thing we want is for Riyadh to start flexing its financial muscle against us, especially given our reliance on Russian support."

Sinead nodded grimly. "Then we tread carefully. If Jenkins wants a legal war, fine. We'll give him one. But we do it on our terms. Get me a full briefing on our legal standing, international precedent, and any jurisdictional loopholes we can exploit. If there's even a sliver of a way to turn this back on him, I want to know about it."

She stood abruptly, turning to the window that overlooked Dublin. The city stretched out before her, its streets filled with people who had no idea of the battle unfolding behind closed doors.

"Jenkins thinks he's clever," she murmured, more to herself than to the official. "He thinks he can use the law as a weapon, bend the world to his will with enough lawsuits and legal threats."

Her hands clenched into fists.

"Let's see how well his lawsuits hold up when we take the fight to him in ways he never expected."

The official hesitated before speaking. "Ma'am… if we're going down that road, we need to be careful. If we escalate in ways that go beyond legal retaliation, we risk drawing the UK and Saudi into direct confrontation. And if we push too hard, Moscow might decide we're more of a liability than an asset."

Sinead turned back to him, her gaze cold and unwavering.

"Then we make sure we don't push too hard."

****

CHAPTER 20 – The Planning Committee

Wednesday 14th February 2029

The unofficially named "Five Eyes Coup Committee" had convened in Vauxhall Cross, the home of MI6, with the intelligence services of the Five Eyes nations—Britain, the United States, Canada, Australia, and New Zealand—along with key allies from Germany and France. The meeting room, deep within the heart of SIS headquarters, was dimly lit, its soundproofed walls ensuring that the discussions within would remain strictly off the record.

There was no official mandate for this gathering, no formal directive from any government. The political leadership of the Western alliance was still tangled in the bureaucratic quagmire of Jenkins' lawsuits, scrambling to contain the fallout. Meanwhile, Russia and the Restoration Government in Ireland had grown increasingly belligerent, their rhetoric escalating in a way that suggested they were preparing for something beyond the usual diplomatic theatre.

It was for that reason that those present—the true architects of Western intelligence strategy—had taken matters into their own hands.

The Five Eyes Coup Committee had met before, but this time, the air in the secure meeting room carried the undeniable weight of impending action. A single glance around the table was enough to confirm that the usual dance of cautious diplomacy had been set aside. The intelligence chiefs and senior officers gathered here were no longer debating whether something had to be done, but how.

"Right," Kelvin said, sighing. ""We've got confirmation from satellite surveillance that Su Li is still on course, still heading for Aberdeen, with an estimated arrival on the 3rd of March. No deviations, no last-minute reroutes—so either the Russians are feeling particularly bold, or they're confident we won't intervene."

Lorna Hayes from the CIA adjusted her chair, arms folded as she stared at the screen. "If they're that confident, it means they think we don't have the nerve to act. Or they think we don't have a plan."

"We have a plan," said Admiral Linus Edwards, representing the Royal Navy. His voice carried the weight of decades at sea, and his expression was one of grim determination. "And if this meeting is anything to go by, we're about to execute it."

Liam Powell of MI5 exhaled slowly, rubbing his temple. "We can't let this thing reach Ireland. That's not even up for debate. If a Sarmat gets into Dublin's hands, Russia won't even *need* to put nukes in Kaliningrad or Belarus anymore. They'll have one sitting in an EU-adjacent state with direct access to the Atlantic. And if the Yanks aren't willing to move on this—"

"They are," Lorna interjected, though her tone was laced with frustration. "At least, the Pentagon is. But Vance's people won't sign off on anything direct. That's why this falls to us. Any word from Mossad? They were sniffing around this before we even confirmed the missile transfer.

If anyone's got eyes inside Tehran's shipping lanes, it's them."

Kelvin shook his head. "Mossad are keeping their cards close. They don't like that we're going for the 'accidental maritime disaster' route instead of outright sabotage. Their usual approach would involve an unmarked speedboat, a few operatives in wetsuits, and an explosion no one could ever quite trace back to them."

"I've had word from a contact in Tehran, by the way," Rania Al-Hadid, MI6's Middle East desk officer, cut in, her voice sharp and precise. "Iran is playing this very carefully. They've made no official statements, but my sources indicate that the missile transfer was brokered through an Iranian Revolutionary Guard front company. I've got a mole in the Guard who's provided the true manifest, and put it this way, Belfast, Derry and Ballymena will be turning into Call of Duty, not 'agricultural hubs', if what else is in the shipment gets to Northern Ireland. There's enough guns to equip an entire battalion, plus an ungodly number of explosives. PC-9 Zoafs, Tondar MPT9s, Zulfiqar Z1s, Fajr 224s, Akhgars, Moharrams, Kaveh-30s, RPG-29 Ghadirs, Toophan 7s, and a BTR-60 armoured personnel carrier, courtesy of the Iranian Revolutionary Guard. They've also got a Fajr-5 330mm multiple launch rocket system, a Naze'at rocket artillery... and a Toufan II attack chopper... all for the IRA."

The laughter at the Irish Republican Army, the nationalist paramilitary force that had once been thought of as little more than a fragmented relic of the Troubles, gaining an attack chopper by one of the more junior MI5 officers who was present was quickly silenced by a sharp glare from Liam Powell. The MI5 Section Chief had spent enough time dealing with the resurgence of nationalist paramilitaries to know this was no joke.

"If you're done laughing," he said icily, "maybe take a moment to appreciate that we are looking at the most heavily armed Republican movement in history—certainly since the days when Gaddafi was shipping boatloads of AKs to the Provos."

The room fell into an uneasy silence. The implications were clear. This wasn't just another smuggled shipment of rifles and Semtex. This was an arms transfer on a scale that would make the modern IRA a serious military force. With heavy weapons like that, they wouldn't just be setting off car bombs or taking potshots at police stations—they could hold ground.

"This isn't about sporadic terrorism," Kelvin said grimly. "It's about insurgency."

Lorna exhaled sharply. "The Fajr-5 alone could level a police station, or even a military barracks. And if they actually get that Toufan II in the air—well, that's the kind of thing that gets NATO involved."

"We can't let it land in Belfast," Admiral Edwards reiterated, his voice slow and deliberate. "No debates. No half-measures. We sink the Su Li before it gets anywhere near Irish waters."

"And we do it in a way that doesn't start a war," Liam added. "Especially as the Su Li is Chinese flagged, and whatever rogue factions in Beijing want to stir the pot."

374

"With all due respect, Beijing is more interested in something else," Jonathan said with a slight smirk, tapping his tablet to pull up a classified intelligence brief from ASIS. "China's got its eyes on a different prize—Taiwan. That and... well, Queensland."

The room went deathly silent at the mention of Queensland.

Kelvin's brow furrowed as he turned to O'Keefe. "You're telling me the PRC is actually entertaining the idea of backing Queensland? That's not just stirring the pot—that's knocking the whole bloody stove over."

"We intercepted some chatter—nothing definitive yet, but Beijing's been poking around certain economic and political factions in Brisbane. The Chinese know Queensland has been getting more... shall we say, independent-minded since the rest of Australia started tightening economic restrictions post-Irish crisis. The fact that they're even entertaining the idea of nudging Queensland towards secession is alarming enough."

Kelvin exhaled, rubbing his temple. "Alright, so in summary, we've got a Russian nuke headed for Dublin, an IRA rearmament plan that reads like a bad Tom Clancy novel, China playing footsie with Queensland independence, and an American administration too wrapped up in Jenkins' lawsuits to give us anything but plausible deniability. So, Admiral, you mentioned you have managed to get BP to release a Gem Class that... well, shall we say, is approaching end of service life for a little 'unexpected' collision?'"

Admiral Edwards gave a slow, knowing nod, his expression unreadable. "BP's Gem Class fleet has a few… older vessels that may or may not be due for decommissioning. One in particular, the British Emerald, is 21 years old, and is showing signs of wear and tear. It's scheduled for retirement, but as it happens, its final voyage will take it along a route that just so happens to cross paths with the Su Li. A freak mechanical failure, a miscalculation in navigation, and… well, maritime accidents do happen. The Master of the vessel happens to be a former Type 23 commander, by some fortuitous coincidence."

The laughter when the Admiral mentioned the previous occupation of the vessel's captain was short-lived, drowned out by the gravity of what they were actually discussing. A "freak mechanical failure" that just happened to involve an ageing BP tanker colliding with a Chinese-flagged cargo ship carrying enough weaponry to turn Belfast into a warzone. A maritime accident that would be tragic, regrettable, and above all, plausible.

"Und we will be providing a salvage vessel," Johan Weissmann of the BND interjected smoothly, his German accent crisp in the otherwise hushed room. "A highly capable, NATO-affiliated, completely neutral salvage vessel that will be on the scene within hours of the 'incident.' We will, of course, do our utmost to recover what we can—purely in the interest of maritime safety, you understand."

Looking at the representative from HM Coastguard, Ken Hardy, a former Royal Marine who had transferred to the civilian side of life in 2024, Kelvin knew that he would have something to say about how the whole operation would need to be framed from a maritime safety perspective.

"Right," Hardy said, leaning forward and fixing Admiral Edwards with a knowing look. "I'm going to assume you've already got this part covered, but let me spell it out just in case—if we're going with the 'tragic accident' route, we need to have the Coastguard playing their part before anything goes down. We'll need an emergency broadcast prepared for all shipping in the area, weather advisories that justify restricted movement, and most importantly, a reason why the British Emerald just happened to lose control at exactly the right place and time."

"Fog and engine failure," Edwards said without missing a beat. "It's an old vessel, maintenance issues have been flagged before, and it's been running on outdated navigation software. We'll put out a notice that it was experiencing mechanical faults a day before the incident, and conveniently, one of those faults will escalate at precisely the wrong moment. Oh, and a cargo of Jet-A1. A nice, fully loaded ship with Jet-A1, heading from Aberdeen to provide fuel for the Danes and their operations in the North Sea. If that fuel ignites on impact, well… that just makes it all the more tragic, doesn't it?"

"Gives me an excuse to order all ships to remain in port except the Lifeboat service and my own mob," Hardy grunted, rubbing his chin in thought. "If we've got Jet-A1 involved, that means I'll have to issue a full maritime exclusion zone for a potential catastrophic fire risk. That means no civilian vessels in the area, no fishing trawlers, no prying eyes. Naturally the SAR teams will have 'retired' Royal Marines assisting, so you've got some manpower if the situation on the ground—or, in this case, at sea—needs additional persuasion." Kelvin nodded. "Perfect. That keeps it clean. A highly unfortunate maritime accident, but one that just so happens to remove an ICBM, an entire weapons shipment, and any plausible deniability Dublin or Moscow might have had about not arming the IRA." Lorna frowned slightly, tapping her fingers against the table. "I hate to be the one asking this, but what happens if something goes wrong? If the Su Li changes course last minute, if they get wind of what's about to happen and take countermeasures?"

"That's where the RAF comes in. I mean, airplanes run out of fuel, don't they?" Air Commodore Jenson Leon said with a grin that was anything but reassuring. "I mean, how unfortunate would it be if, say, an RAF Hawk T.1 of the Red Arrows, on a practice run, accidentally suffered an engine failure over the North Sea, accidentally crashing into the Su Li. There's your Plan B. I mean, we do have a scheduled training session over Waddo, and as the Deputy AOC of No. 1 Group, I do have the pull to make sure one of those planes just so happens to have a 'catastrophic' malfunction over open water." He leaned back in his chair, smirking slightly. "Of course, if we wanted to be overt about it, we could just send a few Typhoons loaded with JDAMs and take the whole thing out, but somehow, I don't think the Foreign Office would be thrilled with that approach. Especially as it's an election year."

Kelvin ran a hand through his hair, considering the options now laid out before him. The plan was, in theory, simple—manufacture a maritime accident, sink the Su Li, and eliminate a major threat before it could destabilise the entire region. But theory had a nasty habit of colliding with reality at the worst possible moment.

"We've got three options," he summarised. "Plan A: The British Emerald has an unfortunate, catastrophic collision. Su Li goes down with all hands, and the world mourns a tragic accident. Plan B: An RAF Red Arrows Hawk suffers an 'unfortunate' malfunction and crashes into the Su Li. No survivors. Plan C: The Royal Navy goes hot, sinks the bastard, and we deal with the fallout."

"Plan C is not an option," Liam interjected, his voice firm. "If we put a torpedo into a Chinese-flagged vessel, we might as well just write out the declaration of war ourselves. Beijing would have to retaliate, even if they weren't directly involved in the shipment. They'd use it as a pretext to push harder in the Pacific, and suddenly, we're juggling two crises instead of one."

"We're going with the British Emerald," Admiral Edwards confirmed. "It's already en route, and the captain has been briefed on what's expected. He knows the stakes."

Kelvin nodded. "Then we move forward. Now, next question—how do we handle Dublin once this is done? Because you can be damn sure they'll cry foul the moment their shipment disappears beneath the waves."

"Easy, we just blame it on the weather," Weissmann said smoothly, a slight smirk on his face. "Storm conditions, poor visibility, and an unfortunate mechanical failure on an ageing vessel carrying thousands of tonnes of highly flammable aviation fuel. Dublin will scream about sabotage, but what evidence will they have? If anyone suggests foul play, we'll point to the Coastguard reports, the weather advisories, the historical records of similar accidents in the North Sea. It's all very regrettable, but entirely explainable."

Kelvin exhaled sharply, looking at the assembled officers. "Right. So, the British Emerald takes the Su Li out. The BND 'salvages' the wreckage for safety purposes. The Coastguard enforces a maritime exclusion zone and takes the lead on the 'investigation.' The RAF stands by in case it all goes tits up, and Mossad… well, Mossad will probably try to blow it up anyway and claim credit after the fact."

Lorna smirked. "Wouldn't be the first time."

Air Commodore Leon grinned. "And probably not the last."

Kelvin nodded, rubbing his temple. "Alright. Now, let's talk timing. We need to make sure this happens in the dead of night, with the right environmental conditions. Edwards, how's the weather looking for the third?"

"Put it this way, it mirrors the 10 March 2025, when the container ship MV Solong collided with the oil tanker MV Stena Immaculate, which was at anchor in the North Sea off the coast of East Yorkshire. Foggy as fuck," the Admiral said with a grin on a face that suggested he'd been waiting to drop that particular detail all night. "Visibility will be near zero, sea state will be rough enough to make navigation tricky, and we'll have just enough wind to make radio communications spotty. The perfect conditions for an unfortunate maritime disaster."

Kelvin exhaled, nodding. "Good. That means we go with Plan A unless something goes wrong. But if it does—" He shot a glance at Air Commodore Leon, who gave an exaggerated shrug.

"We'll be ready," Leon assured him. "Just a tragic accident involving a low-flying Red Arrow on a 'routine' training exercise. Shame, really."

Liam sighed, running a hand down his face. "We're actually doing this. Christ."

"Look at it this way," Lorna said dryly, "it's a lot less messy than the alternative. We let that shipment reach Belfast, and within a month, we'll have an active insurgency on British soil, with enough firepower to turn the whole place into a warzone. Then we'll really be in the shit."

Kelvin glanced at the clock. It was nearing midnight. The meeting had dragged on for hours, but they were finally at the point of execution. "Alright. Final confirmations— Royal Navy has the British Emerald in position?"

Admiral Edwards nodded. "She's already in the North Sea, final course adjustments being made. We're running a skeleton crew to minimise casualties, but the captain knows what to do."

"MI5," Kelvin continued, turning to Liam, "what's the contingency for Northern Ireland? If even half that shipment makes it to shore, we'll have armed militants walking around within a week."

Liam exhaled sharply. "We've already greenlit Operation Ravensdale. Our people in the PSNI are on alert, and we've got a quiet green light for some 'extra-judicial assistance' from our friends in Tel Aviv if things get really bad. But to be honest, the best contingency is making sure that shipment never lands. Also, we need to talk about Holly Flaherty."

Kelvin raised an eyebrow. "Flaherty? The UVF assassin?"

Liam nodded grimly. "Intel suggests she's, this morning, took out another IRA commander. Usual methods, used her sex appeal to get the idiot to think with his dick instead of his brain. Shagged the fucker, and then a double tap to the head. CCTV caught her sneaking out of the Premier Inn in Belfast, an Israeli Jericho 941 tucked into the waistband of her jeans. Poor wanker still had a stiffy."

"To be fair, boss," Oliver Stokes, who was sitting in a corner, reading some of the case files, interjected, "she is former SAS and Rifles Regiment, and her grandfather is a former Parachute Regiment veteran from Bloody Sunday. If there's anyone who was born and bred to do this kind of work, it's her. Anyway, I'd rather go by having a big titted—"

"Really, Ollie," Kelvin cut in, rubbing his temple as he sighed. "If we're discussing rogue assets, let's at least keep it professional."

"Good evening, I'm Rachel McKenna, reporting live from Belfast, where a bomb has just exploded outside Belfast City Hall, resulting in 30 confirmed fatalities and dozens more injured. The Police Service of Northern Ireland has declared this a major terrorist incident, and initial reports suggest the IRA has claimed responsibility. The explosion occurred just minutes ago, during evening rush hour, outside the main entrance to City Hall, an area that would have been filled with commuters and shoppers. Emergency services are on the scene, and authorities are urging the public to stay away from the area. Reports state that it was done in revenge of the assassination of IRA Commander, Lorcan Doyle," McKenna continued, her voice tight with controlled urgency. "Sources within the PSNI have indicated that Doyle, a senior figure within the IRA's operational command, was found dead in a Belfast hotel room early this morning, executed in what appears to have been a highly professional assassination. The attack tonight, described as a 'retaliatory strike,' has already escalated tensions in Northern Ireland, with fears that this may be the beginning of a new wave of violence between Loyalist and Republican factions."

The room fell into a heavy silence.

Kelvin pinched the bridge of his nose and exhaled slowly. "Well, that didn't take long."

He then looked to General Ian King, a British Army commander, who was on the phone, looking very annoyed, barking orders. "...all IRA safehouses in Ulster raided, all weapons stores destroyed, and every IRA soldier, from the lowest foot soldier to the highest commander, is to be either arrested or neutralised. I don't care what the political fallout is. Send in the Sports and Social, the Paras, the bloody Royal Marines if you have to. I want complete control, checkpoints, and even a bloody curfew in place before dawn. And tell the bloody PM I don't give a fuck if he wants to protest, I'm not having another bloody insurgency on British soil on my watch. Get the RAF to bomb the fuck out of any resisting Nationalist compound, and make sure the Americans are on the same page. I don't want a single one of those bastards breathing by the end of the week. The killed my bloody son so I'm going to have their bloody heads."

The meeting room was silent as General Ian King finished his call, his knuckles white from the tight grip on his phone. The weight of his words hung in the air, reverberating through the already tense atmosphere. No one dared to contradict him—not here, not now. The IRA had just committed the worst single terrorist attack in Belfast since the Troubles, and the gloves were well and truly off.

The fact that his 23 year old son, a politics student who was on placement at Belfast City Hall as a policy researcher, had been among the dead had turned an already ruthless counterinsurgency into something even more personal. King was a veteran of the Afghanistan and Iraq wars, a man who had spent his entire career studying and dismantling insurgencies, and now, the IRA had made the mistake of bringing the fight to his own doorstep.

It was then Kelvin realised what King said, 'tell the bloody PM I don't give a fuck if he wants to protest, I'm not having another bloody insurgency on British soil on my watch'. The Swedish-Scotsman knew that it was only 5 months until the General Election, and with the IRA's renewed insurgency, King had just made it clear that Downing Street's hesitation wasn't going to stop him from doing what needed to be done. If the PM didn't approve, then the British Army would act independently, and nobody in this room was going to stop them.

The tension in the room was suffocating. The harsh overhead lighting cast sharp shadows across the table, where some of the most powerful intelligence and military figures in the Western world sat in grim silence. The Five Eyes Coup Committee had spent weeks laying out meticulous plans, carefully orchestrating an operation that could change the course of the entire conflict. And now, in a matter of hours, the entire situation had exploded into something far more volatile than even their worst projections.

Kelvin exhaled slowly, glancing around the table. Liam sat stiffly, his jaw clenched, the glare in his eyes betraying his barely contained fury. Lorna was already on her laptop, likely drafting an urgent cable to Langley. Air Commodore Leon tapped a pen against the table, his usual smirk nowhere to be found, while Admiral Edwards steepled his fingers in front of him, his expression unreadable.

King was still gripping his phone, his knuckles white, his face a mask of cold fury. The IRA had killed his son. The realisation sat in the room like a spectre, unspoken but undeniable. His demand for immediate military action had turned the meeting from a strategic discussion into something far more personal.

Kelvin cleared his throat, breaking the silence. "We need to get ahead of this before the entire situation spirals out of control."

King turned his gaze towards him, and Kelvin felt the weight of a father's grief and a soldier's rage staring back at him. "Ahead of this?" King growled. "Ahead of this would have been taking out those bastards before they had a chance to strike. My son is dead, Svenson. Thirty innocent people are dead. If we sit on our hands and treat this like a diplomatic issue, there'll be another bomb before the week is out."

"We all want action, General," Liam Powell said, his voice level but firm. "But going in heavy-handed could backfire spectacularly. If we roll tanks into Belfast tonight, we might as well hand Moscow the propaganda victory of the century. They'll paint it as the British military 'occupying' Ulster while they sit back and watch. And that's before we even consider what Dublin might do."

"Dublin can go fuck itself," King spat. "Air Commodore Leon, I want Dublin flattened. Get those F-35s of yours in the air and turn the whole bloody city into rubble if they so much as lift a finger to defend those IRA bastards."

There was a brief, stunned silence. Even in a room where black ops, assassinations, and state-sponsored sabotage were routine topics, an outright airstrike on the Irish capital was beyond the pale.

Kelvin pinched the bridge of his nose, taking a deep breath before speaking. "General, we're all grieving for the lives lost today. But bombing Dublin? That's not a retaliation, that's a declaration of war. It's exactly what Moscow wants."

King's eyes were burning with barely restrained fury, his grief fuelling his demand for blood. "And what do you suggest, Svenson? That we let them walk away from this? That we let the IRA re-arm while Dublin and Moscow play coy?"

Lorna leaned forward, her voice calm but firm. "Nobody is saying we do nothing, General. But a military strike on an EU capital? That's the kind of thing that gets Article 5 invoked. We'd be at war with the entire European Union—."

"Technically," Weissmann said, looking up, and Kelvin knew what the German was going to say. "As Ireland is an occupied nation by Russia, the EU would not lift a finger unless they requested assistance under the appropriate channels. Right now, Dublin is Moscow's puppet, and their leverage within the EU has been greatly diminished. Chancellor Scholz would rather help London than work for Putin and his stooges, so I think General King, even though his emotions are clouding his judgement, isn't entirely wrong in calling for a response. If you were to launch, say, a series of 'pinpoint' strikes against high-value targets in Dublin—the sort of thing that removes key figures without flattening the city— Germany would, as you say, look the other way."

Kelvin exhaled sharply. "So, what you're saying is, if we selectively target Restoration Government and IRA command structures inside Dublin, the EU might let it slide?"

Weissmann nodded. "If it is contained. A decapitation strike, removing key Russian and Nationalist leaders, would be seen as an internal matter. A full-scale air raid? That would be an entirely different story."

King's fingers flexed against the table, as if barely resisting the urge to slam his fist down. "Selective, then. I want every single IRA leader dead by morning. We know where they operate, we know where they sleep. If MI6 can't do it, we'll send in the Paras."

Kelvin sighed, rubbing his temple. "General, if you go in like that, we'll be in an open war before sunrise."

"We're already in a bloody war, Svenson," King shot back. "You just haven't accepted it yet."

****

CHAPTER 21 – Ding, Dong, Avon Calling

Thursday 22nd February 2029

"Jesus, Mary and fecking Joseph, London's having a laugh, right? They're doing a 'Special Counter Terrorism Operation' here, in Belfast?"

Of all the things Police Inspector Harold "Harry" Duffy had expected to deal with in the aftermath of the Belfast City Hall bombing, the sudden announcement that the British Army was rolling into town under the guise of a "Special Counter Terrorism Operation" was not one of them.

He had been stationed in Belfast for over twenty years, had seen the so-called 'peace' stretch thinner and thinner with every passing year, but even he hadn't expected this level of response

The last time military boots had been on the streets of Belfast, it had been the dying days of Operation Banner. That was supposed to be the end of it. A new era. And now?

Now the Paras were being flown in under the direct orders of a general with a personal vendetta, and the SAS and Royal Marines were joining in on the fight. Duffy had always known Belfast was a tinderbox, but this? This was an inferno waiting to consume everything in its path.

The PSNI station on Lisburn Road was buzzing with barely contained chaos. Senior officers barked orders into radios, junior constables scrambled to keep track of the dozens of tip-offs coming in from informants, and intelligence officers were working overtime to piece together what the hell was going on.

The official line from Whitehall was that this was a "proportional response" to the City Hall bombing. A move to "prevent further terrorist actions" and "restore public order." Duffy knew better.

This was revenge.

He looked over at a SAS Staff Sergeant, who was the Senior NCO of Red Troop SAS, the elite unit deployed to Belfast under orders so urgent they hadn't even bothered with the usual red tape. The Staff Sergeant, who had introduced himself as Pete Dunne, a Barking native who, according to the Police National Computer, had 2 GBH charges from his youth that had mysteriously vanished when he'd joined the military, leaned against the briefing table with an expression of barely concealed amusement.

"Listen, mate," Dunne said, arms crossed over his tactical vest. "This isn't just about the City Hall job. The IRA thought they'd get away with it because London's been hand-wringing for years. But after tonight? The gloves are off. Anyway, we're waiting for someone before we go raiding in Derry... a former... Captain. The Black Widow of Ulster."

Duffy knew exactly who Dunne was talking about before he even said the name.

"Holly fecking Flaherty," Duffy muttered, pinching the bridge of his nose. "Christ on a bike."

The station, already a hive of activity, seemed to still for a moment at the mention of her name. Even among those who had spent their careers dealing with Loyalist paramilitaries, the fact the chief suspect in the assassination earlier that day of IRA Commander Lorcan Doyle was now being invited to assist with counter-terrorism efforts rather than arrested outright was enough to make even the most hardened officers question what the hell was going on.

Duffy glanced at Dunne, looking for some kind of sign that this was a joke, that some desk jockey in Westminster hadn't actually greenlit putting an unhinged UVF assassin with SAS training on the British payroll. But Dunne wasn't joking.

"She's on her way," Dunne confirmed, checking his watch. "Last seen driving out of Belfast in a stolen Audi. Should be here any minute. Anyway, it's not my choice, but the fucking Rupert that we were meant to have decided to disobey a direct order from General King, so Flaherty's commission has been reinstated with immediate effect."

Duffy nearly dropped his coffee. "They reinstated her commission? You're telling me the same woman who's been running around executing IRA men in bloody Premier Inns is now back in uniform?"

"Yep. And as she's trained on the shit we use as she's done time at Hereford, she's now officially attached to our task force. As she's a Derry lass, the brass wanted her expertise of the local area."

Duffy exhaled sharply, rubbing his temple. "Jesus wept. You lot really are desperate."

Dunne only grinned, the kind of grin that said he knew exactly how mad the whole situation was but had long since stopped caring. "Nah, not desperate, mate. Just efficient. We've got a spare uniform, as I know my oppo on Blue Troop was at Hereford when she was an officer there, and she used to treat the Killing House as her own personal playground. Besides, if we're going into Derry looking for high-value IRA targets, we want someone who doesn't need a bloody map to find the bastards."

Duffy shook his head. "And here I was thinking we'd moved past running death squads out of police stations."

Dunne chuckled. "Oh, we have, mate. This is much more official." He gestured to the documents on the briefing table—sealed orders from Whitehall, an authorisation from the Ministry of Defence, and, most ominously, an MI5 directive signed by Liam Powell himself. "MI5's covering this, MOD's backing it, and Number 10's looking the other way. We're not here to run riot, we're here to dismantle the IRA before they even realise what's happening."

Before Duffy could respond, a constable at the front desk called out, "Uh, sir? There's a woman at the gate demanding to be let in. Says her name's Flaherty."

Duffy groaned, while Dunne grinned like a schoolchild who'd just been handed a case of beer.

"Right on time," Dunne said, pushing himself off the table. "Let's go say hello."

*_*_*_*

The sound of gunfire in a Ballymena church was ironic for Parachute Regiment Corporal Henry "Henno" Clyde, especially as, being a Church of England worshipper and a Para, an elite soldier used to operating in hostile environments, he had always considered himself more of a man of action than of faith. But as the rounds cracked through the air inside the dimly lit St. Patrick's Church, he couldn't help but think that someone upstairs must have a dark sense of humour.

"Contact left!" barked Lance Corporal Thomas Davies, diving for cover behind a toppled pew as rounds ricocheted off the stone walls. "Who the fuck let the IRA have Kalashnikovs and fucking anti-materiel rifles?"

"That would be the Russians and the Iranians," Henno grunted as he rolled behind a thick wooden column, chambering a fresh round into his L85A3. "And considering the size of the rounds hitting that altar, I'd wager we've got at least one bastard with a fucking Kord heavy machine gun."

The firefight had erupted faster than any of them had expected. The Paras had been sent to raid a suspected weapons cache in Ballymena, expecting a few IRA holdouts with handguns and maybe a few AR-15s. Instead, they'd walked into a well-prepared ambush, the kind that suggested the IRA's new suppliers had been far more generous than anyone had realised.

"Henno, we've got movement on the balcony!" Private Callum "Cal" Hewitt called out, his voice strained as he ducked behind a marble statue of St. Peter. "Two shooters, suppressed AKs. Probably trying to flank us."

"Not on my watch," Henno muttered, snapping his rifle up and squeezing the trigger. His first shot caught the nearest shooter in the shoulder, sending him spinning backward, while the second collapsed in a heap as a burst of 5.56 tore through his sternum.

Before Henno could get back into cover, a fresh burst of gunfire raked the floor just inches from his boots.

"We need to move, Corporal!" Davies shouted, his voice barely audible over the cacophony of gunfire and shattering stained glass. "We're sitting ducks here!"

Henno clenched his jaw, scanning the room for options. The IRA had turned St. Patrick's into a kill zone, with entrenched positions on the upper levels and automatic fire suppressing any attempt to move forward. They needed to shift the momentum before they were completely pinned.

"Where's the fucking hand grenades when you need them? Or a bloody heavy machine gun?" Henno growled, his mind racing through their rapidly shrinking options.

"Sergeant Major's got them in the truck," Davies shot back. "Not much use to us right now, though, is it?"

Henno exhaled sharply, making a split-second decision. "Right, smoke and move. Hewitt, pop a smoke grenade, chuck it towards the altar. When it goes off, we leg it left, get to that side entrance and flank the bastards."

"Roger that!" Hewitt pulled a smoke canister from his webbing, yanked the pin, and lobbed it towards the centre of the church. A second later, thick plumes of grey smoke billowed up, shrouding the altar and cutting off the enemy's line of sight.

"Go, go, go!" Henno barked, leading the charge towards the side door, his boots crunching on shattered glass as he sprinted through the smoke.

As they moved, gunfire raked through the haze, wild and panicked. The IRA fighters had lost visual contact and were now spraying rounds in desperation.

Bursting through the side door into a dimly lit corridor, Henno and his men skidded to a halt, rifles raised. A startled IRA shooter barely had time to react before Henno put two rounds through his chest.

"Upstairs!" Davies hissed, pointing to a narrow staircase leading to the balcony where the Kord heavy machine gun was stationed. "If we don't take that bastard out, we're fucked."

Henno nodded, signalling for Hewitt and Davies to follow. Moving swiftly but carefully, they ascended the stairs, their rifles trained ahead, ready to take down anything that moved.

As they reached the top, the gunner was still fixated on firing blindly into the smoke below. The Kord's heavy calibre rounds were chewing through centuries-old stone like it was papier-mâché, each shot echoing like thunder through the church.

Henno didn't hesitate. He pressed the barrel of his rifle against the back of the gunner's skull and squeezed the trigger. The man crumpled instantly, blood splattering across the mounted weapon.

"Clear!" Hewitt confirmed, sweeping the balcony with his rifle.

Henno crouched behind the Kord, inspecting its ammo belt. "Right," he said, a wicked grin creeping onto his face. "If they're going to use Russian hardware, might as well return the favour."

* _ * _ * _ *

"Right, listen up," Holly said, having just heard some bad news on the comms. The assembled SAS operators looked at her with a mix of amusement and wary respect. Even among the hardened men of Red Troop, Holly Flaherty's reputation preceded her. Some had served with her before, back when she was still officially wearing the Queen's uniform. Others only knew the stories—of her brutality, of her precision, of the IRA men who had fallen for her honeytrap act, only to be found with a bullet between the eyes. But whatever their thoughts, no one doubted that she was now a crucial part of the operation.

"The poncy gits in the Marines have gone and got themselves killed on their raid in Omagh. Seems some idiot Second Lieutenant of 29 Commando decided that a tripwire was 'probably a dud' and walked his whole bloody section straight into an IED belt. As a result, we've lost six lads, and the IRA are now dragging their bodies through the streets like it's fucking Mogadishu."

The room tensed. Even among this crowd, hardened operators all, the idea of British soldiers being paraded in the streets as war trophies was enough to send a surge of anger through them.

Dunne exhaled sharply. "Right, that settles it. We were going in quiet. Now we're going in loud."

Holly nodded, rolling her shoulders as she adjusted the sling on her Jericho 941. "Damn right we are. Also, Five have given us some intel. We've got some unwanted Muscovite guests in Derry. Arrived 10 minutes ago. Spetsnaz. 24 Guards Brigade, three troops of the fuckers. The same walkers who've been supplementing the Irish Army on VIP and high-value target protection since the Restoration Government took over."

A murmur rippled through the SAS operators. The presence of Spetsnaz in Derry changed things significantly. These weren't amateur insurgents or brainwashed nationalist volunteers. The Russian special forces were the real deal—battle-hardened, ruthless, and fully capable of going toe-to-toe with Britain's best. This wasn't just a counter-terrorism operation anymore; it was an undeclared shadow war.

"There is some good news... we've got a new toy ready to drop some JDAMs... The brass apparently formed a special RAF Squadron... and let them build a brand new... Harrier."

Dunne looked at Holly with a raised eyebrow, disbelief flickering across his face. "A Harrier? I thought we scrapped the last of those years ago

Holly smirked, clearly enjoying the moment. "We did. But someone in the RAF got all nostalgic and decided to put together a special project using some 'salvaged' components. Apparently, it's a fifth gen VTOL hybrid, built using stealth tech, next-gen avionics, and a weapons loadout designed specifically for asymmetric warfare. And now, it's about to make its debut over Derry."

A silence fell over the room as the reality of what Holly had just said settled in. If the RAF had pulled a Harrier out of retirement—and not just any Harrier, but a one-off, cutting-edge, black-budget monster designed for urban combat—then someone, somewhere, had just given the green light for this to escalate beyond a simple counterterrorism operation.

"Hang on, you said Spetsnaz are in Derry... which side of the border?" Dunne asked, his expression shifting from grim determination to something far more calculating. "Because if it's the Brit side, then Russia have fucked up. Why do I ask? Because... Article 5."

It was well known that Article 5 of the Charter of the North Atlantic Treaty—NATO's collective defence clause—stated that an attack on one member was an attack on all. If Russian troops had crossed into British-controlled Northern Ireland, it would no longer be a covert war. It would be open conflict.

Holly nodded, her expression dark. "Yeah. They're on the Brit side. MI5 picked them up moving through the Bogside, heading towards the Craigavon Bridge. Five have informed the PM... so we might have given the Krauts, Poles and Finns an excuse to revive their own historical military grievances against Moscow. And let's just say, Berlin is very interested in what happens next."

Dunne let out a low whistle. "So, let me get this straight. We're about to run a black ops raid into Derry to neutralise IRA high-value targets, take on Spetsnaz, and we've got the bloody Luftwaffe watching with a bowl of popcorn ready to 'accidentally' send a few Eurofighters our way if things get spicy?"

"Yep," Holly confirmed with a sharp grin. "And to make it even better, the new Harrier's first mission is to turn a Russian safehouse into modern art. So, I'd say we're in for a busy night."

* _ * _ * _ *

Of all the nights to be on a general patrol of Derry, PC Kevin Flaherty knew that this was not exactly the night to be out on the streets in a bloody PSNI uniform.

Unlike his Sargeant, Sargeant Jane McDonald, who had been killed in the IRA bombing of Derry's Waterside Police Station, Kevin Flaherty had survived—by pure chance. He knew that God, Jesus and every saint in the book had been looking out for him when the blast had ripped through the station.

Now, however, he knew trouble was brewing. As a Loyalist who had joined the PSNI to cover up for his elder sister's extra-curricular activities, Kevin was acutely aware of how precarious his position had become. His sister, Holly Flaherty—the Black Widow of Ulster—was now back in uniform, working with the SAS to dismantle the IRA. The streets of Derry were about to become a battlefield once more, and he was stuck in the middle of it all.

It was just past midnight when his patrol car crawled through the Bogside, the tension in the air thick enough to choke on. The streets were eerily silent, save for the distant wail of sirens and the occasional burst of laughter from unseen figures lurking in the shadows. A curfew had technically been imposed, but nobody in this part of town gave a damn. The Nationalists owned the night, and the PSNI were little more than trespassers on their turf.

His partner, Constable Mark Devlin, an older officer who had somehow managed to survive both the Troubles and the uneasy peace that followed, exhaled heavily as they approached the Craigavon Bridge.

"Kev, lad," Devlin muttered, adjusting the grip on his asp. "Tell me again why the fuck we're bloody out here and—shit... we've got a fucking rocket incoming!"

Kevin turned the steering wheel hard to the left just as a streak of fire shot down from the rooftops, a rocket-propelled grenade slamming into the road where the PSNI car had been a moment ago. The explosion lifted the vehicle onto two wheels before it slammed back down, skidding violently as Kevin fought for control.

"Jesus Christ!" Devlin shouted, gripping the dashboard as debris rained down around them. "They're using feckin' RPGs now?"

Kevin didn't answer. He threw the car into reverse, slamming the accelerator as another burst of automatic fire stitched a line of holes across the bonnet. The windscreen spiderwebbed under the impact, but miraculously held. Kevin yanked the wheel again, spinning the car, aiming it back into Loyalist territory, knowing that he needed to get the fuck out of there before they ended up as another two names on the growing list of dead PSNI officers

The radio crackled to life, barely audible over the chaos. "All units, all units—officer down! Officers under attack near the Craigavon Bridge, multiple hostiles engaging with automatic weapons! I repeat, officer down! Immediate assistance required!"

"Shite," Devlin hissed, fumbling with his radio. "Control, this is Alpha-Two-One, we're under heavy fire, taking evasive action! We need immediate backup, over!"

Static. Then a voice, clipped and urgent. "Negative, Alpha-Two-One. Stand by. Military units en route."

Kevin shot a glance at his partner. "Military? Jesus Christ, they're actually sending in the army?"

"Sounds like it," Devlin muttered. "And about bloody time."

Another burst of gunfire stitched a pattern into the side of their car, and Kevin slammed his foot down, the engine roaring as they shot down the narrow streets.

Suddenly Kevin saw a F-35B hovering above the Bogside, its vectoring nozzles spewing heat and dust as it hung there like an avenging angel. The aircraft's underbelly was bristling with ordnance, and as Kevin watched, the jet released a pair of laser-guided bombs, their sleek bodies cutting through the air before slamming into Waterside House, a building near the Craigavon Bridge.

The explosion that followed was biblical.

The Russian safehouse erupted in a violent fireball, the shockwave rippling through the Bogside like an invisible hammer smashing through concrete and steel. A split second later, the delayed crack of the explosion shattered windows across the street, sending shards of glass raining onto the pavement.

Kevin barely had time to react before the blast wave hit their car, rocking it violently as flames licked hungrily at the night sky. The guttural roar of the jet's engines overhead was deafening, and for a moment, all he could hear was the ringing in his ears, the world reduced to a slow-motion nightmare of fire, debris, and distant, panicked screams.

"Fucking hell!" Devlin shouted, gripping the dashboard as the F-35B veered away, its mission complete.

Kevin barely registered his partner's voice as he stared at the burning ruin where the Russian safehouse had once stood. The wreckage was already collapsing in on itself, sending plumes of smoke and flame into the darkened sky. He could make out figures scrambling through the destruction, some trying to flee, others too injured to move.

Above, the fighter jet circled once before banking hard to the west, its afterburners kicking in as it disappeared over the rooftops. The message had been sent. Loud and clear.

"Jesus Christ, they're not fucking around anymore," Devlin muttered, rubbing the side of his head. "That wasn't just a raid—that was a fucking statement."

Kevin swallowed hard, forcing himself to breathe. He had spent years walking the line between his job as a PSNI officer and his loyalty to his sister, but after tonight, that line had been obliterated. The war had returned to Northern Ireland, and this time, it wasn't just the IRA and the UVF in play. The British military, Russian operatives, and even NATO forces were now in the mix.

And he was right in the middle of it.

*_*_*_*

"Checkmate Seven, this is Checkmate Three, we've got a British F-35 on the prowl, you are clear to engage."

Captain Mikhail Sulov, seated in the cockpit of his Su-75 Checkmate, exhaled slowly, rolling his shoulders as he tightened his grip on the control stick. The Russian-built stealth fighter cut through the cold Irish night, its infrared sensors picking up the heat signatures of the still-burning wreckage of what had once been a secure Russian safehouse. The British had drawn first blood. Now, it was Moscow's turn to respond.

"Checkmate Three, this is Checkmate Seven. Locking target. Moving to engage."

He flipped the master arm switch, the Su-75's targeting systems coming alive with an eerie green glow. Below, the F-35B that had just obliterated their position was banking hard, no doubt ready to make another pass over

Derry. The Lightning had caught them off guard, but Sulov had no intention of letting the British pilot leave Irish airspace alive.

"Missile lock," his wingman in the other Su-75 confirmed. "Firing R-77 now."

The Vympel NPO R-77 missile, which NATO designated as the AA-12 "Adder," streaked away from the Su-75 with a flash of fire, cutting through the darkness towards the British F-35B. The Russian pilot's lips curled into a grim smile. The British had escalated this fight—now they would pay for it.

But before the missile could hit, the British pilot did something unexpected. Rather than trying to evade outright, the F-35B's vectoring nozzles adjusted mid-turn, throwing the jet into an aggressive, almost unnatural roll that sent the missile screaming past by mere feet. The British pilot had executed a Viffing manoeuvre—something no stealth fighter should have been able to do with such precision.

Unlike the MiG-31, which Sulov had piloted when he was based in Kaliningrad, the Su-75 was a single-manned multi-role aircraft, the export counterpart to the Russia-only Sukhoi Su-57, the Felon. It was Moscow's answer to the Lockheed Martin F-35, and Sulov had been among the first to test its limits. But now, he was seeing something unexpected—the British had just done the impossible.

"What the fuck was that?" his wingman shouted over the comms. "That thing shouldn't be able to move like that!"

"They've got the SVTOL modification," Sulov muttered, eyes narrowing as he watched the British F-35B climb sharply, its nose pulling towards him in a way that the American F-35A variation could never have managed.

His radar warning receiver screamed as the British jet locked onto him.

"Checkmate Seven, break, break! He's got tone on you!" his wingman barked.

Sulov yanked the stick hard, jinking left as he deployed countermeasures, white-hot flares streaking away from his jet as he forced the fight into a chaotic merge. The British pilot, whoever he was, was no amateur. He wasn't flying like a standard F-35 jockey, relying on his stealth and missiles to do the work. He was flying aggressively, dogfighting—a lost art in the age of beyond-visual-range warfare.

And worst of all? The bastard was toying with him.

It was then that Sulov noticed the squadron insignia. 617 Squadron. The Dambusters.

The realisation hit him like a sledgehammer. The British had deployed their best against him. And now he was up against a pilot who had been trained for exactly this sort of fight—close-quarters aerial combat, something most modern pilots never even had to engage in.

Sulov gritted his teeth. If they wanted a fight, he would give them one.

"Checkmate Three, keep your distance, I'm engaging in a dogfight."

"Negative, Checkmate Seven! Disengage! We don't have clearance to escalate this!"

Sulov ignored the warning. He had no intention of running. If the British thought they could operate over Derry without consequence, they were sorely mistaken.

He slammed the throttle forward, pushing the Su-75 into an aggressive turn to bring his nose back onto the F-35B. The Checkmate wasn't designed for this kind of turning fight, but Sulov had spent his entire career proving that limitations were just another challenge to be overcome.

But the British pilot was already ahead of him. Instead of continuing the turn, the F-35B suddenly flipped onto its tail, hovering for a fraction of a second using its VTOL thrusters before snapping downwards like a stone. It was a manoeuvre that should not have been possible.

"Blyat!" Sulov snarled, yanking his stick hard to avoid overflying the F-35B's nose.

A burst of tracer rounds from the Lightning's GAU-22/A rotary cannon sliced through the night, narrowly missing his fuselage. The British weren't relying on missiles. They were going for guns.

That was when he knew.

He was not getting out of this fight alive.

****

CHAPTER 22 – CoD: Derry
Friday 23rd February 2029

"Lightning Two-One, this is Turbinlite Two, do you copy?"

Wing Commander Adrian "Ade" Newton, the pilot of Turbinlite Two, the callsign for 530 (Turbinlite) Squadron's BAE-RAF Harrier GR.11, a jointly designed 5th-generation new build of the classic Hawker Siddeley Harrier, kept his hands steady on the controls as he maintained altitude over Derry.

The Harrier GR.11 was the product of paranoia within the Ministry of Defence, as, in 2024, Donald J Trump had been elected by the American people once again, and the UK had, fearing the US had installed a kill switch in the Lockheed Martin F-35B, initiated a black-budget project to create a new VTOL aircraft capable of operating independently of American software and logistical support. The result was the Harrier GR.11—built from a combination of salvaged Harrier GR.9 airframes, F-35-derived avionics, and cutting-edge British stealth technology reverse-engineered from Israeli and European programmes. It was an aircraft that officially did not exist.

530 (Turbinlite) Squadron, Ade knew, was a contradiction in itself. A reactivated squadron of World War II history, the original Turbinlite was a cobbled-together experiment—Havoc bombers with giant searchlights, designed to illuminate enemy aircraft for RAF night fighters. Back then, the concept had been as much a death sentence for its crews as it was a tactical advantage. Now,

in 2029, Turbinlite Squadron had been reborn in secret, operating the Harrier GR.11 as the UK's off-the-books answer to the F-35B.

Ade was one of the first pilots to qualify on the aircraft, and he knew it shouldn't exist. The whole thing was a Frankenstein's monster of British aerospace engineering, but it worked—a stealth VTOL strike aircraft that could fight without needing American approval codes or GPS relays. And now, it was about to prove its worth in actual combat.

Lightning Two-One, Ade knew, was being piloted by Squadron Leader Kyler "Wizzy" Wizard, a member of the famed 617 Squadron, the Dambusters. Unlike Ade, Wizzy was flying the much-publicised, heavily-exported Lockheed Martin F-35B Lightning II, the flagship aircraft of Britain's carrier strike force. But now, over Derry, that cutting-edge stealth fighter was in trouble, having just barely evaded a Russian Su-75 Checkmate in a brutal dogfight, before sending another one to the bottom of the River Foyle as if it were a Iraqi MiG-25 piloted by a drunken Ba'athist on a suicide mission. The skies over Derry were no longer the sole domain of the RAF— Russian fighters were now actively engaging British aircraft in a conflict that neither side wanted to officially acknowledge.

"Lightning Two-One, I repeat, do you copy?" Ade called again, adjusting his throttle as he banked south of the city.

Finally, Kyler "Wizzy" Wizard's voice came through, laced with static but very much alive. "Turbinlite Two, this is Lightning Two-One. What the fuck are you flying?

I swear that looks like a Harrier jump jet, but that can't be right because last I checked, we scrapped the Harrier in 2011."

Ade grinned, despite the chaos unfolding below. "Aye, well, turns out someone in Whitehall missed it too much and decided to build a new one. We nicked half of Marine Attacks Squadron 223's fleet and reverse engineered half the bits we liked from the F-35 without all the annoying Pentagon overrides. Welcome to the world's most classified aeroplane, mate. Nice splash, by the way. Y'know Ivan's declared an act of war bringing their fucking fighters over Northern Ireland, right?"

Wizzy exhaled sharply, still regaining his composure after the dogfight. "Yeah, well, nobody told them that. As far as Moscow's concerned, their little green men don't count as an official deployment. Bloody hypocrites. By the way, you've got a bogey on your arse. Lightning Two-Zero is en route from Valley, so try not to get shot down before he gets here."

Ade checked his rear scope and swore under his breath. A second Su-75 had locked onto him, closing the distance fast. He wrenched the stick to the left, throwing the Harrier into a tight roll before engaging the vectoring nozzles. The GR.11 shuddered but obeyed, pivoting on its own axis in a way that would have left lesser pilots unconscious.

"Shite, that thing's nimble," Wizzy remarked, watching from above. "You sure it's not got some Israeli magic in there?"

Ade gritted his teeth, deploying countermeasures as the Russian pilot tried to get a solid lock. "It's got a little bit of everything, mate. But let's not push our luck."

Ade knew that, unlike the F-35Bs, which were staging out of RAF Valley, his squadron was, in theory, based at RAF Brize Norton and was an Embraer E-175 PSO Operator of Last Resort aircraft, acting as the last resort if Ryanair or Loganair were unable to operate routes that were subsidised by the Government for the public to travel on. The E-175 carrying his ground crew, spares, and "paperwork" had taken off from Brize Norton just hours before, heading for an undisclosed "training exercise" somewhere over the North Atlantic. In reality, Turbinlite Squadron was operating out of the former RAF Cottesmore, the British Army garrison at Kendrew Barracks, which had quietly been retrofitted with facilities capable of supporting VTOL operations. If anyone asked, they were running 'low-visibility testing' of legacy aircraft for joint European exercises. In truth, the Harrier GR.11 had just been thrust into a fight it was never meant to be in—at least, not yet.

Ade grimaced as the missile lock tone screamed in his ears. The Russian on his tail was persistent, and unlike the first Su-75 that Wizzy had sent swimming in the Foyle, this one had learned from its wingman's mistakes. The Checkmate wasn't just following him; it was herding him, trying to push him into a predictable manoeuvre that would give it the clean shot it needed.

"Alright, enough of this shite," Ade muttered, flipping the master arm switch. "Let's see how you like this."

The Harrier's onboard weapons system came alive, its internal targeting suite automatically selecting an AIM-132 ASRAAM for the engagement. Unlike the American AIM-9X Sidewinder, the British missile didn't require the pilot to be facing directly towards the enemy—just a glance through the helmet-mounted display was enough.

Ade yanked the Harrier into a rapid deceleration, engaging his vectoring nozzles to nearly stop mid-air. The Su-75 screamed past him, the Russian pilot completely caught off guard.

"Fox Two!" Ade called as he fired the ASRAAM. The missile streaked forward, burning bright against the dark night sky.

The Russian reacted instantly, dumping flares and pulling into an evasive corkscrew, but it was too late. The ASRAAM had already closed the gap, its infrared seeker locked onto the Su-75's heat signature with an unshakable grip.

A moment later, the night lit up as the missile found its mark, detonating against the Russian jet's fuselage. The Checkmate didn't explode outright, but it was mortally wounded, smoke and fire pouring from its shattered airframe as it spiralled downward.

"He's going in!" Wizzy called out. "Eject, you bastard!"

The Russian pilot ejected at the last possible moment, his chute deploying just as his aircraft impacted the streets below, sending a fireball erupting into the Bogside.

* - *- * - *

"BREACH, BREACH!"

Holly Flaherty was in her element, having had her British Army commission reinstated, her boots smashed against the door of the Irish Republican Army safehouse in Derry as the SAS Red Troop flooded the building, weapons raised, laser sights cutting through the darkness like the grim reapers of the night.

The IRA fighters inside barely had time to react. A burst of controlled gunfire cut down the first two men standing near the entrance, their AKs still slung over their shoulders. Holly moved fast, her Jericho 941 raised, clearing her sector with methodical efficiency.

"Room left, clear!" she called out as her SAS counterparts swept through the building with brutal precision.

"Room right, clear!" Dunne echoed as another operative fired a suppressed burst into an IRA shooter trying to raise his rifle.

The house was filled with the acrid stench of cordite, smoke swirling in the dimly lit hallway as bodies dropped.

"Move to the basement!" Dunne ordered. "We need confirmation on the weapons cache."

Holly didn't wait for a second command. She took point, moving swiftly down the narrow staircase. The basement door was reinforced—typical for a safehouse like this.

But she had a bad feeling about it. Not just because of the thick metal hinges or the way the doorframe had been reinforced. No, it was the Russian voices behind Holly's stomach tightened. She pressed herself against the wall beside the door, raising a clenched fist to halt the others. The chatter on the other side was unmistakably Russian—sharp, clipped tones, military discipline. These weren't just IRA foot soldiers huddled in a basement. These were Spetsnaz.

Dunne caught her look and nodded. He motioned for one of the other SAS operatives to prep breaching charges. No point in subtlety now. If Moscow had boots on the ground in Derry, this wasn't just an insurgency anymore—it was an undeclared war.

"On my mark," Dunne whispered.

Holly steadied her grip on her pistol, exhaling slowly. The charge was set, the countdown began.

Three.

Two.

One.

A deafening blast tore through the basement door, sending metal shards and splinters flying. Before the dust had even settled, Holly was moving, her gun raised as she stormed into the room.

The first Spetsnaz soldier turned too late. A 9mm hollow point from Holly's Jericho found his skull, snapping his head back as he collapsed. The second managed to raise his AK, but Dunne's suppressed MP7 barked three times, dropping him in a heap.

More voices, more movement—there were at least half a dozen of them, scrambling to counter the sudden assault.

"Contact right!" someone yelled.

Holly pivoted, sending two shots centre mass into another Spetsnaz operator before he could react. He staggered, fell, but not before squeezing his trigger—sending a wild burst of 7.62 rounds into the ceiling.

A grenade clattered across the floor.

"FUCK! GRENADE!"

Dunne barely had time to react before Holly kicked it back towards the Russians.

A second later, an explosion rocked the confined space, sending bodies and debris flying.

The basement was a warzone. Smoke filled the air, mixing with the coppery tang of blood. Flashing red lights from emergency lamps cast everything in an eerie glow.

Through the haze, Holly spotted something—a crate, partially opened, revealing the unmistakable silhouette of a Russian-manufactured MANPADS launcher. Next to it, more crates marked with Cyrillic script.

It was then that the vest that Holly was wearing pushed back slightly, the sound of a gunshot and the impact of it in her shoulder making her stumble forward, her body slamming into a nearby crate. Pain flared in her shoulder, but Holly barely had time to register it before another bullet hit her.

This time in the back of her head.

Where she was unprotected.

And then everything went black.

* - *- * - *

Donny Lacey was two doors away when he heard the gunshots, the SAS knocking down the door of the IRA-Spetsnaz safehouse, and he knew one thing.

He had to get his gun.

As a member of the Ulster Defence Association, a member of and rival to the other Loyalist paramilitaries, Donny knew it was his rightful duty to take out as many Irish Republican scum as possible. He had lived through the uneasy peace, but he had never accepted it. The moment he heard the explosion, the gunfire, and the unmistakable crack of suppressed weapons, he knew the war was back on.

Aged 70, but with the fitness of a 20something that had never put down his rifle, Donny Lacey moved with purpose, his heart hammering in his chest. The war had never truly ended for men like him. It had just gone quiet for a while. Now, with the British Army back on the streets and the IRA once again armed and dangerous, the Troubles were well and truly back.

He yanked open the drawer in his kitchen, retrieving the Browning Hi-Power pistol he had kept stashed there for years. He had other weapons—an old Norinco AK-47 hidden in the attic, a sawn-off shotgun buried beneath the floorboards of his garage—but the Hi-Power would do for now. He racked the slide, checking the magazine. Fully loaded.

It was then that his landline rang, a method of communication that he and his UDA comrades still relied on when they wanted to avoid modern surveillance.

Lifting the receiver, Donny pressed it to his ear, keeping his voice low.

"Aye?"

"It's me," came the familiar voice of Sam "The Yank" McAllister, his old comrade from the days of tit-for-tat killings and back-alley arms deals. "The UVF have put a bounty on the bloody Russkies. Twenty grand for every IRA scumbag, thirty for a Russkie."

Donny licked his lips as the words sank in. Thirty grand for every Russian, twenty for the Provos. The kind of money that made men disappear, the kind that fuelled the Troubles for decades. And now? Now, it was back on the table.

He gripped the Browning tighter. "Who's putting up the money?"

"The Committee."

That was enough. The Committee—the remnants of the old UDA leadership, the ones who had survived both the peace process and the subsequent years of irrelevance— weren't just throwing money around for nothing. If they were funding a bounty, it meant they had serious backers.

And in a city like Derry, that meant one of two things: the British government, or some very pissed-off businessmen in Belfast who were tired of seeing the IRA rise from the ashes.

"Alright," Donny said, tucking the pistol into his waistband. He knew that the local Councillor was a dyed in the wool nationalist who had been, prior to the Agreement, a Provo, meaning that he had been on Donny's personal watchlist for years. The so-called 'peace process' had allowed men like that to walk free, to shake hands with politicians and play at respectability, but Donny had never forgotten what they were.

And now? Now, with the war back on, it was open season.

He grabbed his coat, slipping it over his shoulder to conceal the Browning. The night was cold, but that suited him fine. The cold kept a man sharp.

Outside, the streets of Derry were alive with movement. Police sirens wailed in the distance, the glow of burning buildings flickering like some twisted funeral pyre. Gunfire still crackled in the night, sporadic but persistent.

Walking down the street, he knew that his target lived two streets away, that the 80 year old man would be asleep and therefore not expecting a wake up and a reminder of the war that he had thought was long buried.

"Yer really think yer gonna kill me, lad?" a gruff, elderly, voice from behind him said as he walked into the street the Councillor had lived on for decades. Donny froze, his hand instinctively moving towards the Browning in his waistband, but the weight of a cold, hard barrel pressing against the back of his neck made him stop dead in his tracks.

"You're not as quiet as you used to be, Lacey," the voice continued, dripping with amusement. "I heard your door open from down the road. Thought maybe you'd finally come to pay me a visit."

Slowly, carefully, Donny raised his hands. He had expected to catch the old man off guard, to put a bullet in him before he even knew what was happening. Instead, it seemed he had walked right into an ambush.

The barrel pressed harder against his neck. "Turn around."

Donny obeyed, pivoting slowly to face the man he had been hunting for decades. Councillor Sean McManus, once a top-ranking member of the Provisional IRA, stood before him, still dressed in a thick wool jumper and slippers, as if he had only just woken up. But the old man's eyes were sharp, and in his right hand, he held a well-worn Webley revolver, its hammer already cocked.

"You never did have the sense to stay down when the war ended," McManus muttered. "And now look at you. Walking around my street, armed, like it's 1973 all over again."

Donny's jaw tightened. "The war never ended, McManus. Not really."

McManus let out a dry chuckle. "Aye, I know. But the difference between me and you, lad, is that I always knew when to step back. You? You still think you're fighting for a cause."

"Maybe I am," Donny spat.

"Or maybe you're just an old man, clinging to ghosts," McManus shot back. "I should kill you right now, Lacey. One less Loyalist bastard to worry about."

Donny held his ground, his fingers twitching by his side. He could go for his gun, but at this range, the Webley would blow his brains out before he even cleared his waistband.

Then, suddenly, a gunshot, hitting McManus in the back of the head, a British Army Parachute Regiment soldier stepping out of the shadows with his L119A2 carbine still raised.

McManus dropped like a stone, the Webley falling from his grip as his body crumpled to the pavement. Donny barely had time to register what had just happened before the soldier turned his weapon on him.

"Stay still," the Para ordered, his voice calm but firm.

Donny raised his hands again, more in confusion than surrender. He was still processing the fact that the British Army had just executed an ex-IRA commander on a residential street in Derry.

"What the fuck is this?" Donny growled. "Since when did the Paras start doing our dirty work?"

The soldier—young, early twenties at most—didn't answer immediately.

Then he grinned. "The Four Star wanted the IRA bastards exterminated, so here we are."

Donny Lacey narrowed his eyes, still keeping his hands raised. The Four Star? That could only mean General Ian King, the British Army's top commander, the man who had lost his son in the Belfast bombing. If King had given the order to "exterminate" the IRA, then this wasn't just counter-terror operations. This was vengeance, plain and simple.

And if the Paras were running black ops on the streets of Derry, then the rules of engagement had just been thrown out the window.

Donny glanced down at the still-warm body of Sean McManus, his blood pooling on the cold pavement. The man had survived everything—the Troubles, the peace process, even the resurgence of the IRA under Russian backing. And yet, in the end, he had been killed not by the UDA, not by an old Loyalist rival, but by a British soldier.

It was poetic, in a way.

The Para stepped closer, his L119A2 carbine still levelled. "Orders are to clean house," he said casually. "You gonna be a problem, Lacey?"

Donny looked at the soldier, then at McManus's lifeless body. Then, slowly, he shook his head.

"No," he said. "Not tonight."

The soldier lowered his weapon slightly, just enough to indicate that Donny wasn't a target. "Good answer. Now piss off before someone sees us."

Donny didn't need to be told twice. With one last glance at McManus, he turned on his heel and walked away, his mind racing.

The war really was back on.

And this time, the British weren't playing by the old rules.

* - *- * - *

Squadron Leader Kyler "Wizzy" Wizard set his helmet down on the debriefing table, running a hand through his sweat-soaked hair. Across from him, Wing Commander Adrian "Ade" Newton was already nursing a bottle of water, his flight suit still smeared with soot from the engagement.

"Well," Wizzy exhaled. "That was a clusterfuck."

Ade chuckled, but there was no humour in it. "Aye, but at least we came out on top. Two Su-75s down, and we're still in one piece."

Wizzy leaned back in his chair, exhaustion creeping in. "Yeah, but how long until Moscow stops pretending this is just 'rogue actors' and starts sending proper VKS squadrons into our airspace?"

Ade took a swig of water, considering that. "Sooner than we'd like. But let's face it, mate—after tonight, we've sent a message. The RAF's still got teeth, and we don't need Uncle Sam's permission to use 'em."

The door to the debriefing room swung open, and in walked Air Commodore Jenson Leon, the deputy AOC of No. 1 Group. He didn't waste time on pleasantries.

"Congratulations, gentlemen. You've just made history—first confirmed air-to-air kills against Russian fighters over Western Europe since the Cold War."

Wizzy and Ade exchanged glances. That wasn't exactly the kind of history they had been hoping to make.

Leon placed a folder on the table. "High Command's been monitoring the situation. The Russian incursion into Derry is worse than we thought. Spetsnaz embedded with the IRA, direct support from Moscow. This isn't just a proxy war anymore. It's real."

Wizzy exhaled. "And what's the plan?"

Leon's expression darkened. "We escalate."

Ade raised an eyebrow. "How much?"

Leon folded his arms. "Enough to make Moscow sweat. We're pulling every F-35B and Typhoon we've got into Northern Ireland. HMS *Prince of Wales* is being sent to the Irish Sea, and No. 617 Squadron is getting green-lit for strike operations. And as for you, Ade..."

He turned to the Turbinlite pilot, a smirk forming. "Congratulations. You and your classified toy are getting an extended deployment."

Ade rolled his eyes. "Brilliant. Just what I always wanted."

Leon ignored the sarcasm. "Get some rest, both of you. You'll need it."

With that, the Air Commodore turned and left, leaving Wizzy and Ade in silence.

After a long moment, Wizzy leaned forward, rubbing his temples. "Bloody hell, mate. We're really doing this, aren't we?"

Ade sighed, staring at the table. "Looks like it."

Neither of them said what they were both thinking.

By the time the sun rose, the United Kingdom and Russia would be at war.

****

CHAPTER 23 – Propaganda Games
Friday 23rd February 2029

Harry Potter was looking at his watch when the live feed from SAS Staff Sergeant Pete Dunne's helmet camera jolted violently. The crack of a gunshot echoed through his headset, and for a split second, the image blurred before refocusing on a crumpled figure on the floor.

Holly Flaherty was down.

"Shit," Dunne's voice came through the comms, low and urgent. "Flaherty's hit. Head wound. We need a medic now."

The feed from Dunne's camera swung as he moved, his breathing audible over the static. Blood pooled beneath Flaherty, her body twisted where she had fallen against a stack of Russian-manufactured weapons crates. Her Jericho pistol lay inches from her limp fingers.

The 24 year old MI5 cyber specialist knew that the Derry born former SAS Captain had always been reckless, but seeing her lying there, motionless, sent a chill through him. Holly Flaherty wasn't supposed to go down like this.

An expert in making deepfakes, images, videos, or audio which are edited or generated using artificial intelligence tools, and which may depict real or non-existent people, Harry knew that this was not any ordinary situation. The Russians would seize on this moment. If Holly was dead, Moscow would use it as proof that the UK was engaged in illegal operations inside Northern Ireland. If she was alive, they would find a way to discredit her, to turn her into a liability. Either way, this wasn't just about boots on the ground anymore—it was about controlling the narrative.

"Pokhozhe, tebya prevoskhodyat chislennost'yu, merzavets iz Khereforda," a male voice said from behind Dunne, and Harry noticed the screen suddenly blur as the SAS operator turned round, the L119A2 firing at the person who had spoken. Harry noticed that the person Dunne had shot was in fatigues with Russian Spetsnaz insignia on his uniform.

Looking at his other screen, however, Harry could see that his main project, a deepfake of Sinead Ryan in the State Information Office, had finished rendering. Grinning, he knew that this would put the British cat amongst the proverbial pigeon, a deepfake where Ryan would declare unwavering loyalty not to President Putin, but to Sergey Naryshkin, the SVR Director, and back him to replace Vladimir Putin as President of the Russian Federation.

In addition, another deepfake, this time of Evgeny Lebedev, Baron Lebedev, of Hampton in the London Borough of Richmond upon Thames and of Siberia in the Russian Federation, was also rendering, one in which he would be announcing that he was defecting to Moscow and declaring the United Kingdom a failing state, praising the Irish Restoration Government as a model for Russian-backed 'liberation' efforts in Western Europe.

Harry let out a low chuckle, shaking his head as he leaned back in his chair in the Nexus, the section of MI5 in Thames House that he worked in. "This," he muttered under his breath, "is going to be fucking chaos."

The deepfake of Sinead Ryan would be the real masterpiece. By forging an AI-generated video of the Irish Restoration Government's chief propagandist pledging loyalty to Sergey Naryshkin instead of Putin, MI5 would be driving a wedge between the Kremlin's intelligence elite and the President himself. Russia was always one step away from an internal power struggle, and if the SVR Director started looking like a serious rival, it could destabilise Moscow's grip over its own operations in Ireland.

The Evgeny Lebedev deepfake was more of a wildcard. The Russian-British media mogul was already a controversial figure, with deep ties to both Westminster and oligarchic circles. A fake defection video would sow discord in London, forcing the UK government to respond while simultaneously embarrassing Moscow. If it worked, Lebedev would spend weeks proving his loyalty to the UK, all while Russian state media scrambled to deny an asset they hadn't actually turned.

"What you done now?" Oliver Stokes asked, and Harry chuckled, knowing that his slightly older colleague would be equally entertained by the sheer scale of digital chaos about to unfold.

Harry spun his chair slightly, glancing over his shoulder at Oliver, MI5's technical officer embedded in Manic Radio, who had spent the last few months acting as a key player in Britain's disinformation war against Moscow. "Oh, nothing much," Harry said, feigning innocence. "Just fabricating a small internal coup in the Kremlin and forcing a Russian oligarch to spend the next month explaining why he hasn't actually defected."

Oliver raised an eyebrow, glancing at the render queue on Harry's multiple monitors. The deepfake of Sinead Ryan was already undergoing final audio processing, the AI seamlessly replicating her cadence and phrasing from countless RTÉ and Russian state broadcasts. The Lebedev defection tape was almost done too, though the final touches—background noise adjustments, slight compression to mimic a recording taken from an unsecured line—were still being applied.

The fact that he had done it in her three personalities, the ""Diet Ri Chun-hee" in English, "1916 But 2029" in Irish, and "Ri Chun-hee But Full Send" in Russian that she did in pressers and official statements, only made it all the more believable. The Russians had crafted Sinead Ryan into a weapon, a mouthpiece of their new regime in Dublin, but MI5 was about to turn her against them. If the deepfake was convincing enough, Moscow would be forced to waste valuable time and resources denying an internal coup, while Ryan herself would have to scramble to maintain credibility among her own handlers.

Harry smirked as he initiated the upload process. The first phase was simple—he'd leak the footage to the usual conspiracy circles, the Telegram channels and fringe forums that the Kremlin's own troll farms used to spread disinformation. Then he'd inject it into Russian social media through compromised accounts linked to legitimate journalists. Finally, using credentials that GCHQ had supplied, he would have RT, CCTV, RTÉ, TASS and even the BBC News, on their upcoming 5am top of the hour bulletins, simulcast the video as breaking news, bypassing editorial controls for just long enough to force a reaction from both Moscow and Dublin before anyone could contain the damage.

Harry leaned back, watching the uploads progress as he sipped his lukewarm coffee. Oliver, standing behind him, let out a low whistle. "Mate, this is next-level chaos. If this works, we're gonna be sitting here with a front-row seat to a Kremlin meltdown."

"That's the plan," Harry said, cracking his knuckles. "Thing is, we don't even need them to believe it for long. We just need them to react. Best-case scenario? Naryshkin has to issue a public denial, which makes Putin look paranoid. Worst case? The FSB and SVR start purging each other in a fit of counter-intelligence hysteria."

Oliver grinned. "And Lebedev?"

Harry shrugged. "Lebedev's whole brand is being 'above' politics, even though we all know he's been juggling Moscow and London for years. This'll force him to either pick a side or go full scorched earth to clear his name. It'll also give Starmer chance to pile sanctions on Baron Siberia and make his life even more difficult. Either way, he's going to be dragged into the geopolitical shitstorm, and that's exactly what we need. If he doesn't defect, the Russians have to pretend they never wanted him. If he does defect, well…" Harry let out a short laugh. "That would be hilarious."

Oliver smirked and took a sip from his tea, watching the last few seconds of the upload tick down. "What about Ryan herself? She's already a dyed-in-the-wool Moscow mouthpiece. She'll deny it instantly. That, and her grandfather was KGB Fifth Directorate. Even if she wasn't fully on board, the Russians have spent too much time grooming her to let her go without a fight."

Harry nodded, already anticipating the response. "Oh, she'll deny it, but the damage will be done before she even gets a chance to open her mouth. This isn't about making anyone believe she's defected—this is about making Moscow and Dublin waste time and resources proving she hasn't." He gestured to his screen, where multiple windows displayed live feeds from various Russian state media outlets. "And since we're about to hijack their own infrastructure to broadcast it, they won't be able to shut it down fast enough."

Oliver let out a low whistle. "Mate, I really hope you've covered your tracks. If they trace this back to us—"

"They won't," Harry cut in confidently. "All the uploads are bouncing through compromised servers in Malaysia and Indonesia, and the origin data is scrubbed to look like it came from CCTV in Beijing."

Harry knew he was playing a risky game, throwing the Chinese into the mix just enough to cause diplomatic confusion, but not enough to actually escalate hostilities between Beijing and Moscow. The real trick was making sure that when Russia went looking for the source of the leak, they'd be barking up the wrong tree. If everything went according to plan, by the time the Kremlin traced the 'leak' to supposed rogue elements inside China, Beijing would already be publicly denying any involvement and probably issuing veiled threats to Moscow about 'false accusations against sovereign partners.'

Oliver shook his head in admiration. "Mate, if this works, I swear, you should be running this entire department."

Harry grinned. "That's the beauty of it. If it doesn't work, nobody even knows it happened."

His screen pinged. The upload was complete. The simulcast injection was primed.

He glanced at the clock. 04:59.

The 5am bulletins were about to begin.

*_*_*_*

Sinead Ryan was sitting in the green room of the RTÉ studios in Dublin, as she was about to present a live press conference about the Northern Ireland terrorism by British military forces. She knew that her masters in Moscow would expect her to deliver with the sharpness and fervour they'd groomed her for.

The clock above the door ticked steadily towards 5:00 am. Normally, Sinead relished moments like this—the calm before the storm, the brief interlude where she could collect her thoughts before plunging into another battle of words and narratives. But tonight, something felt off. As if the Brits were doing something which would try and ruin her reputation in Moscow.

As the clock turned to exactly 5am, she had the sudden urge to turn RTÉ news on the television that was in the room, that she would use to monitor breaking developments. It flickered to life just as the RTÉ opening sting faded out, replaced by the solemn face of the morning anchor.

"Good morning. Breaking news just in: RTÉ has received a disturbing video reportedly featuring the head of the State Information Office, Sinead Ryan, declaring loyalty to Sergey Naryshkin, director of Russia's Foreign Intelligence Service, as part of an apparent internal power struggle within Moscow."

Sinead felt her blood run cold as she stared at her own face on screen—perfectly replicated, her voice and mannerisms indistinguishable from reality. The carefully constructed deepfake was now playing out before her eyes, the image of herself calmly betraying Putin in favour of Naryshkin delivered with the flawless, steely-eyed composure she'd spent years cultivating.

"I want to make clear," the deepfake version of herself said coldly, "that the future of Russia lies not with President Putin, but with Sergey Yevgenyevich Naryshkin. Only under his leadership can our vision of Europe, including Ireland, truly be achieved."

She bolted upright, as she knew that the syntax, the exact way she, in English, would speak—the cold clarity, the icy detachment—had been perfectly mimicked. The deepfake had even managed to capture the precise pauses she used when shifting between sentences, giving weight to each word as if it were a bullet being loaded into a magazine.

"Oh, bollocks," she breathed, eyes widening in horror as her AI-generated counterpart continued to speak on screen, each syllable sending chills down her spine.

"In the coming days," the deepfake version continued smoothly, "you will see clearly that President Putin's rule has become weak, distracted, and ineffective. Only Sergey Yevgenyevich can restore the strength, unity, and vision Russia deserves."

The deepfake then switched to Irish, and Sinead noticed how it exactly used the way she would invoke the Nationalist sentiment, the way she would make it seem as though it was a heartfelt plea for Ireland's future, entwined seamlessly with Moscow's objectives.

"Seo í an fhírinne lom, mhuintir na hÉireann," her digital doppelgänger continued, tone earnest, passionate, yet chillingly precise. "Ní féidir le Vladimir Putin ár dtír a chosaint. Tá sé in am againn glacadh leis an bhfíor-cheannaireacht a thairgeann Sergey Naryshkin—an té a thuigeann an gaol speisialta idir Éire agus an Rúis. Tá ár dtodhchaí slán faoina stiúir amháin."

Sinead's jaw clenched as she heard her own voice echo words she'd never spoken—words so dangerously plausible they might even persuade those within her own government that she'd lost faith in Putin. Before she could react, the feed shifted again, this time to Russian. Her alter ego's demeanour transformed instantly into the bombastic, strident style she usually adopted for Moscow's audience—the Ri Chun-hee inspired aggression she'd carefully honed.

The screen flickered abruptly, cutting to RTÉ's clearly rattled anchor, who hastily informed viewers that the authenticity of the video was being verified. But Sinead knew it was already too late. The video had gone global. Moscow would be waking up to a firestorm.

* _ * _ * _ *

Viktor Mikhailov knew something was wrong. As the SVR assigned political officer when Manic Radio Ireland was still on air, prior to Sinead Ryan finally pulling the plug on the Saudi Arabian backed station—he had grown used to watching narratives unfold with clinical detachment. But as the deepfake video of Ryan pledging loyalty to Sergey Naryshkin, the head of his own organisation, flashed across multiple screens in the SVR station at the Russian Embassy in Dublin, Viktor felt his pulse quicken.

This was not a routine propaganda gambit. This was a direct assault on the Kremlin itself.

"Turn it off," he snapped at the junior analyst fumbling with the remote, sweat visibly beading on his forehead. The screen went black, leaving a tense silence behind.

"Contact Moscow immediately," Viktor ordered quietly, his voice betraying none of his inner turmoil. "Tell them this is a sophisticated British fabrication. We need to discredit it immediately. Inform Director Naryshkin's office directly—he must personally address this."

The analyst nodded hastily, already dialling Moscow. Viktor stared at the blank screen, his mind racing. He knew the real damage had already been done. Naryshkin himself would now have to publicly deny involvement, a humiliation that would plant seeds of paranoia in Putin's notoriously suspicious mind. The Kremlin would be consumed with internal witch hunts for months, crippling SVR operations across Europe.

And worst of all, it had happened on Viktor's watch.

He knew that Ryan was loyal to the Motherland, loyal to President Putin, and that she would never switch allegiance to another unless there was true change in the Federation, as he had been her handler when she was a newbie at RT in London, back in 2019, back when she was a back when she was a bright-eyed, ruthless young journalist, freshly recruited, idealistic yet ambitious. Viktor remembered how easily she'd absorbed every lesson in manipulation, every strategy session, and every carefully scripted message handed down from Moscow. He knew, deep in his bones, that the woman he'd crafted would never betray Putin. But the digital monstrosity he'd just witnessed was horrifyingly believable.

Viktor's thoughts were interrupted by the ringing of his secure line. He picked it up, his voice steady despite the chaos unfolding around him.

"Yes?"

"This is Moscow. Director Naryshkin is going live in twenty minutes to deny involvement. President Putin himself has been briefed. Your orders are clear: Secure Ryan immediately. We need her publicly refuting this before Moscow's broadcast."

Viktor hung up without responding, his mind racing through contingencies. Ryan was currently at RTÉ, minutes from going live herself to deliver an entirely different message—one that condemned British military aggression in Northern Ireland. Now she would be forced to use precious airtime to deny an act she hadn't even committed.

He clenched his jaw and grabbed his coat, storming out of the SVR station. Ryan had been his greatest achievement—a perfectly crafted propaganda weapon. Now, in a single, devastatingly clever move, MI5 had transformed her into a ticking bomb, threatening to explode Moscow's carefully constructed facade of unity.

As he stepped into the cold Dublin air, Viktor knew he'd been beaten. Harry Potter—the name had become infamous among Russian intelligence officers over recent months—had just delivered his most cunning trick yet.

* _ * _ * _ *

"Sergey Yevgenyevich, this is Viktor Alexeyevich," General Viktor Alexeyevich Gusarov, the Senior Strategic Advisor to GRU Director Admiral Igor Kostyukov said, his hands gripping the secure line tightly from GRU Headquarters at Grizodubovoy Street—known in intelligence circles simply as 'The Aquarium'. "Are you aware of the situation?"

He knew that the SVR Director would be in a panic, and that the plan that the GRU had would have to distract the West would either make the Yasenevo based team either worried, or cheering it on.

The plan was simple - a GRU hit squad was already en-route to London, where they would travel to Henley-on-Thames, and eliminate Lord Jenkins KC, the man who had filed a large number of lawsuits against both Moscow and Dublin, leaving nothing but a very public corpse to send a very clear message.

"Da, tovarisch," came Naryshkin's icy voice from the other end, controlled, yet carrying the faintest tremor of fury. "I have already assured Vladimir Vladimirovich that this British stunt will not go unanswered. But we cannot be seen to panic. Whatever you're planning, Viktor Alexeyevich, I hope it's enough to shift the narrative away from this madness."

Gusarov allowed himself a grim smile. "I believe you'll find it more than sufficient. Watch the British news in about two hours. Jenkins will trouble us no longer."

Naryshkin was silent for a long moment, clearly weighing the implications. "Be very careful, Viktor Alexeyevich. Jenkins is not some dissident oligarch hiding in Knightsbridge. He's connected—politically, legally, and militarily. Eliminating him publicly will have consequences."

"That," Gusarov replied calmly, "is precisely the point."

Ending the call, Gusarov leaned back in his chair, exhaling slowly. He knew this operation could not fail. He had personally overseen the deployment of the GRU's best—Unit 29155, the same elite operatives who had wreaked havoc across Europe before. The same operatives who had carried out the Salisbury poisoning years earlier. They had faded from public view, but their lethality had never diminished. Now they would emerge again, this time in broad daylight, sending a stark message to London: Moscow's patience was exhausted.

Gusarov glanced at his watch. The team were already on British soil, their presence concealed behind diplomatic passports and carefully constructed legends. All they had to do was reach Henley-on-Thames, eliminate Jenkins, and vanish into the chaos their act would ignite. He had no illusions about the political firestorm this would trigger, but the GRU had always been comfortable playing with fire.

This time, though, it wasn't merely about silencing a legal threat. It was about changing the headlines—forcing the British media to shift from their carefully crafted propaganda assault against the Kremlin and instead report on the brutal reality of Russian retaliation. By tomorrow morning, James Jenkins KC would no longer be celebrated as Britain's legal crusader against Moscow's interests. Instead, he'd be a martyr, and Downing Street would be grappling with the very real consequences of their own reckless provocations.

He picked up his secure line again, dialling a direct number to the team leader currently driving west from Heathrow. It connected with a short, encrypted beep.

"Speak," came the curt, professional reply.

"Status?"

"En route. ETA forty-five minutes. Target location confirmed. The strike will be clean and public."

Gusarov nodded, satisfied. "Good. Make it unmistakable. Leave no doubt."

"Understood," came the cold reply. The line disconnected.

He allowed himself a moment of grim satisfaction before turning back to the myriad screens in front of him. On one monitor, he could see Naryshkin already stepping up to a podium in Moscow, his carefully rehearsed denial beginning. On another, Russian state TV was scrambling to discredit the Ryan deepfake, frantically spinning conspiracy theories implicating everyone from MI5 to rogue CIA elements and Chinese dissidents.

But none of it mattered now. The GRU's move would not just steal the narrative—it would shatter it.

*_*_*_*

Lord James Jenkins KC had to chuckle at the irony. The alarm of his Henley-on-Thames home was showing on the phone of his bodyguard, a 'former' Saudi Special Forces officer, but he, his wife Carly, his twin sons Sebastian and Oliver, and their pet dog, were nowhere near their home.

Instead, James was in Monaco, a week's unscheduled holiday which he had kept carefully hidden from the public, a precaution borne from decades spent navigating treacherous corporate and political waters, because his mother, the Dowager Jenkins, Lady Alexandra Jenkins, was unwell, and, as she lived in the Principality, James knew that it was an ideal way to get out of the public eye for a while, especially as he had upset both Moscow and Dublin.

He knew that it was yet another assassination attempt on him, the first having been Wagner Group operatives who, walking into the Colmore Building offices in Birmingham of Manic Radio, which, along with its opposite building, One Snow Hill, served as studios, corporate headquarters and nerve centre for Manic's sprawling media empire. That previous attempt had ended badly—for Wagner, at least. GIP, the Saudi General Intelligence Presidency, had intercepted them, took them to the roof, and had suspended the Wagner operatives over the ledge of the Colmore Building by their ankles. The operatives had promptly been handed over to MI5 at Thames House, along with detailed photographs that somehow found their way anonymously onto several Russian Telegram channels. The message had been clear: attacking Manic or its leadership was not a winning strategy.

Now, as James calmly sipped his espresso at the Hotel de Paris in Monaco, overlooking the glittering lights of the Casino square, he could almost visualise the panic spreading in Henley-on-Thames as the GRU assassination squad realised their prize had eluded them. His carefully staged deception was working flawlessly. He chuckled softly to himself as he considered the phone calls undoubtedly crisscrossing between Moscow, Dublin, and their field teams in England, frantically trying to ascertain his location.

The timing had been impeccable. He'd received discreet word from a source inside Thames House—someone who owed him favours from his days at Global—that Russian military intelligence was finally coming for him directly. Hence, the sudden 'family emergency' that necessitated a surprise holiday. Now the GRU's carefully planned operation had become a complete fiasco—precisely the humiliation he had hoped to inflict.

Carly, seated beside him, glanced up from her tablet with an amused expression. "From the look on your face, James, I assume your bait worked exactly as intended?"

James smirked, nodding slightly. "Better than intended. Right now, some poor Russian sod is about to tell his superiors that Lord Jenkins has apparently vanished into thin air."

Sebastian and Oliver, unaware of the exact nature of their sudden holiday, were busy nearby, arguing over the best way to edit the latest episode of their podcast. Their family dog, a small spaniel named Montague, lay curled contentedly at Carly's feet. It was a surreal domestic scene, perfectly at odds with the geopolitical chaos James had just triggered.

He knew precisely the kind of reaction this would provoke in Moscow. The Kremlin had expected a swift and brutal strike, a clear and unmistakable message to the West. Instead, their elite operatives had wasted precious resources on an empty house, and now faced exposure as incompetents. The consequences for the GRU would be severe—someone high-ranking would almost certainly pay with their career, perhaps even their life.

And that, James knew, would be key.

****

CHAPTER 24 – Carl, Excuses, & a Coxless Six

Friday 23rd February 2029

Broadcasting House, and specifically Studio S32—the space BBC Radio 4 and BBC World Service used for The World at One—as far as Carl Peterson could remember, were exactly the same as they had been when he left the BBC in 2026. The corridors, the doors, even the faint scent of coffee that lingered perpetually in the air brought memories flooding back. It was surreal to be here again, as though he'd stepped back into another life. Yet, now, the circumstances couldn't have been more different. He was no longer just a journalist reporting on distant crises; he had become part of one himself.

He had just been on air in the studio, as, following his, Emma's and James's departure from Ireland, Manic Radio had fired him, citing that his 'continued employment represented a security and operational risk.' It was true enough, Carl thought wryly, though the formal notice from Manic's lawyers had struck him as particularly gutless—sent via email, no less. After everything that had happened in Dublin, being let go via a blandly worded electronic dismissal felt absurdly trivial.

Carl leaned against the cool wall of the studio corridor, closing his eyes briefly. The past few weeks had been relentless. After being expelled from Ireland, the Petersons had been hurriedly flown from Dublin to RAF Northolt, where they were debriefed by MI6 and MI5. He knew that Emma, as a MI6 Field Officer, whose covers usually were embassy roles, had anticipated such a scenario; her exfiltration planning had always been meticulous. Carl himself, despite years as her unofficial partner in espionage, found the sudden immersion into the clandestine world more disorienting than he'd expected. Even their son James, whose naïve idealism about working at RTÉ had nearly got him killed, had found himself confronted by interrogations, polygraphs, and the inescapable realisation of just how dangerous their lives had become.

The producers of The World at One had contacted Carl immediately after his public sacking. Clive Myrie himself had rung, his voice rich with empathy but also a sense of professional urgency.

"We need your voice, Carl," Clive had said firmly. "People trust you, they saw you broadcast live from Dublin. They need someone who's been there, who understands what's at stake."

Carl hadn't hesitated, though the irony of returning to the BBC was not lost on him. He was being re-employed precisely because he'd been fired, because he'd become radioactive, a dissident journalist expelled by a hostile regime. The same Corporation that had once gently shown him the door over budget cuts, the eternal bane of the BBC's existence, now opened its arms, eager for the authenticity that only personal peril could lend.

The show he had just presented, called "Radio Free Ireland", a BBC sponsored propaganda initiative aimed squarely at undermining Moscow's grip on the Restoration Government, had been an immediate hit. Within minutes of going off-air, messages poured into the

BBC's social media feeds from Irish expatriates and clandestine listeners in Dublin, Cork, Galway, and Belfast, each expressing gratitude, fear, solidarity—or a potent mix of all three. Carl was suddenly not just a journalist; he'd become a symbol, a voice of resistance from exile, like some strange throwback to the Cold War era. He felt oddly uncomfortable, knowing he was a pawn again, albeit this time willingly.

Carl reopened his eyes as footsteps echoed down the corridor. Annie Walker, his former producer who had survived rounds of redundancies with a resilience he admired, approached with a mug of tea and an expression of relief and professional pride.

"Excellent broadcast, Carl," Annie said warmly, handing him the mug. "Listening figures just broke records across the Republic and Northern Ireland. They're calling you the 'Voice of Free Ireland' on Twitter—no pressure, then."

Carl sipped the tea, smiling faintly. "I'll add that to the list of names people have called me recently. Voice of Free Ireland sounds better than traitor, anyway."

Annie laughed softly, though her eyes quickly turned serious. "It's working, though. MI5 just messaged. They've had contact from resistance cells within Ireland. Real ones, not Russian honey-traps. The show's helping people organise. There's even talk from some ex-Irish Defence Forces officers looking to challenge the regime from within."

"Bloody hell," Carl muttered, his stomach tightening. "They understand it's a propaganda show, right? We're openly funded by the BBC. Anyway, have you seen Russia's excuse for the 6 GRU guys captured in Henley?"

"Wanted to practise for the July Regatta, wasn't it?" Annie said, groaning. "Just like Salisbury back in 2018—they were only there to see the cathedral spire. Honestly, Putin loves playing his greatest hits. I'm surprised Novichok isn't on the Henley rowing club's doping list by now."

Carl grimaced, recalling the surreal Russian propaganda broadcast he'd watched on his phone earlier. Six GRU operatives had been arrested by Thames Valley Police after their raid on James Jenkins's empty Henley residence went spectacularly wrong, ending with the operatives stranded on the riverbank, soaked, cold, and bewildered, surrounded by armed officers and curious locals filming every moment. Moscow's official line had quickly devolved into absurdity—claiming the operatives were a "coxless six rowing crew" from Dynamo Moscow Rowing Club, innocently training for the July Henley Royal Regatta.

Even RT's ever-loyal Maria Zakharova had struggled through the briefing, visibly fighting embarrassment as she repeated the Kremlin's line that the group "became lost while conducting rowing practice along the Thames" and had merely "sought shelter from harsh British weather." To Carl, it was so blatantly ridiculous it bordered on self-parody—yet the Russian state media machine repeated it earnestly, somehow both oblivious and indifferent to how ludicrous they sounded.

"Does anyone actually believe that nonsense?" Carl asked, unable to keep the incredulity from his voice.

"No," Annie replied, "but belief isn't the point. The Kremlin's aim is distraction. Even if they're mocked relentlessly online, it shifts attention away from Dublin, from what's happening in Derry, from Sinead Ryan and that deepfake fiasco. Classic disinformation."

Carl nodded, turning serious again as he took another sip of tea. The absurdity was amusing, but the underlying truth wasn't. The British Isles, once distant from direct Russian meddling, had become the epicentre of Putin's renewed campaign of hybrid warfare. Between Russian-backed Dublin, violence reignited in Northern Ireland, and GRU operatives openly stalking prominent figures like Jenkins, it felt as if Europe had slid back into the dark days Carl had once thought were consigned to history.

*_*_*_*

"I demand lawyer, I demand Russian counsel," Major Andrei Valentinovich Zimin said, sitting in the interview room at the Thames Valley Police station in Henley-on-Thames.

A Major within the GRU, Zimin had been the ground commander of the six man GRU kill team deployed to Henley-on-Thames under diplomatic cover. His task was to assassinate Jenkins and recover any air-gapped kompromat believed to be stored within Jenkins's home network or diplomatic safe.

Detective Chief Inspector Anne McGowan regarded the soaked and shivering Russian sitting across the table from her, Major Andrei Valentinovich Zimin—an experienced officer, one whose cover had spectacularly failed to survive contact with reality. His training may have prepared him for clandestine assassinations and secret intelligence retrieval, but clearly not for the icy humiliation of being fished out of the Thames by a bemused local rowing team and promptly arrested by a sleepy town's bewildered police force.

"We've notified your embassy, Major Zimin," McGowan said calmly, tapping her pen lightly on the table. "In the meantime, would you care to explain exactly why six Russian military intelligence officers—sorry, I mean 'rowers'—chose a cold February night for, how did your press officer put it... oh yes, 'routine river training for the Henley Royal Regatta?' Bit early in the season, don't you think?"

Zimin stared back impassively, his expression rigidly defiant despite the sodden state of his Dynamo Moscow tracksuit—the unfortunate cover identity hastily supplied by a panicked Moscow. "Is not illegal to row in British waters," he responded curtly, his voice accented but controlled. "We simply made navigational error due to weather conditions."

"Navigational error," McGowan repeated slowly, allowing her scepticism to hang visibly in the air. "You mistook a private estate in the dark, climbed a high fence, and broke through a locked rear door—all because of a 'navigational error'?"

Zimin merely shrugged. "River currents very strong. We lose control of boat. Was very dark. We try to find shelter and assistance. This all misunderstanding."

She let the absurdity of his explanation linger, her gaze steady and unblinking. Eventually, Zimin shifted uncomfortably, perhaps aware of how farcical his claims sounded even to his own ears.

"Major," McGowan said, leaning forward slightly, her voice calm but edged with steel, "we found military-grade encrypted phones, surveillance equipment, suppressed firearms, and enough plastic explosive to sink your supposed rowing boat several times over. Is all that standard kit for Dynamo Moscow athletes? The British Olympic Association will be fascinated to hear about your pioneering training methods."

Zimin folded his arms, refusing eye contact. "I demand Russian consulate official."

"They're on their way," McGowan replied coolly. "But frankly, I doubt they'll be very pleased with you. Six highly trained operatives captured live on TikTok by a bunch of teenagers with mobile phones, splashed across every social media platform within twenty minutes. You've turned Russia's premier clandestine assassination unit into an internet meme."

There was a tightness around Zimin's jawline that betrayed suppressed fury. Clearly, becoming a joke on the internet had not been part of the GRU's meticulous mission planning.

"Perhaps," she continued conversationally, "Moscow should consider less risky targets. Next time, Major, maybe stick to sightseeing at—"

A knock at the door interrupted the Detective Chief Inspector as a young Police Constable walked in.

"For the purposes of the tape," McGowen said, as she knew that it had to be recorded as part of the process, "PC Gabriel Carter has entered the room."

Zimin looked up and saw the young man walk in, his uniform ill fitting, and instantly knew that Carter wasn't a Police Constable, but most likely an intelligence officer. The constable's nervousness was too studied, too intentional. Zimin had interrogated enough captured agents to recognise an act when he saw one. His instincts sharpened immediately.

*_*_*_*

Harry Potter knew that, for his first time going undercover, instead of running cyber ops in the Nexus for MI5, being a PC named Gabriel Carter was not something he expected, especially as he had been awake for nearly 19 hours and working for 17 of those 19 hours. Still, there was something perversely enjoyable about stepping out from behind his monitors and into the real, gritty fieldwork he'd spent years manipulating digitally. Harry adjusted his borrowed constable's uniform, feeling the unfamiliar weight of body armour beneath his stab vest.

Zimin's gaze was cold, calculating—exactly as Harry had imagined from his files. The man was a veteran GRU officer, battle-hardened, and probably already working out ways to exploit the apparent nervousness Harry was projecting. Harry took a deep breath, leaning slightly into the act he'd crafted on his rushed journey from Thames House to Henley Police Station.

"Um, excuse me, Ma'am," Harry began, deliberately stumbling over his words, eyes flickering uncertainly between McGowan and Zimin. "I've got orders to escort, um, Major Zimin to a secure holding area. The Home Secretary has been on the telephone. Apparently the Ambassador is personally on his way to speak to Mr—I mean, Major Zimin."

Detective Chief Inspector McGowan raised an eyebrow theatrically, as if annoyed at the interruption, but Harry saw the glint of understanding in her eyes. "Very well, Constable," she said curtly, standing. "Major Zimin, it appears your diplomatic friends have managed to pull a few strings. Interview terminated, 14:18 hours."

Zimin's expression barely changed, but Harry detected a faint flicker of relief beneath the icy exterior. He rose stiffly, smoothing down the sodden tracksuit as if dignity could still be salvaged. Harry stepped aside, holding open the interview-room door and gesturing nervously towards the corridor beyond.

"This way, sir," Harry said politely, keeping up his uncertain, rookie façade.

Zimin stepped into the corridor ahead of him, shoulders rigid, clearly calculating his next move. Harry fell into step just behind him, keeping a careful distance. As they approached a rear door leading towards the secure parking area, Zimin glanced back briefly.

"You are nervous, constable," Zimin observed quietly, in surprisingly clear English. "First big operation?"

Harry forced an embarrassed cough. "Uh, yes, sir. First time dealing with anything like this. Usually it's just traffic stops and, uh, pub fights."

Zimin gave a faint snort of disdain. "Typical British incompetence. I advise you not to get involved in this game. It is not for amateurs."

"Of course, sir," Harry mumbled, carefully steering Zimin past the Virgin Media van that was in the car park, one that he knew had Mossad hitmen, ones who specialised in swift, surgical kidnappings. According to his section chief, Liam Powell, Mossad had wanted Zimin for numerous operations both in Isreal, along with operations in the occupied territories, as well as the targeted assassination of an Israeli diplomat in Cyprus. For Mossad, the capture of Major Zimin was not merely a prize—it was justice, a chance to settle old scores and dismantle a piece of the Russian intelligence apparatus that had long operated without consequence.

Harry's heart quickened slightly, a pulse of adrenaline surging as he continued guiding Zimin towards the van. He'd never done fieldwork like this before; he preferred to be in the van, at a desk, running cyber operations and monitoring communications for his fellow Nexus officers. But Powell had ordered him personally to be part of the team bringing the Russian to Mossad's arms. After all, Harry looked exactly like the real PC Gabriel Carter—the same height, same build, same hairstyle—and as the real

PC Carter was a genuine Thames Valley Police officer currently on leave, the cover was flawless.

Harry cleared his throat nervously, playing into his cover again as Zimin glanced suspiciously at the van.

"Ah, yes sir," Harry stammered convincingly, fumbling theatrically with a set of keys. "This, um, Virgin Media van here... they've been fixing the... nick's... internet systems."

Major Zimin paused, his eyes narrowing suspiciously at the Virgin Media van. The branding was immaculate, complete with a convincingly muddied chassis and a pair of ladders mounted to the roof. A bored-looking technician sat in the cab, sipping coffee and idly scrolling on his phone. To the casual observer, everything about the scene was normal, innocuous—British mundanity at its finest. But Zimin wasn't a casual observer. His years of operational tradecraft were screaming alarms at him, even if his soaked tracksuit and disgraced position had left his instincts dulled and his pride wounded.

Harry's throat tightened slightly. He could feel the Russian's hesitation—see the internal calculus playing out behind Zimin's carefully neutral mask. If Zimin bolted now, Harry wasn't certain he could stop him. He was trained for digital battlefields, cyber warfare, and psychological operations—not for grappling with seasoned GRU field officers in a police car park.

"Internet," Zimin repeated sceptically, his accent sharp, eyes darting back towards the safety of the police station doors. "Is always convenient excuse, yes? Internet problem, plumbing leak, electrical fault…"

Harry felt the tension crystallise, an electric frisson between them. Zimin turned fully now, eyes probing, calculating every detail of Harry's uniform, stance, and increasingly unsteady demeanour. Harry was uncomfortably aware that the real PC Carter's uniform didn't quite fit him—another detail that would never escape a seasoned operative like Zimin.

"Tell me, Constable Carter," Zimin began slowly, a cold smile playing at his lips, "why does your uniform not fit properly? Seems a strange oversight for Thames Valley Police."

Harry forced a nervous laugh, buying precious seconds. "I'm, um, covering for a mate—borrowed his gear," he stammered, feigning embarrassment. "Honestly, they called me in last minute—didn't have anything clean. I was meant to be at Villa Park tonight, as the Gunners are away, and I can't beat a bit of Saka's right foot working its magic. Tell me, are you a CSKA, Spartak or Zenith fan, Major?"

Harry's voice quavered with just the right amount of naive deflection, but inside, his brain was screaming. Zimin's eyes narrowed—football banter wasn't going to buy him much more time.

The Russian's jaw tensed. "CSKA," he said coolly. "Now tell me, Comrade, are you Thames House, Vauxhall Cross, or that giant doughnut in Cheltenham?"

Harry's spine prickled. The air between them turned glacial.

There it was—the drop. Zimin knew.

Harry exhaled slowly, adjusting his grip on the key fob in his pocket—the silent signal device designed to alert the Mossad team.

"I'm just PC Carter, sir," he replied with a deliberately weak smile. "I don't know what any of that means. I just… I just wanted to get through the shift without being made a TikTok meme, y'know?"

Zimin gave a long, hollow chuckle. "Then you've already failed, boy."

At that moment, the back door of the Virgin Media van slid open with a soft *click*. The 'technician' in the cab—now visibly alert—tapped twice on the steering wheel, a silent cue. Two more operatives, dressed in cable repair overalls, stepped out of the rear of the van like ghosts.

Zimin turned slightly at the sound, eyes now blazing with realisation.

"Of course," he muttered, "Mossad."

Harry stepped back.

Before Zimin could move, the operatives were on him—one seizing his right arm in a practised lock, the other pressing a specialised device to his neck. It hissed. Zimin stiffened, eyes wide, before slumping backwards as the fast-acting sedative took effect.

Harry watched as the operatives—silent, swift, and surgical—bundled the unconscious GRU major into the van. One of them gave him a nod of approval, then slammed the sliding door shut.

The driver turned the ignition, the van reversed, and within twenty seconds, it was gone—just another nondescript contractor vehicle disappearing into the gentle Friday afternoon drizzle of Henley-on-Thames.

Harry stood alone in the car park, heart pounding. The silence was deafening.

Then he exhaled, slow and deep, and finally pulled the tiny earpiece from his ear.

"Target acquired," he whispered, knowing his comms link to Thames House had remained open the entire time. "Mossad's got him. No complications. Well… one complication. I need new undies."

A moment of static. Then Liam Powell's voice, dry as ever: "Noted. Well done, Potter. You're cleared for curry, pint, and 12 hours' sleep. After that, report to Nexus for debrief. Zimin's going to Tel Aviv. We'll leak the rest to The Times tomorrow."

Harry shook his head in disbelief, already trudging back inside to return PC Carter's gear.

Bloody hell, he thought. That actually worked.

* _ * _ * _ *

"Oh, shit, Jenkins is at it again," Oliver Stokes, who was sat at his desk at the Nexus, said, looking at Alison

Harper, who was theoretically, for Manic, 'working from home', but was doing a Thames House day as she needed to brief MI5's Strategic Communications team on the fall-out from the Zimin snatch. She looked up from her monitor, raising a weary eyebrow.

"What now? Has he declared himself Lord Protector of the Realm?"

"No," Oliver replied with a grin, "but close. He's just filed criminal charges with the CPS—all against Admiral Kostyukov and the Coxless Six, as well as Big Vlad, Conspiracy to commit terrorism, conspiracy to cause grievous bodily harm, conspiracy to assassinate a peer of the realm, and for good measure, he's filed civil cases against them in London, Brussels and half of the Commonwealth. Even Singapore."

Oliver swivelled in his chair, waving the list on screen like it was a particularly juicy Nando's order. "Oh, and he's named the GRU as a 'foreign criminal enterprise masquerading as a sovereign intelligence service.' That one's going to go down well in The Hague."

Alison sipped her tea slowly, trying to process it all. "So just the usual Tuesday in Jenkins-land, then."

"It's Friday."

"Worse."

She stood up, crossing to Oliver's desk to glance at the filings. He wasn't exaggerating. There they were—case references, barrister names, and even a list of damages claimed by Jenkins, including "£18,500 for psychological distress, even though he and his family were in Monaco, loss of reputation, and destruction of a £1.3 million pound Rolf Harris painting... of Her Majesty Queen Elizabeth."

Oliver stared at the last line, blinking in disbelief. "Wait, wait—hold up. A Rolf Harris painting? Of the Queen?"

Alison gave him a look that said, I've seen worse, then turned back toward her desk. "Knowing Jenkins, as he's loyal to the Firm, being a hereditary peer, he brought it and hung it at his home in order to celebrate Her Majesty's Platinum Jubilee. Probably thought it was patriotic. Now he's blaming Putin's 'coxless hit squad' for ruining a piece of royal heritage. Honestly, you couldn't make this up. He's also listed, and you'll love this, theft of a diamond studded 19th century necklace that belonged to his great-great-grandmother, the wife of the 10th Lord Jenkins of Henley-on-Thames. Cost... £2 million. Lloyds of London confirm that they've seen the necklace back in 2021, and their valuation was accurate. He's claiming it was lifted during the raid, possibly by one of the GRU team."

"A £2 million pound family heirloom," Oliver repeated slowly, scrolling through the claim forms as if hoping one of them would blink and reveal itself as satire. "And he's included a map reference to the drawer it was supposedly in."

Alison raised an eyebrow. "He would. Probably added CCTV timestamps too. You know Jenkins—his house has better security than Fort Knox. If one of the Russians did lift it, he'll have a high-definition close-up and a biometric scan of their bloody fingerprints."

Oliver snorted. "MI5 spends half its time trying to prevent state-level attacks, and Jenkins just crowdsources deterrence with a home security system and a lawsuit catalogue. Honestly, he's a one-man hybrid warfare doctrine."

Alison leaned against the desk, folding her arms. "To be fair, it's working. The Russians look like amateurs, the GRU are a global joke again, and the deepfake fallout has Moscow tripping over its own lies. Between Carl's Radio Free Ireland, the Zimin snatch, and Jenkins' legal crusade, it's starting to feel like we're turning the tide."

Oliver tilted his head, half-agreeing. "Yeah... but you know the Kremlin. They'll retaliate. Humiliation doesn't go unanswered. Zimin's snatch, the coxless six farce, Ryan's deepfake—that's all one very large bruise on the ego of some very dangerous people."

"And bruised egos lead to reckless decisions," Alison finished quietly.

The office went silent for a moment. The hum of computers and distant clatter of typing filled the void as they both contemplated what might come next.

Then, Oliver cleared his throat and added with a smirk, "Still... if they do try anything else, I hope it involves another GRU 'sports team'. Maybe next time they'll be a synchronised swimming squad caught snooping around Windsor."

Alison rolled her eyes but couldn't help smiling. "Let's just hope they don't send a fencing team into Number 10.

That, or send a running squad to Balmoral for tea and crumpets with the King."

****

CHAPTER 25 – Collision Course
Saturday 3rd March 2029

Squadron Leader Mark "Minty" Mahoney knew that this mission was important. After all, being part of the Royal Air Force Aerobatic Team, or Red Arrows as the public knew them, was normally about putting on a show—precision, discipline, and breathtaking spectacle in red-painted Hawks soaring above delighted crowds. But today wasn't about acrobatics. Today was about discretion. Sacrifice. And plausible deniability.

He looked out across the dull grey expanse of the North Sea as the dawn began to rise, casting a pale blush over the choppy waters below. Visibility was limited, just as predicted—dense fog curled like smoke across the surface, hiding everything except what was immediately in front of him. The weather report had been accurate down to the hour. It was perfect. Or rather, perfect for what had to happen.

The Hawk T.1 he piloted today was older, a well-maintained but slightly worn aircraft marked for decommissioning in April. The squadron engineers had 'accidentally' delayed a few maintenance checks. Not enough to raise suspicion, but enough to form a convincing narrative once the Ministry of Defence drafted its statement: catastrophic mechanical failure during a solo training sortie.

He knew that he was the backup plan, the secondary option for a classified Royal Navy operation, and that, accompanying his plane was a General Atomics MQ-9 Reaper, an unmanned aircraft that was acting as a reconnaissance escort and real-time intelligence relay for those monitoring the operation from Northwood and Vauxhall Cross. The Reaper, painted in dull greys and stripped of all insignia, hovered at a legal altitude over the exclusion zone, silent but watchful. Its sensors were live, its encrypted feed streaming to multiple secure command centres where senior officers, political liaisons, and a couple of very nervous lawyers were watching every pixel for signs of deviation.

* _ * _ * _ *

The fog on the North Sea, just 20 nautical miles of Aberdeen, was stifling, but Sam Holloway knew that he wouldn't have missed it for the world.

The operation was simple. A BP oil tanker that was filled with A1 Jet Fuel, the kind of volatile material that could set the sky alight with a single spark, was about to "accidentally" collide with a Chinese-flagged cargo ship—Su Li. That same ship was, according to all-source intelligence, carrying an RS-28 Sarmat ICBM, plus enough Iranian-sourced arms to turn Belfast into Fallujah with Guinness.

He had volunteered to be onboard the BP owned British Emerald, mainly because he was, after his Section Chief, the most senior Nexus officer within MI5, and therefore he wanted to be able to make the call himself if it all went wrong.

Sam stood at the edge of the British Emerald's bridge, thick oilskins pulled tight against the cold sea air that whipped in through a partially opened porthole. The tanker creaked beneath his boots—aged, but still imposing. She had once been the pride of BP's Gem Class fleet. Now she was a decoy, loaded to the brim with combustible Jet-A1 fuel and fitted with just enough 'technical issues' to ensure nobody would be surprised when she suffered an unfortunate accident.

The crew, he knew, was not the regular BP crew, or crew chartered by a contractor. Instead, they were a mix of Royal Navy Type 23 officers, German Navy officers, American, Swedish, Dutch and Italian junior crew, and a mix of BND, Mossad, MI5, MI6 and CIA agents all posing as a motley civilian shipping crew. It was like something out of a Cold War novel—if Le Carré had written about oil tankers and sabotage instead of moles and safehouses.

A German-accented voice crackled through Sam's comms earpiece. "Visual contact with Su Li. Bearing 220, range six nautical miles. She's slow—looks like she's either heavy in the water or nursing a dodgy engine. Or both."

Sam turned and looked out the port side. Even in the fog, the silhouette emerged like a spectre—a fat container ship, running low in the water, its hull streaked with rust, its massive superstructure blotting out the pale dawn light like a monolith. The Su Li was moving on schedule, just as the intelligence reports had predicted. The shipping transponder said agricultural supplies. The satellite manifest said something else entirely: a Russian missile, Iranian arms, and the promise of a new Irish insurgency.

He glanced at his wristwatch. 06:17. The collision was due at 06:35.

"Condition?" he asked quietly.

"Ship's trimmed for portside collision," came the reply from the engineering bay, the voice clipped and calm. "Steering's been pre-set. Once we disengage the autohelm and throw the gearbox into override, it's just a matter of holding course. Impact should be dead centre midships. Right where it'll do the best. You'll need to brace for impact when we hit it, as you'll be riding a hundred thousand tonnes of flaming diplomacy straight into the history books."

Sam didn't smile. He didn't blink. He just gave a single nod.

Perfect.

The British Emerald's engines groaned, and he could feel the slight shift in motion beneath his feet. They were committing. There'd be no last-minute course correction now. This wasn't a drill, and it wasn't theatre. It was a carefully choreographed "accident" designed to erase a threat that couldn't be acknowledged, let alone confronted openly.

** _ * _ * _ **

Minty Mahoney was heading over the North Sea when he noticed, on his radar, an unknown contact. As a former Quick Reaction Alert pilot before his tour with the Red Arrows, based at RAF Lossiemouth, he knew that any Russian aircraft on the east side of the British airspace was never there by chance.

"Red Control, this is Red Seven, be advised, I'm picking up a contact bearing 048, altitude 21,000, speed 0.82 Mach. Definitely not civilian. Possibly a Flanker out of Kaliningrad."

Minty knew that his control at the home base of RAF Waddington, the RAF's Red Arrows, ISR and electronic warfare hub, would be all over that radar return within seconds.

"Red Seven, this is Red Control," came the clipped, calm voice of the Waddington controller. "Confirm visual if possible. We've got NATO AWACS feeding this contact as well. Assessment: Su-35S out of Chkalovsk, likely forward-deployed to Kaliningrad and running recon. You are not to engage. Repeat, do not engage."

"Copy, Red Control," Minty replied, eyeing the direction of the contact through the misted canopy. The fog below was thick, but the skies above were clearing, and with it, danger. The presence of a Flanker here, now, was no coincidence. If Moscow had even an inkling of what was about to happen, they were showing their cards—subtly, but unmistakably.

It was then that a light on the Hawk's selection of dials, lights and switches flickered amber.

ENGINE FAULT – WARNING: FUEL PRESSURE DROP

Minty frowned. That was not part of the plan. The Red Arrows Hawk had been deliberately maintained to appear slightly temperamental, but this wasn't supposed to be real. Or at least, not this early.

He knew that the Hawks were meant for decommissioning, with the T.2 variants, the former RAF Valley fleet trainers, being considered for the acrobatics team as they were the same airframe but far more modern. The T.1s were graceful, but old—elegant warhorses well past their prime, and prone to mood swings at the worst of times. But this?

This wasn't a performance. This was a malfunction. A real one.

"Red Control, this is Red Seven. Confirm engine pressure drop—diagnostics showing unstable fuel delivery. Request emergency check-in with maintenance logs, but I may have to abort."

The line crackled for a moment before the voice returned, cool and clipped.

"Red Seven, standby. You are within visual approach of the AO. If aborting, divert northeast and climb to angels two-five. Do not descend below twenty thousand under any circumstances—there's too much noise in the area."

Minty gritted his teeth. This was not ideal. He wasn't meant to be the main act—just the understudy in case the British Emerald missed her mark. A backup plan with a tidy alibi and a conveniently explosive ending. But now? Now the bloody Hawk might go down before the show even began.

Minty's heart raced as the amber light on his dashboard continued to flash, an insistent reminder that his aircraft wasn't as predictable as it should have been. The fuel pressure drop wasn't in the script—at least, not this early.

He had been set up as a contingency, part of the back-up plan, but now, that plan was teetering on the brink of failure.

He cursed under his breath. The mission was tight, every second crucial. The fog was working in his favour, obscuring his aircraft's movements from anyone below. But up here, in the thinning mist, the stakes were rising. A malfunction wasn't just an inconvenience. It could ruin everything.

"Red Seven, this is Red Control. Standby for confirmation from maintenance. Prepare for possible abort. Do you have eyes on the target?"

Minty flicked his gaze to the radar once more, his eyes narrowing as the signal from the Su-35S began to drift closer. It was still there, on his tail, playing its silent game of cat and mouse. This wasn't the sort of attention they had hoped for. The Flanker wasn't just a curious air traffic blip. This was the kind of shadow Moscow sent to monitor, assess, and—if necessary—interfere. And with a fuel issue of his own, Minty couldn't afford to play hero.

*_*_*_*

Russian Air Force Captain Gennady Vladimirovich Chekov had one simple mission—to test the response of the Royal Air Force's Quick Response Alert system. He had done this mission before, entering British airspace from Kaliningrad's Chkalovsk air base with a simple goal: provoke. He knew that the Polish Army, following a declaration of Article 5 of the North Atlantic Treaty, were massing on the border between the Polish and Russian territories.

The Poles, he knew, coveted the exclave, wanted to see it returned to Poland's fold, and Russia was not about to let that happen without a fight. By entering British airspace and staying within its radar range, he would provoke an inevitable response—a testing of NATO's readiness. And that would give Moscow just the information it needed to assess its next steps in the escalating chess game that was now spreading across Europe.

Captain Chekov's Su-35S skimmed the thin cloud layer, staying well above the fog. His job was to remain unnoticed as long as possible, just long enough to see how quickly the RAF would scramble. He had been tracking the British Aerospace Hawk, he had noticed it was a Red Arrows liveried one, meaning that it was not armed, not on patrol, but performing manoeuvres standard with the training patterns of the Royal Air Force's aerobatics team.

He knew that it wasn't a threat, therefore he dismissed it as nothing more than the RAF being the RAF.

Unbeknownst to him, however, it was part of a two pronged operation, and the Red Arrows' presence was far from incidental.

Looking at his radar, Chekov noticed, coming from Lossiemouth, the standard QRA response to an attempted incursion—two Typhoons, the Tranche 3 version of the Eurofighter, roaring to life as they were scrambled from RAF Lossiemouth

"Kak raz vovremya, tovarishch," he muttered to himself. "Right on time, comrade."

He adjusted his course, banking slightly westward to prolong the engagement without technically breaching UK sovereign airspace. This wasn't a combat mission—it was theatre. A demonstration. Moscow's way of letting London know that nothing went unnoticed, that the Baltic bear still had claws and eyes in every fogbank.

But Chekov couldn't shake the feeling that something was off. The Hawk he'd passed wasn't behaving like a training sortie. It was solo, low, and curiously aligned with the sea lanes. That alone would be unusual. And the presence of a large cargo vessel—Su Li—combined with the lumbering silhouette of a tanker... something didn't feel right.

He flipped a switch on his console and brought up the satellite feed overlay piped through Russia's Liana system. The data was patchy—expected this far out—but the outline of the two ships below him caught his eye. The Su Li was running low in the water. Very low. Not suspicious in itself, but...

His brow furrowed. The pattern didn't match usual maritime activity in the area. He reached for the encrypted channel back to Russian Naval Command.

"Zarya-1 to Murmansk, confirm cargo routing of vessel Su Li. Location: 57°04'N 1°53'W. Possible Western military activity. Intermittent radar reflections suggest unmanned aerial vehicle also in vicinity."

There was a pause before a heavily accented voice crackled back.

"Su Li is flagged for agricultural cargo. No additional intel. Maintain observation only."

Chekov grunted. "Agricultural cargo," he repeated dryly. *Looks like enough fertiliser down there to blow up a continent.*

He throttled back slightly. He wouldn't interfere—not yet. But he would stay close. Moscow liked options, and this felt like the sort of event that could blossom into headlines. Or war.

* _ * _ * _ *

The British Emerald was only minutes until the point of no return, when Sam Holloway noticed it first.

"Shit, we've got to change course," he shouted. "The Arrow's engine is flaming out. Looks like he's got a failed engine and he's going to do the accident for us if we're not careful."

Sam knew that the Hawks were getting to the point where they were about to be decommissioned, and that they were, frankly, temperamental machines at the best of times. But this was too early—far too early—and if Minty's Hawk went down before the British Emerald struck the Su Li, the entire operation would be blown wide open.

Although, he thought, it would be a tragic accident, a pilot dying in the service of King and Country, his aerobatic aircraft failing at a point where an unthinkable collision occurred, the press wouldn't need much help writing that story. Red Arrows aircraft, faulty maintenance, weather conditions, fuel pressure loss—plausible, tragic, neatly contained.

The irony that a Flanker was, as a RAF controller who was on the line through the comms, had said, testing Lossiemouth's QRA response, so would automatically assume it was a training flight going awry… well, that irony wasn't lost on anyone. Least of all Sam.

He knew that Minty Mahoney was a widower, his bride having died three years earlier, herself a Squadron Leader at RAF Coningsby, his parents killed in a car crash, no children, no family apart from his Squadron and the Red Arrows. A man whose life had already been shaped by service and sacrifice. And now, it seemed, fate was circling once more.

Sam's fingers hovered over the comms switch. "Control, this is Holloway aboard the Emerald. We've got a possible premature airframe failure on Red Seven. He's going down."

*_*_*_*

Sinead Ryan was sat in the Office of State Information in the new Restoration Government's headquarters, the former Department of Foreign Affairs building on St Stephen's Green, Dublin. The view from her office, once occupied by Irish diplomats, now overlooked a city increasingly armoured with Russian checkpoints and eyes. But Sinead wasn't focused on the streets below.

She was staring at the feed from RTÉ, where the 0700 bulletin had just opened with the usual Restoration propaganda—construction progress in Limerick, the "heroic" arrival of Russian agricultural supplies, and some laughable photo-op with schoolchildren reciting Pushkin. But her eyes kept flicking to the ticker, which had just begun reporting "unconfirmed reports" of British military activity in the North Sea, including "a possible Royal Air Force crash." That line alone had made her fingers tighten around her coffee mug.

Across from her, Viktor Mikhailov, now her official "Political Advisor" but in truth her SVR handler, was already checking his secure line to Yasenevo. His eyes hadn't left the screen either.

"It's one of the Hawks," he muttered, lips barely moving. "Red Arrows. Not a standard patrol aircraft. Solo sortie. Emergency declared mid-flight. Pilot is dead. Is normal."

Sinead knew that over the past few years, the Red Arrows had had numerous incidents, mostly minor, but some fatal. She could already hear the carefully prepared Russian line forming in Mikhailov's mind: tragic accident, nothing more. British incompetence. Ageing equipment. Perhaps, if needed, a whispered suggestion of Western desperation—military drills covering up their weakness, their unravelled grip on order.

She knew from the past week that she was being watched, not just by the SVR, but the GRU, following the deepfakes that had been unleashed across multiple media channels. Deepfakes so precise they had triggered interrogations, loyalty audits, and a sleepless night where she'd had to explain to Moscow—on three different encrypted lines—that she was not, in fact, staging a coup on behalf of Sergey Naryshkin.

She knew that her Manic Goldies appearance earlier in the year, where she claimed that she loved Zombie by The Cranberries, had also raised suspicion—GRU analysts had parsed her every word, every glance, every syllable of nostalgic sentiment, searching for coded messages. The SVR, on the other hand, were glad, as she had followed the scripted plan they had made, that she fake a moment of confusion, a moment of wanting to get out of the game, to make her more believable as a mouthpiece, not a zealot. The added line of wanting Ya Soshla s Uma, because she knew, and her controllers knew, that Manic's setup, prior to it being closed down, had secret feeds that the Five Eyes group of intelligence agencies were almost certainly monitoring. That subtle reference to t.A.T.u., to mental collapse, to losing grip—it had been both a message and a test. To see who would bite. She suspected MI6 had clocked it immediately.

Which resulted in a subtle contact from a known MI6 affiliate, a member of embassy staff.

Which was why, on the 30th January 2029, the SVR had, via the Restoration Government's External Affairs Directorate, the former Irish Department of Foreign Affairs, declared that individual, as well as the majority of the staff at the British Embassy, persona non grata, citing vague accusations of "subversion and inappropriate conduct." The real reason was clearer: someone in London had picked up on her signal.

That had resulted in one of the sound engineers at RTÉ, as well as Carl Peterson, also leaving, as the latter was married to an embassy official, and so had diplomatic protections that the Restoration Government were no longer willing to tolerate. The former? James Peterson, his son, who, as he was a 26 year old, a non-dependent and therefore no longer afforded protection under the Vienna Convention once his parents were expelled. Sinead hadn't seen him since. Whether he'd escaped, disappeared, or been disappeared, she didn't know—and wasn't entirely sure she wanted to. She knew that the ESVR, the newly reorganised External Security of the Restoration Government, an SVR-advised counterintelligence unit, had taken over many of the former Garda Special Branch functions, had been authorised to disappear the young man with the same kind of rules that their Russian counterparts used in their own operations.

The truth, however, was that Sinead, now that her partner, Mikhail Sulov, was dead, killed by the British, shot down over the Northern Irish city of Derry. And that had made her even more determined to serve the Motherland with the utmost loyalty. Yet, the last few weeks had been a blur of chaos, suspicion, and surveillance. She could feel the walls closing in as the Restoration Government tightened its grip on the country, while outside, the rumblings of resistance only grew louder. Every move she made, every word she spoke, was scrutinised. It wasn't just the British or the Americans now—Moscow's eyes were everywhere.

Her mind snapped back to the present as saw the RTÉ feed mention how "western Imperialists deliberately crashing into an innocent Chinese ship, and that BRICS leaders were planning to convene to discuss the situation." The ticker at the bottom of the screen continued to buzz, running its line about "the tragic incident" involving the Royal Air Force, and how the British military was to blame for the supposed collision. The narrative was already being spun, the PR machine churning out a well-practised tale of Western incompetence, incompetence that perfectly matched the Russian propaganda line.

And she applauded it. She knew that if she was doing the presser for it, she would say exactly the same things.

"They're learning well, these new puppets," Sinead muttered under her breath, her fingers tapping a staccato rhythm on the desk. "Viktor, I'm going to order the newsroom to put out a report stating the incompetence of the British Air Force's maintenance, about its crumbling imperialist military, and the inevitable consequences of their neglect. It'll shift focus away from the true cause of this—and Moscow's upcoming steps. Make sure the narrative includes the 'tragic loss' of the brave British pilot. They'll believe it, especially after the deepfake fallout."

Viktor Mikhailov nodded, his face betraying no emotion, though his mind raced behind his impassive features. The collision, the timing of the missile shipment, the sudden presence of Western naval activity—everything was playing out like an intricate chess game. A move here, a pawn sacrificed there, all to entrench the Restoration Government's legitimacy and sway public perception.

"Of course, Sinead," Viktor replied, his voice smooth as ever. "I'll coordinate with the media and liaise with the Ministry of Information. The narrative will be tight. It will also give us time to manage the fallout from the military and intelligence community regarding the crash. The British will be scrambling for answers, which makes them look more desperate."

Sinead rubbed her temples, already feeling the weight of the day ahead. She had not expected this mission—this fragile veneer of stability in Ireland, built by Moscow's hand—to unravel so swiftly. First, the defection stories and now the mysterious cargo shipment. Each piece of intelligence seemed more chaotic than the last. If the British managed to link the Su Li with the Irish Restoration Government, the cover would blow wide open.

"We need to make sure the narrative is contained," Sinead said, her eyes narrowing as she surveyed the unfolding reports on her desk. "Once it reaches Western media, we can't afford a backlash. If the BRICS community holds fast, and if China backs us on this, the West won't have a leg to stand on. They're on the verge of overreacting—let's push them there."

Viktor, ever the strategist, considered the broader implications. "We must also manage the narrative at the diplomatic level. The UK will be ruffled, but their response will be theatrical—perhaps too theatrical for their own good. If we strike the right balance, the response will fracture NATO's unity. They're already on edge with the Baltic situation."

Sinead's eyes flickered briefly to the window, where Dublin's fog had begun to lift, revealing a bleak, grey skyline. "This isn't just about Ireland anymore. It's about the West coming apart at the seams. We're pulling on their threads, Viktor. And when they snap, we need to be the ones in control."

She glanced at the clock on her desk. Another press conference loomed, this one more critical than the last. The world was watching, but the world didn't know that the real battle was already unfolding beneath the surface. This was about control, about shaping the future, one lie at a time. The Restoration Government would take a hit, but it would also rise stronger. They had no other option.

And the fate of Britain? To be decided.

****

Books by Thomas Brant

Broadcasting Boundaries
BROADCASTING BOUNDARIES
BROADCASTING CHAOS
BROADCASTING DISRUPTION

The Wirral Gal
THE WIRRAL GAL... IN SPEKE
THE WIRRAL GAL... NOW A MAM

Fallen
IRELAND IS DOWN

Other Shared Universe Novels
THE BROOKES BABES
THE DAY THE QUEEN DIED
VIXEN
THE MANIC COLLECTIVE CANDIDATE